If you could live
forever, would you?

PRAISE FOR REMAINING AILEEN

Remaining Aileen is that perfect blend of heart-pumping suspense, unexpected humor, and bittersweet and beautiful truth. Aileen's struggle to figure out who--and what--she is as both a vampire and a mother, is poignant, and the love she holds for her family versus the reality of what she's become will rip apart your heart and then mend it back together a dozen times over. This book shook me--in the best possible way--proving that debut novelist Autumn Lindsey is a force to be reckoned with.

— AMANDA LINSMEIER- AUTHOR
OF *OUR WILD MAGIC*

Remaining Aileen blends women's fiction with a bite of paranormal to produce a metaphorical vintage genre that works. Who knew vampires made the perfect metaphor for moms?

— JOY RANCATORE- LOGOS AND
MYTHOS PRESS, QWERTY WRITING
LIFE PODCAST

This book was written for every mom who's struggled with finding herself after having children.

— SARAH ARMSTRONG-GARNER-
AUTHOR OF *THE SINKING TRILOGY*

Autumn creates the perfect parallel in Aileen's journey to discover not only who, but what she is and the disconnect mothers can feel when they too, embark on their new journey of motherhood and attempt to adapt this new role into their existing lives.

— NICOLE RUBIO- AUTHOR OF
SOMETHING WICKED

Remaining Aileen was the perfect blend of intrigue, heart, and humor.

— EVERLY REED- AUTHOR AND CO-
FOUNDER OF WRITER MOMS INC.

Remaining Aileen addresses the difficult and sometimes heart wrenching situation women find themselves in as we grapple with where we fit into the world, especially after becoming a mother.

— HEATHER REESE- GOODREADS
REVIEWER

This book was such a treat to experience. The setting and the characters are vividly drawn, the pacing excellent, and the ending made me gasp! I would call this "women's fiction with a paranormal twist" and if that sounds intriguing, you should absolutely check this one out. It's a wonderful escape read while also feeling firmly rooted in reality.

— BRADEIGH GODFREY-
GOODREADS REVIEWER

Lindsey provides new nuances to vampire lore as she twists Women's Fiction and vampire paranormal to produce a unique blend that is at times light-hearted, and at others vampire-dark.

— SUANNE- GOODREADS
REVIEWER

Right when I started reading I felt *Twilight* vibes and that continued through the story which made me ecstatic. It's a debut novel... thrilling, paranormal adult fantasy. I was so invested in the story I just kept turning the pages craving to know what happens next.

— TERESA- GOODREADS REVIEWER

REMAINING AILEEN

REMAINING AILEEN

BOOK ONE

AUTUMN LINDSEY

"If you could live forever, would you?"

COPPER XYLOPHONE PUBLISHING CO.

This is a work of fiction. Names, characters, places, and incidents either are the product of the author's imagination or are used fictitiously. Any resemblance to actual persons, living or dead, events, or locales is entirely coincidental.

Remaining Aileen. Copyright © 2020 by Autumn Lindsey. All rights reserved. Printed in the United States of America.
For information, address Copper Xylophone Publishing Co., Po.Box 574 Pine Grove, C.A. 95665

No part of this book may be reproduced in any form or by any electronic or mechanical means, including information storage and retrieval systems, without written permission from Copper Xylophone Publishing Co., except for the use of brief quotations in a book review.

Cover Design: Dionne Abouelea

Hardcover Edition ISBN: 978-1-7350536-0-8
Digital Edition ISBN: 978-1-7350536-2-2

Second Edition

For my husband and children—You are my forever.

LETTER TO READERS

Dear Reader,

If this is your first time reading Aileen's story, welcome! If you have visited before, welcome back! Some changes have been made, a few special things have been added to this book's edition but the story remains the same.

If there is one thing that writing *Remaining Aileen* has taught me, it is to never give up on my dreams. To keep writing, even when it hurts. Even when all seems lost.

Thank you for your support. I truly hope you enjoy this story.

Love,
  Autumn Lindsey

CONTENTS

REMAINING AILEEN

DIRTY THIRTY

Socks, underwear, swimsuit.

Right, *swimsuit*.

Thunder rolls in the distance as I stare at the plain black bathing suit laying on my bed, now wishing I had gone with the vintage-style two-piece instead. A glance at the clock reveals there's no time for this now. I throw the suit in my carry-on with a few other non-mom outfits I grabbed from Target's end-of-the-season sales racks. I pull the zipper shut, pinching my finger in the process, and try not to cringe at the idea of actually having to wear this suit on the beach… around people.

Aside from stretch marks and lack of a normal belly button, I look decent for having birthed two giant babies, I'll give myself that. But as I look in the mirror at my raised eyebrow and pursed-lipped frown, I know I'm failing at convincing myself.

After one more scan across my neglected room, I find my toiletry bag peeking out from under the corner of the disheveled bedspread. I stuff it in the front of my carry-on before I decide to change my mind about this trip. One weekend away every ten years will be good for me, or at least that's what I've been telling myself. Eight years of parenting warrants a chance to sleep— uninterrupted by kids— however late I want. I can't pass up this opportunity; I also can't disappoint Jordyn who's been begging Phil and me to visit her beach house for years. This should be fun, even if he can't make it.

"PHIL! Where are you? It's 7:30 already!" My voice sounds foreign to me. When did yelling become the only way I communicate? But today it seems, even my "mom" voice goes unanswered. I swear I'm a ghost sometimes.

I check my reflection one last time in the barn wood mirror Phil made me, hoping I'll pass as a presentable adult. Assessing my jeans, worn-out T-shirt, and hoodie, and navy Vans, I suddenly doubt I'll blend in with the fashionable Miami crowd. Presentable adult is not the right description; semi-functioning will have to do.

And now that I'm in self-conscious mode, I can't help but notice how much my eyes have dimmed— the green barely showing through the hazel these days — and how pale and uneven my skin tone has become complete with faint, blue shadows that have

2

taken up a permanent residency under my eyes. Sleep deprivation will do that to a person, I guess. Even with makeup on. There isn't enough concealer in the world that could hide these dark circles. Needless to say, parenthood has taken its toll on me more than I care to admit. The fact I'm turning thirty is beginning to take its toll as well. I didn't realize when I entered into this whole motherhood phase of life how quickly I'd lose sight of that well-rested girl I used to be.

My phone dings with a text from Jordyn.

JORDYN: You on the plane yet? Hurry up and get here!

Thunder claps, almost making me jump out of my skin. I can't believe I'm about to fly in this weather. Maybe I'll just go back to sleep. I longingly stare back at the rumpled bed and contemplate hiding, from this birthday, nestled close to Phil, snuggling with my girls— safe. I sigh, and text my life-long friend back with a lie I'm urgently trying to convince myself of as truth:

Leaving now! So excited.

Only excitement isn't the right word. Sick to my stomach would be more accurate.

Quickly, I bend forward to shake some volume into my long, ashy-brown locks, grimacing as my loose

3

stomach skin leftover from pregnancy gives way to gravity and brushes against the soft fabric of my shirt. I adjust my stomach, a habit I've formed over the years, tucking it quickly back into my mom-jeans as I stand. One thing I am thankful for is high-waisted jeans actually being back in style. I figured, if they're being sold to sixteen-year-olds at least I'm sort of on-trend, minus the cute crop tops I always see them paired with.

With my carry-on in one hand and green cross-body purse slung firmly in place, I grab what's left of my self-esteem and head out of the room. My luggage drags down the hall over the remnants of the girls' adventures from yesterday, from the whole week really, cluttering the old hardwood floor. I could have cleaned up last night— Phil would have appreciated that. But, no, it's his house too, and he knows how to clean. He can handle this, I'm only going to be gone for few a days.

At the end of the hall, I stop. Our usual Saturday mornings consist of the girls snuggling on the couch, layered with blankets from their bed watching cartoons. I then make some comment on how they should use the ones in the living room and how they will need to put them away when they're done, but today the couch is empty and the room is quiet, too quiet. A momentary rise of suspicion and worry begins to seep into my already anxiety-ridden system until the pleasant scent of warm vanilla catches my attention.

"Surprise, Mommy!"

My heart skips as I spin a one-eighty toward the kitchen. Two excited, giggling girls stare back at me. Tears well up, threatening to fall, and all my anxieties temporarily melt away as I read the handmade sign hanging above them over the front door in the kitchen. A bright purple, "Happy Birthday Mommy, We'll Miss You!" banner covered in large splats of blue paint on stapled-together printer paper. Davina's sweet four-year-old face is, as usual, covered with food— this time yogurt, which her older sister Imogene takes notice of and grabs a rag to clean her up. Imogene, my sweet little eight-year-old going on eighteen.

"Happy birthday, Mommy! Are you old today?" Davina asks, swatting her hands at her sister, who's determined to clean every last bit of breakfast from her face.

"Oh sweetie, I love you, " I say, giving Davina a big kiss on the cheek before smushing those sweet little cheeks between my hands. "But let's be clear: Mommy still has two more days till she's officially old, okay?" She giggles at me as I switch the subject, "Did you paint the pretty blue dots?" Her big cerulean eyes light up as she nods.

"Humph," says a scowling Imogene, green eyes narrowed, with arms firmly crossed in front of her chest, a brown paper lunch bag clutched in one hand, her pre-pubescent attitude clearly already well established. "Well, it *was* perfect, Mom, till Sissy messed it up. This is for your flight, in case you get hungry."

She thrusts the bag into my hands as warm brown sugar, vanilla, and chocolate surrounds my senses and I secretly thank myself for teaching her how to bake cookies.

"Thank you, sweetie, and the sign is perfect because you both made it for me." I can imagine in a few years Imogene will be rolling her eyes at statements like that. But for now a satisfied smile stretches across her face.

"Now, where is your daddy?" With the Sacramento airport being over an hour's drive away and my flight scheduled to depart in an hour and a half, my apprehension returns with a vengeance. Either we leave right now or I'm staying home.

"I don't know," Imogene says in a sassy tone before she goes back to eating her yogurt and granola.

"Do you have to leave, Mommy?" Davina asks, grabbing onto my leg and sliding down to the ground in protest.

"No, I don't have to but—"

The slider in the living room squeaks open cutting off my train of thought as Phil steps inside. Having overheard Davina's complaint he finishes what my thought should have been, "But Grandma gave Mommy a really nice gift."

Right, the *gift* of not being mom for a weekend. My heart aches a bit at the thought. Torn between how much I love being Mommy and knowing I need this break. It's hard to admit but I'm scared of this always tired, grumpy, quick-tempered parent I'm becoming.

"Where have you been? And where *is* your mom?" I hide my nerves behind impatience as I snap at Phil.

A very fit, six-foot-one, one hundred and eighty pounds of smoking hot husband joins us in the kitchen. His grey-blue eyes glisten like the ocean after a storm breaks and his smile can bring me out of any mood no matter how foul. He doesn't rise to my bait, only turns on the sink to wash his hands. "The chickens were out of food."

"Well, thank you." My mood improves slightly as I lean into him for a hug. He grabs me, squeezing me tight with damp hands and a devilish smile. A pleasant warmth fills me from within, calming my nerves. I point with the bag of cookies still in my hand up to the birthday banner. "So, this is what you've all been up to this morning?"

"Well, aside from *our* little early birthday celebration in bed, yes," he purrs in my ear. Goosebumps once again cover my body, only this time in a much more welcome way.

Heat rises to my face thinking of what we did; it's been a while since morning has been a time for grown-up kinds of fun. It's nice when the girls decided to "sleep in" until 6:30, instead of their usual 6. We learned very quickly after becoming parents to take whatever window we could get.

"That *was* a nice birthday present. Thanks for still wanting me in my old age," I say with a wink, even though I'm still trying to convince myself thirty isn't old.

"Well, babe, you can't stay young forever!" He winks back, smacking me on the behind as he goes to make some coffee.

He's right, dammit.

"Hey! We have no time for coffee." I peek out the window in hopes my mother-in-law/childcare for the day, will appear due to my efforts of simply willing her to arrive. But all I see are puddles of water pooling on the empty driveway as the rain begins to fall.

Phil gives me a look, the kind where his face draws a blank as if he is about to dramatically expire. He closes his eyes and after a deep, long, exaggerated breath he replies, "Aileen, there is always time for coffee."

He struggles to hold onto the seriousness of his tone before his heart-melting smile breaks through the ruse and he pours himself a mug full.

I should know better, being that I married a caffeine addict with third-wave coffee shop taste. No quick and easy "Mr. Coffee" machines in this home—only pour-over systems or French presses.

"Want any?" he asks with a taunting expression, knowing full well we are out of Half-n-Half and that I wouldn't drink that stuff black to save my life.

Shaking my head, I glance back outside, nerves zipping through me as the rain falls harder. It's now mixed with tiny beads of hail. Thunder booms, echoing through the house and the girls run screaming into the living room to hide under a blanket. I debate joining them as look back up at the ominous sky above, the same sky I'm going to be flying through less than two hours from now.

"It's alright, girls," I call out to them, trying to ease their fear of the storm. Maybe trying to ease my own as well.

Phil's phone buzzes, vibrating our wooden dining table he crafted himself in his garage workshop. The call another reminder of the fact I'll be flying alone today, thanks to his job's constant need of him to fill in for their lack of personnel. He's never one to turn down being needed at the fire station, which leaves me battling the sting of my own selfish desire to keep him to myself.

"It's too bad your shift got changed. I wish you were still coming with me."

"Fires don't fight themselves," he says, sipping his coffee and shoving his phone into his pocket after a quick reply to his text.

"True." *But thirtieth-birthday vacations don't happen every day, either.* I swallow that last thought— no use

9

starting am argument now. Not when I'm about to leave.

"Where is she?" I ask, my impatience growing as I stuff half a cookie into my mouth. Stress eating is my last defense against my pre-flight anxiety now. Maybe the weather won't be like this in Sacramento. Unlikely.

"She'll be here," he answers just as her car pulls into the driveway with a honk of the horn. I cringe at the honk, wondering what neighbor will complain this time, probably Mr. Gerigson from across the way, as always.

"Grandma's here!" the girls yell, running back into the kitchen. They love their grandma and they should: Small, annoying traits aside, Ana is one fantastic human. When my own mother turned her back on me, Ana fully accepted me as her daughter, and she loves these girls more than anything.

The front door opens with a loud, singsong, "Happy Birthday, Aileen!" Ana's soft, warm, motherly arms embrace me, then shove me back just as quickly. "Now get going! You'll miss your flight!" She motions me toward the open door.

Rain continues to fall hard from the dark foreboding sky. I'm not ready to go, not yet.

"Thank you for the trip, but you really didn't have to." I shut the door once she clears the doorway reminding her, again, that she didn't need to do this for me.

"Nonsense. I know what it's like to be a mother of young kids. A nice weekend on a warm beach will do you some good. You'll come back a new woman ready for anything! Now scoot!" She would know, single-handedly raising two boys thanks to a husband who preferred his booze over his family.

She's right— I do deserve this. I hug my girls one last time and I try my best to hold back tears; heaven forbid I ruin the eyeliner that took me forever to apply. I kiss each of them on the top of their heads, breathing in the soft soapy scent of their shampoo, and they run back to their TV show. Ana follows them with a smile.

It dulls the sting of leaving a little, knowing they'll be in her capable hands.

PHIL DRIVES FAST as we head down the highway out of our sleepy little town toward the Sacramento airport through sheets of rain in my old mom-van. Old gas receipts and snack wrappers litter the floor-boards. Outside the water-streaked window, the blurred green, grassy hillsides and old, worn-out buildings zip by as I say my silent goodbyes to my mundane life, feeling almost excited for a weekend of carefree living. That is until flashing red lights blink in the side mirror followed by sirens coming up from behind us.

"So much for making my flight on time," I say sarcastically, secretly hoping I might actually miss it as lightning trails across the darkened sky. I shiver, convinced it'd be for the best. Jordyn would understand, right? But I knew she wouldn't. She's been trying to get me to, as she put it, "escape from the drudgery of motherhood" for years now. Of course, her definition of fun is vastly different than what any married mother should be doing in my opinion. Until now, I've successfully put it off by using the excuse that the girls needed me home. In reality, it's me who needs to be home with them, safe in the comfort of my house where I don't have to face how much motherhood has changed me. Because who am I now without them?

"I wasn't going that fast." He flicks on the blinker and pulls over to the side of the road.

The sheriff's white and green Ford Explorer zooms past us, followed by a fire engine and an ambulance.

"Lucky me," I whisper under my breath as my momentary hope this would make me miss my flight dissipates. Phil nods to his passing coworkers and drives back onto the highway following behind them.

Not too far ahead we catch up with the sheriff and the rest of the emergency crews. Jon Harker is there, Phil's closest friend and the deputy sheriff, standing in the rain observing the scene, head shaking. He may be forty-five but the years he's spent in law enforcement have aged him at least a decade more. It doesn't help his mustache is speckled with more gray than the auburn tone it used to be, stresses of the job I'd imagine. Regardless of how afraid I am of seeing something I'll regret, I can't help but stare at the ugly car wreck steaming on the left side of the narrow two-lane highway. From the bits of twisted metal and glass of a former vehicle and evidence of a cabin fire put out by the rain, it doesn't look good. My heart twists in sympathy.

"People can't drive in the rain," Phil mumbles, eyes firmly set on the road ahead.

"It's not like we get it that often. I guess we're all out of practice." I peek back at the flashing lights behind us, watching them fade into the distance and realize I only saw one car. Perhaps they hit a deer. Another cookie makes its way into my mouth from the bag at my side, the buttery-chocolate flavor melting momentarily overriding my fears of flying.

"You're awfully quiet this morning," Phil says a few miles down the highway, stealing one of my cookies in the process.

"I should be spending my thirtieth birthday with you and the girls." My words catch in my throat.

"We can celebrate when you come back." He rests his warm hand on my knee, the effect is calming and much appreciated. "The girls and I have something special in mind. Besides, tonight you and Jordyn have reservations at that place you said she's been dying to get a table at."

I gasp, taking bits of cookie down with the air.

He pats me on the back, laughing. "Death by cookie would be one way of avoiding your birthday."

I try to answer, but instead, cough, hacking up the cookie crumb at fault. "But The Royal! She said it has a six-month waiting list. How did you get us in?" Finally, something else besides sleeping and sun to look forward to. According to Jordyn, the steak there melts in your mouth. Except it costs a hundred dollars a plate and I worry about how this is going to fit into our budget.

Phil gives me a sly look. "I have my ways. You only turn thirty once; party it up, girl! I want it to be a birthday you'll never forget, to, you know, carry you through your old-lady years."

This makes me laugh, but not before slapping him on the leg. Phil smiles at me with the same goofy smile he had the day I fell in love with him. It captivates me, bringing me back to a time when we were both nineteen, so young and free like it was only yesterday our summer camp romance began, and not ten years ago.

"We never really age, do we?" My mind lingers in the past, how cute he was when we met. This tall, lanky kid with sandy-blond hair, offering his hand to help me out of a rowboat, even though I was perfectly capable of getting out on my own. I remember the collective sigh from the middle-school-aged girls I was counseling as they stood at the edge of the lake, dreaming of when they'd find their own summer camp romances. That girl I was then is a stranger to me— and someone I often wish I could be like now. I miss her fit, thin frame, unencumbered by the thralls of motherhood, able to comfortably wear whatever swimsuit she wanted without hesitation. She had her days and nights all to herself, open for whatever adventure awaited her next. I find myself missing her sometimes, in the night when the house is quiet and I'm alone with my thoughts, and I wonder how I lost her, when I lost her. Guilt ripples through me, I love my daughters more than anything, more than the girl I used to be, I don't want to seem ungrateful.

"Feeling sentimental now, are we?" He steals another cookie from my bag, shaking me from my self-wallowing. Despite everything, I'm happy with the choices I made. I might have been young, but I was eager to escape my dull Midwestern existence and overbearing mother for the excitement of California with the sandy-haired boy from summer camp who stole my heart.

My nerves settle a bit the rest of our hour-long drive, as we talk about the girls, the latest gossip at the fire station, and Phil's new obsession with woodworking. He can go on for hours about wood curl and crotch feathering, I giggle every-time he says the phrase, but I don't mind— his voice is soothing.

He pulls up to the curb at the airport right at 8:56,

still leaving me with time to find a restroom before the micro-sized airplane bathrooms become my only option. Thankfully I have no bags to check. The gusty wind blows my hair across my face as Phil grabs my carry-on from the back of the van and wheels it over to me.

With one last lingering embrace I bury my face into his shoulder and breath in the clean, soapy scent of his Old Spice Sport deodorant.

I groan, "I don't like flying." This trip was far more exciting when both of us were going to go.

He kisses my forehead gently then presses his head against mine, our noses touching. "Everything will be fine. People fly every day." Phil knows this always makes me laugh, how being this close makes it look like he has one cycloptic eye. I smile.

We part heads as Phil hands me my carry-on. "Happy almost birthday. I love you!" He blows me a kiss and walks back to the van.

"I love you too. See you soon."

I push back the sudden flood of emotion, swallow down my nervousness, and push anticipation of a vacation to the forefront of my mind. Get a grip Aileen, I scold myself, It's not like I'll never see him again. This is my birthday trip to Miami, a place of fun in the sun, and it really wouldn't kill me to try and enjoy the break. With a wave, I watch him drive off, and my phone dings with another text from Jordyn. I can already picture her standing at the airport baggage claim, drinks in hand. She hasn't changed much at all since we were in high school. Her unruly hair, which without any effort, ends up looking amazing. Her affinity for sundresses and the highest heels she can wear to offset her five-foot-two stature. It's no wonder she moved to Miami as soon as she was eighteen.

JORDYN: Gahhh! I seriously can't wait to see you!

Realizing how much I miss my old friend and all the good times we shared growing up I type back eagerly:

At the airport. Be there as soon as I can!

Finally, I feel it: excitement, adventure. Thunder booms again. Nope, terrified. I feel terrified.

GOODBYE, JAMES BOND

eople fly every day, right? Phil's words echo in my mind, but they bring little comfort as I scan over the sleek Boeing 757 tube of terror I'll be stuck in for the next five hours. Looks safe enough I guess.

The packed plane is abuzz with people scurrying to find their seats while flight attendants assist in stuffing giant carry-ons into overhead compartments that clearly won't fit. Disinfectant lingers in the recirculated air, mingling with burnt coffee and sweat. I look to my ticket even though I've already memorized my seat— 21-B— and take a deep breath. The last time I flew anywhere was my honeymoon, and obviously, I wasn't alone. And the last time I flew alone, I was escaping my life in Ohio to work a summer in California at Sunny Days Summer camp. My overbearing parents didn't know I had no plans of returning home, and with the excitement of starting a new life, I didn't have time to be scared of a plane flight. But I'm no longer that girl. I'm *Mom* or *Mommy*. Outside of that role, I don't know who I am anymore.

I walk through first class and admire the soft, faux leather seats complete with ample legroom, warm towels, and fizzy complimentary mimosas. My growing envy of the first class passengers momentarily distracts me from the shaking in my knees as I pass through the doorway to my final destination in coach. Except, every step I take past the narrow, claustrophobic rows of coach seating, I grow more confident that if humans were meant to fly, we'd have been born with wings.

I spot my seat finally, grateful to see it's an exit row, yet surprised to find it already occupied. A beautiful woman about my age with thick, golden-blond hair sits there. Her long locks perfectly frame her creamy yet very pale face before cascading down off her shoulders in soft waves. Her attention is firmly placed on the book in her manicured hands. She doesn't seem to notice as I walk up to her and I can see why when I notice the earbuds in her ears, foot-tapping along to whatever she's listening to. Her few belongings, a notebook, magazine, and small clutch, are stacked neatly on the window seat beside her—Phil's seat, or what would have been Phil's seat.

"Excuse me," I say, stuttering through my words.

A line of impatient passengers begins to form behind me.

The woman looks up at me with mesmerizing lavender-blue eyes. Smiling with a set of glistening teeth that seem to glow from behind her full pink lips, I wonder if she isn't some sort of supermodel or actress. She pulls out one of her earbuds, and I'm almost embarrassed to be disturbing such a perfect looking person and wonder if I should just shut up and take the seat beside her.

"I'm sorry, my music." She laughs, taking out the other earbud. The ring of her laughter calms the growing heat of embarrassment in my cheeks. "Thank God, you look normal! I was worried I'd get stuck sitting by some weirdo the whole flight."

"Oh no. I'm sorry, I meant you're in my seat. 21-B?" I hold up my ticket, feeling like an idiot.

Her smile fades and her brow furrows. "That's strange, I could swear——" she says, digging through her clutch. "Where are you, ticket? I just threw you in here— oh, there you are!" She reads it to herself, lips moving along with her eyes. "Oh! My bad. I'm *41*-B."

She smiles again, allowing it to fade quickly before she effortlessly swoops up her things and stands.

"I'm sorry," I repeat, although I'm unsure why I'm the one who should be sorry.

"Nice meeting you." She glides down the aisle to her seat in row forty-one, right next to a rather large, hairy man in a tank top and looks back at me like we're old friends, shrugging her shoulders with a silent giggle, in a "go figure" kind of way. The man sneezes, wiping his nose with the back of his bare hand. She frowns, her nose wrinkling in disgust as she plops down discontented into her seat, and pops in her earbuds.

After stuffing my carry-on in the overhead bin I take what would have been Phil's window seat instead of my assigned one and settle into the plush fabric. The short interaction with the lavender-eyed woman replays in my head. The more I think about it, the more embarrassed I feel to not have just shared the row with her. I toss my purse under my seat, along with thoughts I no longer need, and fasten my seatbelt — safety first— even though we aren't moving yet.

Raindrops run down the foggy window and I sit with my head leaned against the cold plastic pane, waiting to get on with this torture, reminding myself how much fun I'll be having five short hours from now. I wouldn't doubt if Jordyn is already at the airport waiting, a day of spontaneous fun already mapped out. Probably wearing something bright and sexy that will put my mom jeans and T-shirt to shame.

My mind wanders to the only two times I've spent away from my kids— well, just Imogene. It's sad, really. There was that one night I spent in the hospital when Davina was born, no vacation by any means. And the time before that when Phil took me on one last trip while I was eight months pregnant. I laugh silently to myself, remembering how he picked the worst hotel. The first room came with a lovely blood-stained floor and the second room . . . well, at least the people next door were having a good time. All. Night. Long. So much for discounted hotel room web deals.

Thinking back on all this I realize it's pretty pathetic I haven't ventured out on my own sooner, considering I've been a mom for eight years now. Though I guess I convinced myself there wasn't anything else worth doing. I've been too anxious to leave them, worried that if I did something could happen to them, or me. I can imagine my pre-moth-erhood-self looking down from wherever she went, shaking her head over what I've let myself become: someone run by fear, no longer seeking the adventure I once longed for. Adventure I never got the chance to experience once I saw that positive pregnancy test. I take a deep, calming breath through my nose, and the scent of a very pleasant men's cologne kindly improves the already semi-expired airplane air, erasing the negative thoughts from my mind.

A man's voice, smooth and soothing with a slight British note, interrupts my wallowing, "Pardon me, madam, I believe I am seat 21-A."

The distinguished voice belongs to a tall, very handsome man with coffee-colored, unkempt hair that falls perfectly down either side of his temples. My heart stops, and I debate jumping out the emergency exit. His dark-chocolate eyes contrast well against flawless, stone-like skin. The right amount of next day stubble frames a perfect smile. He's only dressed in simple jeans and a white T-shirt, but the vintage leather jacket makes him appear unconventionally refined, like a runaway billionaire.

"S-s-so sorry. I thought this seat was empty." It was dumb of me to assumed Phil's last-minute cancellation would mean his seat would remain unfilled. My mind reels once again with embarrassment. First, someone takes my seat, then I take someone else's. Sounds about right. I was wrong— embarrassment doesn't even begin to cover what I'm feeling inside. After staring way too long, I lower my eyes and fumble to unlock myself from the seat.

"Need some help?" he asks.

His voice causes my skin to tingle. Maybe it's the accent or the way he said the word "need". I take a breath to steady my nervous heart and already hot cheeks. "No, I'm fine." Relieved to finally free myself from the restraint I move toward the aisle. But I make matters worse as my right foot catches on the strap of my purse, throwing me in the direction of the handsome stranger's arms. He graciously steadies me, his touch cold even through the sleeves of my hoodie, bringing relief to the heat building from my on-going embarrassment. I realize my hands are tightly gripping his biceps, hard under the soft leather of his jacket. But I can't move, intoxicated by his warm, inviting cologne, my eyes inadvertently lock with his before I can stop myself.

"I'm sorry," I mumble, my senses overwhelmed, hypnotized by his stare. What is wrong with me?

"Whoa there, love, not a problem." His breath is sweet. "Would you rather have the window, darling? I'd hate for you to hurt yourself over it." A passenger waiting in the aisle, witnessing my horrible people skills, rolls his eyes and looks at his watch.

Love? Darling? Who is this guy, James Bond? I'm too mortified to accept, so I shake my head no as he flips us around, his movements like a graceful dance even in such a confined space and positions me in front of my actual seat.

Stunned, I blurt out a delayed, "No, please, sir, it's yours." Did I just say, sir? His accent demands the title. The spell of what just happened fades and all I can do is pray I didn't forget to brush my teeth this morning. A sudden hyper-awareness of every inch of my being waves over me as I mentally do a face-palm, wondering who in their right mind let me out in public. This is why I haven't left Amador County: I've forgotten how to be a functioning adult.

He moves to his seat, brushing past my legs causing a pleasant tingling sensation all over my skin. I distract myself with my phone, a safety measure to ensure no more embarrassment happens on my behalf.

But wishes are futile today. The man clears his

throat and I glance up, again caught in his hypnotic gaze. My phone slips from my fingers, landing on the floor by his finely shoed feet. Who is this guy?

He swiftly picks my phone up and smiles. "You seem a bit nervous." If I were him, I'd want to laugh at me right now. He has to know the effect he has on women. No one that good-looking can be oblivious to the way people react to them. His cold fingers brush mine as he places the phone in my hand shooting tingles down every nerve of my being.

"Oh, no, I'm fine," I lie. Hell yes I'm nervous! Like the seventh-grade girl who just got asked to the dance by the cute eighth-grade boy. Only I'm almost thirty, and very happily married. As if this flight didn't have me worked up enough I'm simply reminded that disaster seems to follow my birthdays. When I turned twenty-one, the neighboring county burned up. On my sixteenth birthday, an earthquake destroyed my grandparents' home. Here's to hoping my embarrassing people skills are as bad as it gets for thirty.

The way-too-handsome-for-my-own-good seat buddy calls the nearest flight attendant over, and I can't help but wonder what he's doing in coach. First class seems more fitting of his profile. "Please send over two of your finest glasses of wine, as soon as you're able." I'm surprised he didn't ask for a martini, shaken, not stirred.

His charm works on the unsuspecting attendant, who seems to react much like I did and blushes at his request before nodding and stumbling off to continue her pre-flight tasks.

"Thank you, for my phone, and the wine," I say, grateful I'm faring better than the poor girl next to hairy tank-top guy. At least I got seated by a handsome man who just might be 007 himself. I sneak a glance behind me and catch the guy coughing up something questionable, the lavender-blue eyed women's seat beside him empty. I wouldn't blame her if she'd asked to be moved.

The fasten-seatbelt sign dings and a well-rehearsed woman's voice begins to speak. A man performing a choreographed routine stands in the aisle beside me. I sink back into my semi-comfortable seat, grateful to find reprieve through this interruption of my social ineptness.

"Ladies and gentlemen, the captain has turned on the fasten-seatbelt sign. If you haven't already done so, please stow your carry-on luggage underneath the seat in front of you or in an overhead bin. Please take your seat and fasten your seatbelt. Make sure your seat is straight and folding trays are in their full, upright position . . ."

I can feel 007's stare burning into the side of my face, and though I try my best to ignore it on the outside, my heart races inside my chest. It's probably all in my head anyway; he seems nice enough, but I'm unsure why a guy like him would be interested in me.

Maybe he is he flirting? I'm unsure what flirting even looks like anymore.

". . . if you are seated next to an emergency exit . . ."

The flight attendant looks at me—

". . . and if you are not capable or do not wish to perform the functions described in the event of an emergency, please ask a flight attendant to re-seat you."

I turn to look at 007. He winks and smiles at me. This is definitely flirting. Perhaps I should move seats, but I'm too mortified to do anything else but sit still and wait for the plane to land in Miami for fear of what else I might do embarrass myself.

The roar of the plane's engines increases as we begin to taxi down the runway.

"Sure is dreadful weather we're having today," 007 says, resting his chin on his hand, eyes facing the waterfall flowing over the small oval window.

I twist my wedding ring around my finger nervously. Talking about weather seems safe enough. I can talk about weather.

"I'm hoping the flight won't be too bumpy." I look at the soft stubble lining his firm, square jaw, how his lips are the oddest shade of washed-out pink, and his coffee-colored hair that waves but doesn't curl, almost touching the collar of his leather jacket. He doesn't look at me but I almost see his mouth turn up into a smile. I face myself forward, before he can see how awkwardly I'm staring him, a *stranger*, and focus on the narrow slit in the first-class cabin curtain.

The rain runs horizontally across the window as the plane rolls faster down the tarmac.

"Flight attendants prepare for takeoff," says our hopefully adept pilot, his voice garbled by the loud-speaker.

We speed down the runway, engines roaring. I press my back into my seat until I can feel the seat's fibers poking through my shirt and my hands grip the armrest as if holding on might be the only thing in the world keeping this plane together. As the plane leaves solid ground, a heaviness flips in my stomach, and I realize I'm holding my breath.

Calm as can be, 007 looks through the emergency protocol pamphlet from the pocket in the seat. Outside the window, water streaks past until the rain is replaced by dark grey wisps. As we ascend through the clouds the plane bumps and jolts as if the clouds were speed bumps instead of water vapor. I clutch the armrest a little bit tighter. This must be what it's like to be a passenger on a toy plane flown by a toddler.

"So, what are you headed to Miami for on this fine-weathered day, business or pleasure?" 007 asks still looking casually through the pamphlet. I turn my eyes back to the seat in front of me.

Talking to him would be a nice distraction from

the bumping and jostling going on, and suddenly I find his voice to be calming even if my heart skipped a beat when he said the word "pleasure".

"Pleasure. My mother-in-law gifted me this trip for my birthday, actually."

"I see. What a kind woman." His eyes turn to me and brighten as he smiles. "So you're spending your birthday alone?"

"No, not alone," I answer quickly, but I'm caught in his smile.

The plane jolts, taking my breath with it, as we're both thrown forward in our seats. My hair flings across my face, but I leave it alone, gripping the armrest tighter, fearful again of what might happen if I let go. 007's hand gently brushes the strands off my cheek and places them behind my ear, sending a tingle down my neck as he smooths the rest of my hair before returning his hand to his seat where it belongs.

"There, that's better." His voice is calm, soothing my fears of the bumpy flight. "You have a most lovely face, my darling. No need to keep it hidden." He smiles again, bigger, and this time almost seductively. "You were saying you're not alone on your holiday?"

"I'm meeting up with an old friend of mine."

His eyebrows rise, creasing his forehead— the only creases his face has, come to think of it.

"My husband was going to come with me but—" The plane jolts again. My knuckles turn white gripping the armrest, and I silently pray for the plane to steady. I swallow the lump of nerves growing in my throat and continue, "But his work schedule got shifted, and I have two kids at home, so it's a girls-only weekend now."

My face reddens as his dark, thick-lashed eyes stare deep into mine. My heart beats faster till the sound of blood pulsing through my ears competes with the sound of the plane's engines; if this turbulence doesn't do me in, he surely will. He leans forward toward me on the armrest, his eyes narrow almost as if he's examining me.

He angles his body closer to my seat. "You look far too young to be a mother."

I remove my hand from the armrest we share, leaning as far away from him as I can without falling into the aisle. He's coming on to me. Why jeans, a T-shirt, zip-up hoodie, and Vans are something to stare at I don't know— not the sexiest combo of clothing. Maybe I should switch rows. I sneak a look up over the back of my seat. Every seat is filled minus the empty space where the lavender-blue-eyed woman was sitting. Perhaps she's in the bathroom, made sick from this flight— or her seat buddy.

Lightning flashes, illuminating the cabin. A deafening boom hits the plane, knocking me once again into 007's firm, leather-clad arms. The man beside me braces me back to sitting, his hands linger on my shoulders longer than necessary. The smell of him once again invades my senses.

"Sorry, again." I steady myself, kindly brushing his hands off me while the plane rattles and shakes all of us passengers within.

"My goodness, this is some weather to fly in." He looks almost giddy, as if we're on some theme park ride and not flying through the air without a lifeline.

A woman behind me begins a frantic, whispered rendition of the Lord's Prayer which sends the hair on the back of my neck on end. I'm not the only one nervous about this storm. My cold, clammy hands glue themselves to the shaky armrests once again, and I try to quell the panic rising in my throat. Another flash and the shaking intensifies. Thunder echoes through the cabin, drowning out the roar of the engines. The lights flicker on and off like a strobe. 007 sets his hand on top of my wrist. My eyes fill with tears as I look at him. I try my best to summon up any tiny bit of courage I might have— something to keep me strong, something to feel okay, but find myself lacking.

"There, there, love, this will pass as soon as we reach cruising altitude. Nothing to worry about," he says in a calm, monotone voice that no longer comforts my fears as we rise further into the turbulent storm clouds.

After a ding, a garbled voice speaks over the inter-com: *Ladies and gentlemen, this is the captain speaking.*

Please remain calm. We will be turning the plane around as we need to make an emergency land—" lightning strikes again, hitting the plane, as power cuts out. For one quick moment all seems still as static electricity radiates around me in the darkened cabin. Illuminated only by tiny orange emergency lights lining the aisle, I strain to see the worry growing in the faces around me.

Another jolt disrupts the stillness, followed by an explosion louder than the thunder. The lights flicker on then back off again. My stomach knots as the plane drops rocking us back and forth like a ship riding over stormy seas as the pilot tries to regain its stability.

But the shaking only worsens. Then, as if in slow motion, I watch the oxygen masks fall from above. My heart stops. This can't be happening.

Chaos swarms around me as flight attendants fight to stay upright in the unstable plane, rushing up and down aisles to help passengers with their masks. Their pale, sweaty faces are illuminated by more flashes of lightning, assuring me this isn't going to end well.

"Everything is fine!" one flight attendant yells next to me over the noise of the storm to the two hundred frenzied people around her. "This is just a precautionary measure." She helps stretch the mask over my head and onto my face, but I can feel it in the shake of her hands that this is no precaution. The lights flicker back on, then off again until our still-ascending plane loses all power. An eerie stillness of finality blankets the cabin in morbid terror as everyone sits frozen and silent. For a moment, it's as if the clouds try to suspend us in the air as long as they can, but the plane begins to fall. Simultaneously lightning flashes as a chorus of screams follows another explosion from somewhere near the front of the plane.

Panicked, bloodied passengers from first class try to defy the pull of gravity as they race past me up the aisle. Grabbing the seats as they struggle to climb to the back of the plane. Clouds of thick black smoke follow them into coach.

"FIRE! FIRE!" yells a man in a suit, gripping tight to my seat as he struggles past me and up the aisle with the others.

The plane shakes in its violent decent causing some to lose their footing, screaming as they fall past me back towards the fiery hell they were trying to escape. The horror of it all begins to set heavy in my chest as my mind tires to catch up with the reality of what's happening.

Terror rises as passengers continue to lose all sense of sanity. More exit their seats only to fall to the front of the plane. I turn away and lock eyes with 007, his hand tightly holding my wrist, possibly the only thing keeping me from escaping to the back myself. A moment of peace settles over me as his unmasked face stares back. A smile appears on his lips and then the moment is over. My stomach knots as we fall faster.

Smoke penetrates my oxygen mask, forcing me back to the bleak reality of this flight from hell. I press my head back into my seat to not fall forward myself. Sick to my stomach, warm bile rises in my throat. I choke it back down and squeeze my eyes shut. 007 leans his head close to mine. His lips brush my ear sending a shock of emotion through me.

"You are going to be fine."

"No! We're not!" I yell from behind my mask, tears welling in my eyes.

I try to pull my arm away from his hold, but he holds tighter. So tight it almost hurts. But I welcome the grounding it brings. He grabs the back of my head with his other hand and presses his forehead into mine. An intimate gesture that in a different situation would not be welcomed. But I know my end is near and I allow myself to take comfort in this stranger. My breath tightens as the air thickens with smoke. I close my eyes tighter, his cool, calm head against my sweaty one, and listen as he repeats rhythmically, "You'll be okay, you'll be okay . . . "

With that, the chaos around me fades and Phil's words from earlier come to mind: *Everything will be fine.* Only everything isn't going to be fine. I open my eyes as 007 releases his hand from the back of my head and removes his forehead from mine leaving his other hand firmly planted on my left arm. My mask is failing as fogginess replaces my fear with a lack of oxygen. Smoke clouds my vision and I watch my mysterious seatmate disappear behind a veil of darkness.

My chest rises and falls, struggling for air as my seatbelt painfully cuts deep into my hip bones. It's the only thing keeping me from falling into the seat in front of me.

Not that it matters. I'm going to die today.

Tears fall free, stinging my eyes as they mix with the hot smoke billowing around me. Amber flames creep slowly up the aisle toward my feet. And I wonder how bad it will hurt when it ends.

All the other passengers who didn't fall into the first-class cabin yet, are still trying to climb to the back of the plane. Their bodies break over the seats as they try to fight their way to the rear, trampling over each other like animals. Flames creep closer, and my self-preservation kicks in. I pull at my arm, trying to free it from my captor. But he only grabs tighter.

"Stay where you are," he says calmly, over the noise.

"Let go of me!" I rip off my useless mask with my free hand, confident if I hold tight enough to the seats I can climb to the back as well.

"We'll hit the ground before the flames reach us. You'll have a better chance of surviving if you stay in your seat. You'll be crushed back there or fall in the flames."

He's right. I stop fighting him and focus on my struggle for air. The shaking of the plane is unbearable. My chest tightens as I cough and wheeze no longer able to breathe anything but smoke. Images of Imogene, Davina, and Phil swarm through my head as I search for each of their perfect faces. Desperate to see them one last time, but nothing will come into focus. I can't even say goodbye. I think of finding my phone, but the disturbing reality of what they would hear in that call breaks me. Their last memory of me shouldn't be filled with the audible terror of my death.

I'm leaving them without a mother.

Emptiness fills my soul.

Suffocating, I hyperventilate as my lungs search for air that is no longer available.

There is no way out of this.

007 grabs my wrist so hard the bones begin to squeeze together, yet I still find comfort in not being alone. I don't even know his name. My eyes are now too dry from the fire for tears, but burnt sobs of breathless sorrow release from my heavy heart while my soul and the plane fall deeper into hopeless despair.

"BRACE! BRACE FOR IMPACT!" echoes faintly over the crashing metal as we finally hit ground.

The plane folds around me. In a violent instant, the whole ceiling disappears. Pieces of seats, metal, and luggage smash into me as the plane searches for a final resting place.

Forward, to the side, the other, upside down and

around. I'm whipped about, held in only by the flimsy fabric belt across my hips. I watch as the sky and ground trade places over and over again. A blur of clouds, smoke, and dirt. The plane tumbles and continues to shatter, losing pieces, and people, as it goes.

Something hits my arm cutting deeply into my wrist. A searing pain radiates through my body. Heat burns into my skin. And I notice 007, as well as his seat, and that whole side of the plane, is gone. Everything stills. And I'm left alone, upside down, hanging from my seat, still buckled in. My body bashed and broken. The pain too great to feel anymore.

There's no air to scream as the world begins to darken around me. All is still and silent; only a ringing in my ears and a burning in my breathless lungs remain.

3

ANYTHING BUT ALL RIGHT

Beep, beep, beep, beep.

I snuggle deeper into my warm sheets, pulling the down comforter up over my ears. It can't be morning yet. Regardless of my efforts to drown it out, the alarm continues to shout out its repetitive beat. I swat at it, knocking it off the night-stand to the floor with a thud. It's still beeping as I try to shake the horrors of last night's dream. I am never flying again, ever.

Sitting up, I swing my legs off the edge of my bed. The cold air settles on my bare skin and goosebumps to prickle up and down my legs. I shiver and glance down at the clock laying face up at my feet. It's only three-a.m. Annoyed, I pick it up and push the stop button, but the alarm blares on. It must have broken in the fall. I cringe, wondering how Phil is still sleeping through it. When I glance at his side, all I see is an empty divot and tousled sheets; he must be working tonight. I touch his spot and find it cold. Frowning, I don't remember him leaving. But he probably received a call sometime in the middle of the night and left without waking me. A sense of unease settles in the pit of my stomach. He always wakes me before leaving. Always brushes my cheek with his lips as he whispers good-bye.

I pull the alarm clock's plug from the wall, but the beeping continues, even without power. Maybe it has a back-up battery? Before I can look, an odd flicker of light catches my eye, reflecting in the barn wood mirror on the wall to my left. It dances like the flame of a candle, calling me from my bed, teasing me to come closer. Heart thumping, I tuck the incessant beeping clock under my pillow and walk to the mirror.

The tiny flame grows, filling the mirror with a raging fire as I approach. Hot air stings my face as if this fire is real, but it can't be real. A woman appears in place of my reflection within the flames. Her body is burning and mangled beyond recognition. I try and scream at the horror that stands before me, but nothing comes out. Again, I try, forcing air up from my lungs, but still no sound.

My scream remains silent.

I try to run, but my legs won't move. It's as if my feet have fused with the floor, cruelly forcing me to watch as the woman in the mirror burns. Her vacant eyes meet mine, staring from her blistering face. She doesn't seem to fear the fire or feel the pain of her melting skin. Sweat beads on my forehead, dripping down my face. The fire crackling and popping before me. Her mouth begins to move in a rhythmical motion as if she's chanting the words of a sinister spell. But the sound of her voice is drowned out by the roar of the flames. Her lips stop moving as she reaches her arms out toward me. She flicks her wrists and the mirror bursts sending fire and glass shooting into me. Finally freed, the woman screeches an ear-piercing call that reaches over the roaring blaze. She grabs my wrists, digging sharp, claw-like nails deep into my skin. Screams release from me as well, as searing pain burns into my arms radiating up into my body.

She smiles as she yanks me hard towards her, pulling me in through the broken mirror. Into the flames.

BEEP, beep, beep, beep.

Gasping for breath, I wake up again, unsure if I'm still dreaming or not. The constant, annoying rhythm continues to beep, keeping pace with the pounding beat of my heart. I lie still for a moment, in sweat-drenched clothes that aren't my own, staring at a bright ceiling covered in white square tiles and rectangular fluorescent lights. As I try to sit up, a tug on my right forearm draws my attention to the IV line taped to the inside of my elbow. I look to my left arm — this one's wrapped in a white bandage. I try to curl my fingers into a ball but the mere flinch of my pinky shoots pain up my arm and into my shoulder, and I remember the plane.

The crash.

Death.

I'm alive? Pushing myself up in the hospital bed, I read the band cuffed around my wrist:

Aileen Ross

Birthdate 10/19/1985

El Dorado County Hospital

I stare around me, stunned, breath caught in my throat. Dingy-white tile borders the bottom half of the sea-foam-green walls as a grey and black speckled linoleum tiles the floor. To my right, the window shades are open, revealing a high-rise view of a sunny, cloudless sky. On the sill sits a line of hand-drawn cards and vases filled with cheery, colorful bouquets. Drooping 'Happy Birthday' balloons that struggle to reach their full height are tied to a peach-colored vinyl chair. Empty.

Beep, beep, beep, beep. My only companion.

My mind races as I try to figure out if this is real or another dream. I remember my bones breaking and the metal that cut into my skin as the plane tore itself apart upon impact. But I feel fine aside from an ache in my throat and the pain in my left arm. No other markers from the crash mar my skin, anywhere that I can currently see. I remove the heart monitor pinching my index finger and rub the bridge of my nose while enjoying the silence of the empty room for a brief moment before an even louder chain of alarms is set off instead.

Squeaky shoes race from outside my room as a panicked nurse in baby-blue scrubs bursts through the hospital room door.

"Oh, thank heavens!" she says with a slight draw to her voice, one hand over her nurse's badge and the other on the wall to support her as she catches her breath. "Nice to see you up, sunshine. Been out for two days now." She walks over, promptly placing the monitor back on my finger. "Now, what were you thinking taking this thing off and scaring the hell out me?" Beads of sweat form on her forehead. She smells like peppermint and hand sanitizer.

I open my mouth to apologize, but a deep burn in my throat stops me.

"Take it easy, sweetie. They just took you off the ventilator this morning. Your throat might be tender for a day or two." Her tired eyes shine as she smiles, and I wonder how long she's been waiting for me to wake up. Oh, that's right. She said two days, but my brain is having trouble grasping the fact two days are missing from my life.

I mouth the word "sorry". Even the movement of speaking hurts.

"Don't you worry, sweetie. Let me get you some ice chips." She steps out of the room for a moment and yells at someone, then drags a big cart full of medical monitoring equipment from the far corner of the room to my side.

"I just don't want a beautiful young woman dying on my watch. You're a miracle, you know that? When they found you, well, I heard it didn't look good." She shakes her head and places a blood pressure cuff on my arm. "The dogs found you near the wreckage buried pretty deep under the mess, charred as could be. At first they assumed you were burned up like the rest of them, bless their souls. Open please." I open my mouth; a cold metal thermometer is jabbed under my tongue. We wait in silence.

As I wait, I stare into her baby blue scrubs and see a purple pen poking out of the pocket on her chest. Lavender eyes flash before me as my head buzzes. The room grows dark around me. I fall back onto soft, wet earth, looking up into a blackening sky clouded by thick smoke. Icy rain pricks down onto my skin from above. The air thins, and it's hard to breathe. Frozen I watch as thorny vines covered in black, rotting roses reach up from the earth beneath me, wrapping around my neck, my arms, my legs, entangling my entire body. I try to yell for help, but the burn in my throat is too great. The woman with the lavender eyes stands over me and smiles a wicked smile. She plucks a rose dripping thick black oil from its stem. She tilts her head watching it drip slowly down her arm before suddenly disappearing into a cloud of smoke. Terrified, I shut my eyes as the thorns from the vine extend, biting into my skin. The earth shakes.

In the distance dogs bark and a man yells, "We found one!"

Once more I try to cry out but the earth gives way, and the thorns tighten their grip, stealing my last labored breath as the earth swallows me whole.

"Sweetie? Aileen?" The cold touch of a wet towel on my forehead brings me back to my chatty nurse. "Wake up, you fainted."

"I'm okay," I say with a hoarse whisper, surprised that the ache in my throat has subsided. I try and sit up again, wincing from the pain still in my arm, radiating from under the bandage on my left.

"You are pale. You should really stay lying down," she says. "I know this must be a lot for you to take in all at once, but I'm glad your throat seems to be feeling better."

"No, really, I'm okay, I'd like to sit." She helps me up the rest of the way. Tucking the pillows behind my back while eyeing me carefully.

"You're the talk of the town, you know." She begins the process of checking my vitals all over again. "Reporters are all lined up outside just trying to steal a peek at the 'Miracle Woman of Flight 29!'" She shouts this like some old action movie title, complete with arm gestures. "The EMT's brought you here since we're the closest hospital to the crash site, we cleaned you up, and you won't believe it— soot! You were just covered in soot! It really is a miracle that all you got was a little scratch on the wrist."

Scratch on the wrist is an understatement. A sharp pain shoots up into my elbow and an unwelcome clamminess creeps over me as reality sets in. *I survived. This isn't a dream. This pain is real.* Bile rises to my throat as memories assault my mind. Grinding metal, people screaming. I clasp my hands to my mouth in hopes of holding in the horror I so desperately need to vomit out.

"Oh, honey, let me get you something. You're as green as a frog!" She holds a bedpan under my chin as I heave into it over and over again until there is nothing left but memories of a day I'd much rather forget.

I wait, my face hovered over the bedpan as I muster up the courage to ask a question I don't really wish to know the answer of. "Are there others?" She hands me a tissue to wipe my mouth.

Hope clings to my question. After all, I survived.

The nurse looks at me in silence as she sets aside the bedpan, the warmth quickly fading from her face. My heart drops. I already know the answer.

She gently rubs my shoulder as if it might dull the bite of her words. "You're the only one."

Bile rises again, and she hands me a fresh bedpan. "I'll leave this with you. I need to let Dr. Harmon know you're awake and doing all right, considering."

I am anything but all right. More memories push their way up, this time riddled with guilt. The woman with the lavender-blue eyes, and 007— or whoever he was— and countless others are gone, and I survived.

My body shakes, and I drop the empty bedpan, pulling the thin hospital blanket over me. It doesn't bring much warmth for this hopeless chill forming within my bones, but I find comfort in my temporary hiding place. I shouldn't be alive. All those people are dead. I blink, waiting for the tears to release the huge lump lodged in my throat, but nothing happens. I can't even cry yet.

Footsteps echo down the hall from the open door. A strong, familiar smell of happier times and Old Spice Sport enter the room. My heart pounds as a corner of my hiding spot rises and Phil peeks his head in under my blanket, and finally, the tears come.

Tears form in his eyes, which are a more vibrant blue than normal from the redness surrounding them. "Thank God you're awake." Signs of sorrow too deep for words are carved into the creases of his forehead. He thought I had died.

I'm unable to return the smile. "Hi."

He lifts the blanket off of me and sits down on

the bed, his warm arms wrap me in a gentle embrace. I could spend the rest of eternity here, with him holding me. He pulls back a bit, and his soft, tired, red eyes hold mine. His gaze offering sweet solace from the storm of emotions swirling inside my head. But I can't accept it. His lips crash onto mine in a passionate kiss rivaling any great romance novel. One hand cups my face and the other tangles into the back of my greasy, ratted hair. I want to return the kiss with the same fervor and heat it's being given. I want to pour myself into him with every ounce of love I have— every ounce of the love I thought I'd never live to give again— but I can't. My arm aches as I rest my hands on his shoulders. He stops.

"I'm sorry, I shouldn't have done that." His voice quivers as more tears form at the rim of his bottom lashes.

"Don't be sorry." I force out what I can of a smile to bring him some comfort. "Where are the girls?" I ask, wanting nothing more than to hold them all in my arms forever and never let go.

"They're with Mom. She's already on her way." He looks down toward the floor, I take his hand with my good arm and take a deep breath. "I talked to your mom," and before I can respond, he adds, "I had to. I'm sorry— she called when she saw the news. Recognized your description from the damn reporters. She thought you were— we all thought you

. . . " He can't finish, his words lost in a bad memory of his own as he sits on the bed beside me.

I haven't spoken, really spoken, to my mom in years. Brief calls or emails here and there to announce the birth of another unvisited granddaughter, but after my dad's death and her refusal to attend Phil's and my wedding, we haven't had much to say to each other.

"Is she coming?" The hope is long gone from my question. He shakes his head in a sorry no, and I let out a sigh of relief. I have enough to deal with at the moment.

Our attention turns toward the door as a tall, goofy-looking middle-aged man with wiry, unkempt hair enters the room. White coat. Clipboard in hand.

"Hello there," the man says as his eyes scan his clipboard. "Well, what do you know? Your chart says today is your birthday. You are one very lucky lady Mrs. Ross." He walks to the foot of my bed.

Phil stands to greet him. "Hello, Dr. Harmon."

"Well Phil, you must feel relieved." Dr. Harmon turns his attention back to me. "Aileen, this man hasn't left your side since you arrived. You got yourself a good one." Dr. Harmon pats Phil on the shoulder. "Now if you don't mind, I'd like to ask you a few questions." I nod, and he continues. "Can you tell me your full name and date of birth?"

"Aileen Elizabeth Ross, October 19th, 1985."

He smiles as he jots down notes on his clipboard.

"Very good, that was an easy one. What year is it currently?"

I think for a moment, "2015."

"Good. Now, are you experiencing any pain or discomfort?"

I mentally scan myself, still in disbelief of my physical state after falling from the sky. "Just my wrist. And my throat is a bit tender."

He writes a few more notes before politely excusing Phil from the room so he could talk me confidentially for a minute.

Phil steps out into the hall, hand on the doorknob. "I'll be just outside the door." I can sense his hesitation in leaving me as he slowly closes the door behind him.

Dr. Harmon sits down in the vinyl peach chair to my right and takes a deep breath. "Aileen, I am puzzled but pleased to say that aside from your arm and the brief coma, we could find nothing wrong with you. Normally an incident like you were just in would cause massive trauma to the body and brain but every X-ray, CAT scan, and MRI we did showed nothing besides the injury to your left wrist. If I didn't know any better, I'd question if you were even on that plane."

I remember the seat belt cutting into my pelvis. My body being crushed by the tumbling aircraft. "I was definitely there," I answer. Though now, even more so I wish I hadn't been.

"Let's have a look at that arm of yours, shall we?"

He removes the bandage, and I cringe while the sticky gauze tugs and pulls at the raw, bloody gash on the underside of my wrist. The iron tang of my blood is overwhelming. I turn my head and hold my breath.

"Huh. Interesting." He gently twists and turns my arm, I wince. "Sorry," he says, looking confused. "It's healing quite well." He sets my arm on my lap before he flips back through my chart.

I look down at my left hand and notice my ring finger is bare. My wedding ring gone.

Dr. Harmon taps his pen on the clipboard confused. "Hmm. It's not at all as deep of a cut as the ER doctor mentioned here. There is a note of possible amputation watch. But I see no reason why he would have mentioned such a thing."

I don't say anything, saddened by my missing ring. Still in shock over the fact I survived.

Dr. Harmon presses the nurse call button.

A tall, male nurse in navy scrubs pops his head in the doorway. "Need something Doctor?"

Dr. Harmon stands. "Elmer, grab some ointment and gauze for Mrs. Ross, please, and have Judy come wrap this back up."

"So, I'm okay?" I ask, suddenly picturing myself with one hand. My stomach lurches at the thought, it could have been so much worse.

He writes a few more notes in my chart. "Shockingly, yes."

A nurse, who I assume is Judy, comes in. She quickly wraps my wrist and leaves.

"Thank you, Judy," Dr. Harmon says to the nurse.

"Does this mean I can go home?" I ask, my wrist throbbing under the tight bandage.

"I'd like to keep you overnight, just for observation."

"I'd really like to go home." *Home*. A place I thought I'd never see again with my family who days ago was forced to assume the worst. I want to leave this all behind me as quickly as I can. Starting with getting out of this hospital gown and taking a nice hot shower.

"Well, Mrs. Ross— " There's a hint of disappointment in his voice. "I strongly suggest you stay another night but have no immediate reason to keep you. I want you to promise to take it easy. Don't be surprised if you start to see bruising. Watch for signs of internal bleeding or severe headaches, and return immediately if you experience anything out of the ordinary. Your paperwork will have some more info on what to look for. We have a counselor on-site for you as well. Also, someone from the National Transportation Safety Board has been waiting to talk with you. I'll go start your discharge papers and let them know you are awake."

"Do I have to talk to them now?" The last thing I want to talk about right is the crash with a stranger.

"It is important you speak with them, especially

since you are the only one they can speak to, but I'll let them know you need a few days, okay?" His smiley demeanor returns as he points toward the door. "Looks like you have visitors."

My heart swells as Davina's sweet little face peeks through a crack in the partially opened door and I break all over again just as I did seeing Phil.

Ana opens the door further. "Go on in, sweetie." She herds Davina and Imogene into the room, followed by Phil.

Davina runs to my bed, jumping up into my arms. "Mommy!"

"Hi baby." Tears flood into my eyes at the feel of my sweet girl in my arms.

"I thought you might need these." Ana's voice cracks as she sets a bag full of new clothes on the floor by my bed.

"Thank you." I wipe my eyes with the shoulder of my hospital gown as Davina hops down off the bed and begins to play with the balloons by the window.

Imogene stays back by the room door, her face red and puffy, staring at the floor.

"Mommy's okay," Phil reassures her, but I can hear the waver in his voice as if he still doesn't believe his own words. He takes her hand, and they walk together to me.

I can only imagine how hard she would have taken this and my heart breaks even more. I crawl out of the bed as far as my IV line will allow, and kneel down in front of her, holding her beautiful, sad face in my hands. "I'm okay sweet girl. See? I'm okay." She places her hands on either side of my face. Examining me as tears fill her eyes. She looks as if she's aged five years while I was out.

"Mommy?" Imogene questions before bursting into tears of her own. She hugs me tight. "I thought you died," she sobs into my shoulder.

"I'm okay baby," I whisper tearfully in her ear, rubbing her back to calm her. I thought I died too.

"Mommy! We got to use a secret passageway into the hospital!" Davina shouts over the noise of her thumping a rather large birthday balloon into the wall, clearly not as aware of how close she came to losing me, and part of me is grateful for her innocence.

Ana cuts in, almost as excited as Davina though I know it's only a face she puts on when emotions run high, "I called Jordyn for you; she was happy to hear you're alive. And if you hadn't noticed, you are quite the fuss these days. Reporters have been staking out this hospital since they brought you in. One was extra nosy— pretty little thing, had very unique eyes, almost purple . . ."

My head rings as lavender eyes and a sinister smile once again flashes before me. The image from my dream. I blink.

Ana continues, not noticing my unease, "But anyways, being pretty doesn't mean you get to butt into people's lives like that. I told them all to mind their own damn business." She stops, pursing her lips as tears fill her eyes, her walls crumbling with the tears falling loose down her cheeks. "Oh Aileen, I should have never made you go on that trip."

"Nonsense Mom, you had nothing to do with this." Phil wraps his arm around his mom's shoulder.

"Well, I'm sure as hell glad you're okay. I don't know if I could live with myself if anything worse had happened to you." Her voice high-pitched and barely audible through her now uncontrollable sobs.

I clear my throat in hopes of lightening the tone of the room. I can't bear to see the pain in each of their blood-shot, puffy eyes. "Well, I do believe today is my birthday."

I finally accept this is no longer a dream as they each come to my side and we embrace in a family-sized hug.

I breathe out a sigh of relief.

I'm alive.

THE STEAM from the hospital shower fills the small bathroom with warmth as I dig through the bag of clothes and toiletries Ana brought for me. She picked out an eclectic mix of various oversized sweatpants and loose-necked shirts in case I was in too much pain to dress in anything constrictive. Oddly enough, I'm in no pain at all aside from the wound on my arm. I take one more mental scan of my body and find nothing out of the ordinary. Weird. Maybe even miraculous.

Turning back to the clothes, I settle on a light pink scoop-neck tunic and navy sweats and set them on a towel-covered toilet lid. With discharge papers all signed and vitals taken one last time, I was given the go-ahead to get cleaned up and dressed. Phil already untied the top string of my hospital gown before he took Ana and the girls to the cafeteria for some dinner, and as I tug on the last remaining string with my one good arm, the gown falls to the floor as I stare in disbelief at my reflection. I knew there was already no cuts or bruising showing up on my extremities, but I was sure there would be some proof of the ordeal I went through from the seat belt across my lap. A band of bruising. Cuts. Something. Yet . . . there's nothing. No bruises, no cuts— and most unsettling of all my stretch marks are gone. No more crinkly loose skin around my belly button. The proof of carrying my girls, gone. I pinch myself hard, hoping if this was still a dream I'd wake up to reality, only reality might be much worse than this. Perhaps I should be grateful and accept that for whatever reason I'm okay. Maybe this really is a miracle.

Still, as I shower then dress, I can't stop my hands from shaking or quiet the little voice inside my head whispering, *there is something very wrong here.*

4

OIL AND WINE

Accompanied by hospital staff and local law enforcement, Phil, the girls, and I, push through a loud crowd of reporters, and cameras, and blinding spotlights. In a blur the hospital security helps load us up into a black, unmarked SUV. They drive us far away from the hospital to my mom-van parked just outside of El Dorado City. Phil takes us the rest of the way home. As the city falls far behind us in the rearview mirror, I'm grateful to be heading toward our small-town country seclusion. Far away from the big cities and nosy news station reporters.

Just as we pass over the Amador County line I yawn. Exhaustion is finally taking over from the excitement of the day. I glance over to Phil in the driver's seat. He notices and rests his hand gently on my knee. Behind me girls are sleeping, Ana sits between them. She smiles and whispers, "We're almost home."

Home.

I wait in the car while Phil and Ana carry the girls inside. My eyes too heavy to keep open any longer. The last thing I remember is Phil laying me down on our bed, covering me up with our cozy down comforter, and kissing my forehead before sleep finally takes its hold.

I AWAKEN ON THE PLANE, next to the dark-haired 007, a cheery flight attendant stands in the aisle beside me. The sky is blue outside the small oval window, not a cloud or storm in sight.

"Here's your drinks you requested, sir," she says with a southern lit, handing my seatmate two glasses of pungent red wine. "Is there anything else I can get y'all?" Her lipstick matches the blood-red liquid within my glass.

"No, thank you," 007 says.

I look at him, confused, I remember him ordering wine, but I don't recall falling asleep after. What happened to the storm?

He motions to the small glass in my hand. "That should help calm your nerves."

"Thank you?" I say more like a question. Maybe my anxieties over flying exhausted me out more than I was aware. I raise the wine to my lips, remembering how much I embarrassed myself moments after take-off, and then to fall asleep? It only adds to my social ineptness. I can't form my thoughts right. Maybe he's right and the wine will help.

I empty my glass in seconds. He looks at me, one eyebrow raised like he knows what I'm thinking; one isn't enough.

He hands me his untouched glass. "Looks like you could use another."

I drink this one just as quick and set my empty glass next to the first one in the tray in front of me when a large burp makes its way up and out of my throat. 007 looks as if he wants to burst into laughter but gives me a gracious smile instead. I can feel warmth rushing into my cheeks.

"Sorry, I don't know what's gotten into me."

He leans in close, too close. His face only inches from mine, his eyes are blazing with fiery desire. My pounding heart overpowers my screaming thoughts to move away from his perfectly chiseled face. The wine kicks in and fogs my mind. Sensations ignite a burn from deep within me, matching the desire in his eyes. His mouth inches closer and closer, passing over my lips, teasing its way to my ear. The stubble of his beard is pleasantly rough against my cheek. "Maybe this will help, too," he whispers.

Electric currents tingle through me as he nibbles my ear, my mind too buzzed to listen to my better judgment. He picks up a wine glass and trails it down the left side of my neck, to my shoulder, then down my bare arm. The cool sensations of the glass send goosebumps all over me, exciting my senses even more. I close my eyes in sweet surrender and moan as he sucks on my earlobe, his breath cool against my neck. He stops. I protest with a purr.

"Shh." He holds a finger to his lips.

I grab his hand and suck his fingers into my mouth a payback of sorts for all his teasing, ignoring the questions screaming in the back of my mind.

"Mmm. But, no, not now." He takes his fingers back. "I want to show you something." He lifts the wine glass, holding it up in front of us before crushing it effortlessly with his hand, tiny flecks of glass glittering down onto his lap.

His eyes darken and with a wicked smile he looks up at me a piece of the glass still in his hand. My heart pounds even harder as fear replaces my adulterous desire. He grabs my left wrist jabbing the shard of glass into me. Slicing through my skin, exposing my veins. I wait for the pain to strike, but it doesn't come. I can only watch in horror as a thick, black oily substance oozes out of me.

His smile widens. "Not so bad is it, love?" His eyes lock with mine. I stare back at him frozen, as he licks his tongue slowly up my arm, tasting the black ooze dripping down from the gash.

A scream forces its way to the front of my mind. I

jerk my arm back and cradling it against my chest wondering what I can use to stop the bleeding. Panicked, I look around in hopes someone might help me, but none of the other passengers seem aware of my cries. With madness in his eyes 007 laughs. Black blood, *my* blood, drips from the corner of his mouth. Suddenly I realize I'm shaking— no, not just me— the plane shakes violently. 007 ceases his laughter as the plane begins to fall—

I SIT UPRIGHT IN BED, drenched in sweat, heart banging within my chest until I realize it was only a terrible nightmare.

"Honey?" Phil asks, half-awake, nudging me. "You okay?"

Gathering my senses, I mumble something noncommittal and look at the clock on my nightstand. It's three-a.m. I'm exhausted, and I can tell he is as well. I rub my wrist over the bandage. My wound is still a little tender, but at least there is no black ooze leaking out of it.

"I'm okay," I whisper, speech returning again. "Go back to sleep."

But instead, his arms reach out and pull me close to his side. Despite his warm and comforting embrace I can't fall back asleep.

The next night I find myself in another nightmare. A similar one to the night before but this time I'm aware I'm dreaming. I'm once again on the plane with 007, only the woman with the lavender eyes is here now. She holds in her hand a black rose. The long green stem is covered with sinister thorns. I watch, helpless as the blossom bursts into flames, setting the plane ablaze as we plummet to the ground.

Phil gently wakes me from the nightmare, again. He's become hyper-aware of my every movement since I woke up in the hospital. While I appreciate the attentiveness, I worry about him going back to work tomorrow with no sleep.

He flops back down on his pillow. "Another bad dream?"

"It's okay, I'll be fine. Get some sleep."

He replies with a snore.

A stipulation for discharge was a phone call with a psychologist the doctor recommended, to make sure I was managing okay. I agreed to one phone call. One. I called her about the first nightmare I had about the woman in the mirror. According to her, adjusting to normal life might be a challenge after what I went through, and I should expect night terrors. But the terrors of these dreams feel far too real.

As I crawl out of bed to head out to the living room so Phil can sleep, something catches my eye in the window. I freeze, staring at the dark silhouette of a person staring straight back at me. All I can see of the shadowy figure is the moonlight glinting off the corner of their eyes.

My heart stops, and I scream.

"What's wrong?" Phil flips on the light on his nightstand as he sits up shielding his eyes from the light.

I look closer out at the window and see nothing but my own reflection. "Sorry, I thought I saw something." God, I need sleep.

"Do you want to talk about it?" His voice is hoarse with a hint of understandable annoyance at being woken up, again. But he's thoughtful, doing what the doctor suggested: *"Don't push her into telling you what's wrong, but make sure someone is there for her to talk with when she's ready."* Will I ever be ready?

He pulls me down back on to the bed. "You aren't sleeping. Do you want to speak with the psychologist again? We can call her in the morning."

I give him a quick kiss. "No, thank you. Two nights really doesn't seem like anything to worry about." Compared to the fact I survived a plane crash.

Only I'm not fine. It's three-a.m. Tuesday morning, and I haven't slept through the night since Friday, the night before my flight. It's not just sleeping that's wrong. I haven't told Phil but I've completely lost my taste for food. I'm hungry and tired, which is makes me constantly grumpy. Every time I dress and see my new flawless abdomen my unsettled feelings worsen. I haven't told Phil about my stomach either. I stuff it all inside, for fear he'll want me to go back to the hospital. I don't want to go back there ever, if I can help it. Being home gives me separation from the realities of that day. The hospital only sits as a reminder me of where I should be right now, dead and buried under the wreckage with the other passengers.

Phil turns out the light and in seconds he's snoring. That man can fall asleep anywhere, anytime, anyway. It's a skill I've always been jealous of, especially now. I look back toward the window and see nothing. My stomach turns realizing it couldn't have been my reflection I saw.

Maybe I'm losing my mind.

Tiptoeing down the dark hall toward the living room, I detour to check on the girls. Both of them lie fast asleep in beds that rest parallel to each other, with just enough space between them to walk. I kneel down between their beds and place a hand on each of their warm, blanketed backs, feeling the soft rhythm of their little heartbeats. Their little bodies rise and fall with each slow, sleeping breath. This has been a ritual of mine since they were born. Even now while they are sleeping, I can still imagine their tiny, sweet newborn faces. It brings me back to the moment I first held Imogene in my arms. All the promises of what being a mom could be. The promise of being different than my own mother. It calmed me, gave me hope that I could have the family

I've always dreamed of. Giving birth to Imogene, holding her in my arms— it was just the beginning; my beginning, and I was in control of how things would be.

But am I different? I rush too much, spend too much time focusing on things that don't matter. I lose my patience too quickly over the small stuff. I control too much and by doing so I fear I've taken my girls, my family, and my life for granted. Falling from the sky, facing death, forces me to be grateful for second chances. The fear of my nightmare fades as I'm filled with the hope that comes with new beginnings— the same hope that filled me the first time I held my Imogene.

I sneak quietly out of their room to the living room couch. Walking through such a tidy house is strange. Toys aren't strewn about like usual, not with Ana being here every day. *When in crisis, clean* is her motto, and she's kept a spotless house for years. Sadness rises within me as I realize I'm the crisis, the reason these floors are tidy.

But sleep finally calls to me now, as I curl up on our well-worn leather couch. I pull up a granny-square afghan my grandmother made years ago and let the night take me, regardless of what dreams may come.

POKE-POKE-GIGGLE. Small fingers jab my side. "Is she dead again?"

"No, Davina, Mommy was never dead, she was just sleeping. Like she is now." Imogene says in her bossiest big-sister tone.

The heaviness of sleep pulls me back down, but Davina's giggles tap at me from the world of the awake. She pokes me again, and I want to wake up and partake in the fun she's having, but I'm just. So. Tired.

"Davina, leave Mommy alone. Let her sleep," Imogene scolds.

Finally, a moment where sleep feels simple again, a moment untainted by terror and guilt, and I'm forced to choose between my daughter's needs and my own. Such is the life of a mother. I was even having a pleasant dream about running through the forest's crisp night air. I hate running, but it was just so peaceful. I felt alive, free, unhindered by worry as the cool forest air filled my lungs with life. But judging by my last few dreams, no doubt it would have turned into a nightmare of me running from something. I yawn with a roar. Stretching my arms and legs out, I force myself from my slumber.

"Who dares to wake me!" I speak in a loud, playful growl, startling the girls as they take off screaming and laughing down the hall.

I stand to chase them, but my vision fades to black, and I fall back down onto the couch.

"You can't get me, Mommy!" Davina yells from somewhere down the hall.

"Oh, I'll get you!" I holler, waiting for my vision to return to normal.

Low blood sugar. That's what this is. My tired body yells at me to lie back down, to sleep longer, maybe even forever. But I stand again and this time my vision holds long enough to get myself down the hall to the entry of my room where the girls are playing on the bed. I pause. My heart pounds in my ears while air squeezes through tight airways into my lungs and I wonder if the fire on the plane damaged them. I catch my breath and smile, seeing two giggling lumps under the comforter next to an exhausted Phil, who has sandwiched his head between the pillow and mattress. I'm sure sleep will take precedence over the game for him.

"You look comfortable," I say to Phil, who groans as Davina and Imogene dog-pile on top of him. He gives in and joins the fun as I hold tight to my weakening consciousness. My heart is full seeing my family happy and quite honestly, there is nothing more I could ask for right now. Okay, I lie. Sleep. I could ask for sleep— or coffee, a nice hot cup would make this morning perfect.

A car honks in the driveway. "Grandma's here!" Imogene yells as she and Davina rush out of the room to greet her. Phil slowly digs himself out of the pile of blankets and pillows left by the girls as I smile, then follow the girls down the hall.

"Hello!" Ana sings from the kitchen, letting herself in and bringing with her the delightful aroma of coffee and maple donuts.

Drawn to the heavenly smell, I join them in the kitchen. Coffee always works wonders when sleep is lacking, and it's the only thing that's tasted right since waking up in the hospital. The girls pick out their donuts and run to the living room where Disney Channel awaits, Ana hands them napkins along the way. Normally I'd forbid junk food for breakfast but being in a plane crash is quickly affecting how much I care about the little things. If they want to eat donuts and watch TV before school— at least for this week— I can be okay with it.

"Thank you for bringing all this."

Ana gives me a big hug and steps back, giving me the once-over. "You look tired," she says, setting plates out on the table before handing me my coffee. "Half-n-Half and honey, right?"

"Yes, thank you."

She sits, and I join her with my coffee at the table. I take a sip of my liquid sleep, in awe of how the creamy warmth fills my mouth, the only thing that still excites my taste buds. As I swallow, it's as if I can feel the coffee spread throughout my body. With each sip, I awaken little by little, until I've gulped the entire 16-ounces.

Ana eyes me with a crooked smile. "Rough night again?" She slides her coffee in front of me. "It's black, but you clearly need this more than I do. I got you more Half-n-Half at Phil's request; it's in the fridge."

"No, really I'm fine." I politely slide the coffee back even though I would kill for more right now. "Once the caffeine kicks in I'll be right as rain." Already it zings through my veins, waking each and every cell along the way.

"Mhmm." She draws a long, blissful sip of her own coffee. "How about I take Davina to the park after I drop Imogene off at school? Give you some time to rest up a bit."

I yawn again, contemplating brewing more coffee. "I might have to take you up on that offer."

Ana takes a bite of a big, soft maple bar and my stomach growls. Maple bars are my favorite and remind me of the happier parts of my childhood when my grandma would bring fresh maple syrup from her farm up north. There's one still left in the box among a few glazed ones. I take it, salivating over the sweet maple syrup and fresh doughy-carb deli- ciousness before shoving it into my mouth. Only instead of a mouthful of soft yummy goodness, I gag on the foul-tasting excuse for a pastry.

Ana hands me a napkin. "Donuts too?"

"Maybe something is wrong with the donuts." But I know it's not the donuts. It's me.

Phil walks in as I'm wiping donut residue off my tongue and stares at me with the same crooked smile his mom gave me while I chugged down my coffee. The kind that asks gently, *Are you okay?* without actually saying it. He grabs a glazed donut out of the box, smells it, and stuffs half of it in his mouth. My stomach sours as I watch him swallow.

"Tastes fine to me," he says, stuffing the other half in his mouth.

Thinking maybe it's just my donut, I lift the last glazed one from the box and try a bite, immediately spitting it out and gagging in the process. Phil laughs at what I can only assume is my disgusted face; that always brings him good laughs. He says I look like a pug because of how far my nose turns up compared to how deep my lips pull down into a frown.

"It's that bad? Really?"

"Here, you taste it." I hold out the donut to him.

He takes the glazed pastry from my hand and devours the whole thing in one bite. "Nufing wrong wif this one!" I dodge the pieces of donut flying out as he talks.

"You are so gross." I can't help but laugh at how ridiculously funny he looks right now. Cheeks puffed out like a chipmunk, I can almost imagine what he looked like as a pudgy-cheeked toddler.

"Maybe you hit your head in the crash and your taste is just a little off," Ana says reassuringly.

"Maybe."

"Give it some time, I'm sure your taste will return soon." Phil gives me a quick kiss on the top of my head. "I need to get going. Are you sure you're okay with me going back to work this soon?"

"I'll be fine," I promise. In reality, I'm terrified of him leaving, unsure if I'm mentally ready to be on my own for the next few days. But with the station low on staff, someone has to be on-call in case of an emergency. The life of a fireman's wife.

"I'll take good care of her, dear," Ana says as she heads to the kitchen sink.

Phil grabs his duffle bag. "Thanks, Mom." He gives her a quick hug and goes to the living room to say goodbye to the girls.

I glance at my mother-in-law as she stands with her back to me rinsing some dishes. Thank God for Ana. I don't know what I would do without her.

WITH PHIL GONE, Imogene at school, and Ana and Davina off at the park, I lie in bed, awake, dreaming with vain hopes I might return to the peaceful place of slumber I was in this morning. Where sleep came easy, and it was harder to stay awake then to give in to sleep's request. Only now, every time I shut my eyes I re-live the images of those people in terror and the thought of sleeping sends me into a panic. Maybe it's the coffee. I heard it makes anxiety worse and I've been drinking far more of it than usual.

The wound on my arm starts to itch. At first it's mild, but the second I touch it the itching worsens, burns even. Though my bandage needs to be changed, I've been unable to muster up the courage to face the damage it hides. Wounds always send a shiver of disgust through me, especially if they're mine. Phil would have changed it for me before he left. I should have asked. Perks of having a firefighter-paramedic as a husband, especially when blood makes you queasy. I suck it up and peel off the dirty gauze when I'm hit with the rotting smell of a festering wound. The putrid stench growing stronger with each rotation of the bandage until it's off, and my eyes behold the horror of what lies underneath.

Just like in my nightmares, an inky black substance oozes out over my wound. I watch in shock as it drips off the underside of the old, saturated bandage. Not caring if it will hurt, I grab a wad of tissues from my nightstand and frantically wipe the ooze off of my arm. It doesn't hurt, in fact, there is no wound at all. Nothing but a jagged, crescent-shaped pink scar. The dirty tissues fall from my shaking hand to the floor. The room begins to spin around me. Waves of nausea hit hard, knocking me from the bed and onto the floor. Cramps consume my stomach making me writhe in pain. I scream for help. Only there is no one there to hear me. No one to help.

The pain worsens, stealing my breath as I crawl across the floor to the bathroom. Chills ripple across my clammy skin as the strongest urge to vomit I've ever felt forces me to my feet. I run. Barely making it over the threshold of the bathroom before I lose my rotten donut and, worst of all, my coffee into the poor, unsuspecting toilet.

The cramping and nausea subside once my stomach is empty. The pain is gone as if it never arrived. Exhausted and sweaty, I slump back against the wall beside the toilet and run my finger over the jagged scar on my completely healed wrist as a dark and dreadful feeling stirs within me.

I survived a crash that no one could survive. My stretch marks are gone. Food no longer tastes as it should. The more things I list off in my head, the more the feeling grows that something is very, very wrong with me.

5

OH BABY

Wednesday through Thursday rendered me useless. Thankfully, Ana was more than willing to come stay and take care of the girls. As long as I stayed away from food, I was fine, but with Ana around not eating is not an option. Every time I'd throw up she'd go on a rant about the uncleanliness of hospitals. How I probably picked up Ebola or some other dreadful disease she's heard floating around the news. I assured her it's likely just a flu.

The news is another thing that's tough to avoid when Ana's around. She's always watching it. My name and the plane crash circulated around the national news circuit for two days straight. Reporters, panelist, and experts analyzing each and every bit of information. Finding anything they could possibly scrounge up to feed the morbid curiosity of their viewers. At first I found it helpful— at least it confirmed the crash really happened, I'm not crazy. But when they held an evening special in honor of the victims, showing names with faces I recognized— the flight attendants, even the hairy, tank-top man— George Williams, 56, flying to Miami to visit extended family— even Ana turned it off.

The Sacramento-area news never went into as much detail as the national media but stretched the coverage out a bit longer than they needed to, in my opinion. It wasn't until yesterday, Thursday, five days after the crash that something else caught their attention. It caught mine too. An unidentifiable female, thought to be late 20's, with no ID, was the victim of an alleged head-on collision Saturday morning in Amador County. I remember the steam rising from the hot car as rain fell upon it, and Deputy Sheriff Jon Harker shaking his head off to the side of the road as we passed by on our way to the airport. The next thing the report confirmed was my own question from that day: detectives could find no evidence of another car's involvement, only that the damage sustained lined up with most head-ons. The report ended with pleas for anyone with any information to call. My bothered mind loops after seeing the wreckage again. Wondering if maybe it was an omen of events to come. What if we stopped to help and I missed my flight? One seemingly small decision would have changed *everything*.

It's Friday morning and while I didn't sleep a wink last night, for the first time in the last week, I actually feel pretty good. Well enough even to relieve Ana of her watch. It took some convincing but she knows Phil will be home by evening. And I think we both know we could use some time to ourselves.

However, by lunchtime my nausea returns, with a vengeance. All it took was opening the can of tune while making the girl's lunch to send me back in front of the toilet. Imogene graciously took-over making sandwiches.

By evening I was useless as a parent. I let them skip their bath and watch more TV than usual and in return they both promised to put themselves to bed early.

Around eight-o-clock, just as I'm taking a breather from this evening's vomiting marathon, Phil returns home from his shift.

"Aileen?" I hear him drop his bags on the kitchen table, then walk down the hall.

"I'm in here," I say softly, trying not to wake the girls. While my nausea seems to have momentarily subsided, staying close to the toilet seems like a good idea.

"What happened around here? The place is a mess." He enters the bathroom, face wrinkled in puzzlement. He's most likely confused since his mom *was* here after all. I neglect to tell him I let her go early. It only takes a few hours for the girls to undo everything she cleaned. He stops as he sees me resting my head on my arms, draped over the toilet. "Sick again?"

"I think I ate something bad, that's all——" and at the mere thought of food, my vomiting break is over. I don't want to tell him I might have the flu; he'd take me to the hospital immediately.

"Well, what the in the world did you eat? You look terrible."

"I don't know what I ate and thanks." I don't hide the sarcasm. "Nice to see you too." I heave again.

"Sorry you feel bad. Maybe you should see a doctor." He kneels down beside me to help hold my hair as I throw up, his warm fingers threading through the strands, making goosebumps break out on my neck from the chill that has yet to leave my bones since waking up in the hospital.

"What is a doctor supposed to do for food poisoning?" I groan, my throat is raw, and my stomach feels like it's been shredded from the inside out.

"I'm pretty sure this is something far beyond food poisoning." His hand slides onto my sweaty forehead. "Well, you don't have a fever, but we should get you checked out just to be safe."

"I'd rather just go to bed." I wish he would just leave me to suffer in peace. I know he means well, but I don't feel like going to the doctor, mainly because I don't want to leave the comfort of my puke palace.

Phil frowns. "You haven't been yourself since

you've been home. You're not sleeping well or eating much of anything. I can see you're losing weight. This isn't normal, Aileen. I really think you need to see a doctor." His brow furrows, pain residing deep within his stormy, ocean-blue eyes from his now constant worry of my wellbeing.

"Surviving a plane crash isn't normal," I remind him. Nothing about me still being here is normal. But he's right: who else throws up everything they eat, can't sleep, and has developed a strong sense of smell, regardless of being in a plane crash? Panic shoots through me as pregnancy alarms ring off in my head. How has this not crossed my mind yet? Right. Probably because Phil had a vasectomy two years ago. But what if the vasectomy reversed— what if I'm pregnant? When was my last period?

"Aileen? You okay? You look even paler. Please let me take you in."

"Would you get my phone, please?" Phil looks at me like I just asked for the moon, but I don't care; I need a calendar and the only one I have is on my phone.

"Would you consider seeing a doctor, please?" he says again, concern rising on his tone. "Plus, you don't have a phone, remember?"

"Right." Mine burned up in the crash. Along with my clothes, luggage and wedding ring. "I'll get yours."

I hold down whatever might be left in my stomach and slowly rise from my post at the toilet. Pins and needles tingle through my feet and up my legs. I straighten my rumpled-up sweats, smooth my hair, and attempt to walk out of the bathroom. My numb legs are proving to be a bit of a challenge, and the urge to purge again grows stronger with each step I take toward my room.

"Stop, it's right here." He pulls it from his pocket and hands it to me. "I'm going to go shower in the other bathroom," he adds, flipping on the vent fan before walking out of the room. I don't blame him, vomit doesn't smell great.

I slide back down to the floor and scroll through the calendar on his phone. 28, 29, 30— I should have started on Wednesday, which would have been day 28, and today is Friday. Not too late I guess; the trauma of the crash could've delayed things. Maybe I'm not pregnant after all.

The thought of another baby feels strange, like an uninvited guest in my home. I never thought of parenting more than two and at this point, I'm terrified to start over. My heart twinges, thinking about the possibility though. But we could start over. A new life to celebrate life wouldn't be the worst thing in the world. I lie down on the bathroom floor to stop the room from spinning around me. The tile cools the heat building in my clammy cheeks as the idea of pregnancy begins to settle, bringing with it a strange comfort. If I am actually pregnant, maybe nothing is wrong with me after all. I try to push the idea out of my mind while I wait till Phil gets out of the shower. I should probably take one myself. Instead, I push myself up and settle for brushing my teeth and running a brush through my greasy hair. Then I remember the last shower I took was at the hospital on Sunday, I'll take one tomorrow.

Cupboards open and shut from the kitchen, and I make my way out of the bathroom, my mouth tasting like mint instead of sick. As I turn to enter the kitchen I see Phil leaning against the sink, eating a bowl of cereal. A shirtless profile backlit by the dim canned lighting above. His low-sitting charcoal sweats nicely emphasize his well-maintained core and the beat of my heart stutters as I walk towards him, catching me off-guard. An unwelcome, shocking bolt of pain shoots throughout my body with an uneven heartbeat.

I clear my throat, setting my heartbeat back to normal as my thoughts refocus on Phil's bare torso. He looks at me and nods after inserting a huge spoonful of Honey O's into his mouth— a mouth rimmed by soft, kissable lips. Suddenly, the only thing I'm thinking about is how much I want him, even after spending the last few days partnered with my toilet. My heart flutters again as lust zips down my body, leaving a deep, dull radiating pain through my chest and up my scratchy throat, but I don't care; nothing else seems to matter but him. I clear my throat again as Phil looks back at his bowl, dipping his long, hard, silver spoon into the milk.

God, what's wrong with me?

Swallowing the discomfort, an urgency fueled by primal needs compels me toward him. Like a lioness hunting her prey, nothing could stop me from wanting to devour him.

"Oh, hello," I say, running my hand lightly down his firm bicep. Tingles run up my finger and settle somewhere pleasantly deep within me.

"Well, hello?" His brows raise as he sets down his cereal bowl and wraps his arms around my waist. He's falling right into my trap.

My lips meet his in a firm, seductive kiss for a moment before I trail more kisses down to his neck. He breathes in deep. I hear his breath catch as my tongue meets his skin and draws up towards his ear. A strange and powerful hunger consumes me as his pulse pounds under my tongue. With each beat of his heart, a sweet aroma pours into my senses, filling the room around me and intensifying my hunger for him.

He grabs me by the waist, spinning us around as he lifts me up and sets me on the counter. I wrap my legs around him as his lips kiss mine; I have him right where I want him.

"You seem like you're feeling better." He smiles.

"Much better, actually." I bite my lip, eager to move this part along and get on with the good stuff.

"Dare I ask if you're hungry? I can make a mean bowl of cereal."

The thought of food leaves a sour taste in my

mouth, but desire for him quickly settles it. I lean in, close to his ear.

"Oh, I'm hungry," I whisper seductively, still wondering what in the world has come over me. I'm not usually this forward; my insecurities don't usually allow it, at least not without a couple drinks in me first.

Heat builds in the air around us as I nibble his ear, then trail my tongue down the side of his neck, tasting the sweet salt and remnants of soap on his skin and letting out a soft moan under his ear just for him.

Phil puts his hands on my shoulders, distancing himself from me. My heartbeat painfully skips its rhythm again. I ignore it and move in for a kiss, but he stops me.

"I don't know if we should be doing this yet." He pulls his head back before my lips can meet his.

I process the sting of his rejection, but my hunger pushes me not to give up, not till I'm satisfied. "It's been almost a week now, since we last, you know—" I move in for another kiss but stop short.

His face looks pained as he shakes his head. Not what I was aiming for. My disappointment must show as he hugs me instead and sighs.

"I want to. I really do." Phil rests his forehead on mine. "But I don't want to hurt you or anything. It's only been a week."

I don't want to push my husband into having sex with me, but this burning need for him is overpowering. I try to reassure him. "For whatever reason, I'm here. And last I checked I'm not broken; all the scans and tests at the hospital confirm that." On the verge of tears, I give seduction one last try.

He holds me close, my hunger for him raging at me to take him. Hovering my lips near his neck, I let my hand run down his chest to the rim of his charcoal sweats. My hand pauses for a moment, summoning up its own courage to dive in. His pulse quickens loudly as he gives in with a pleasured groan.

"Oh, Aileen, I've missed this. But——" he whispers, caught up in the ecstasy my hand is offering him.

"No buts," I say, quickly pulling my hand out of his pants and smiling like the sexy she-devil I feel inside— I'm winning, I think. I hop off the counter and turn around, shaking my rear at him, giving him his favorite view as I hook my thumbs into the top of my oh-so-sexy sweatpants and slide them down toward the floor. Thank God I wore semi-decent underwear today. I watch as his eyes light up with passion. He grabs hold of my protruding hip bones and pushes himself against me, pressing me forward into the counter, kissing the side of my neck.

My heart pounds, stuttering once more with a painful burn, but again I ignore it as he pulls down my underwear, his lips tickling the backs of my legs with soft kisses as he goes. With one swoop he flips me back around with his strong arms, placing me up on the counter amidst the toaster and French press. I wrap my legs around his hips, stirring up an even deeper need for him to be inside me. He tastes my lips with a flick of his tongue before crushing his mouth into mine. His lips migrate to my neck, biting softly as he heads towards my collar bone, one hand cupping my breast over my shirt. I move my hands to slip down his sweats to free what's waiting for me inside, but he stops me.

"Arms up," he commands with a carnal glare, now waiting to devour me.

I close my eyes as he lifts my shirt up over my head— then nothing. I open my eyes as Phil stands there, the lustful glare now replaced by a contorted look. A look I've never seen from him before, especially during sex. He lets go of my shirt and I watch it float in slow motion to the floor.

"What?" Un-summoned tears build behind my lashes. His eyes fixate on my stomach. "Oh."

My stretch marks and sagging skin have returned since inexplicably disappearing after the crash. Only now, my stomach is a mass of bruised skin, and instead of the stretch marks appearing as their usual silvery-white slits, dark-maroon-colored streaks surrounded by faint blackish-blue lines outline my veins, with yellowing around the outer edges. Anyone in their right mind would react how Phil did. It looks painful, but I don't feel any discomfort— only disgust.

My nausea returns as bile burns its way up my tender throat once again. With one hand over my mouth, sickened, naked, and embarrassed I race for the bathroom, leaving Phil's paling face behind me. I make it into the bathroom and lock the door behind me just in time to dry heave into the sink. For Phil, my body is an unwelcome reminder of the day he almost lost me. For me, it's more proof that there's something terribly wrong with me. I need to be alone right now.

A cold sweat covers my body. It's not just my stomach that's changing; if I look close enough, my whole body is cast in a sickly green-tinged hue. Maybe it's just the poor lighting in my bathroom or my lack of a proper meal for days, but the woman I was before the crash seems to be disappearing. Only a glimpse of her holds on in my bloodshot eyes, crying out to me for help.

It's no surprise now, Phil's hesitation to have sex with me in the first place. I'm so thin and frail it looks like I would break with one wrong touch— and my stomach, it looks like I was in a plane crash. Must be from the seat belt on the plane; it has to be. My fears switch from worrying about pregnancy to finding out one might be ending. That would explain all this, right? A miscarriage? Tuesday's cramping that jump-started all my throwing up would make sense. Only there's been no bleeding.

My heart stutters again but this time doesn't stop with clearing my throat. Agonizing pains wave through my chest and down my arms and legs. I stumble, trying to grab the counter as I fall, hard, to the tile floor. My heart takes on an unsteady, painfully sporadic offbeat pace. I hit at my chest as hard as I can, hoping this will help it regain its normal rhythm. But instead, my heart stops.

I panic, pounding my chest with weakening fists, my breath tight, willing my heart to beat again. "Dammit!" I scream, mustering every ounce of strength I have left to lift my fists and pound them into my chest one more time.

My heart regains a normal rhythm, and I catch my breath. Lying face-up on the bathroom floor, cold sweat dripping off me. The pain dissipating slowly from my chest until it's gone completely. My heart ticks on like nothing happened.

"Aileen!" Phil pounds on the door, rattling the knob. "Let me in. You okay?"

I don't answer; I don't know how to answer. Did I just have a heart attack? He bangs on the door again. I reach up and grab a towel and wrap it around my shivering, naked body.

"Aileen? Open the door!" But his voice trails away as he speaks. The next minute the knob rattles and the door opens. The key we keep above the bedroom doorframe in case the girls ever get locked in held in his hand. I sit up quickly.

"I'm fine." I hide the quiver in my voice as I tuck my disheveled hair behind my ears. "No, actually, I think I just had a heart attack." Strangely, I almost laugh.

He kneels down beside me on the floor, rushing his hands to my neck to feel my pulse. The warmth of his hands burns into my chilled skin.

"Any chest pain or discomfort? Or pain in your right arm? Can you take a deep breath?" he asks frantically.

I breathe in deep. Everything seems fine; I feel stupid for even mentioning a heart attack. "No, not now, I feel fine."

"Then I doubt it was a heart attack. When I was an EMT, I got lots of calls for heart attacks that turned out to be panic attacks. I wouldn't be surprised with what you've been through. But I am worried about you. You have extensive bruising on your stomach." He sighs. "We should get you to a doctor just to play it safe. What if something ruptured? Delayed from the crash?"

"No, I'm fine. Really," I say, determined to avoid a trip to the hospital. Memories of rude reporters wanting the first story on the *miraculous sole survivor of Flight 29*, who tried to take advantage of the worst day of my life, remain burned into my brain. My name just cleared the local news circuit, I don't want to stir it back up again. Or worse, I find out from the doctor I am pregnant— or miscarrying, or worse, I'm dying. I can't process the idea of losing any more life right now.

"Well, if you won't see a doctor, will you at least

let me look you over to make sure there's no internal bleeding? My bag is in the car."

"Of course."

He rushes out to grab his medical bag while I lie down on my bed, still in a towel, convincing myself my heart didn't really just stop. I place two fingers at the pulse at my neck. Normal.

Phil returns with his bag and my clothes from the kitchen.

"Don't put these on yet, I want to check you over." He lays out the contents of his bag on the bed beside me. So clinical and professional. This is not the kind of doctor I was hoping to play tonight.

He pokes around my stomach. It doesn't hurt, but I cringe each time I feel the sag of my skin move under his fingers. He's never cared that my stomach didn't return to a perfect, pre-baby state, but I can't escape the images thrown around this world of what women are "supposed" to look like, and as much as I know I shouldn't buy into that, it's often hard not to.

He sits me up, checking my temperature, blood pressure, and pulse. "I guess you seem okay. Your bruising seems about right placement-wise with where your seatbelt would have been." His voice wavers slightly and I can only imagine how painful it must be for him to think about me being on that plane. He clears his throat. "I'm surprised you haven't noticed it yet."

"I haven't exactly been paying attention to my looks lately."

"How's the nausea now?"

"I feel okay," I say this to keep Phil's mind at ease. However, my own mind is far from okay. The more I think about it, the more I'm convinced what I just experienced was no panic attack. I just know it, my heart stopped—

"Aileen?"

"Yeah?" I ask, realizing he had just said something.

"I said let's get some sleep," Phil repeats, "Need anything, water maybe?"

"Sure, thanks." I sit up on our bed, in shock from my potential epiphany of doom.

He heads out of the room while I put back on the clothes I so eagerly shed in the kitchen moments ago. Since waking up in the hospital last Sunday, I've pushed away this one question clawing at the back of my mind, and after tonight, I can no longer ignore it. I run through my checklist of things not right with me, adding possible heart attack and bruised abdomen to my list. What if my so-called miraculous survival wasn't a miracle after all? What if instead, I've somehow tempted the fates? Somehow disturbed the very balance of life and death, and the powers that be aren't happy about it?

What if I'm falling apart because they want me back?

6

BUMPS IN THE NIGHT

T he old wooden Adirondack chair creaks as I sit back and admire the clear night's sky. Stars in abundance twinkle back at me as I search for the only constellations I know: the Big and Little Dippers. Sleep, once again, brought only nightmares. It's no surprise considering my heart stopped only hours earlier. Shock does funny things to people, I guess. I can't help but wonder, what if I'm making this all up? What if my mind's attempt to cope with such a powerful near-death experience has left me broken beyond repair. It wouldn't be surprising given what I've been through. A light breeze picks up, brushing my hair across my nose, bringing with it an odd yet delicious smell. My mouth waters and my stomach grumbles again, reminding me how long it's been since I've had a meal— especially one that smells this wonderful. Perhaps one of the restaurants on Main Street is already prepping for their morning customers.

A stronger gust of wind passes by and my stomach churns violently as I'm consumed with a hunger I can no longer ignore. Primal urges take over my senses, compelling me off the deck and into the wind in search of the source of the intoxicating scent. Regardless of how ludicrous it might be to search for random food in the early hours of a Saturday morning, outside. It's crazy, yes, confirming the brokenness of my mind. But in the madness I feel a glimmer of hope. Maybe finding *something* to eat— something that I won't throw up— something that will help my strength return so life can go back to normal, is too real to pass up.

Weakly I stumble through the yard, following the delicious smell. I stop when I get to the chicken coop in the back corner of my quarter-acre lot. Puzzled as to why it smells as if someone left an entire Christmas dinner within. The breeze picks up again, mixing in another scent. A vaguely familiar one, yet I can't place where from or what of.

The coop door is off-kilter. Hanging only by its top hinge, and I cringe. Something must have gotten into the coop again. A plume of dusty feathers flies out towards me as I open the broken door. I cough, squinting in the dark as I prepare myself for the worst. Only nothing could have prepared me for the carnage waiting inside.

Thick, dark, blood shines in the waning moonlight, coating the inside of the coop walls. Ripped-up carcasses of what used to be my hens scatter across the sawdust floor. Worse than the massacre of what were my chickens, is the undeniable fact the delicious odor is from this mess. Perhaps it's the hunger, or delirium from my lack of sleep, or the shock of my find, but I realize I'm holding one of my sweet, Dominique hens. Her lifeless, sticky body weighs heavy in my tired hands. Tears fill my eyes, I loved these chickens, and now they're gone. I hug her in close to me, her soft feathers against my cheek, and the delicious mystery smell is revealed: it's them. My chickens. My raw, bloody, torn apart, chickens smell better than Thanksgiving. My mouth waters as a strange and powerful thirst overrides my hunger. A thirst I fear no amount of water would be enough to quench.

The breeze blows again, and on it, the words, "Eat it," dance into my ears.

The chicken falls from my blood-covered hands as I back away from the coop, almost tripping over an old oak tree stump in the process. I'm ashamed to admit how badly I do actually want to taste my poor dead chicken. No, not taste—devour. Every last bit of her. I'm dreaming again, I have to be.

The wind shifts and the familiar, yet unplaceable scent draws into my nostrils bringing with it misplaced memories and an odd sense of uneasy peacefulness.

My stomach flips as piece by piece the scent falls into place; vintage leather and men's cologne. And not just any men's cologne: 007's, his scent still burned into my memories from the crash. But he died that day, along with the lavender-blue-eyed woman, and the rest of the 200 passengers on flight 29, now one week ago today.

The bloody chicken triggers more than just my memories of the flight, it inflames my survivor's guilt as well. Scent is a powerful memory and right now my brain is too tired and malnourished to process anything currently happening as reality. I close my eyes, wishing away memories I'd like to forget. They open as the snap of a twig echoes across the yard and my heart jumps from my chest. A dark silhouette of a tall man, seemingly similar in stature to 007, or what I remember of him, leans against a tree in the field just outside my yard. He doesn't move and neither do I. This has to be a dream. I rub my tired eyes, and with that, the shadowy figure disappears. My fight-or-flight awakens as I turn and run toward the house, lungs burning, weak legs moving as fast as they can, chased by the ghost of his memory. I look back and, though I see nothing, I keep running until I reach the back-slider, dive in, lock the door, and duck down behind the back of the couch. Pulling the old granny square blanket off the top I place it up over my head to hide from my nightmare and wait for the sun to rise and melt away the darkness.

THE MORNING SUN shines bright through the hand-crocheted holes of the blanket I still have placed over me like a shroud of protection. I struggle to breathe, winded from running into the house hours ago. Still unsure if I'm in a nightmare or if this is reality.

"Aileen? Where are you? You okay?" Phil's footsteps and voice fade in and out of our room, the girls' room, the guest bathroom, as he makes his way down the hall, searching for me while the girls play throughout the house, unaware of their missing mother.

He sounds worried and I wish I could help, but I'm not sure where I am anymore. Who I am anymore. I took off running after seeing a ghost in a dream and I fear by now I'm too far gone to ever be found again.

His footsteps come closer and stop in front of me, blocking the light that was shining into my fortress. He slowly lifts up the edge of my blanket tucking under himself and joins me in my hiding place.

"Hi." His tone masked by humor but his concern is palpable. "What are you doing under here?"

I burst into laughter at my situation, or at least try, my breath too weak to laugh. It's more a sick chuckle. Phil stares at the ghost of a woman beside him.

"I'm a thirty-year-old woman who can't sleep, can't eat, my body is weird, you won't have sex with me, and I don't blame you. Also, I've been hiding under this blanket since four a.m., stuck in a nightmare I can't wake up from."

His previously teasing smile turns disturbingly stark. "Is that blood on your face?"

My attempted laughter increases until I wheeze, "I almost ate a chicken, and— please don't think I'm crazy when I tell you what I saw."

"What can be crazier than you almost eating a chicken?" he asks hesitant, one eyebrow raised, one knee up ready to stand.

"I saw James Bond in the forest."

"Can we go back to the chicken?" His face draws blank and I notice the color fading from his cheeks. "Why is there blood on you?"

"Something got into the coop last night. I found the chickens dead inside, I picked one up and for some reason," I pause and hide my head in my knees before adding, "It smelled really good." I know what he's thinking: *She's lost her mind*. I laugh again in a nervous, psychotic sort of way. Phil doesn't seem amused.

"I think you're hallucinating from a lack of sleep."

"The chickens, yes, but 007— that's what I named the man who sat by me on the plane. I never got his real name. I swear I saw him in the field, out by the oaks. I saw his ghost." Confessing this out loud seems to ease the hysterical feeling I have from last night.

Phil stands up, taking the blanket with him,

mechanically folds it, then sets it on the couch. "Let's find you something to eat. Maybe some broth for starters." He smiles at me in a way I'm not sure I've seen before. It's almost a cross between *Get me out of here* and *What the hell*. I don't think he wants to hear any more about James Bond, or the chickens.

"I'm fine, really. I'll wash up, then find some food." My stomach growls, reminding me of the delicious-smelling, dead chickens. Horrifying to admit, it takes everything in me to *not* taste the dried-out remnants of blood still on my fingers.

"Alright, but if you start throwing up again today, I will take you to a doctor." The strange new smile still lingers as he watches me stagger my way into the girls' bathroom off the hall. "And please find something a little more normal to eat."

Red runs down the drain as I scrub at my hands, which seem to be permanently stained. For whatever reason, the usual tangy coppery smell of blood is missing, replaced instead by a sweet, vanillaesque tone. The strange thirst from last night returns, I sip some water in between scrubbing the blood from my cheek, but it only dulls slightly. I stare at my face, making sure I've cleaned everything off it and find myself looking into my fading, greying-green eyes. Hauntingly thin translucent skin stretches over protruding cheekbones, the fullness of life now long gone from my face. I understand what Phil's strange new smile must mean: he's losing me. In fact, I look far worse than I did last night— if that is even possible. It's as if my life is fading before my very eyes.

My heart stutters as a painful possibility crosses my mind. I try to push the thought aside but it keeps pushing to the surface: I'm dying.

I grab one of the girls' brushes sitting on the counter to remove the feathers stuck within my hair. Instead of feathers, a large clump of hair pulls out with ease from my scalp.

Silencing the scream that threatens to rise, I throw the brush with all my strength at this image of a starving, broken, ghost-seeing woman. The mirror shatters the image into a spider web of faces.

Tears rise, but I won't let them fall. I can't let this defeat me— I'm not dying, I'm fine, I *have* to be fine. My stomach grumbles, reminding me there's still hope. I escaped death in the most profound of ways. Surely, I can find something to eat that will stay down. Something to help me feel human again. I leave the bathroom, my brokenness, and the now shattered mirror behind and take my determination to the kitchen.

My heart aches as I walk past the girls' room and listen while they play together. All I wanted was a weekend to myself; to recharge, regardless of how anxious I was to go. Now, I have nothing left within myself to offer them, except this renewed will to go on. As I pass through the living room, Phil walks across the yard with a shovel towards the chicken coop. I make a silent promise to him, the girls, and myself, to try every food in this damn house until something stays down. For a brief second, I wonder if the chicken might still be worth a try. After all, it smelled so good. I shake the thought, disgusted by the reality of what I'm actually thinking. I'm not a monster.

A fresh-baked loaf of Ana's honey wheat bread sits on the kitchen counter. My stomach does not agree with the yeasty odor that comes as I slice a thick piece and coat it with butter. When I take a bite, a rotten, moldy taste fills my mouth. Bile forces its way up my raw throat, but I choke it back down and grab a glass of milk to wash away the taste lingering in my mouth. The milk is worse than the bread— rancid, curdling the moment it enters my mouth. I spew out the souring milk in the sink and watch as both the milk and my hope of not going back to the hospital swirl down the drain.

Back to the refrigerator, I open the door and stare into its bright interior fully stocked thanks to Ana. The motor hums its tune while I look over my options. Nothing looks promising. A half-empty carton of eggs on the top shelf reminds me of the chicken. Meat, maybe I need meat. On the shelf below sit two nicely marbled slabs of beef. Perhaps I'm anemic. Maybe I'm protein deficient. That might explain the hallucinations.

"I'll try you," I say out loud to the beef. My rumbling stomach seems to agree with my choice.

With the iron skillet heating on the stove, I unwrap the sweet-smelling meat. Usually the feel of raw meat in my hands disgusts me, but as I hold the cold slab of muscle, its juices dripping through my fingers, I don't mind. It's weird and unconventional, but I can't help but see it for the life-giving gift it promises. I set it slowly into the hot skillet as the meat sizzles and cracks, but the once sweet-smell from only moments ago turns rank as it cooks. I hold my breath to avoid throwing up from the putrid smell, slamming the skillet lid down with one hand and flipping on the overhead vent fan with my other hand. I then hold my breath in hopes the stench will dissipate before my nausea returns. It's too late— bile rises, but I refuse to let go. I have nothing left to purge anyway.

The other piece of meat sits in the package on the counter next to me. I give it a sniff and smile as the pleasant aroma calms my stomach and revives my hunger. Salivating uncontrollably, I wrap my fingers around the cold, pink piece of steak. It's heavy in my weak hands. Fueled by my will to live and a strange new instinct, I know what I need to do. Cringing in preparation for the worst, I take a bite.

My teeth sink in with ease, cutting through the cold, solidified fats as the delicious raw steak dissolves with each chew. No bile-inducing horrid taste, no nausea forcing me to spit it out. Just the satisfying sensation of a good meal. I take another bite, and then another until the whole twelve-ounce steak is nothing but a memory. I say a quick prayer of gratitude for finally finding something to satisfy my hunger and hope I won't die of E. coli. Like a miracle, my strength returns immediately. My breathing easier, my heart steady, and for the first time in days my legs feel firm in their stance.

"Hey, you're looking better. Steak, huh?" Phil says cheerfully as he walks into the kitchen to wash his hands. I look up, almost guiltily. Thank goodness he didn't walk in sooner.

"It sounded good. That one is for you." I motion to the stove as I scour the fridge for something more to eat. Although Ana filled the fridge, meat is one thing she won't buy. All that remains as far as meat goes is a pack of chicken. My stomach turns, thinking of how much I wanted to eat my beloved dead hens. Definitely a no on the chicken. I need more beef.

"I was thinking of heading to the store; we're out of beef, you know how your mom is."

He lifts the lid off the skillet and raises an eyebrow at me like I'm crazy, which I might be. The smell of the cooked steak wafts over to me, making my stomach uneasy again. The last thing I want right now is to lose the first meal I've had in days.

"I'll go, you should rest." He pokes at the meat with a spatula.

"No, I need to get out for a bit." I almost gag as

Phil flips his steak. Desperate to not throw up again, I grab my keys and purse and head toward the door. "Some fresh air will do me some good."

"Hey, you might want to change first." He grabs a plate from the cupboard, eyes glancing at my shirt.

I look down. My shirt is filthy with pieces of feathers and smears of chicken blood all over the front. Yeah, I might want to change first.

7

CAN'T STOP THE BEAT

A crisp autumn wind blows through the car windows as I enjoy the short drive down the sleepy highway to the small but helpful market just outside of town. Fall has always been my favorite time of year here in the Sierra foothills, especially as the air grows cold, scented with cozy wood-burning stoves and cedar. The winding highway road that leads out of town to the market is lined with bright red-leafed dogwood trees, tall, yellowing black oaks, and pines that hold tight to their dark-green needles. Though this October has been unseasonably wet, today the sun is shining in the bright blue sky, not a cloud to be seen for miles. Most of all, I love the old homes and buildings still standing from the gold-seeking founders that provide small glimpses of a simpler time before cars and cell phones. Speaking of cell phones, I'm beginning to miss mine.

The parking lot at the market is full— the down-side to only having one place for groceries. Not wanting to waste time looking for a close spot, I keep it simple and park in the far outer edge of the lot. The warm sun beams down through the cool air as I walk towards the entrance, almost burning my bare arms, causing the strangest sensation of hot and cold all at once. I've never noticed my skin feeling this sensitive before, but after eating raw meat, I've given up on keeping a list of the weird things happening to me. I'm simply happy to have finally found a food that makes me feel better. Even just after the one steak, my overall appearance has noticeably improved. I grab a cart and head into the store, noticing the skin on my arms is a little pinker than before. Strange, that the short walk through the parking lot could have given me a sunburn.

Inside, herds of people pace up and down the aisles, mechanically harvesting boxes of cereal and canned fruit off the shelves. A frail old lady with white hair, an empty cart, and an even emptier gaze walks past me. Her perfume grabs me by the throat and I cough to clear out the potpourri scent. She's probably used the same one for decades and is unable to smell it herself anymore— unfortunate for those around her. There is something about her empty gaze that terrifies me though. Perhaps it's pity for the old woman who looks lost and forgotten, or the recogni-tion of my own frailty I see in her. Or maybe it's the fear of not ever having the chance to be old and wander around the grocery store, torturing fellow shoppers with my perfume.

I shake off my thoughts of morbidity— near-death experiences will do that to a person— and resume my mission toward the butcher. As I approach the freezers, I'm thoroughly disappointed that the beef smells gamier than my steak at home. Here's hoping it's simply the stain of the old woman's perfume lingering in my nostrils. My nausea threatens its return; as great as my breakfast tasted, the thought of eating meat raw *is* utterly disgusting. But I have no choice other than doing what I can to stay alive, to do what I must to heal whatever it is that's wrong with me. I grab more than my fair share of beef shoulder and flank steak— up close, both smell hopeful and both are on sale.

Embarrassed by the amount of meat, and only meat, I have in my cart, I avoid eye contact with the other shoppers as I weave my way toward the check-out. Not that it matters. People tend to prefer keeping to themselves anyway. And thanks to a sinus-clearing walk past the coffee section, I can finally smell the unadulterated sweet, sweet aroma of hope and survival piled high in my cart. My stomach growls. I'm tempted to forget all societal norms and devour every last vacuum-packed tray of meat right here and now.

"Aileen! Hello! Oh my god!" A woman speaks

with a most unpleasant vocal fry. I turn around to find Genevieve, a mom from Imogene's school. We were almost friends once, back in the day when we'd have coffee together while our babies played. I met her through the local mom's club but soon lost interest when it became more drama club than a support group. I see her from time to time on social media, or the occasional PTA meeting I manage to attend but otherwise keep my distance. Dressed in her characteristic expensive brand-name athletic wear, she pushes her cart toward me from the other end of the aisle. My hands stiffen on my cart handle.

I stare, momentarily forgetting how to socially interact with others. "Hi Genevieve," I say cordially, regaining my social senses as she stops her cart right in front of mine.

False concern plasters across her face. Although she was always one of the nicer moms, she has a knack for collecting private knowledge to use as social leverage. Now that I've been through one of the more-recent national tragedies I'm sure she's hungry for information.

"I am so sorry about what happened to you!" she whispers excitedly, like the crash is some dark secret, even though it's been blasted all over the media for days now. "How are you?"

How am I supposed to respond to things like this? Where is the guidebook for how to talk to people after your plane crashes and you're the only one to survive? "I've been better."

Genevieve laughs, the sound even more annoying than her voice. "We've all been so worried about you!" she says, reigning in her morbid excitement. We, as in the mom's club. Worried, as in everyone is gossiping about me. I don't like being the center of attention.

"It's okay, really. Thank you." I try to smile, but my nausea begins to threaten its return.

When she realizes I'm not willing to say any more on the matter she takes a quick glance at her phone. "Well, I better get going. You having a barbecue?" She points to the mounds of meat in my cart.

"No." I laugh, trying not to sound nervous. "It's on sale; thought I'd stock up."

"Well, you let me know if there is anything we can do for you," she says with a smile, already heading toward the meat section. Not many moms I've met can turn down a sale.

I walk the opposite way, drawing in a deep breath of relief that my social encounter is over, and stop dead in my tracks. My heart pounds and my knees weaken, adrenaline rises, as once again the haunting fragrance of 007's ghost hits me.

I glance around and don't see him. But his scent remains and each step I take toward the end of the aisle it grows stronger. My body shakes as urgency courses through my veins. I turn around and decide on a different route in hopes that my ghost of survivor's guilt will pass so I can refocus on my mission: groceries.

Five aisles down seems safe enough; I turn at the frozen food aisle. The cold air thickens again with leather and cologne. There is no denying it's real, and here, but how? Suddenly I'm trapped in a tornado of hallucinations, and I see *him*. No shadowy silhouette, no see-through ghost-like apparition, but 007, himself in the flesh. Just the same ol' runaway billionaire in a leather jacket, opening the door of the freezer where the ice cream is kept. He turns his head and smiles at me, but his eyes are dark and foreboding. Either he's, in fact, a ghost haunting me, or he's somehow alive too.

The fluorescent ceiling lights spin above me. The floor becomes Jell-O under my feet. I steady myself against the cool glass freezer door, and once the floor is still again I look down the aisle where he was standing— he's gone.

"Are you okay, dear?" the old perfume woman asks me, pulling my cart which seems to have run away, back to me. "You don't look so well. Can I find someone to help you?"

"I'm fine, thank you."

She nods and walks away. Even over her perfume I still smell him. Was he here? Or am I completely losing my mind? The overpowering scent emanating from the old woman mixing with the cologne of my ghost ignites my nausea with a vengeance. I ditch my cart as the sickness waves up and down within my chest and run from the store, nearly knocking over the kind, odorous old woman as I race past. Whatever strength my breakfast gave me is gone. Breathlessly, I run towards my car.

Defeated I let go, of my breakfast— my last chance at hope— into the bushes at the far end of the parking lot. At least I didn't waste a bunch of money on beef shoulder. Nausea has its way with me and leaves almost as abruptly as it came. Once again, I'm weak, panting, exhausted, and starving. I should have known better than to eat raw meat, and now I probably have E. coli or salmonella to add to my list of maladies. Without a cell phone, I can't call Phil to give him the joy of taking me back to the hospital. Instead, I lie alone on the warm asphalt, behind the bushes at the outer edge of the grocery store parking lot, watching the buzzards circle above me in the clear blue sky.

Suddenly, the wind blows an icy veil across my sweaty skin and with it, vintage leather and men's cologne. I'm too tired to clearly think through my options of whether he's real or I'm hallucinating, and I'd much rather lie here watching the scavenger birds fly in the most hypnotic sort of patterns. Someone will find me, eventually, and hopefully call an ambulance. Until then I'm contented to lay here listening to the whooshing sound my pulse makes in my ears.

It must be around noon now, at least. I've been lying here long enough to watch the late October sun slowly drift higher in the sky, burning down on my cold skin. It's not enough of a burn that it hurts, but it's not comfortable, either. It more just itches, but I can't bring myself to move. The faint sound of a woman's cry, so quiet it's as if she barely had the breath to call out at all, drifts across the parking lot. This breaks me from my stupor as I finally find the strength to rise and peek up over the side of my car. The smelly-perfume woman is just a few rows over, sprawled on the ground between her car and the one next to it. The contents from her bag of groceries scattered on the ground beside her. My breath catches in my throat at the sight of her still body.

The most wonderful smell, better than the chicken coop or the raw steak, seeps into my senses. Salivating, my stomach hungers, and my throat rages with a deep and desperate thirst. Instincts more vicious than at the chicken coop take over; like an animal on its hunt, nothing matters to me right now except finding and eating whatever it is I'm being drawn towards. The scent drifts from the poor old woman— it seems to be coming from near her, probably something she just purchased from the deli. God, I hope it's not raw. The closer I walk toward her, the more my mouth waters. My stomach twists violently as my whole body, not just my throat is in the throes of agony with the most intense pangs of hunger and thirst I've ever experienced.

I reach the woman in a daze, my weak legs wobble with each step I take. There she lies, frail and unconscious. Her white hair stained a deep crimson from the nasty gash on her forehead.

My concern for her well-being battles with my selfish desire to fulfill my hunger. "Ma'am, are you okay?" I glance over her spilled groceries. Nothing but toilet paper, floor cleaner, and bananas. She doesn't respond. I check her pulse, pressing my fingers to the side of her neck, sticky with warm blood. Her heart is beating. In fact, I can hear it loud and clear. My thirst increases as I stare at her blood, dripping from my hand.

My hands shake as my hunger rages. What the hell is wrong with me? Before I can stop myself, my blood-coated hand rises to my mouth. My lips close around all four dark red glistening fingers, licking and sucking off every last bit of her blood, filling my mouth with the most delectable taste I could ever imagine. Her blood tastes divine; sweeter than honey and vanilla, a welcome taste for my starving tongue. With all lines now blurred between right and wrong, real and unreal—

I reach out for more.

But before I can move my arm, powerful vibrations wave throughout my body. My heart pounds, speeding faster and faster, skipping a beat here and there, worse than the heart attack. I try and catch my breath but each time I inhale, my pulse races even more, painfully radiating through my chest. Every muscle in my body cramps and pulls away from me like a rubber band about to snap, as if my bones want to break out of my skin. I try to call out for help, but all the air is locked tight within my lungs.

"Okay, that's enough," says a familiar male voice with a slight British note. "You're coming with me." With little effort, 007 grabs me around the middle and hoists me up over his shoulders like a sack of potatoes, whisking me away from the elderly woman in a flash. Lava sears through my veins with each excruciating heartbeat as I watch the bleeding woman and grocery store parking lot fade off into the distance.

"What are you doing? Let go of me!" I growl. I should care more about the dead man who is grabbing me, but all I want is more blood.

"I'm saving you. You need to feed, but I can't have you causing a scene your first time." He runs so fast the scenery flies past me in a blur.

And it's confirmed, I'm still in a nightmare. People don't run this fast, especially dead ones. Or the only other explanation my foggy mind can come up with is I'm officially dying and he must be the Grim Reaper, dragging me into the afterlife. Maybe he forgot me; I was too buried in the wreckage after the crash for him to find. Maybe that's why I survived. It was only a delay, not salvation. My focus shifts from wanting more blood to my plummeting heart rate. Each beat thumping slower than the last, each one more painful than the one before. I try to breathe but my throat is tight and unforgiving, allowing only a small stream of air to wheeze through at a time. Fear grips me. This is it. It has to be.

"How are you alive? Or am I dead? Are you taking me to heaven?" I choke out in a whisper, delirium swarming into my fuzzy brain.

He laughs. "Darling, there is no heaven for us. Just hold on, we're almost there."

The pain now is worse than the impact of the plane hitting the ground. "What is happening to me?" My heart beats slower.

"I'll explain later; it's started, and we don't have much time."

"What's started?" The speed, the pain— my head spins as my consciousness begins to fade. All light begins to suck away from the blurry world around me.

"Hold on, we're there."

Where is *there*?

We stop. *There* is an old white farmhouse alone in a field, not much different than the fields behind my house. He brings me inside, each step amplifying the burn flowing through my veins. He lets go, and I drop with a thud onto an ancient, musty velvet sofa that matches the era of the nineteenth century home.

"Sorry," he says, running— no, whooshing is

more like it— out of the room, my vision fading in and out. People don't move like that.

I try to look around, gather my bearings, but my mind keeps slipping away from me. My eyelids too heavy to hold open for much longer. He returns in seconds with a large red thermos, the contents of which share a common odor to the injured woman's blood, minus the perfume. He holds it out to me; I want nothing more than to have the sweet-tasting silk it holds inside, but my foggy mind yells out one last refusal. *This is wrong.* What I've done, tasting a poor helpless woman's blood, is wrong. I close my eyes tight and shake my head. I need this to stop before I go too far.

His cold arm props me up higher as he sits beside me, cradling me in his lap he holds the thermos to my mouth. "Quick, drink this. You don't have much time."

I cover my mouth with my hands and freeze, crying out in pain as my stiff elbow joints pop and crack. Remnants of the stranger's blood stain my fingers, I recall the tiny taste and how it so quickly brought me momentary healing, how divine it was. Then I remember the state I'm in now. This must be my punishment. A moment of clarity sets my panic in motion—

"This is blood!" I yell with what little breath my lungs allow.

He chuckles as I lie in his arms, unamused,

holding on to each painful beat of my heart, wondering which one will be my last. *Blood*. Reality hits me like a ton of bricks. I just tasted blood. And worse, I want more. "This is blood," I repeat.

"*This* is your life force. *This* is what will sustain you throughout eternity. Without it you are nothing, but with it," he leans in close to my face and his dark-brown eyes light up as he whispers, "you are all-powerful, unstoppable, immortal."

"What kind of freak are you? People don't drink blood," I gasp. Only I *want* it. I want it more than I've ever wanted something before. As my pain over-powers my fear of my captor, my heartbeat pauses— I am dying. He said I don't have much time.

"Why, darling, I'm no freak. If you want to know what I am, just look at yourself." His voice is calm and gentle. The same voice that brought me peace during the plane crash. He smiles as I lock eyes with his, fear radiating as deep as my pain. "I'm the same thing you are."

"What? No!" I cry as a wave of panic shakes through me. I wish I could run, far, far away, wake up from this nightmare, but the pain is too great, pinning me to the couch. I'm afraid of the answer to the question I'm about to ask. He said *thing*. *THING*, I don't want to be a *thing*.

"What am I?" I whisper through clenched teeth as tears begin to fall down my cheeks, my heart again stalling as I gasp for breath.

He answers, two words: "A Vampire."

My head spins even faster. "This isn't real." I try and will myself to move through my pain but I can't.

"Yes, it is, and I'd really like you to live; I happen to fancy you, Aileen." He holds the red thermos back up to my lips. "You don't have much time, now drink!"

There is honesty in his urgent request, but I can't understand it. Tears of frustration burn my eyes. I don't want to die. My struggling will to survive forces its way to the surface of my mind, telling me to drink, telling me he's right. Thirst comes, overpowering the surges of pain. For the first time since the crash I long for this to just be another nightmare, and if this is only a bad dream, what do I have to lose? I nod, too overcome with fear, thirst, and pain to move.

He grabs my face with one hand, squeezing my cheeks till my lips part, and pours the contents of the red thermos past my lips. My senses delight as warm vanilla and honey, similar to my earlier taste, yet with hints of cinnamon, sweetly fill my mouth. And I stop, pursing my lips shut and look up at 007. His dark eyes are full of urgency.

"I'm the reason you survived the crash, Aileen." He gently strokes my hair. His cool fingers on my forehead bring a moment of relief. "And this is the way you will survive now. You *must* drink this. Trust me. Aren't you thirsty?"

More tears come as the taste on my lips over-powers my fears, and I drink.

"I'm sure you are full of questions." I listen as I swallow mouthful after mouthful of thick, warm blood. "We will address them, I promise. Also, I have yet to properly introduce myself to you. I am Donovan Sellars."

I lift my eyes to him— Donovan— in acknowledgment, but I can't remove my lips from the thermos. It's nice to know he has a name. The blood courses through me, soothing my throat, heart, and stomach, flowing through my arms, legs, fingers— every little bit of me finds relief from my earlier pain.

"It's good, right?" A wide, eager grin stretches across his face, exposing his vibrantly white teeth. His perfect, stubbled face, millimeters from mine, brings me back to the day I met him. The day of the crash.

It's more than good; it's amazing.

I sit up with his assistance, taking the thermos for myself. My strength returns as I gulp the blood down, quenching this new, uncontrollable thirst, all my weakness melting away.

"When the plane hit the ground, I was unfortunately torn away from you. I never meant for you to go this long without completing your change. And in case you're wondering how you died, you burned alive . . . well, you were mostly alive. You would have passed out from a loss of blood first. Do you remember any of that?"

I shake my head.

"Thanks to my bite you healed quite nicely, and fast too.

Rubbing my wrist, I run my finger over the jagged pink scar. "You *bit* me?"

He nods, pleased. "Notice how quickly they let you leave the hospital? However, your immediate regeneration only lasts about a week, as you would now know judging by today. Without first replacing your dead blood with new blood, your transition to becoming a vampire would be incomplete. If you had waited any longer, it would have been too late, and your body would shut down and die."

As ludicrous as it sounds, what he's saying makes sense— *if* what he says is true, *if* I don't wake up from this nightmare, but I can hardly think clearly. The thermos is empty, but I'm still thirsty. Even more so now than before I drank it. I thrust the thermos at him.

"You need more." He nods, taking it from me. "Hold on."

Donovan disappears into the other room again, and in seconds, returns with the red thermos refilled. I snatch it from his hand and drink greedily.

"Slow down, darling." He sits down in an old, burgundy parlor chair that matches the sofa, facing me. "You have all eternity now, no need to hurry." The advice seems strange coming from someone who moves so incredibly fast.

I don't want to think about what this means if it's real. All I want is more blood. I chug this one down faster than the first, only the soothing comfort it first brought me disappears. My heart races again, pumping fire through my veins. Each swallow burns hotter as it flows down my throat, hotter than I can bear. Still, my bloodlust pushes me to keep drinking till every last drop is gone, hoping maybe the next swallow will bring back the soothing relief it brought before. But none comes as I quench my wretched thirst through the pain till every last drop is inside me.

Bolts of electric current shoot from my heart into my limbs, pulsating painfully with each beat. Screaming, I throw down the empty thermos and fall to the floor, shaking, twisting, yet still begging to God I don't throw up this blood. I cry out in long, anguished wails of distress, disgusted with what I've done, yet all I want is more. Knowing full well I'd endure far more pain— do anything, even crawl through the depths of hell if I have to, for another refill. I'm addicted.

He picks up the thermos and sets it on a side table.

"That should do it."

I stare at him, fire behind my eyes, yelling, screaming like a mad woman for more, as I roll around on the floor, doubled over in pain. He sits back in silence on the sofa, watching with a smile on his face.

"What did you do to me?" I growl, my heart

beating out of my chest, shooting stronger and stronger currents of torture through me with each beat. Have I been poisoned?

"I know, it's quite painful. Give it a minute. You're almost there."

My mind numbs from the overload of trauma happening inside me. I shut my eyes tight and wait for death to relieve me from this, but doing so only amplifies the pain. My chest tightens and then, my heart slows its pace. Each beat pounding one long, horrific pattern of, *buuu-bump, buuu-bump,* holding progressively longer than the one before it, as I gasp for breath between screams.

My heart stalls on an up-beat, the most painful part of its unsteady rhythm. I pound into my chest with everything I have left, crying for it to start again, but it remains stuck, leaving my chest feeling as if it's being squeezed in a vise with no hope of relief.

This man is not my savior. People don't drink blood, monsters do. Perhaps he is the Grim Reaper after all. I bet he'll take pleasure in watching me die, enjoying every minute before he can take me to hell. I begin to accept this is the end for me. The flames have come again to claim my body as they were supposed to on the plane, only this time I'll burn from within.

I try one last time to pound my fists into my chest, but my arms won't move. I look up at him. "Help me."

As the last bit of air leaves my lips from my cry, the beat lets go, and my heart stops.

An icy river of relief silently washes through me as I lie still on the floor. A lonely tear trails down my cheek. Donovan kneels down behind my head, leaning his face over mine. He smiles sadistically and strokes my hair as he watches his victim die. Except for one thing—

My heart stopped beating, but I'm not dead.

8

FOREVER TWENTY-NINE

"I said relax, darling! Good lord, your heart's stopped; it's not as though the world did," he says as I sit rocking back and forth on the floor, hyperventilating. "And darling, you don't need to breathe anymore."

I draw in a sharp breath and snap back, "I can't help it!"

"From here on out air is only of use to a vampire for speaking and smelling. But go ahead, continue your panic, I'll be here when you're done."

With each and every inhale and exhale I can feel, see, and smell the particulates mixed with the air. I'm completely overwhelmed by even the smallest of my movements. They're strange, foreign even, as if my brain has been thrust into a new body, not one I've owned for the last thirty years. Donovan paces the floor telling me again to call down, everything will be okay. What did he expect? That I'd shower him with thanks? Everything is one-hundred-percent *not* okay— and it's his fault. I should have died in that crash. I should be gone and buried right now. At peace. Not this . . . torment. Not this torture. I am a *vamp*— I can't even wrap my head around it enough to say the word. Instead, I glare at him, seething, waiting for him to *do* something, say something. Help me. Fix me.

Finally, he slumps down onto the sofa, his walking back and forth only amplified the number of things I'm feeling; the vibration of the floorboards, the clouds of dust that plumed as his feet touched the old wooden planks, it's all too much. He sits back, arms stretched out across the sofa, settling his feet on the floor near me sending a ripple straight into the part of my backside touching the floor. At that, I still my rocking, and all the movement around me calms. I listen to the air sifting through his own lungs and know he is about to speak, as he leans forward looking down at me.

A hint of a smile appearing on his face as if he knows exactly what I'm feeling. "See? It's better when you relax. Stop fighting it. This is who you are now."

I stand up and escape across the room to the fireplace to give myself some distance from him while I figure all this out. I'm caught off guard by the second it took me to stand. The zinging sensation of air whipping past me, to the sudden halt as I thud into the mantle above the old brick fireplace. A large, ornate mirror sits on the wall and I catch a glimpse of myself, or who I think is supposed to me. She looks more like a stranger than myself. Or maybe someone I could have been had I obsessed over diet and exercise, someone you see in the "after" photos on Instagram. Not me, Aileen, a thirty-year-old mother of two. My un-beating heart begins to ache at the thought of my family. How can I still be a mom now?

"This is not me. What did you do to me?" I look away, not wanting to see more of that stranger, that monster with an un-beating heart, who drinks blood.

"Well, you sound grateful." He doesn't hide his sarcasm. "Would you rather I left you to die on that plane? Or worse, left you to rip that poor old woman to pieces from your imminent bloodthirsty rampage, leaving me to clean up your mess?" Donovan loses his smile as he leans back against the sofa again, clearly annoyed with my reaction to this new "living situation."

What does he want me to do, run into his arms? Lavish him with praise for saving me? I'm not ready to accept this as a reality, not yet. But he's right, I didn't want to die on that plane, and I certainly don't want to have ripped apart that poor woman.

"So, I'm cursed then, right? *Night of the Living Dead* status?" I find an interesting knot in the wood on the mantle top to swirl my finger in fighting the urge to look back at my reflection, terrified it will still be that stranger looking back at me.

"No, not cursed. Quite far from cursed really," he answers.

"How is being a— how is this not a curse?" I can't bring myself to say the word, let alone believe this is true. "I can't ever go outside again."

"And why would you think that?"

"Won't the sun turn me into dust?"

"Well, darling, we may be a little more sun-sensitive. But turn to dust? No. I was outside with you today after all, and see," he holds out his arms, "no dust here."

I watch as he sits deeper into the couch, making himself comfortable. My eyes linger longer than I'd like on his slightly stubbled porcelain-like chin; nothing about him has changed since before the plane crash.

"And garlic bread?"

"Well, you shouldn't *eat* it. You shouldn't eat anything now for that matter, but garlic won't hurt you. As for your diet, only blood as well as a few other liquids, if you must, for keeping up with social appearances. I don't recommend straying from blood too long. You'll become weak, susceptible to injury, possibly even die without it."

"Great."

"Don't look so grim. I think you'll find blood has a vast array of flavors, like wine. And you seem to have acquired a taste for, how should I put it, more vintage varieties." He smiles.

I cringe at the thought.

"Well, what if Buffy comes along and stabs me with a sharpened broomstick?" I rub my finger over a rough patch on the mantle's edge. "Will I die from a splinter?" I stop touching the wood, just in case. He said without blood I *might even die.* Questions I don't want to think further into flood into my mind, as I quickly try and push them aside.

Donovan looks at me with narrowed, dark eyes then bends down and yanks up the old wooden end table next to him by the leg. The table explodes as he smashes it on the floor, splintering the antique into pieces until only the leg is left, jagged and broken in his hand.

"Buffy, huh?" He contemplates the table leg like it's a dagger in his hand. He whooshes over to me, backing me up against the mantle, and taps his palm with the dagger. My breath catches on the scent of his cologne. There is danger in his eyes, but also something else, something I've seen before. It's the same devilish look he had in my dream, before he sliced my wrist with the shard of glass and strangely, seductively, licked the ooze from my arm. I brace myself for the worst; if he is anything like the 007 from my dream I wouldn't put it past him to either stab me or kiss me. My lips tingle at the thought. He smiles, almost as if he knew what I was thinking about him, and says, laughing, "I used to watch that show; it was a fun way to end the nineties. Let's have a demonstration, shall we?"

He backs up, removes his leather jacket, tossing it aside. Without even a moment of hesitation he plunges the wooden dagger into his chest. Falling down, he cries out in pain at my feet. Then he stops, lying still as death on the floor as I stare in shock, unsure whether I should run away from him or to him. A moment passes, and then a smile reappears on his face. I let out a ragged breath before he shoots back up to standing and pulls the piece of wood out of his chest. I can tell by the expression on his face that it hurts him to do so, but he quickly hides it and drops the dagger to the floor. The tip is covered in the same oily, black substance from my dream and my bandage.

Donovan laughs. "Oh, Aileen, your face!" He points to me, doubled over. "See, I'm fine." He stands up, arms out, and does a spin and I wonder how often he likes to show this part of him off. "Perfectly fine. You really can't believe everything you see in those TV vampire shows."

"What is wrong with you?" I wait, still backed up against the wall, watching him as he gathers his composure from his little circus act. He's more like a giddy high school boy at the moment than the dark, sexy, super-creepy undead stranger from my dream.

"Sorry love, just having a little fun. This is a big

day for you! You've been reborn! You're a vampire! We should celebrate!"

"Your idea of fun and mine are very different, and I don't feel much like celebrating. You're dripping, by the way," I point out, icily, as more of the inky-black substance drips down his white shirt.

"Right." In a whoosh, he disappears to the other room then returns in seconds with another thermos, a blue one this time. "Now this is the really cool part." He rips off his shirt, exposing not just his oozing wound but a smooth, perfectly sculpted chest and abs as well. I'm shocked and disgusted by a strong sudden urge to run my hands carelessly all over his hard, muscular body. He drinks and I watch, amazed, as the wound on his chest closes up in seconds before my eyes.

His smile grows larger after seeing the one that's popped up, unbidden, on my face. "Brilliant, right?"

I correct my mouth back to a firm line. "You could say that." With how excited he was to stab himself, I begin to wonder what type of person— creature— I'm mixed up with. I'm leaning toward mentally unstable— dramatic to say the least. But showoff or not the self-healing thing is *brilliant*, I will admit.

"Thought you might like to see what you're capable of." He returns to his spot on the couch, motioning for me to join him. I keep my distance, safe by the fireplace. He made me nervous on the plane

with a shirt on; now he's shirtless and I'm terrified—
in so many ways.

"Is this how you always are? Slightly psychopath-
ic?" I look at him, and he smiles again. There's something about his smile that makes me want to
reciprocate. I suppress the desire and once again focus
on the knot in the mantle trying to ignore my own
knot forming deep within my stomach.

"To be completely honest, I've never changed
anyone before. It's going to be nice having another
vampire to pal around with." He casually crosses his
leg over his knee like the world hasn't suddenly been
turned upside down.

I'm his first . . . ? Interesting— almost flattering.
Yet the knot in my stomach tightens at the thought of
what "pal-ing around" with him entails. Am I
doomed to wander eternity with an unstable "pal"
creating bloodbaths in parking lots? I knew my
survival from the crash was no miracle. I was
supposed to die that day, and now here I am, this—
thing, alone in an old farmhouse with a shirtless
stranger I thought was dead only hours ago. I want to
cry. I want to scream. I want to go home— but can I
go home? I'm sure by now Phil is wondering where I
am, but, if I *can* go home, is he going to want a blood-
sucking monster for a wife?

My anger flares. "Did you ever think that maybe I
wouldn't have wanted this?"

Donovan's brow furrows as he processes my question as if the thought never even crossed his mind. "If I'm honest— and Aileen, I swear to always be honest with you— no. I never considered if you would want this or not."

"Why would you assume such a literal life and death thing?"

"Who wouldn't want to live forever? We are gods now, the divine immortal, all-powerful— nothing can harm us. Who wouldn't want that? I saved you from death itself." He pauses waiting for me to agree and when I don't he pops up from his relaxed position on the couch and stands. "Regardless, it's too late. Your change is complete. There is no need to bother yourself with this matter."

He's right. I've changed. It's done. I drank the blood and now I'm stuck here on this earth— forever. But the alternative would have been to die. To forever be wiped from this world. The knot tightens more as I try and accept my new fate. Perhaps I should be grateful to him, at least a little. That is *if* I can go home and be with my family. What is eternity without them?

He clears his throat and starts where we left off before his Buffy killing re-enactment. "Let's touch back to what you eat now, shall we? The most important thing is to keep your meals . . . quiet."

Quiet, huh? I cringe again, thinking about what that means exactly. Quiet as in low-key, don't draw attention? Or quiet as in don't let them scream? An unsettled queasiness replaces the knot. As Donovan continues his instructions my thoughts drift and I accidentally look into the mirror I've been so carefully trying to avoid. I catch him saying something about needing to eat at least once a week, but this strange woman I see in place of my old self captivates me. Why was I so afraid to look before? Never have I seen such beauty, not even on Instagram. Her skin, so pure and smooth as if it's made from the same porcelain Donovan seems to be made from. Her eyes glow an iridescent green, like emeralds, as they catch the last rays of daylight floating in from the window to my right. All my fears, worries, questions fade into the background of my mind as I try to accept this might really be me.

"No reflections, huh?" I ask, in a daze, hypnotized by my own reflection. Too lost following the lines of long, thick, auburn hair flowing from the crown of my head to my chest, to care about his answer.

Noticing the crease deepening between my brows, I relax my face. Not a wrinkle or blemish in sight. I touch my supple rosy lips, as my other hand slides down my neck to my chest, cupping my re-inflated breasts. My hand continues down to my stomach and under my shirt; it's smooth as stone. I look down at my belly— no more bruising, no more sagging skin, no more stretch marks. The physical memory of ever having carried my daughters wiped clean from my body. Tears run down my cheeks as my dead heart sinks a little deeper. Donovan appears behind me, placing his hand softly upon my shoulder.

"There, there. It can be a lot to take in at first, darling." He rubs his hand up and down my arm.

"This isn't me," I whisper, wrapping my arms around my stomach.

"Oh, but it is you, love. You are a most magnificent creation; you were even before your change. Only now can you see yourself for how you truly are, without the limitations of your old, insecure human understanding. What you see, right now, is no different from how the world saw you before, just a little brighter perhaps, a little more refreshed. You are beautiful Aileen, and I certainly wasn't about to let someone as perfect as you go down with the ship, or plane, as it were."

He runs his hand down the back of my hair, still staring into my reflection. His dark brown eyes soften, filling with compassion. He must know what this is like; he's changed once too. I should be happy I'm alive (well, sort of), and this is how anyone would want to look, right? I glance back at myself and then look away, my feelings lost somewhere between violated and grateful.

"Come." He steps back holding out his hand, extended from his still-shirtless torso. I wipe my tears, reverting my eyes back to his. "Come on, I'm here to help you." He smiles, and his voice is warm, soothing the cold that has permanently settled inside me. Just like on the plane, there is something about him that brings me peace, like the comfort you get from an old friend. "I won't bite," he adds to nudge me out of my thoughts.

"Very funny." I slip my hand into his, which is now the same temperature as mine.

He leads me to the window. Outside the sun sinks behind familiar green, rolling, Amador County hillsides under a pink-and-orange cotton candy October sky. Oak trees spread their gnarled branches wide over grazing cattle as they eat their evening meal. If I didn't know any better, I'd think I was in my own backyard. I remind myself I'm not, I may never be again.

"Empty your lungs and stop your breath," he commands, drawing my attention back to my reality in the old farmhouse.

I do as he says, my breath escaping slowly past my lips until every ounce is released. He lets go of my hands. They fall gently to my sides and then, everything is still. Nothing in my brain urges me to breathe, no familiar burn from my lungs to inhale. No beating of my heart. No blood flowing through my veins, or swishing pulse keeping rhythm in my ears— just a perfect, silent stillness. The thick evening air hugs me like a blanket as the warm rays of the setting sun dance on my cool skin through the window. A genuine smile forces its way to my lips. Donovan smiles too.

Suddenly, I'm filled with such immense peace. This is incredible.

"Now close your eyes."

I hesitate; every time I've closed my eyes lately the amplification of sound becomes unbearable. But again, I feel this sense of trust that usually comes with time well spent with someone. My lids close and the darkened world around me springs to life with noise— no, not noise, music! Cows chewing their cud, a fly buzzing in the corner of the room, birds flapping their wings as they fly from tree to tree. Each sound, from within the house and out, work together in harmony, forming a chorus of such organic beauty it would shame even the greatest composer.

I hear the parting "pop" of Donovan's lips as he opens his mouth to draw in air. I can tell he's going to speak before a single word exits his vocal cords.

"Now, keep your eyes closed and breathe in slowly, very slowly, through your nose."

Again, I do ask he asks, thoroughly enjoying the discovery of my new abilities. Inhaling deep, the air rushes down my airways and into my lungs. First, I notice his cologne: sandalwood, patchouli, cedar, mingling well with the seasoned leather fibers his jacket must have left behind on his skin. The musty velvet sofa, the well-worn, dusty nineteenth-century fir floors, the remnants of blood in the empty thermos. A fire bursts into my throat when I think of the blood and I realize air is no longer my life force but simply a necessity for speaking and smelling. A tool for finding my newest necessity for living: blood. All sense of peace and wonder fade as I open my eyes, my arms wrapping around myself in hopes of finding an ounce of warmth from their embrace. But my cold, lifeless arms offer nothing.

"Please, tell me this is a dream." I wonder if *dream* is really the right word for this. Perhaps nightmare might better fit the bill, I am an undead monster now after all.

"I assure you *this* is no dream, darling."

"Then I'm hallucinating." Looking up to the ceiling I contemplate a trip to the roof. If it is a dream, maybe I can fly, too, amongst other absurd things I can think of. His dark eyes squint at me analytically, as if he's trying to read my mind.

"You seemed to be enjoying yourself there a moment ago," he says his face once again puzzled at my lack of gratitude. "But go ahead, be in denial. I understand it's a lot to take in. But beware, denial is the fastest way to harm the ones you love. Example, your family."

The word echoes loud in my mind. Ricocheting of my better judgement. My family— what am I going to tell my family? How can I be what I am and a mom? What happens if Davina cuts her finger, or when Imogene one day starts her period? Or Phil— he's going to know something isn't right the moment he touches my cold skin or my flawless belly—

"I can't go home, can I?"

The room darkens as the sun sets behind the hills. I should have been home hours ago.

"Of course you can if you wish to. However, the blood you drank won't last you long. Would you stay for another drink?" Donovan asks with a hopeful glint in his eye.

I get the feeling he doesn't have much company. My throat burns at the thought of more blood, but the idea of drinking *human* blood leaves a sour taste on my conscience.

"No, I can't hurt innocent people. The blood, from the thermos, that was a person."

"Darling, I promise, that blood was not innocent." He pauses. "So, you don't wish to be a humanitarian, then?"

I look at him, unsure of how to answer.

"Humanitarian?" he asks again, smiling. "You know, one who likes to eat—"

"I get it," I say, cutting him off. Clever, I'll give him that. "No, I don't wish to eat humans."

"Okay, well, the deer population upcountry could use some control. You won't like it as much, though," he wrinkles his nose at me as he says it, "it's like the human equivalent to being a vegetarian actually."

The thought of eating Bambi isn't any better, even if it makes my mouth water to think of a different source of blood. "Bambi it is then," I say.

From the darkness outside, and being that it is

near the end of October, I realize that it must at least 7:00. Phil will be worried sick— only the thought of what might happen when I go home sickens *me*. "Will I be safe around my family?"

Donovan quickly steps up to me, close— too close. His perfect shirtless body is less than inches from mine, his eyes soft and hopeful, and a broad grin barely exposes his vibrantly white teeth that I notice contain no fangs. I want to reach out and touch him, kiss him. I try to shake the thoughts, but with him so close my mind grows fuzzy. "Well, if you're worried, you are more than welcome to stay here. Till you get all *this* under control," he says with a wink as he reaches his hand out toward me, sweeping my hair behind my ear. His touch sends a tingle down my spine. I want him to lean in closer, to feel the scruff of his face on mine. I barely know him, yet this draw to him is strong. Why? I take a step back instead.

"I need to leave," I say, fighting an odd and unwelcome urge to kiss him. I head toward the front door. He races ahead of me, faster by seconds, and opens the door for me like some old-timey gentleman. I join him at the door and end up "whooshing" as well, without even realizing it. Moving this fast will take some getting used to, yet it feels no different than walking as I normally would.

"I apologize, that was too forward of me being so close to you. I don't mean to make you uncomfortable. You've had a long, and I'm sure, confusing day. You will be fine with your family. The blood you drank should last at least a few days." He pauses, staring out the door into the dark night sky. "But one last thing. *This,*" he points back and forth between the two of us, "is our little secret." He strokes his hand down the side of my face, and the urge to throw myself at him returns. "No one can know about this, understand? No one."

"They wouldn't believe me anyway," I say, breaking myself from this odd hold this stranger has on me before I get any more urges to kiss him. I once again move way too fast without meaning to and whoosh out the door into the piercingly cool evening air.

Within seconds I'm yards away from his house, standing on an old dirt walkway that connects to an uneven, overgrown dirt road. Phil would think I'd lost it, probably lock me away in some asylum if I told him what just happened. I barely believe it myself. Although something within assures me this is all real, I still hold out for hope I'll wake up tomorrow morning in some hospital and learn I simply blacked out from lack of sleep and dehydration.

"We will meet again soon, my love. There is much for you to learn still," he says from the doorway. He didn't speak loudly, but I heard it as if he was right beside me.

I wave my hand at him politely out of habit and walk, making an effort to keep a 'normal' pace, down the desolate country road in search of anything familiar to find my way back to the parking lot. I don't want to go back for directions.

EVERYTHING IS DARKER without the moon, yet despite the lack of light, I can see almost as well as in the daytime. The nightlife shifts and stirs all around me, yet I fear nothing. If anything, I'd be the predator now, I guess. It wasn't until I had already spent hours wandering aimlessly down the old country highway I remembered I have no keys, no purse, all of which are lying on the ground in the market's parking lot. There's a good chance it's all been stolen by now. Maybe it's a sign I'm not meant to go back home. Maybe they will think the crash was too much for me and I just kept driving. Or maybe it's my only excuse for my tardy entrance when or if I ever find my way home.

What kind of mom can I be now, anyway? I'm a monster. And not just any monster: I'm a monster that might easily trade the ones she loves most for one more hit of her new addiction. The thought of turning my family into nothing more than a meal sickens me, but my throat flares up at the mere thought of blood regardless of who it belongs to. I disgust myself.

"I. AM. A MONSTER!" I scream into the darkness.

The words scratch through my dry, burning throat and up into the star-filled sky. I fall down hard to my knees, like the tears falling fast down my face, waiting to feel the sting of the hard blacktop as it tears through the knees of my jeans. One day in and already I'm longing for a simple reminder of my humanity, only I feel nothing. I lie down across the double yellow line and shut my eyes tight, hoping any minute now I'll wake from this nightmare.

Vibrations rise from my bed of asphalt, growing stronger by the second, signaling the coming of a car — the first one I've seen all night. I don't care to move; if I'm invincible as Donovan says, then I'll be fine. If not, well, it would solve a few of my dilemmas. I won't have to choose to go home. I'll never have the chance to physically harm my family. Tires grind over the pavement as I open my eyes and stare into the growing brightness of headlights till all I see is light around me and wait for impact.

9

LIAR, LIAR, YOU'RE A VAMPIRE

The lights swerve across the highway to the shoulder on the other side of the road. Tires burrow into the dirt, flinging bits of gravel onto the road as the vehicle comes to a stop, engine still running. A siren bleeps, followed by red and blue flashing lights that reflect off the pale skin on the back of my hand.

"That's her, Jon! Oh, God, that's her!" Phil yells from inside Sheriff Jon Harker's white Ford Explorer.

I sit up so he won't think I'm lying dead on the highway and almost laugh out loud at the thought; I *am* dead, lying on the highway. Instead, I calm the mania building within me and hide my head in my knees and try to think of a plan for how I'm supposed to explain all this. What was I thinking to leave Donovan so soon?

"How in the hell did she end up out here?" Jon

says, his footsteps crunching in the gravel as he exits his Explorer. "They found her van miles in the opposite direction."

Jon moves the spotlight on his car, pointing it right at me. I stare straight into the light, unflinching. Phil runs toward me across the lane. Standing, I straighten out the front of my wrinkled T-shirt, brushing the dirt from my torn jeans, not that it matters. Panic sets in the closer my husband gets. With each step he takes, the scent of his blood burns stronger through my nose enraging my thirst.

"Stop!" I yell over my parched lips. I have speed now— I could run, leave everything. My family— everyone— would be safer that way.

But Phil doesn't stop walking toward me and I can't make my feet move. The sadness in his ocean-blue eyes, the furrow in his brow, the love I have for him it keeps me frozen in place as he approaches, as his warm arms wrap around me. His heart beats from his chest into mine, and for a moment I feel as if mine is beating again. A lump forms in my throat and I choke back a sob.

The overpowering smell of his blood is soured, probably with stress and worry. I don't blame him. I'd be upset, too, if he disappeared without a word. I cease my breath, gently pushing myself away from Phil. Not breathing helps dull the burn of my ever-growing thirst.

"What were you doing lying in the road like that?"

He grabs tight to my arms, tears welling up in his eyes. "What happened to you? Did someone hurt you?"

I'm at a loss for words. Any speaking requires breathing, and breathing means I'll want to eat my husband. What am I supposed to say? *Hey, guess what? I'm a blood-sucking monster now! So that's cool, right?* Instead, tears let loose as the full reality of my situation envelopes me. I don't want to leave the ones I love most— I can't. They *need* me. My girls need their mother. Only my urge to feed sparks hotter and hotter with each heavily breathed sob. I open my mouth to say something— anything— but nothing comes out.

"No, no, it's okay, everything will be okay," Phil says, rubbing his warm hands up and down my arms. The warmth of his hand is a nice distraction from the overwhelming thirst building within me. In fact, this is the first time I realized how cold I am out here compared to his warm body. Phil notices too. "Your skin's like ice!" He turns to Jon, who moved to stand near his SUV. "We need a blanket!"

The sheriff digs through the back of his vehicle and tosses the blanket to Phil, who wraps it around me. The blanket is old, made of dry, scratchy wool, loaded with the scents of dog and dirt. It helps tone down my lust for Phil's blood though, and my sobs ease.

"I'm fine," I finally say, choking down the burn in my throat that remains. I grab hold of the blanket as I step back, holding it tight to keep the last bit of warmth left from his hands on my arms.

Jon joins Phil in the road and they both look at each other, then back at me and kicks into Deputy Sheriff mode. "Aileen, I'm going to need to ask you some questions. Would you please come sit in the car?" Jon inches towards me at a crawling pace and I put it together, they probably think I was assaulted in some way, or kidnapped— or worse.

"I really am fine. Nobody hurt me." I'm doing all I can to focus on the foul-smelling blanket and not the two warm, life-sized thermoses of human blood standing only feet away.

"There was a woman in the parking lot at the market, where you were last seen. She was, well, she was in bad shape. And that's all I can say about that. Your van was found this evening, in the neighboring county—"

"You can't be fine." Phil cuts him off, his voice anxious and I can tell he's worried. I'm almost more worried now about that old woman. "It's nearly ten pm and you're lying in the middle of a dark highway. You've been missing all day. Please tell me if someone hurt you."

My poor Phil. Once again, I've put him through a terrible day. First the plane crash, then he finds out my van is stolen, and I'm missing. I want to embrace him, hold him close and tell him everything is okay— only everything is not okay. There is now a part of me, a very strong part of me, that would love nothing more than to sink my teeth into his neck. But I've been able to control myself so far. Perhaps there is hope after all. Maybe I can fight this. I have to.

"It's hard to explain, but I promise I'm okay."

Phil runs his hands through his sandy blond hair, frustrated, "You're miles from the market, your car! This doesn't make any sense. Maybe you're in shock. We should take her to the hospital, Jon."

"No, please!" I panic, the last place I need to be is in a hospital, probably the bloodiest place in the county. I scan my thoughts for something, some explanation that will placate him for now. "When I left the market, my van was already gone. I didn't have a cell phone, so I panicked and thought maybe I could walk home. I guess I got lost. I'm sorry, I haven't had much to eat, and with being sick, and not sleeping, maybe I'm not quite in my right mind today."

His eyes soften and his heartbeat slows to a more regular rhythm. I can't tell if he believes me or if he's just humoring me. "Let's just get you home, and warm."

He holds his hand out toward me. I don't dare take it, do I? He needs to know things are fine. I bunch the blanket up to my nose and hold my breath, and place my icy hand in his. Phil opens the door to the front passenger seat, and I slide in. He carefully shuts the door. On the other side of the glass, Jon places his hand on Phil's shoulder, leading him to the back of the cruiser.

"I know she says she's fine," I hear Jon whisper, "but things just aren't adding up. I have a feeling more happened today than she's ready to tell you. The plane, and then this? She's been through a lot. You might need to give her some time."

Been through a lot is an understatement. Jon opens the rear passenger door, his mustache turned down in a frown, helping Phil into the seat like he's in custody, then takes his seat up front with me. Flipping off the roof lights, he puts the Explorer in gear and we head toward home.

Home.

One week ago I thought I'd never see it again. Now, home is a place I never thought I'd want to be further from.

The ride is silent except for the tires trolling down the road and old country music playing softly over the radio. I'm grateful for not having a need to breathe. No conversation means I don't need to suck in any dog-blanket-blood-scented air. Eventually, I'll need a better reason why I was missing all day and laying in the middle of a highway. We pull up to the curb of our small, craftsman-style bungalow. Ana's car sits crooked in the driveway right next to my returned stolen van. Knowing Ana, she would have done all she could to shield the girls from today's events, which would only add to the stress I'm putting her under.

I get out of the car and head toward the front steps before Jon has a chance to let Phil out of the back seat, careful to make my movements slow. Again, I overhear Jon speaking with Phil and I linger with my hand on the doorknob of the house to listen. "Hey, I don't want to meddle, but surviving a crash like that— all sorts of strange, uh behavior, can be expected. I have a good friend with PTSD; he says seeing his shrink helped him. Maybe that will do her some good too."

I doubt seeing a *shrink* will do me any good. An exorcist maybe. I take a seat on the steps and wait for Phil.

"Thanks, Jon. For everything," Phil says. "I owe you one."

"You don't owe me anything."

Phil nods and pats the side of the SUV as Jon drives off, waving at me as he goes, worry etched in his tired, aging face.

The curtain in the front kitchen window to the left of the door moves. No doubt it's Ana, giving us our privacy but still curious as to my state. My only hope now is that the girls are sound asleep. Phil sits down by me on the steps, setting his arm over my blanketed shoulders. My body is rigid and still— too still. I need to breathe, to appear alive, to remain human. I take a breath as fire flows into my lungs from the smell of him. The sound of my new obsession beats through his veins. Each pump pounds loud in my ears. His neck, so close I can see the flicker of pulse throbbing under his thin skin. He leans into me, bringing his neck even closer to my lips. Suddenly, nothing else matters except for quenching my thirst— I shoot up from the steps, tossing the blanket over his head, giving myself some much-needed distance from an urge to sink my teeth into his neck. Maybe I don't have as much self-control as I hoped.

"Now what was that for?" he asks, confused, as he pulls the blanket off his face.

"I thought I saw a spider," I lie, attempting to loosen up my tense stance. "Sorry."

"Can we talk?" He pats the step next to him for me to sit.

"Shouldn't we get inside? Your mom's probably worried sick." Phil remains on the step, unmoving. I sigh but stay planted where I am. "I'm fine. Really. I promise."

But I see it in his eyes, the same look he had upon seeing me in the hospital. My stomach sinks; I could never hurt him physically, could I? I sit back down beside him, determined I can be stronger than this thirst inside me. Surely love conquers all? But the thought of the thick, warm, sweet syrupy blood as it coated my tongue, soothed my aching throat, sits more like a vivid aftertaste than a memory. And I want more. I regain control over my thoughts as best I can.

"You know I love you," Phil says, "And *I* know

you've been through so much. You need to talk to someone about this." His eyes are tired and glossy.

"I love *you*, no matter what. You know that, right?" I ask, taking over the conversation. I bend down to him, my hands holding either side of his warm face. I fight past the pain of each word following my every breath, but the flames of my thirst lick up my burning throat. What choice do I have besides fighting this? I'd do anything for Phil and the girls— I escaped death for them. Learning how to live a normal life again, even *this*, pales in comparison to no life with them at all.

"Of course I do."

"No matter what?" I prompt, still holding his face. He nods, and I continue, "I need you to trust that I'm okay. Please?" I stress, the burning feeling becoming more and more bearable as I relax my body into each breath I take. "I just got lost. I will be more careful from now on. I wasn't taking good care of myself this past week. The shock of the crash . . . it really messed me up. I just need some time."

"Okay, fine," he says far too easy to believe it's actually *fine*. He places his hands over mine and pulls them down off his cheeks. "You're right; we should get inside. Your hands are freezing."

Ana opens the door before Phil's hand can close around the knob. She embraces me the second my feet cross the threshold. Red, puffy, hazel eyes look back at me. Tear stains mar the makeup on her slightly leathered cheeks. The whole time I'm repeating to myself over the pounding of her heart, *I will not hurt my family, I will not hurt my family,* until my thirst subsides and I once again feel more in control.

"What in the world— you're freezing!" She pushes me through the kitchen into the living room, where a soft, warm glow flickers from our trusty wood stove.

Above my protests, she presses me down into the couch, draping a blanket over my lap. Past spills, forgotten cheese puffs, and remnants of countless people who have sat here over the years waft up around me from the cushions. It's truly repulsive. Had I noticed the stench of this room sooner, I would have gotten a new couch. Or at least washed this blanket. The downsides to my more sensitive senses are adding up fast. I slide the repulsive blanket off the side of my lap and hope Ana doesn't notice.

Phil heads into the kitchen and Ana follows impatiently behind.

"Let me get you two something to eat. You must be starving." She tries to race past Phil to the fridge nudging him out of her way.

"I'm fine, Mom. You want anything, Aileen?"

"No, thanks." God, if they only knew what I really wanted right now. *Um— yes, please, can I have your carotid artery?* The bad joke sickens me.

"You're so cold, how about some tea, or coffee? I have water heating on the stove," Ana adds, speaking from the kitchen, already neck-deep in the cupboards where I keep the mugs.

Coffee seems like a normal human thing to accept. Donovan did say other liquids were okay. I'm still a mom, after all; it seems cruel to end my life *and* take my coffee. "Coffee sounds great, thank you." I try to keep my voice down as to not wake the girls. I'm not ready to face them yet. I'm almost nauseous at the thought. Hurting them is not something I can handle.

Hushed whispers echo from the kitchen as I hear Ana asks question after question: "Where did you find her? What was she doing? Where in the world was she all day?"

Phil shushes her. She pauses as she turns on the coffee grinder.

"No, I need to know," she says hastily once it stops, her volume rising. "Is she okay? Should you have taken her to the hospital? She's so cold, she might have hypothermia or something."

"Mom, stop," he says, no longer whispering. The kettle whistles.

"No one in their right mind wanders off like that, without something terrible having happened first, especially not a mother of two." Their voices rise like my current body temperature absorbing the heat from the room.

"What do you want me to do— she says she fine. There isn't anything else I can do," he says, lowering his voice. "I can't force her to do anything. Jon suggested we give her some time to come around to us."

She doesn't answer. They're both upset, I don't blame them— they've been through hell today, but so have I. Only there's no one for me to talk about it with, no one except for Donovan. For a moment, my skin tingles from my lips to my toes at the thought of seeing him again, before my stomach knots back up into a tight ball of anxiety. I hate him for what he did to me. But I should be grateful, he did save my life.

"Here you go, sweetie." She hands me a hot mug of coffee that I know definitely did not perk nearly long enough. "This will warm you right up."

The black liquid in my hands steams up through my nostrils, reminding me of the thermos of blood from earlier. I raise it to my lips; it's weaker than I make it, but it pleases my wanting tongue. With each sip my body fills with warmth, soothing my aching throat, somehow partially satisfying my craving for blood. Perhaps a normal life may be possible after all.

"Oh no, I forgot your Half-n-Half." She rushes back toward the kitchen.

"It's fine."

She stops her in her tracks and stares at me critically before sliding down into the maroon wingback chair to the right of the sofa, between the living room and kitchen.

If only I could read minds. After endless moments of watching Ana and Phil exchange silent glances interspersed with sips of their coffees, Ana opens her mouth to take a breath but stops short of speaking, deciding instead on an overtly fake yawn. I drink the rest of my coffee, feeling the most human I've felt all day. I'm suddenly empowered with the sense I can do this, and life can go back to what it was, and from this sensation, a small smile escapes my lips.

Ana's eyes light up in frustration. "And what are you thinking about, young lady?" Her manner unfriendly, which throws me off-guard. Phil shoots her a warning glance.

"Just happy to be home, I guess." I hide behind a sip of coffee from my empty cup. Her eyes narrow at me, scanning me as if she were trying to read my thoughts.

Ana is all sweet and smiles— except when she's worried. Then she becomes an unstoppable bulldog. She clears her throat. "That's all?"

I cringe, wishing I could crawl inside my cup and hide.

"What's that supposed to mean?" Phil says for me, unbridled annoyance in his tone.

"She's just *happy to be home*?" The tension in her voice rises along with the pitch and volume.

"Mom, stop!" Phil commands.

"Don't you *Mom, stop* me," she scolds. "Am I the only person here who can clearly see something is wrong? I have been worried out of my mind all day! God knows what happened to her because she won't

151

talk about it!" She's now speaking to Phil as if I was invisible. I almost wish I was.

"Now is not the time for this." He glares at her.

Both their faces are red, blood pressures rising, inviting the return of my hunger. I hold my breath.

"If not now when, huh? What if whatever happened whoever took her comes back! But we won't know how to help her because she won't tell us!"

"Ana, I'm fine, really. No one took me," I answer, but she ignores me and stares at Phil instead as if he might hold the answers she seeks.

"Mom!" he shouts, clearly reaching his limit with his mother.

"— Or better yet, when you find her *dead* on the side of the road, frozen to death?" Ana stands, her heart pounding a furious beat in her chest.

"Maybe it's time you go home and give Aileen and me some time to process this, okay?" Phil tents his fingers over his eyes.

"I will not cower away and ignore this like you are," she says with a lowered voice for effect.

"Is that what you think? You think I'm ignoring this?" He stands up, facing his mother. "She was in a plane crash! Her van was stolen, a woman was assaulted in the same parking lot. What's there to ignore?"

Ana, clearly hurt by her son's lack of support in the matter, seems to realize her defeat. She straightens her blouse and clears her throat. Her hot-headed attitude turns a one-eighty as a pleasantly forced smile settles on her softened face.

"I can see when I'm no longer needed. There is freshly baked bread on the counter, and the laundry is in the dryer. Goodnight." With a nod and pursed lips, she gathers her things and heads out the door.

Even Phil seems shocked at what we just witnessed. He turns to go into the kitchen. I can see by the determined, tense set of his shoulders that he's trying to process it all. She may be spirited, but I've never seen her this upset, and it's my fault. I can't help but wonder if she is blaming herself for the crash and that's why she's taking this all upon herself.

"Thank you," I say to Phil, joining him in the kitchen.

He rests his head against the back of the door and lets out a heavy breath. "Are you honestly sure you are fine?" he asks head still resting against the back of the door.

"Yes." *No. Maybe?*

"Then why do I feel like there is something you're not telling me?" He turns to face me, frustration painted across his furrowed brow. A tendril of sandy-blond hair falls across his eye. He rakes his fingers through his hair to place it back where it belongs. It doesn't listen.

"I told you, I was not thinking straight earlier. It scared me that the van was stolen, I got lost walking home with no phone to call you. I don't know what else you want me to say."

"I'm exhausted, you must be too. Let's just go to bed," is all he says.

Phil mechanically locks the front door, flips off the light in the kitchen and then the living room, and walks down the hall to our bedroom without another word. He doesn't turn around or ask if I'm coming. The room falls silent except for the clicking of the wood stove, its warmth now fading, casting a blood-red glow across the wood floor.

Phil knows me better than anyone which is exactly why he knows I'm not telling him the truth. I've never lied to him before but I have to now, for his own good. Even though I hate myself for it.

I am dead, harboring a dark secret I have no idea what to do with. And I'm alone.

The door to our bedroom creaks open. The sheets of our bed rustle and the bed frame squeaks as Phil settles in. The thought of enclosing myself in a small space with him sounds like a bad idea; instead, I head outside to the back deck where I can breathe.

The crisp fall night air is soothing after all the heat festering inside. Stars shine in abundance from the moonless sky. If there is one thing I can be proud of tonight, it is how well I can control myself. I know I can't hold my breath forever without drawing suspicion from Phil, but I'm taking the wins where I can. A breeze picks up and dances toward me the scent of vintage leather and men's cologne, bringing with it a slight sense of comfort knowing Donovan is near. But the relief is temporary as the slider opens behind me. Phil's sweet-smelling blood is stronger than Donovan's cologne, and it takes all I have to keep my thirst at bay. To prove to myself that I'm not the monster Donovan forced me to be.

"What are you doing out here? I thought you were coming to bed. It's freezing." Phil's breath escapes like clouds from his lips as he rubs his bare arms to keep warm.

"I just wanted some fresh air. I'll be in soon."

"Are you hell-bent on freezing to death tonight?"

I turn toward him, wishing he could know how funny that question is. And then I wonder if this new life is a secret between only Donovan and me, could Phil not maybe become a part of it too? The what-if's itch up under my skin; *What if Phil can know, what if Phil can be this too?* I need to know.

"If you could live forever, would you?"

"Can we go inside, please?" He frowns. His body shivers in the doorway.

"Can you answer my question, please?" I plead, matching his tone, the urge to know growing quickly inside me along with a hope I so desperately need.

His face turns red as he holds in a breath, then, releasing it slowly, he answers. "After everything that happened today, you're asking me *that*?"

"Yes. If you had the choice to live forever, would you?"

"Right now, I'm making the choice to go inside, where it's warm. You should too." He walks toward me, grabbing my hand. "My God, you're like ice— come *on*."

"Fine." I follow him in. "Then can you answer my question?"

If Donovan could change me, surely Phil could change, too. The sudden thought of spending eternity here on earth without Phil is too unbearable a reality to accept. And what of the girls?

Oh, God, the girls. The thought of losing my family overwhelms me and the glimmer of hope that was growing begins to shatter at the reality of it all. I can ask this of Phil, maybe. He's an adult. But not the girls. I am going to lose them no matter what I do. I am no master of time and I would never choose *this*, the life of a bloodthirsty monster, for them. I shouldn't want this for Phil either. But my fear of being without him festers in the back of my mind.

Once we're both inside the warm living room, he shuts the slider and locks it. "No," he says from behind me.

I turn to face him, looking painfully into his saddened eyes. "No, you won't answer my question or—"

"No, I wouldn't choose to live forever. Can we go to bed now?"

"Why not?" I hold back tears that are waiting to fall as I focus on picking at a perfect fingernail.

He breathes out an impatient sigh. "Aside from the fact that we aren't meant to live forever, life is exhausting. Take today, take this last week, for example."

"What if you could freeze yourself, just as you are now?"

"No." His tone softens as he slides his hands around my waist. To my surprise, a smile forms on his face. "I'd rather grow old with you, play with our grandkids, do things old people do, I guess. That is if you'll stop scaring me half to death."

I nod, and a tear falls down my cheek. He wipes it away and kisses my forehead.

Looking up into his stormy-blue eyes I ask, "But what if I wanted to live forever and knew how, would you want the same? To stay with me? We could live forever, together? Think of all the amazing things you could do. The things you could see— the things *we* could see, together."

His laugh is small. "You may have survived a plane crash, but you aren't invincible. And since that isn't how life works, I don't think it's something we need to worry about. We can live life together here and now, and then, when we're old we can pass on quietly into the hope of something more."

He wipes another tear from my cheek as his smile

fades to worry. He takes a deep breath. "What really happened today?"

I shake my head and bite my lips as the burn returns to my throat. "Nothing." I push myself back from him, wishing the world would go back to how it was before all this.

"Let's go to bed then." He turns in the direction of our room. "You coming?"

I shake my head no, choking back the tears stinging my eyes. Silent, he continues down the hall to our room, glancing back one last time as if he had something to say but instead disappears into the dark.

I can see it just then, in his eyes. A look of pure, immeasurable sadness. The silent type that rises from the darkest parts of your heart and is never quick to leave. All caused by actions I cannot explain, a new existence I'm unable to share with my own husband.

I want to join him. To lie in bed with him, snuggled up, pretending my life is normal again. But what is normal about being a monster?

Phil wants to grow old with me. That's what we were supposed to do together, not this. Tears like I've never experienced before fall to the floor along with me, and I bow my head in surrender to my sadness. Silently crying as to not wake the house. Realizing the full extent of my loss of eternity with the ones I love, stolen by the only man who truly knows what I am. This is hell, and I'm stuck here forever.

10

ELIXIR OF LIFE

The rain began falling not long after I ran out of tears. The dry burn in my throat eventually forced me off the floor and into the kitchen where I remembered how soothing the cup of coffee Ana made earlier was. How it so easily tempered my cravings for blood. So I make more and do the only thing I can do: busy myself with, something. Four cups and a deep-cleaned kitchen later, I sit here alone at the table, cup number five in hand, as I listen to the rain fall with my new, more acute hearing. It's odd how I can focus on each individual drop as they hit the tiny leaves of the old valley oak just outside the kitchen walls. The usual pitter-patter of rain is replaced by pings and zings. I can clearly hear the drops slosh their way off the leaves and whiz down through the air as they fall to the ground below.

Out the window, dark clouds begin to glow from the breaking dawn somewhere behind the storm.

I raise my cup to my lips for another sip knowing fair well it's empty, but out of hope and habit, I go through the motion anyway. On the counter sits an almost empty half-gallon jar of coffee beans, complete with the word "beans" etched on the side. By the looks of it, I'd guess there is enough for one more pot.

The ritual of making coffee is usually Phil's specialty, but I've watched him enough to know what I'm doing. I start by turning on the kettle and putting the beans in the grinder. Day one of this so-called new life. Day one of doing everything I can to fight this blood-sucking beast within me so I can find a new normal. The only solution to my current dilemma? More coffee. Perhaps I could simply live off of it. Sounds reasonable enough. If it curbs my craving for blood, maybe it's all I really need. Donovan left out blood-sucking 101 in his introduction to this new, *life*, and I'm glad— sort of. The thought of drinking blood is repulsive. If only it didn't taste so good.

Needing to get my thoughts off blood, I grind the beans, praying the sounds won't wake the girls. While there's a lot I don't like about my new life, and a lot I will need to get used to, the truth is I am here, some-what alive and right where I wished— no, begged— to be as the plane fell from the sky: home with my family. The family I'm now terrified of accidentally making my breakfast.

Even over the sound of the grinder, I hear Phil rise from our creaky bed. The suck of air as he inhales, preparing for a large yawn. The tread of his feet as they walk down the hall and into the girl's bathroom. How his hand thuds against the cupboard door under the vanity, the squeak as its hinges open, and the rustle of plastic. We must be out of toilet paper in our bathroom.

"What the—?" he mumbles to himself, and stomps back up the hall to our room, closing the door firmly behind him.

I cringe as I dump the grounds into the coffee press. He must have seen the mirror I shattered yesterday. Talk about bad luck— I thought a broken mirror only brought you seven years of it, not curse you for eternity. Joke's on me, I guess. As I pour the hot water from the kettle over the grounds in the French press, up rises the sweet aroma of hope. Hope in my ability to hide what I am and not hurt anyone in the process. Now, if only coffee will also grant me the strength I need to get through today. I close my eyes and listen for the girls, thankful that all I catch is their tiny beating hearts in rhythm with their slow, sleeping breaths.

Our bedroom door groans loud as it opens up slowly and Phil walks out of the room and down the hall. I prepare myself for seeing him as I pour myself another cup of coffee.

He enters the kitchen and through habit grabs a

mug, setting it down immediately onto the counter as he leans in on his hands. Eyes closed, he takes in deep all the air left in the room, then exhales a thick fog of tension in its place.

I want to run up to him, hug him tight. To apologize for my selfish idea of wanting to make him immortal, like me. I can't keep him forever like some relic of my former existence. Sadness waves through me again at the thought of life without him. I push it aside. Never have I wanted to be so close, yet so far from him at the same time. I clear my throat to test for urges— coffee's still working for now. Phil looks in my direction.

"Morning," I say. He stares at me for a second in silence, like I'm a ghost— did he not notice I was here? "We need to get more coffee," I add after a few more moments of silence, unsure if he's upset about the mirror, yesterday, or our conversation last night. Maybe all of the above.

His pulse quickens as he stares out the kitchen window, his arms still pressed firmly in place, a stiff extension of the white-tiled countertop. The dim light of the rainy-morning sunrise reflects on his furrowed brow. I stare back, hating every part of this cold, closed-off worry-filled version of Phil. I could attempt to clear the air with the truth of what I've become— except why in the world would he believe me? I'm still in denial myself.

"Are you okay?" I ask out of habit. I know he's not

okay.

"Coffee, you said?" The words as glassy as his blank looking eyes.

"Yes, we're out." I stand and point at the now-empty jar on the counter to his left.

"You think I'm going to let you out of my sight after spending all day looking for you yesterday? Do you know how worried I was?" By his tone, I can tell he's hurt. He knows I'm not telling him something. He's not normally the type to control where I go and what I do.

I sit back down, already weary from the conversation that's barely begun.

"You were in the middle of the road! They found that poor old woman murdered in the parking lot—"

I gasp. "She's dead?" My soul, if I still have one, sinks down further into the depths. Did I kill her? Her heart was beating when I touched her.

"Sorry, I shouldn't have shared that. Jon wants it kept under wraps. I just, I don't—" Flustered, he takes a breath, picks out a mug, fills it with the last of the coffee from the French press, and sits down across from me at the table. "There might be a serial killer on the loose, and I thought I lost you, again."

"A serial killer? Who else was killed?"

"You know Jon overshares, I shouldn't have mentioned that."

"I'm sorry," is all I can say. I mean it, though. I never meant to put him through all this.

He sips his coffee. "You didn't come to bed last night."

"No, I couldn't sleep." I take a sip of my own.

"I know there is something you aren't telling me about yesterday." He stares into his coffee cup. "If you won't tell me will you at least call the therapist from the hospital back? Maybe you could tell her?"

The worry in his brow, the drained color from his once sparkling blue eyes, tugs at my frozen heart. He's right, I'm not telling him what happened, but I can't tell a therapist either. "I'll consider it, okay?" It's all I can think of to say.

We sit in silence, each of us lost in our own thoughts, sipping our coffee. The rain has stopped and a fresh blue sky peeks out from behind fading dark clouds. I almost see a smile in Phil's eyes. Maybe it's just the coffee, but a peace settles over us, quieting my uncertainty. This is normal— drinking coffee with my husband is normal. A grin stretches across my cheeks as I inhale the sweet hopefulness of this moment. Maybe life could be normal for me after all.

Phil's gaze is as warm upon my face as the rising sun outside the kitchen window.

"You drank the last of my coffee," I say with a smirk.

A real smile forms on his lips.

"*Your* coffee? Since when do you like coffee so much anyway? And without your precious Half-n-Half, I see?"

"Well, you know what they say, strange things can happen when you almost die in a plane crash." I laugh out loud at the irony of my statement. I wish drinking coffee black is the strangest thing to happen to me. I missed this. "It's been a long week."

"I miss you," he says, his demeanor turning serious.

Phil's dampening eyes meet mine as he stands and moves to my side of the table. I know what he means — I miss me too, and perhaps somewhere deep inside, my life as it was before still has a chance of returning. Downing my last swallow of coffee, I hold my breath and embrace him hard. I don't care what my hunger does. I need him— I need him to know I'm still here. I need him to help me feel alive again. His warm arms encircle me as he lets out a huge sigh. Any minute now I expect him to notice my cold, life-less body, but he only hugs me tighter. I could stand holding him forever, the beating of his heart pulsing through his chest into mine brings comfort. I shut my eyes and summon every ounce of willpower to fight off the small flare of hunger returning to my throat. No, not now.

"Oooh!" Phil says, breaking our embrace while shaking out his arms.

"What?" I ask, wondering if he noticed my missing heartbeat or my lack of body heat.

"Gee, girl, you got a grip!" He rubs his bicep with a wince.

"Huh?"

"My arms were going numb," he laughs.

Great, I'm stronger now too— another thing I need to keep secret and keep under control to protect my family. "Are you okay?"

"I'm fine." He hugs me again, this time placing his arms over mine.

The scent of his blood grows strong as it pools into his injured arm muscles, rising to the surface as a juicy bruise across his outer biceps. My nostrils burn with my inflamed thirst and my bloodlust returns with a vengeance. All I can think of is taking a bite out of his arm. I push myself gently but quickly away.

"What, do I smell bad?" he asks, sniffing himself.

If he only knew how good he smells. Hunger pangs rise to my throat, giving me two choices: feed or run. I smile through the burn, through the desire to tear out his throat. Then, I hold my breath and give him a silent wink as I head out the kitchen toward the hall, leaving Phil and his delicious bruises safely alone.

"You smell fine," I say as soon as I feel there is a safe enough distance to catch some air to speak, adding a friendly chuckle. I round the corner to the hall; he follows me. "But I sure don't. I'm going to take a shower."

Rushing into our bedroom before he gets to the hallway, I lock the bathroom door behind me, I turn on the shower and contemplate actually getting in. I give my underarms a sniff— no foul odor here; in fact, I don't think I really smell like anything at all anymore.

The girls start yelling at each other in their room. They're awake and grumpy. The thought of three blood-filled bodies on the other side of my door is too terrible a thought to bear.

Phil knocks on the bathroom door.

"Yeah?" I ask, stuffing a towel over my face. That flimsy wooden door doesn't seem like nearly enough protection from me right now. I need to regain control and fast.

"Since we're out of food, how about I take the girls to breakfast, then get some groceries so you can rest?"

"Yes, get coffee!" I shout through the pain of my raw, dry throat, horrified by this instinctual urge to break down the door and satisfy my thirst. I let the shower run, steam fogging up the mirror till I can't see my reflection anymore, counting the seconds till they leave.

"Bye, Mommy!" echoes through the house mere moments later. The front door shuts and I wait until I hear the car leave the driveway before breathing a sigh of relief and shutting off the water. Plopping myself down on my bed, I lie on my stomach with my head at the foot, staring out the window. Coffee is no match for blood. I need to find a more reliable solution to my hunger problem, and soon.

TALL PINES DANCE in the crisp fall breeze on this soggy, late Sunday morning. Ironic to call today Sunday since the sun has since hidden behind the next batch of rain clouds. I hope Phil grabbed the girls' jackets. Across the street, my elderly neighbor Mr. Gerigson sits in his usual spot at the top of his driveway sheltered under his open garage door.

Ever since his wife passed, there he sits, day in and day out, rain or shine, watching the world pass by. For about an hour around noon each day, he closes his garage door and goes inside for lunch, only to return to his post afterward. Throughout the day cars toot their hello's as they drive past. He waves at them and then continues his watch. But most of the time, like right now, he's sleeping. If it weren't for the fact I can see the rise and fall of his shoulders with each of his breaths, I'd say he looks dead. Sometimes I wonder if he sits out there simply because he's waiting out his days— waiting for his moment to die and be reunited with his wife.

My thoughts grow darker. If he *is* waiting to die, wouldn't I be doing him a favor? Only I have no idea what I'm doing. It can't be that hard, right? Bite and suck. Do I have to bite? I run my tongue over my teeth; they feel like normal teeth. No pointy fangs like in the movies. Maybe I should watch some of those movies, try to get tips. I sneak to my window and crack it open, breathing in deep the scent of his blood.

"Smells good, doesn't it? Has a hint of old tobacco pipe to it." says a familiar voice, his British accent charming as ever. I shut the window and jump to my feet. My senses are overwhelmed with the mix of his signature scent and warm blood, but not Mr. Gerigson's blood, different blood. Donovan stands at the doorway to my room, in his vintage jacket, blue jeans, and a white shirt, red thermos in his hand.

"What are you doing here?" I ask, unsure if I should kick him out or hug him for bringing me breakfast. Mr. Gerigson would be grateful as well. Not only is it fundamentally wrong to kill your neighbor by draining him of blood for your nourishment, but it's also just plain gross.

"Thought you could use this." He whooshes closer and places the thermos in my hand.

His scent is hypnotic; warm sandalwood, amber, and leather. I take the thermos, but my conscience gets the best of me— "And who am I drinking?"

"Do you really want to know?"

I cringe and change the subject. "No. And you can't be here." I thrust the thermos back toward him.

Donovan smiles a crooked smile as he tucks my hair behind my ear, leaving the thermos in my hand. "Why, you expecting someone?"

My ear tingles from the touch of his hand. I move away from him, closer to the window.

"Yes, my family. They should be back any minute now," I say, debating whether I should just jump out the window and leave. The last thing I want to do is explain who Donovan is to Phil.

His smile grows bigger.

"So you didn't eat them yet, I'm assuming? Well, good for you!" he says as he sits down on the edge of my bed, bouncing on it as he makes himself comfortable.

"It's not hard to not want to hurt the ones you love." Only I wish that statement were true. I glance down at the thermos in my hand, knowing full well it's the only thing that will truly keep them safe. I have to feed on something.

"Right," he says sarcastically as he stands and heads toward the doorway. "I recommend you drink the whole thing. It should get you through today— tonight we hunt."

"Hunt?" Hunt what?

Donovan disappears without a sound just as Phil pulls into the driveway. Get me through today, huh? It doesn't sound as promising as I had hoped, and the idea of hunting doesn't sound any better. I down the thermos in seconds, and like the coffee, it takes the edge off, but a dull ache remains deep within me. I pray I can make it through the day without hurting the ones I love most. I force a smile onto my face and go to greet Phil and the girls, licking away the last remnants of blood from the corners of my mouth.

11

COLD NOSE AND BLOODY TOES

Not only did Phil remember coffee, but he also picked up a new iPhone for me while they were out as well. It's shocking how many unread texts poured through. Some from people I barely know, all wondering how I'm doing. Some with belated birthday wishes. A long drawn out one from Jordyn. I ignore them all. And then there was a voicemail from the Transportation Safety Board — three voicemails, actually— from a kind-sounding woman named Angela Summers. I ignore those too.

Thanks to the blood Donovan brought me and the coffee beans Phil picked up, my cravings remained manageable. I even felt comfortable enough to participate in the girl's bedtime. Terrifying as I was, no one was hurt. I even hugged the girls goodnight and almost cried at how normal it felt, my confidence growing in my ability to control this new thirst growing even though deep down I know I could never hurt them. But now, everyone is asleep and the house is quiet, and as I'm sitting here on my side of the bed watching Phil sleep, the burn of my hunger slowly rises to the surface of my thoughts. My foot taps incessantly on the floor as I stare at the clock. One-forty-seven-a.m. The night is long when you don't sleep— even longer when you're hungry. And a bowl of cereal isn't going to fix this late-night craving.

My foot stops. What did Donovan mean by "hunt"? I'm not about to go out and stalk people in the night if that's what he's thinking. My phone dings with a text; I turn the sound off quickly, not wanting to wake up Phil.

555-743-2253: Ready, love?

Who is this?

555-743-2253: Seriously? It's me. Where do you want to go for dinner? Downtown Jackson?

I should have known better. I can hear his accent in his texts.

I'm not eating people if that's what you're implying.

555-743-2253: There's a pretty scuzzy pub there full of ...exotic flavors.

No people.

I don't care how "scuzzy" they are.

555-743-2253: Upcountry it is then. Meet me in the woods just before Silver Lake. Run, don't drive, and don't stop till the houses are gone.

Run. Is he crazy? Silver Lake is a five-thousand-foot climb in elevation from here. With all the rain we've had here in the foothills I'll be surprised if snow isn't already blanketing the ground up there. But then again, it's not running I do. I whoosh, faster than human eyes can see. I'm stronger, too, and don't need to breathe, so the climb should be easy. Plus, there is nothing covert about starting up a car at this hour of the night. I save Donovan's number in my phone as *007*. I hate to admit it, but if I'm going have any chance of maintaining any sense of a normal life again, I need him to teach me how to do this whole undead thing.

Phil snores. The sounds emitting from him are barely human, and I wonder— *how did I ever sleep through that?* Quietly, I toss on a pair of black yoga pants, a charcoal fitted tee with a lightweight hoodie, and my barely used, multicolored Nikes. I tuck my phone into the waistband of my pants and sneak through the house to the back door. The last thing I want to do right now is have "dinner" alone in the woods with another man, and a somewhat creepy man at that. Actually, really creepy, come to think of it.

With a snort, Phil rolls over, his snoring amplified in his new sleeping position. It's time to go.

I run out the back door without a second thought, into the yard, past my empty chicken coop, and leap over the back fence like it's nothing, into the fields behind my house. With each step I allow myself to run faster and faster till I am whizzing past the sleeping homes and neighboring fields. The sleepy old town becoming a blur beside me while the path before me stays perfectly in focus. In minutes, I hit the highway and start the fifty-mile run upcountry toward Silver Lake, taking the forested edge that runs alongside the asphalt. Memories of summer days spent picnicking on the lake's rocky shores with the girls are quickly blackened by the motivation behind this visit: my hope of finding non-human options to satisfy my new "diet." None of this sits well with me, and I don't think it ever will. But in this moment I'm so hungry I could eat a bear, or maybe two. God, I hope I don't have to settle for squirrels.

I blast through the tall, dark pines offset a bit from the highway. Occasionally a quick blink of a car drives past. It's been a few minutes since I've seen any homes and the last sign I saw read *Silver Lake Five Miles*, so I head deeper into the forest away from the road. There is no snow up here yet, but the temperature has to be close to freezing, if not lower.

As I come upon the tree-lined edge of a small clearing I stop. For years Phil and I have hiked around this area but tonight I find myself I'm in a part of the forest I never knew existed. Frosted tips of pine branches glisten in the faint light of a thin, waxing, sliver of a moon glowing above. Truly a sight to behold. I imagine it's rarely if ever, seen by humans. My glittering hand catches my eye. Mesmerized, I wave and wiggle my fingers in the barely-there moonlight. Just like the frozen, icy branches, each one of my fingers is delicately adorned with ice crystals— each one perfect and beautifully frozen like winter jewels upon my hands.

With this, a new curiosity is birthed within me. Perhaps my new life is not all death and blood, but a new beauty of its own. Could this curse be, instead, a gift? One thing is for sure: my human self would not have found freezing, dew-covered fingertips— or standing alone in a dark forest— as fascinating as I do now. All the pain of dying, marriage, motherhood, and hunger begins to fade into the clearing as I stare at my frosted hands. Is this a glimpse of what my new life might be? A *life?* And for the first time since yesterday I realize, maybe I don't have to be *alive* to still *live.*

Alone in this shadowy world of wonder, I inhale the chilly night air and blow it out, waiting to see the cloud of breath that always brought me joy as a kid— who am I kidding, as an adult too— only nothing shows up. Disappointment sets in once again by the fact I am still a non-living being. No more internal body heat equals no warm exhaled-breath clouds. Fear settles in the back of my mind, as I wonder if my humanity in its entirety might one day gone as well.

A soft breeze glides across my face, bringing Donovan's scent with it— he's here. Happy but hesitant, I push aside my existential worries and questions I don't yet want answers for and look for him. Maybe he already caught something and will save me the dirty work. My eyes dart to every corner of the forest but only the faintly-lit frozen trees glitter back at me.

"Where are you?" I whisper. He gives no answer and his scent disappears. Maybe I imagined it. Part of me would rather do this without him present, and maybe that's his plan. Let me see what I'm capable of doing on my own.

I dash off across through the clearing and head deeper into the forest, still amazed by my new-found freedom and speed, no longer hindered by human constraints. A stabbing pain of thirst in my dry throat reminds me of my only real restriction— a sinister and cruel one at that. Unsure of where to start, I close my eyes and listen to the forest. I only hear silence and the faint lapping of waves from Silver Lake a few miles behind me, closer to the highway. Frustrated, I open my eyes. I had hoped this would be easier than it's turning out actually to be. Yet my determination to succeed, to feed, to find this new normal I so desperately want, urges me to try again. This time I shut my eyes and concentrate harder, searching deeper into the silence.

Suddenly, a concert of sounds rises from all around me as thousands of little drums begin to beat. No, not drums. Heartbeats. Some fast but weak, others smooth and steady. Some sounds are grouped together, while others whiz past me in the air above. The longer I listen, the more I'm able to pinpoint where each sound is coming from. So this is how I'll find food. An excitement over learning more of my abilities shoots me into action. *Here we go.* Eyes still shut, I hone in on a group of slow, even beats not far to my right. Not about to run with my eyes closed, I open them and proceed toward the sound, trying to listen as I go. The more I focus, the more I can hear with my eyes open. Louder and louder the beats grow until I come upon a herd of deer in a thicket. Ten, maybe fifteen of them lie still on soft beds of dirt. All of them sleeping, unaware of my presence. I kneel beside a large buck. His heartbeat is strong; the scent of his blood is stronger. It's gamey and not nearly as sweet as the human blood from the thermos, but my thirst has risen to a point where it could taste like dirt and I'd still drink it. I lift my hand up to its neck and hover it over his fur, warm heat radiates onto my icy hands. My throat burns and I want to bite, but my heart cries out to spare the poor creature. I push myself back, away from the buck, snapping a twig in the process and alerting the herd who, in seconds, thunder away from me.

"Try again," a voice whispers from somewhere behind me.

I turn expecting to see Donovan, but no one is there.

A rustling in the bushes to my left draws my attention away from the whisper. I dash after the quick-paced rhythm of a rapidly-beating heart as a fox with a mouse dangling from its mouth darts out of his hiding place. This time I don't think about it. Invigorated by the chase, I run my fastest yet, following the fox back into the clearing. He stops to set down his own meal and clean his paws; like the deer, he too seems unaware of me. Perhaps my lack of body heat helps me blend into the scenery. My throat screams at me to take advantage of my camouflage and I snatch the fox up by his soft tail. The creature in my hand emits a foul stench of fear and squirms, screeching a loud, horrified call into the night. Its hot breath steams in quick bursts from its panicked breathing.

Again, I can't bring myself to make the kill as his

dark glossy eyes look into mine, wide and full of terror. I set him down as he grabs his meal and escapes out of the clearing to the safety of the forest. I doubt a fox would be big enough to satisfy my ever-growing thirst for blood anyway. At least he got his meal.

I fall to the ground in defeat. Donovan's laughter rings out from the forest edge. This is a nightmare, like one of those dreams where you need to find a restroom so bad, but all the toilets are in the middle of crowds so you can't bring yourself to use any of them despite the discomfort. Then, a new beat catches my ear not far to my right, back in the trees. I skirt to the edge of the clearing and wait. The strong, sturdy beat grows louder and closer, each thump emanating its warm, rich, earthy-toned blood. Just like the deer, it's not as sweet-smelling as a human's, but my hunger burns the same and this time I don't think it's going to let me back down.

Moving toward the sound of my prey, a large, round boulder begins to move. I freeze as a huge black bear turns toward me. My instinct should be to run, but instead, I stand firm as the beast pauses to sniff the ground at my feet. I pray he doesn't notice me, like the deer and the fox, and I'm relieved to see he doesn't.

"Take it," Donovan whispers.

The bear snorts as he finds a suitable stone and digs into the ground with its mighty paws.

"It's yours, they're all yours!" he says, still a faint whisper in the breeze.

It's exhilarating being so close to such a powerful creature who, with one swipe, could take me down, just like that— if I was still human, that is.

"Come on already! You're killing me, love!"

"But he's so cute," I whisper back. Then I realize, if I'm a failure at this whole hunting I can at least enjoy this— I reach out my hand toward its soft fur—

"I wouldn't do that," Donovan warns.

Too late. The coarse, warm fur under my hand rises, and I'm faced with a nine-foot-tall startled black bear who's now very aware of my presence. He gnashes his teeth and growls a terrible growl, and his angry eyes peer deep into my soul as flames ignite inside me. I have no fear or desire to run, only a strong instinct to attack. To fight. Growling back at the bear, I stand my ground as he bats at me with a giant, clawed paw. Dodging it without contact I look toward his neck. I can hear the strong beat of his heart. And as I wait for the right moment to strike I dodge his blows as I focus the rise and fall of his fur as his quick pulse races underneath.

"Now we're talking, love!" Donovan stands behind the bear, right in my line of sight.

Distracted by his outburst, the bear knocks me down off my feet with his powerful paw. I look up to him towering over me with his arm drawn back, ready to release again, and an old sense of self-preservation kicks in— fetal position, cover your neck. It was something I remember learning in summer camp. Fight or flight. I should run, but I can't.

"What are you doing? Get up! Take the bear!" Donovan yells.

A wrecking ball slams down into my back as his claws tear through the top layer of my shirt, painfully grinding into my back like nails running down a chalkboard. I scream as an unsettling cold, gooey thick, dampness coats my back, and I picture the oily black ooze that is now my blood soaking into my shirt. Frozen with fear, I curl up on the pile of pine needles beneath me, hoping it won't hurt too bad as I become this bear's dinner. The bear growls again, its battle cry deafening. I shut my eyes and wait for the worst, but instead of another blow from the bear, a terrible squealing and gasping replaces his deadly roar. I wouldn't be surprised if the sounds were coming from me; I'm too afraid to look.

"Come on, you! Think you're so tough, huh?" Donovan grunts.

My eyes open and there he is once again— my savior, Donovan, riding on the back of the bear with a chokehold around its neck. The bear, struggling to breathe, tries its best to fight him off its back, but Donovan is stronger. The beast bucks, gasping for air, spit flying from its massively sharp teeth. The event is hard to watch, but I'm fascinated by the display of strength before me, and I wonder if I too am as powerful as Donovan. He gives him one more squeeze around the neck and with it, the bear's dark eyes dim with the last, faint beat of his heart. They both collapse together on the ground with a mighty thud.

"Why did you— what did— you wrestled a-a-a—"

"A pain in the ass." He gives the bear a kick and laughs.

"Don't do that," I scold, staring down at the once-mighty creature.

"Why not? It's food now. Hungry?" His accent accentuates his smug tone, although his smile speaks for itself. He stands up and brushes his hands on his pants before ripping off a chunk of fur from the bear's neck. He goes in for a taste.

Tears begin to build under my lashes in mourning of the conquered beast. "What is your problem? Have some respect!" I've never killed anything before, let alone seen anything be killed. I don't think I'm cut out for this kind of life.

Torn between sadness and hunger, I watch. The bear's blood is pungent, comparative to a strong, baked brie. I never liked brie, but my mouth waters regardless, and my thirst burns like an inferno in my throat. I move toward the steaming, warm artery in the neck Donovan has ever-so-kindly, yet insensitively, opened for me.

"It's really not so bad," he says. "It's flowing still, jump in." He smiles as he pulls a tattered-up handkerchief from his pants pocket, dabbing blood from the corners of his mouth. So proper for having just wrestled a bear.

Kneeling down beside the creature I dig my hands into the coarse fur on either side of the wound. His skin is still warm. I close my eyes, take a breath, and as the scent of the blood fills my senses, urgency compels my mouth to the bleeding gash in the bear's throat. The salty, dirty skin doesn't faze me as my lips clasp over the wound and warm, fresh blood fills my mouth. Any and all disgust fades as euphoria takes its place. Each gulp flows down my throat like thick honey, quenching my once-endless thirst. I drink and drink until the bear runs dry and its skin begins to cool. My own skin warms as the bear's blood settles within me. I feel the wound on my back close up like a zipper. Pushing myself off the dead carcass, I fall back onto the frosty, leaf-littered, forest floor, smiling, laughing even. Every inch of me fills with joy.

I feel alive again.

"Feel better now?" Donovan sits beside me stroking my hair.

Not bothered at all by his touch, I lie there, staring into the frozen, starry night. He has given me life—literally—multiple times now, and at this moment I'm so high from my fill, nothing could bother me.

"I feel incredible, fearless. And most wonderful of all, I feel like *me!*" I exclaim, sitting up beside him, letting my eyes softly meet his. He no longer intimidates me, not like when we met on the plane, and as he smiles I throw my arms gratefully around him, knocking him over in the process.

"Sorry." I laugh, embarrassed by my outburst of affection toward him. I stand up and brush the forest floor off my clothes, yet something inside me wants to sit back down beside him.

"Don't be." In a flash, he rushes at me and pins me between himself and a large pine, its bark rough against the semi-exposed, fully healed skin of my back. Donovan's body is heavy against me as he leans closer. His lips barely brush mine, leaving me breathless.

We stand there, frozen like the icy world around us, his body and lips still warm from the bear, ready to melt into mine at any moment.

"What are you doing?" I'm unsure of what to do, of what he might want to do to me. Afraid of what I might *let* him do to me.

Donovan's lips are almost touching mine as he speaks, "You have kill on your face." He traces the rim of my bottom lip from edge to edge with his soft tongue then stands back, staring at me with a wickedly sexy smile. He slowly sucks the last of the blood he stole from off his bottom lip. My stomach twists— from delight or horror, I'm not sure. Maybe both.

"Forgive me, darling. You're irresistible." He lets out a sigh as he steps back. "Your family is safe. That bear should keep you satisfied— for now. Let's do this again soon, shall we?" And in the blink of an eye he disappears into the night.

If I needed to breathe, it would take me all night to catch my breath after that. Why must he be so hot? And worse, why am I so drawn to this stranger? My hunger is replaced with guilt, as a darker part of my thoughts linger on being sandwiched between Donovan and the tree and his tongue as it slid across my lips. Although I am indebted to him for saving my life, I never asked him to do it. I owe him nothing. But still, I'm drawn to him.

I'm venturing into this strange new world, and my only companion is a British vampire with no respect for personal space. What matters most now is this freedom from my thirst for blood. With the dread of the past few days gone and Donovan nowhere in sight, tears of happiness flood my eyes. I am over-whelmed with the assurance I'll be safer around my family. That I can still be mommy to my girls. Maybe even take some much-needed time away with Phil. Despite the piles of secrets and accumulating guilt, I brush off the tree bark from my torn shirt back and whoosh back toward the highway, ready to give this new life of mine a chance.

Halfway home my phone begins to ding, and ding, and ding, and ding— I'm back in a cell service area. I grab my phone from my back pocket and brush the dirt off it, I too am covered in dirt. There is also a substantial amount of bear blood and fur all over the front of my shirt and my own bloody, claw-shredded back. I have multiple texts and missed calls from Phil, all wondering where I am, dating back to three forty-five a.m. It's now five a.m., the stars above fading from the faint light of dawn breaking up over the mountains behind me. I send him a text and hope he's not already out searching for me:

```
Went for a run, couldn't sleep,
I'm fine. Sorry! Was out of cell.
Be home in 15 min.
```

I stash my phone and dash down the highway as fast as I possibly can.

Not far from my house, Phil and Jon are chatting, passing the time on our front porch. It's only ten minutes after I texted him— what's a few more? I take advantage of my speed, and sneak around to the back of the house, through the slider and into my room. I ditch my bloody, hairy, dirty running clothes for a pair of sweats, so my alibi can be slightly more believable, being that it's a late October morning, and a cold one at that. In the bathroom, I check my back for claw marks, surprised to see nothing but smooth skin. My hair is already messy-looking enough to pass for running hair. I pick out a few remaining pine needles from my ponytail, rinse my face from any remaining bear blood, then dash out the back door, over the fence, and around to the street with a few minutes of my estimation to spare. I rein in my speed to a slow and steady walk and labor my breathing, stopping to "catch my breath" as I near the men. Phil and Sheriff Harker are now leaned up against the side of his patrol SUV parked on the curb in front of our house.

"Well, Phil, looks like she's home, safe and sound," Jon says, crossing his arms in front of his chest.

"Safe yes— sound, I question," Phil answers, not knowing I can hear him. Jon laughs.

"Hi!" I shout. My lingering high from the bear's blood leaks out through my over-enthusiastic wave, however inappropriate it may be for this situation.

Phil gives a stiff wave in return. His tired, blood-shot eyes stare at me, cold as the dawn. Only a few feet away from them, I breathe in the sweet odor of his human blood, and thanks to the bear, my thirst stays satisfied. He, however, looks like he may want to kill *me*.

"So you're a runner now?" Jon gives Phil a nudge with his elbow.

Phil eyes me like I'm a stranger but who am I kidding, I *am* a stranger. The woman I was is dead, gone, burned up in a plane crash. This woman only today learned how to properly find a meal— even I don't know much about her yet.

"I'll take it from here, Jon." He pats Sheriff Harker on the back.

"Bye, Jon. Sorry. . . again." I wave.

Phil and I stand parallel to each other at the curb in front of our house as the sheriff's car drives away. Without a word Phil looks at me then walks into the house, leaving the door open behind him. I follow his lead, closing the door behind me, thankful that at least Ana isn't here this time. The house is pitch-black; it didn't seem this dark when I snuck in to change just moments ago. A faint glow appears in the hallway, and I follow the light into our room. Phil sits like a statue on the bed, his face hard and cold, arms crossed at his chest. His pulse is racing, but his breath flows in a slow, concentrated rhythm. I sit beside him, not sure what else to do, and stare at my once-multicolored Nikes now browned with mud. Phil's warm hand smacks my forehead and rests for a moment, then pulls away just as abruptly as it arrived.

"What was that for?" I ask, feeling the warmth from his hand soak into my skin.

"Seeing if you have a fever. Trying to understand this erratic behavior of yours." His brow furrows and his eyes narrow, staring into me as if he's trying to read my thoughts. Part of me wishes he could. I hate lying to him.

"I'm sorry I should have left a note. I couldn't sleep and thought I'd go for a run." I grab hold of his hand in his lap, shocked by the temperature and color contrast between us. I didn't realize how pale I now am; I'm hoping he doesn't either.

"A note would have been nice. Or a text, something to let me know you where you were going."

Frowning, I realize how reckless I was. I think of the woman in the parking lot, the woman from the car wreck, and remember there is a killer out there. "You're right, I'm sorry."

Phil picks up my other hand and holds them both between his. "Your hands are like ice." He breathes his hot breath onto them like he does with the girls when they play in the snow without gloves. As my hands warm from his, so does the look on his face.

"Well, it is pretty cold outside." I gently taking back my hands, the warmth quickly fades. "I'm fine though. Next time I'll wear gloves?"

"Next time? Since when do you like running anyway?"

"I read running can help you process trauma." I look down at my dirty shoes. Playing the plane crash victim card got me off the hook yesterday; maybe it will work again today. He takes a deep breath and gently rubs my back, across the spot where the bear should have left a nasty mark. The heat from his hand is soothing to my icy skin.

"I bet the therapist from the hospital might know a thing or two about dealing with trauma," he says, still rubbing my back. "I think it would help you."

Wouldn't I be an interesting patient to have: *Hello doctor, what's my problem, you ask? Well, as you know, I survived that crash. It just so happens I found out I'm dead, but not dead, and I crave blood. Is something wrong with me?* I almost laugh out loud at the thought. Not the best idea.

"No doctors. I know I've been acting weird since the plane crash, but after running this morning I'm actually starting to feel like myself again." This isn't a lie; I really do feel wonderful. Plus, this could be a great excuse for when I'll need to feed again. "I'd like to give my running therapy a try first."

"What is it with you and not getting help?"

"I can do this myself. Besides, running *is* my help."

"Well, you do look much better. More rested maybe? I'll give you that." His smile is tinged with doubt.

I'd like to think I look better than *rested*. That woman I saw in place of my reflection yesterday was gorgeous! "Thanks," I say in a tone he quickly picks up on, raising a confused eyebrow at me. My ego is slightly hurt by his inattentiveness.

"Far better than the other day. . . " I can almost see his brain sifting through what he should say next. "When we— never mind, forget that," he mumbles. He didn't sift very well.

"The day we were going to have sex and I looked on the verge of death?"

My bluntness trips him up for a second, but he recovers. "It's nice to see you're feeling like your spunky, beautiful self again," he says, throwing in beautiful to make up for whatever it was he might have said wrong.

I can't help but smile at his fumbling and the memory of what we were trying to do that night. "I'd like to finish now what we started then," I say, running my fingers up his arm.

He scoots closer and cups my face in his hands, kissing my forehead. The breath from his nose heats my cold head, and I wait for the flutter in my heart he always causes with his kiss, suddenly remembering it doesn't beat anymore. Regardless, my excitement ramps up the same, perhaps better even with all my new senses and abilities. It's nice to have his face so close without feeling the overwhelming urge to bite him. Only a small, manageable burn sits quietly in the far back of my throat.

"We should get some sleep before the girls wake up." He gives me a chaste kiss on the lips.

I kiss back, my hands on each side of his face, indulging in his mouth with my tongue. He tastes divine. A primal drive takes over and I push him down on the bed, straddling him as I toss aside my muddy shoes and let down my ponytail. His eyes grow wide with surprise and intrigue, caught off guard even. But the heat I feel rising underneath me from him, reassures my actions. I lean in again and devour him with my kiss, intoxicated by his taste, his smell, the heat of his body. He groans, but not a groan of pleasure— I stop.

"Are you sure you're okay to do this?" His face is taut with frustration. "Last time we tried . . . " he motions with his eyes to my shirt covered stomach.

Right.

"I was dehydrated or something." I hover my mouth over his. "I'm fine now."

His eyes light up, so I kiss him again, hot and deep. He moans this time with pleasure as his firm hands grab my arms, flipping me onto my back.

"I've missed this," he says planking above me, and returns to kissing my lips, my neck, my collarbone. He pauses once more to remove my pants. The sensations amplified as the soft fabric glides down my legs. Tingles that vastly rival any ones Donovan has given me vibrate through my body as Phil runs his hands up from my toes to my waist but I'm careful to leave my top on. I'm not ready to explain my flawless belly.

A spark of passion ignites inside me— a passion I feared I'd never be able to share with him again. I ignore any lingering desire to bite his sweet, sweaty, pulsating neck as I wrap my legs around his body. But as my lust for Phil grows stronger with each thrust of his hips, my lust for his blood increases as well. Yet, the burn inside only intensifies this pleasure all the more. There's no stopping now, and I'm not about to ruin this moment with my secret by giving in to my darker desire. Instead, I moan as our bodies melt into each other again, and again, and again.

THE PROS AND CONS OF IMMORTALITY

"Come on sleepyhead, wake up," I say to Imogene, sitting on the edge of her bed and watching her face twitch as she tries to open her heavy eyelids. "Monday morning, time for school." A second later her alarm begins to beep, and I lean over to the dresser at the head of her bed to silence it, not wanting to wake up a soundly-sleeping Phil.

She scrunches up her face and rises to her elbows, squinting her eyes at me, head cocked to one side. "Mom?" she asks, as her face brightens. I stop a tear threatening to fall. I'm usually the one to wake her up for school— really, I'm usually the one who does most everything for them. For the first time in forever, it's nice to do this without the nagging exhaustion that *usually* accompanies motherhood.

"Who else would it be?" I wink. She smiles bigger.

"Good morning, Mommy," Davina says, stumbling out of her bed. "I'm hungry." She rubs her eyes and sleepwalks out of the room toward the kitchen. I already set out her favorite breakfast, granola and yogurt, for her to find.

"Are you going to start taking me to school again?" She smiles as she crawls out of bed and grabs the clothes she must have laid out last night from the top of her dresser.

"Not this morning, sweetie. Grandma will be here soon to take you." Her smile fades. Even with my hunger satisfied, I'm still terrified of what I'm capable of. I witnessed what Donovan did to that bear; I have that power in me too. Beyond my new-found monsterdom, I'm also worried about facing all the other parents, who by now all know about the plane crash, thanks to the media and Genevieve. "How about I pick you up from school instead?" Donovan said the bear would last me a while, but I'll need to prove that to myself first. If I am still hunger-free by the afternoon, I'll consider it safe and feel more comfortable being around other humans.

Imogene's smile returns, and she skips off to the bathroom to get ready for the day.

At seven-thirty sharp Ana comes and goes in a whirlwind of remembering school lunch and homework. Davina insists on going along for the ride as well, knowing Grandma will take her to the Main Street Café for a yummy treat. This morning is normal; life goes on as it should, and my cold dead heart is happy.

Smiling from ear to ear, I sit at the end of our bed and stare out the window, watching as Mr. Gerigson takes his morning post in his driveway. Sheets rustle behind me.

"Hey." Phil yawns, sitting up in bed on his elbows. His shirtless body gives me a much better scene than looking out at old Mr. Gerigson.

"Good morning." More tingles flood through me at the memory of earlier this morning.

He rubs the sleep from his eyes. "What time is it?"

"Mr. Gerigson just came out, so it must be eight."

"God, I'm tired— you have to stop keeping me up all hours of the night." The comment stings a little, which he must see on my face. "Come here," he says, holding out his arms.

Snuggling up beside him he shudders as my skin touches his bare chest, but he doesn't say anything. I soak his body heat into mine, and adjust to his temperature, resting my head on his shoulder. I'm thankful to the bear for allowing me the closeness I feared I wouldn't be able to have again. As long as I feed, I can be a wife and mother. As long as I feed, I can be *me*.

"Thank you," I say, tears welling up in my eyes.

"For what?"

"Being so understanding, patient, and so good-looking." I laugh, sending a sentimental tear down my cheek.

"You're crazy. And cold!" He hugs me tight, pulling the comforter up over the both of us. Resting my head over his booming heart, my eyes relax shut. I lie there, curled up next to Phil, listening, almost completely free of my bloodlust minus this slight ever-present burn I'm slowly growing accustomed to, to each booming beat of his heart while the heat from his body radiates through mine. I thought my lack of body temperature would be an issue, but it seems I'm more adaptable than I thought, and I'm again in awe of the beauty this new body and life of mine holds, however unconventional.

A roar rivaling a chainsaw rips out from beside me. I look at Phil, once again asleep and snoring. I tuck a lock of blond hair behind his ear, seeing for the first time how much its golden tone has faded over the years. One white hair pops up near his temple and Phil's life flashes through my mind. Will his life become but a moment to me in light of my eternity? I watch my fragile human sleep, every second growing older, growing closer to death. Closer to the moment we will be separated, forever. That time could come any second, especially in his line of work. He could burn in a fire with no Donovan to save him from the flames.

I push the thought from my mind and place a kiss between his eyes. His sleeping brow furrows under the coolness of my lips. He purses his mouth and rolls over to his side with another loud snore. I gather up a pair of jeans and a loose grey T-shirt and head into our bathroom, closing the door softly, leaving him to get some much-deserved rest since he begins his next shift this afternoon.

It's my second inhuman day, and I turn on the shower to start it in the most human way possible. Under the water I stand, letting it fall straight on my face, covering me completely like I'm standing in a waterfall. I've never experienced a shower quite like this before, mainly because breathing was of utmost importance in my human state. I close my eyes, each drop of water touching my skin as if they were falling one at a time— my skin tingling all over as the water's warmth soaks in. It's a pleasant distraction from my new life's predicaments and gives me a moment to figure out how to enjoy each moment as it is, one at a time, like the drops of water raining down over me.

The door to the bathroom opens, stirring the steam that has filled the room into little swirls in the air. Phil walks into the bathroom, heart booming as he opens the shower door standing there with nothing on but a smile. By the smell of it, he could use a shower, but by the look of it, he has other ideas. I move aside and welcome him in, but he jumps out just as quickly.

"HOLY HOT SHOWER, BATMAN!"

I turn my stomach toward the shower wall. He may not have noticed more subtle changes, like my new taste for blood or lack of body temperature, but I have a feeling my unmarked stomach might be a bit more obvious, especially contrasted with the last time he saw it.

"Did you just yell 'Batman'?" I laugh, looking over my shoulder.

"My *God* the water is hot!" He reaches in and turns down the heat. The warmth felt great to me.

"Sorry! I read hot showers help firm your skin." I step out of the shower, keeping my back toward him till I can grab a towel. "It's all yours." I smile, blowing him a kiss as he steps in and shuts the door.

"I'm pretty sure cold water is supposed to do that!" he bellows over the shower door. "Sure you don't want to join me?" he adds, disappointed.

"I'm still recovering from earlier. Plus your mom will be back any minute with Davina," I say, smiling as I rub the towel through my hair, loving everything about how ordinary this moment is too. I throw on my clothes and brush out my damp mane, facing the beautiful stranger whom I am still getting acquainted with in the mirror. My face disappears behind the fog. I grab my hairdryer and blow the steam off the mirror till I can see myself, then start drying my hair. The weight of the wet hair on my brush, running it under the heat, is calming. Slowly, it turns from heavy to light as the ends falling down dry around my shoulders, formed into a slight curl. For once I don't feel the need for makeup. Today my face seems perfect without it, and a part of me wonders if maybe it's always been that way.

"What do you want for breakfast?" I ask Phil, peeking my eyes over the frosted shower door and raising my eyebrows up and down in regards to the view of his gorgeous, naked body.

"Cereal's fine, weirdo." He laughs and smiles as he rinses the shampoo off his head.

"Good," I tease. "You can get that yourself when you're done." And I leave the bathroom to make my way to the kitchen for step two of feeling human and normal: coffee.

My phone dings from the kitchen counter beside me, loud and clear over the noise of the coffee grinder. It's Donovan. I want to ignore him, continuing to enjoy my day of normal— he is anything but normal. My phone dings again. Guilt settles into my gut at the thought of his tongue tracing my lips, and worse, how much I enjoyed it. This is all so new. I haven't been myself, literally. I grab my phone before it can ding again.

007: Last night was fun.

007: Well, funny actually, watching you fail miserably at hunting.

I can't help but smile. I was pretty terrible at it.

Haha, very funny…How long can I go
between 'meals'?

007: A bear that size, maybe a
week.

Good, a week away from him is much needed. I
dump my grinds into the press and slowly pour in the
hot water, hoping Donovan is right about the bear
lasting a week.

See you in a week then.

007: Until then love, I'll drink
to the taste of your lips.

Phil shuffles down the hall, humming a pleasant
tune. Disgusted yet flattered, I delete the conversation from Donovan. I press the coffee down and
pour myself a generous portion, being careful to
leave some for Phil. Ana's car pulls into our
driveway with an annoying double tap on the horn,
but brings with it Davina's sweet voice bellowing out
a song— something my normal ears wouldn't have
been able to hear from inside the house. I peer from
the kitchen window as Ana helps her out of her car
seat.

"Mommy!" Davina yells, bursting through the door and running at full speed straight for me.

"Hi, sweetheart! What did you and Grandma go do?" The small burn settled at the base of my throat flares for a second as she rushes into my arms but I easily push it aside.

"She got me hot chocolate!" I already knew that from the rich chocolate scent she's saturated in. She hops out of my hug and stares at me, studying my face with squinting blue eyes. Her sweet head tilts to one side, then the other as she plants her soft, warm hands on each side of my face, squishing my lips together and giggling. "You look like Mommy again." She smiles and takes off running for her room, singing the same sweet melody from the car.

"You do look more like yourself today," Ana says, setting her purse on the table as she settles in.

"I feel like myself. Coffee?"

"Please," she says, while Phil gives her a brief hug and they both have a seat at the table.

"Imogene do okay getting to school today?" Phil asks.

Ana chuckles. "She did just fine. It's fun being around them a little more than usual, reminds me of when you boys were younger. Only this time I'm older!" She dramatically wipes her brow, smiling big.

With a laugh, I set her coffee in front of her and take a seat with the both of them. The joy from my almost normal morning sours as I realize how out of the loop I've been in my own daughters' lives since the crash. It's been a long week.

"Thank you," she says to me, yawning over her coffee mug. "You really do look like you're feeling better." She takes a drink. "No offense, but you gave us a scare there. You know with the crash, and then you . . . disappearing for a day— I ran into Jonny at the cafe, he mentioned you're a runner now too? He told me about this morning." She raises an eyebrow at me.

Phil glares at her. He takes a breath and looks at me with his new odd smile, the same one Ana is wearing as well. Leave it to Jon to overshare to the people of this family.

"Listen, it's not every day you find yourself the only survivor of a plane crash—" I pause, and unwelcome tears well up. "—I still can't help but feel I'm not supposed to be here." My tears flow freely; nothing is more human or normal than crying over upsetting things. Phil and Ana come to my side, putting their arms around me.

"I'm so sorry, sweetie," Ana says, comforting me. "This has been hard on all of us."

"It's okay," I sniff.

"Mom! Mom!" Davina yells, running into the kitchen. "Come see what I made-ed for you!"

"Okay, I'm coming." I wipe my wet face with my sleeve, following my sweet baby girl to her room. Her favorite blanket is laid out on the floor, and on it is placed every item of food from her toy kitchen. The ensemble is complete with coordinating pink and purple plates and bowls.

"Oh baby, you made this for me?" I ask, placing hand over my heart.

"Mmhmm." She giggles and grabs my hand and then sits, pulling me with her to the floor by her setup. Her face is beaming with excitement as she fills my plate with every sort of concoction her four-year-old self could come up with. I could sit here with her forever, picnicking away on the floor of her room. Then, between a serving of plastic mac and cheese and rubber donuts, her sparkling topaz eyes catch mine, and as she smiles at me, a realization too painful for words stabs into my heart. Not the physical type of pain, but the mental kind that manifests itself as real, genuine, gut-wrenching agony. I will never age. What will happen when I'm supposed to look fifty, but instead remain thirty? Will I have to leave them to keep my secret and miss out on their lives? A vision of Davina's life suddenly flashes before my eyes and my dead heart shatters.

"Why are you crying, Mommy?" Davina asks, dropping her plate as she snuggles by my side. She looks at me, her eyes big and round. I slow my hiccuping sobs as best I can and hold her close.

"Sweetie, thank you for the yummy food. Can I have Daddy come play with you for a little bit?" I sniffle back the snot about to run freely down along with my tears.

"Okay." She clears my plate and yells for Daddy to come join her.

I sneak out of the room and meet Phil in the hall.

"What's wrong? You're upset," he says, stopping me with his hand on my shoulder.

"I'm feeling a little emotional. I'm going for a run if you don't mind. I'll be back in time to pick up Imogene from school." Thinking of Imogene only strengthens the realization fueling my heartache as the air thickens around me. I have to get out of here.

"Okay." He smiles his odd little smile and hugs me. "Wear a sweatshirt; it's cold out."

I throw on some cold-weather-appropriate running clothes. "Be back in a few!" I yell as I walk past Davina and Phil's picnic, then rush into the kitchen toward the door.

"Where are you going in such a hurry?" Ana asks, washing the coffee dishes from earlier.

"Therapy!" I shout on my way to the door.

Ana pauses her rinsing. "I was thinking we should do a nice family dinner this weekend before—"

I dash out the door with her words trailing behind me. My little house fades into the distance.

———

THE LATE-MORNING AIR is crisp and clear as I run

down my quiet street. Chimney smoke and rich old oaks scent the world around me. I assume almost everyone is away at work or in school. Mondays are a fairly dead day here in Amador County, but not dead enough to zoom full-speed-ahead without drawing some sort of attention. I keep my pace at what I hope looks like a normal speed through the main street downtown, turning east up a lonely road, hoping it to be less busy than the highway. The warm sun shines down upon my face, making it sting my more sensitive skin a bit as I run, but it's bearable. The quaint old historic homes turn to newer track homes, then disappear into open, grassy hillsides as I run out of town towards a hilltop mixed with oak and pine trees that line the upper ridges under the clouds.

I run faster and faster down the road, pushing through the stabbing pain within my heart. I knew Phil would grow old without me, I hadn't let myself dwell on the fact the girls will too. So here I am, running to Donovan— the only one I can turn to, the only one who might possibly understand. Donovan, whom I'm still trying to hate and yet can't stop myself from wanting to see. Donovan— whom I have no idea how to find.

My feet stop as still as my aching heart. I forgot my phone; no doubt Phil will be texting me like crazy if I take too long. Falling back onto the grassy hilltop I stare up at blue sky as I hit the ground with a thud. The tall pines sway in the cool fall breeze as I lie here wishing there was a way to make this pain in my heart disappear, but there isn't. I doubt even Donovan can save me from this. My spirits lift as I pick up the scent of vintage leather and he lays down beside me without a word. Each time I see him, my desire uncomfortably increases, and even though I love my husband more than anything, I can't deny there is something strong, something dark, that draws me to Donovan.

"Are you still stalking me?"

"Stalking? No. I saw you run out of your house in a hurry. Thought something might be wrong, so I followed you," he says with his smug grin, propping himself up on his elbow.

I laugh, giving him a playful push, surprised by the shift in my mood. I'm growing accustomed to the eccentricity of his personality. He falls onto his back, crying out in pain, one hand on his shoulder.

"I'm so sorry! I don't know my own strength yet." I lean over beside him, trying to see what damage I might have caused.

He grabs my shoulders as he smiles and flips me onto my back, the weight of his body pinning me down.

"Get off me!" I try and squirm out from under him but he's clearly stronger. The strange feelings I have for him are growing stronger as well.

Passion blazes in his dark eyes as he brings his face close to mine. Once again, too close. Pausing, his lips inches from mine, his eyes so near it's all I can see of his face, and we're frozen together in what I'm sure would be an awkward scene for any passers-by . . .

"Get off me!" I say in a harsh, unfriendly whisper. The passion cools in his eyes; his brow furrows and he sits up, straddling my middle.

"Something is bothering you, isn't it?" In his tone lies genuine concern as he slides off my body.

"How can you tell?" I ask, not hiding the sarcasm.

"Well, being the stalker I am, I can tell these things." His self-satisfied smile returns, causing me to question why I needed him so much moments ago.

"I need to go. School will be out soon and I'm picking up my kid." I try to move but the heartache festering inside me forces me to stay.

"I saw the relief in your face when I showed up." His face lights up. "You needed me!"

I push him, and he falls to the side, smiling like an idiot.

"You . . . needed me . . . again!" he says, lying on the ground like a giddy schoolboy, his daydreaming face beaming up into the sky.

"Forget it. This was a bad idea." I brush the dirt off my clothes and start to walk down the hill towards the road. He rushes to my side and stops me.

"I'm sorry. Please? I like that we're friends now. What's wrong?" Concern fills his face for a moment until he suddenly lights up again. "Did you kill someone?"

I walk away.

"You did, didn't you! Was it that old man across the street?"

"Oh, God, no! What is wrong with you? And 'friends' is stretching things a bit." I quicken my pace and he catches up. Not only is he stronger than me, but he's also faster than me too.

"Okay, okay, sorry. Forget I said that. Please? Come." He streaks up to a rock on top of the hill beside us, motioning for me to join.

I look down at the road at the base of the hill, both ways; no one's around. I run up to the rock, taking a seat beside him only out of desperation for someone to talk through all this with.

"Would you look at that view," Donovan says, changing the subject.

What an ass. But he's right about the view. From here I can see all of Amador County, still and quiet on this lazy Monday under the bright noon sun. My house should be somewhere to the left and Imogene's school is off to the right just up the next rolling hill. The world falls silent— empty, as I let an eternity pass before me, gazing over my little town like God looking down on creation. My heart fills again with pain and bittersweet tears burn their way to the surface to rain down on my town. The silence breaks.

"Would you please tell me what's wrong?" Donovan asks, cupping my face with his hands, much like Davina did earlier.

The tears fall harder at the thought of her. I push his hands down and take a deep breath. This is, after all, why I ran out to find him. "I'm going to live forever."

He looks at me, confused. "You just realized this?"

"I was sitting with my four-year-old. She made me a picnic in her room, complete with place settings and all her little plastic food." I laugh, wiping tears off my face with my sleeve, trying my best to focus on a cloud to steady my sobby-cry voice.

"You don't feed your children real food?"

I punch him in the arm. He pretends it hurt.

"It was perfect, that moment picnicking with her on the floor of her room. Until I saw a vision of her and me, years from now. She was lying in a Hospice bed, and I sat there beside her, still frozen as I am now at thirty, holding my sweet Davina's frail, wrinkled hand. She could have passed as my great-grandmother. Her eyes were still the same sparkling topaz blue but filled with a lifetime of memories. Her crepe paper face was framed in a halo of soft, white hair, still curly. Then she smiled at me, her cheeks folding deep into the corners of her face. And with one single breath, I watched as the glow in her eyes began to dim. She couldn't speak but gave my hand one last weak squeeze and I knew that squeeze held the words, 'I love you, Mommy.' And then her hand fell limp as she drifted away from this life into the next, without me. She would have been the last to go. Everyone else in my family would already be gone— and I knew I was alone."

His hand grabs mine as unstoppable tears cascade down my face, threatening to flood the tiny world below me.

"I'm going to watch my children, my family, friends, Phil— people I love— die at the hands of time. And then what? I'll still be here, on this godforsaken earth, completely alone." I wipe my face with my sleeve.

"You never have to be alone," he says, brushing the back of his hand across my tear-stained face.

"Phil, Imogene, Davina? I'm cursed to watch them die! Is this the price I pay for my life being spared? This pain isn't worth it."

"Way to look at things in a positive light," Donovan says, a confused look stuck on his face.

"And worse! Unless they know and accept me for what I am, I'll be forced to leave them long before they grow up, left to watch them die off from a distance as I stay young forever!" I throw my hands in the air in defeat.

"This is ridiculous," he says, incredulous. "You were going to die; I spared them the sorrow of losing you!" I can almost see his thoughts scrambling to understand me, trying to say the right thing to win me over to his way of thinking.

I sneer at him. Obviously, he's unaware of the complexities of loss. "They could have mourned me and one day years from now we would be together in eternity." Anger boils up within me; this is all his fault. "Now I'm stuck here, forever."

"Well, you have me," he says, sadness falling over his face. He rushes to me, holding my head in his hands and, without notice, kisses me. Passion, sadness, anger, and a million other emotions flow from his lips onto mine. He pulls me close, his hard body tight against me— a prisoner of his uninvited affection. I want him to stop, but also keep going. As if I'm suddenly torn in two. My new life here with him, and my old one struggling to remain firmly with the ones I love— where I long to be forever.

"Stop!" I try to push him away, but he holds on tight. "Stop," I cry again in a whisper.

"Sorry, I don't know what came over me." He loosens his hold. "I can't bear to see you hurting."

"So then naturally you kiss me?" My sadness turns to anger. "You can't keep doing things like that," I scold, breaking his hold and stepping away to keep a safe distance from his lips.

"But don't you see? With me, you will never be alone."

"We can be friends, Donovan, but that is all. I really need to be just friends with you." I take his hands in mine. "Who else do I have to share this part of my life with but you?" I can't stomach the thought of losing the only person I can turn to because he can't stop being such a narcissist.

His face sags in defeat. I let go of his hands and we both look out across the miniature town before letting another eternity pass in silence.

"I had a wife once." He breaks the silence. "My sweet, beautiful Rebekah," he adds as he fidgets with his ring-less left finger. The confession somehow stunning me. He is aware of the complexities of loss after all.

I can tell it hurts him to think about her. Seeing him like this almost hurts me as well; he's never looked so sad or human to me before. "She had a beautiful name," I say, now hoping to learn more about married, human Donovan.

"Yes, she did." He smiles, lost in his memories. "We were happy too. It was the spring of 1866, April I think. We had emigrated from England during the gold rush in hopes of finding our fortune in a new world. So we got a small plot of land near our claim and I began my life as a miner." He stops and looks around. "Here, follow me it's over here." He grabs my hand and we whoosh off into the hills, not too far from the rock we were just sitting on. In seconds we stop at a large pile of boulders laying against a steep, shaded hillside overgrown with poison oak and ivy vines.

"Here is where it happened." I don't ask where we are. Instead, I watch in silence as his face darkens. "It was dusk. I was getting ready to head home from the mine when something attacked me. So quickly did it move I couldn't get a good glimpse of what it was. The last thing I remember after my bones were crushed, and limbs twisted, was sharp teeth ripping open my neck and leaving me for dead before I passed out from the pain. The next morning came, or what I assumed was the next morning, and I was surprised to still be alive. In fact, I found I was completely healed aside from the wound on my neck left. I wondered if it was only a dream. I often slept here, right under that tree actually," he points to a huge valley oak not far to our right. "So, I figured Rebekah wouldn't be too worried and went back to work in the mine.

"Then the nightmares started— I'm sure you are familiar with those. And because I couldn't sleep, I stayed at the mines and worked day and night until time became a blur and delirium set in. Or so I thought. When the wound on my neck opened back up and began to ooze a black, oily substance I knew something was wrong. A burning hunger no food would satisfy drove me to madness, and I wandered through the tunnels in the mine, alone and scared. Every sound I heard I'd wonder if the creature was coming back for me. I was hoping it would— to finish me off, to end my suffering, but it never did.

"By the fifth day, Rebekah must have begun to worry. A group of miners showed up looking for me. My name echoed through the mine shafts along with an unnaturally loud, booming of their heartbeats. With each beat a fire grew within me, taking over my body, and as soon as I smelled them near I attacked them at speeds I never knew were humanly possible. I killed them, each and every one of them, feeding on their blood. Tearing the men apart. When I drank as much as I could, I was forced to my knees by the pain of my transformation. And as my heart stopped beating I collapsed to the ground, again waiting to die. I deserved to die after what I did, but death didn't come. Soon all the pain left me, and so did the hunger. Confused and covered in blood, I stood up and stared mortified at the seven bodies lying at my feet— each one of them a friend."

He stops. Shame creasing his face.

I can picture it all like I was there. Captivated yet horrified by his story, I look to him in hopes he'll continue. Now more torn than ever in my feelings for him, especially learning how he came to be, changing all alone— Donovan didn't leave me. He saved me from this. The dead miners— that could have been my family. Another tear falls down my cheek. I can forgive him for his kiss; I have to. Moments pass till finally he takes a breath to continue.

"I knew I wasn't alive— my heart wasn't beating — but I wasn't dead either, and I wasn't about to be hung for killing the seven men. So I collapsed the mine with what dynamite I had left, forever hiding my regrets with the cover of a common accident." He walks over, touching one of the boulders in reverence to the men who died. Who he killed. "I was a monster."

My heart now aches for Donovan and suddenly all I want is to hold him in my arms. The connection I feel to him deepens, knowing we aren't much different. "You couldn't help it," I say, joining him by the rubble blocking the mine. "Did you ever go home?"

"I missed my wife deeply and needed her words of comfort. She'd always been an understanding soul and I was sure she'd keep my truth. She was my soul mate, my one true love."

He stops again, looking as if there was still a knife in his heart that had yet to be removed. He turns his head to me, studying my face with his glassy dark-brown eyes.

"What do you think your Phil is going to do once he finds out what you are?"

"I thought you said never to tell my secret," I say, unsure how to answer.

"Good girl." He pats me on the back. "See, this is what happens with honesty when it comes to creatures like us. At the sight of Rebekah, I broke down, told her everything that happened to me, everything I had done, just as I told you. She saw the blood covering my clothes, realizing what— who it was from, and screamed, *Demon! Monster! Murderer!* The warmth in her eyes left, replaced by repulsion. She was terrified of me and ran into town for help. I took off running as well in the opposite direction and didn't stop till I was way up in the high country and found solace in the forest near Silver Lake; no one would dare look for me there. And I was alone, a lonely monster, indeed."

A single tear falls from his cheek onto the ground, and his nostrils flare for a moment with a long, drawn-in breath. I know the feeling well. I am a monster too.

"What happened to Rebekah?" I can't help but think of Phil. What this truth might do to him. To us.

"I watched her from a distance. Watched as her grief forced her to find comfort in other men, lover after lover, until she picked one, the local banker, and moved on with her life— a life without me." A smile grows on his face and his dark eyes shine a bit brighter as he looks into mine. "But now I found you, Aileen. You, whose light shone from within. You with your cute, clumsy humanity, tripping into me on that plane. Listening to your nervous heartbeat each time I looked at you. I could smell your terror when we crashed. I couldn't let you die— not like that." He tucks a lock of my hair behind my ear and smiles. "Aileen, I can be your forever."

I close my eyes, lost in a whirlwind of emotion, desperate for a moment to catch a breath I don't need. I wouldn't blame Phil if he left me too, even if I never massacred people— at least not yet. I empathize with Donovan. To lose the one you love, to be left alone for all eternity. . . no one wants to be alone forever, not even a monster.

My eyes open to a pile of boulders: the tomb of the men he killed, no Donovan in sight. I know now, he understands what I'm going through. Only, a darker fact arises I never wished to have confirmed— he's is dangerous, and if I am what he is, that makes me a danger as well.

13

SHATTERED SCREENS

My lips burn from the stain of Donovan's kiss as I stand at the foot of my driveway. My clothes now saturated with his scent, and I'm thankful Ana is not still here. If anyone is going to notice a strange, other-man-smell, it's her. The front door creaks and pops as I open it, announcing my entrance, much to my dismay.

"Hey, how was your run?" Phil asks, startling me as he rounds the corner into the kitchen.

"Fine," I say, still lost in thought. I shut the door behind me and step inside.

Phil rummages through the fridge; it must be lunchtime.

"Want some?" He pulls out a bag of leftover pizza.

"Maybe later." The smells coming from the

opened refrigerator are repulsive to my sensitive nose. "When does your shift start again?"

"As soon as I'm done eating. Why? You kicking me out?" His voice takes on a more serious tone as he sits at the table. Beside him is his bag, all ready to go for the station. Only it's the extra-large duffle bag he takes when he knows he'll end up with overtime.

"No. Why did you grab your overtime bag?" The guilt festering on my lips teases that he somehow knows what I did and is ready to leave me. Reality reminds me they're short-staffed at the station.

"No overtime. You took my other bag on your trip, remember?"

"Oh, right." A chill runs down my spine as I think of the fiery fate of my carry-on. Relieved this has nothing to do with Donovan, I watch in amazement as Phil stuffs half the slice of cold pizza in his mouth.

"You sure you don't want any?" he mumbles through a mouthful, smiling.

"No thanks." I laugh, but the deep breath in from my laughter brings with it the strong scent of Donovan's cologne, reminding me I need to get out of these clothes before Phil notices.

He starts to speak, and a chunk of pizza slips out of his mouth. He catches it; I laugh again, partly grimacing. The sight of him trying to talk with half a pizza in his mouth is impressive and also incredibly off-putting.

"Okay then. I'm going to get out of these stinky

running clothes now." Phil wipes pizza sauce from his chin as I slink my way out of the kitchen, staying as far away as I can from him. He doesn't seem to notice I stink like a cow who walked through the perfume section of the mall, and I wonder if it's perhaps simply my guilt amplifying what I smell. Perhaps it's not as detectible by his human senses.

"Mom!" Davina's sweet voice sings from her room as I pass by her door.

"Hi sweetie, did you eat lunch yet?"

"Yes." She motions to the picnic in her room. The room is a mess, but to her, it's proud perfection. One day we'll master the cleaning-up part of life.

"Have you eaten real lunch?" I smile as she shakes her head side to side. "Go ask Daddy for some pizza."

"Okay!" She rushes past me and into the kitchen. I cringe at how sweet her blood smells, like honey-suckle on a spring afternoon. It amplifies the ever-present burn in my throat and reminds me again that I am nothing short of a monster.

Defeated, I whoosh into my room, thinking about warm melted cheese on soft crust, topped with pepperoni instead of the sickening fact no one is safe from my thirst for blood. I toss my Donovan-soaked running clothes onto the ever-growing pile of laundry on my bedroom floor. The irony of it all makes me laugh. I'm an invincible vampire-mom who can clean the entire house in minutes, except for laundry— no matter how fast I am, I'm still at the mercy of my washer and dryer.

A fresh pair of jeans slide with ease over my hips up to my smooth stomach. No more stuffing my saggy belly skin in before buttoning. I was starting to appreciate this part of my change, but instead of feeling thankful for my repaired stomach my mood worsens, and once again I hate Donovan for what he did to me. He stole my humanity without asking. Even though Phil had a vasectomy and I was happy not to have to worry about pregnancy anymore, I always knew my body was still *able* to create life. My stretch marks were a reminder of that. Now my body only brings death.

I blink back tears standing in front of my closet, ripping out every shirt I own and throwing them to the floor, taking out my frustration on each worn out, out of style shirt. The last one left is a mustard-yellow V-neck, and I take a breath to calm down and finish getting dressed. I grab a light blue infinity scarf and a chunky knit sweater from the floor— an attempt at blending in. The afternoon air will hold a late October chill, and the rest of the moms will be bundled up accordingly.

This is the first time I've gotten dressed in something besides sweats since the crash. I'm pleased with how human I look. It eases my frustrations and once again I remind myself that I can do this. I glance around the room, now with two piles of clothes. I kick the clean one back into the closet and shut the door—

I'll take care of that later— and look for the laundry basket for the dirty pile. It's missing again. I'd bet money it's in the girls' room. Instead, I gather as many items of dirty laundry as I can carry, stuffing the smelly Donovan clothes into the middle and head to the laundry room in the kitchen.

"Don't we have a basket?" Phil asks, working on another slice of pizza, Davina at his side.

I walk past them, giving Davina a silly face. "Oh I'm sure it's *somewhere*."

She giggles.

"Need a hand, then?" Phil rises, making his way toward me and my suspicious-smelling laundry pile. I remind myself again, he likely won't even notice.

"I got it!" Just in case, I hurry to the washing machine, smiling enthusiastically while dumping the clothes in and slamming the lid down. I flip on the machine and as I turn to walk out of the laundry room I'm stopped by Phil. He's standing there with his strong arms stretched up to the top of the entryway door to the room. His fingers hooked, arms hanging casually from the door frame, blocking my way. A sliver of his bare, toned stomach peeks out from in between his pants and shirt. A different kind of hunger flares up and I focus up to his ocean blue eyes instead. Not now.

"Aren't you going to use detergent?" There's a hint of laughter in his question.

"Right." I whirl around, quickly fill the little cup

with detergent, and toss it in, trying my best not to open the lid too far. Even that little bit reeked of Donovan to me.

"Now *excuse* me please." I smile, motioning for Phil to get out of my way.

"What's the hurry?" He wraps his arms around me, and I return the embrace, being careful not to crush him this time.

"Hi," I mumble, my face pressed into his shoulder. He squeezes me tighter.

This feels so good, so right. We fit together like a puzzle, with my head resting just right in the crook of his warm neck— the smell of him— a mixture of clean soap and a lifetime of memories. All of it reminding me of the security I had in our love. And now, I am the one threatening that security.

"I love you." It's all I can say before tears well up in my eyes. An hour ago I was kissed by another man. A man who not only stole my humanity but made me a monster of a mother. A man who has feelings for me as well as deep, profound emotional issues. And to make things worse, I have an ever-growing desire for him. A man I barely know. The idea of Phil learning my secrets and losing him sooner than necessary is unbearable. I'll figure this out, I have to.

"What's wrong?" Phil's voice is soft as he cups my face in his hands. He wipes a tear with his thumb then embraces me again. "Bad therapy session?" His hands gently rub my back.

"You could say that." I press myself up against him, my ear resting on the side of his neck. Phil's pulse beats in a steady, calming rhythm, soothing my frazzled nerves. Compared to Donovan's cold, lifeless, invincible body— heck, compared to mine— Phil's is soft and warm, yet weak in comparison. Another morbid reminder that he isn't going to last forever— we aren't going to last forever. My soul whispers to confess everything. He of all people would understand, right? We would find a way. We may not share eternity, but we can share what time we have left, openly and honestly. I might chance being miserable with him knowing the truth over this false, semi-curated life of secrecy— but would he? It would be fair for him to have the choice: leave me, accept me, or possibly— one day— join me.

Instead, I lie, again. "Nothing's wrong, I'm okay."

Phil hugs me tighter as I find my resolve. I'm lost in limbo with no clear path. Donovan's recollection of Rebekah's words echo in my mind and I stifle back the sobs that threaten to escape my adulterous lips. Maybe secrets can be a good thing.

"Your hair smells different. New shampoo?"

"No, same shampoo." Guilt flushes back through me as I gently leave his embrace. Wiping the dampness from my eyes with my sweater sleeve.

"I guess I just never noticed it." He looks at his watch. "It's one. I'm so sorry, but my shift—"

"It's okay, you shouldn't be late."

"Are you sure you're all right with me going back to work?"

"Yes, I'll be fine." I force a smile and playfully nudge him toward the door.

"No more running off—" He stops himself from saying any more. I don't blame him for thinking it, but it does sting a little nonetheless.

"I would never leave the girls alone if that's where you're going with this," I reassure him with a passive side of guilt.

"I know." He kisses me on the forehead and does the same to Davina, who's still picking, uninterested, at her slice of pizza, before grabbing his bag for the fire station.

The front door shuts like the lid of a coffin, sealing me in. My first time picking Imogene up at school, my first night alone with the girls since the plane crash— since knowing I'm a blood-sucking monster. At least the bear seems to be holding me so far. No more than my tiny, ever-present burn sits in the back of my throat, bearable to say the least. I can do this. I *need* to do this, be mommy again, regain control of myself no matter what future may lie ahead.

"All done, sweetie?" I say to Davina, clearing her plate for her.

"Can we go to Target?" she asks. It's her favorite store, but it's also almost an hour's drive away.

"Not today. Get your shoes on; we need to get

your sister soon." Her face drops as she shuffles to the shoe bench by the door.

I spot my missing phone by my purse, face-up on the kitchen counter. My fingers automatically pull up the home screen and, of course, a text from Donovan is waiting for me.

007: Talk felt good, sorry about the kiss.

My brand-new phone falls from my hand onto the floor, as a crack spreads across the pristine screen. My heart might be still but after today my nerves sure aren't.

Laces flick-flacking with each step, Davina runs back to the kitchen and stops next to my fallen phone.

"I need you to tie my shoes!"

I kneel down and grab her laces, wishing Phil had gotten a case to go with the new phone.

"Okay, let's go." I pick up my phone and tap the screen. The crack splits straight down the center, splitting the screen into two sides, much like my own life currently.

THE SCHOOLYARD IS SILENT, minus the chitchat of parents waiting to pick up their children. Everything is decorated for Halloween: spider webs filled with plastic spiders sit in the school hallway corners, and cute posters of ghosts and vampires line the walls. I laugh to myself. Vampires are definitely not cute. Well, one is pretty handsome. I mentally slap myself for that thought. *What is my problem?* His kiss was like poison, seeping beneath my skin, sinking him deeper into my thoughts.

"Hey, what do you want to be for Halloween?" I shake off my darkening thoughts as I ask a skipping, carefree Davina. She loves Halloween. Both girls do. In the chaos around me, I'd completely forgotten about it. Apparently so did Ana and Phil.

"I want to be a ninja!" She pauses to stomp in a puddle.

"We need to get our costumes soon, don't we?" I whisper to her. I hope they have something left but with Halloween five days away and the celebration our town holds a day sooner on Friday, we don't have much time. A trip to Target this week might be refreshing— if I don't end up wanting to kill everyone in the store. She smiles and grabs my hand, pulling me as fast as she can toward her sisters' classroom. I've missed this.

"Oh my God! Is that her?" a female voice whispers. I glance over to see two moms from Imogene's class— the whispering one is Genevieve from the grocery store— sitting on a bench, watching as their younger children play nearby.

"She looks good. Too good for just being a plane

crash," the other woman replies in a snooty tone. "Are you sure she wasn't getting, you know, work done?"

"You know, I ran into her at the store on Saturday. She looked terrible then but much better now."

Both women chat on, blissfully unaware I can hear them. And it's not only their voices I hear from across the yard. I hear their heartbeats as well, loud and booming. The more they spew their gossip, the stronger the scent of their blood becomes as it drifts toward me. I'm not used to being the center of others' conversations, and I really don't like it. I try to tune them out but, all around the school other people stare at me with dagger-like eyes as if they could pierce their way into the secrets of my life. Each of them nodding their head at me as I walk by, all with the same solemn expression and sorry little smiles. *Freak show* comes to mind. If only they knew the whole story. There's a soft click of a camera off somewhere to my right. I breathe a sigh of relief when I see it's just an upper grader taking photos of the school decorations. Thankfully, the local journalists haven't bothered me since I left the hospital. It's been nine days since the crash, and already the national news seems to have moved on to other things. I can't wait till I become old news to all the mom groups too.

"Come on, Mommy!" Davina demands as we press on towards Imogene's classroom.

The school bell rings and the halls come to life with the buzzing of children. Davina takes off, running ahead to find her sister. The whispers and stares of others fade away as Davina runs into Imogene's classroom and my girls embrace each other in a hug. I never had any siblings and I'm grateful they have each other. Sadness settles briefly within as I realize they will still have each other someday, at least, if I ever for whatever reason, have to leave—

Imogene's teacher, Ms. Cooper, rushes up to me, cornering me between the classroom door and her desk. A desk that happens to be covered with towers of ungraded papers and trinkets from students. It's welcome distraction for now, pulling me away from things I'd rather not think about.

"Welcome back, Mrs. Ross! Imogene said you'd be picking her up today." Her voice is loud and overbearing, scraping like glass against my sensitive ears, which is odd coming from such a petite young woman. "It is so good to see you in one piece. The minute I heard your name mentioned on the news I just couldn't believe it! I was so heartbroken for your girls, you can only imagine how happy I was to hear you were okay. I'm so sorry, look at me blabbing like an idiot. *Blah blah blah.*" She laughs with an awkward shrill, mimicking herself with her hands. "So how was your trip— I mean, sorry— I mean, how are you?" She takes a deep breath and clears her throat.

"I've been better." I offer her a smile in hopes of putting her at ease. My brain tries to play catch-up with her babble. I'm anything but okay— same goes for the 200 other passengers and their families affected by the crash. I try to remind myself she means well.

A crimson hue flushes her face, and my hunger burns more than I'm comfortable with. I bite my tongue and hold my breath.

Imogene hands Davina a set of plastic vampire teeth; they must have had a Halloween-themed day or something. I watch out of the corner of my eye as Davina runs around the room, growling and chasing after her sister, coming dangerously close to bumping into Ms. Cooper's disastrous desk.

"Well, that's—" she begins to say.

"Davina!" I yell, cutting Ms. Cooper off as I stop a stack of papers from crashing to the floor with my hands.

Ms. Cooper stares wide-eyed at her desk, then at where I was standing just milliseconds ago. "Wow, I've never seen anyone move so fast!" She rushes over to grab the papers from my hands and attempts to reorganize the mess that is her desk. "How did you—"

"You know what, I need to get going. Come on girls," I say, guiding Imogene and Davina toward the door. "It was good seeing you, Ms. Cooper. Have a nice day."

"Can we go to the costume store now?" Davina asks, the plastic vampire teeth still in her mouth. I give her my mom glare and she gives me one back.

Imogene's eyes light up. "Costume store?" I give

her a look too as we head into the hall. I am in no mood for shopping.

"What?" Imogene asks in response to my look.

"But Mommy, you said we need to get costumes!" Davina whines again as we reach my outdated mom van. I open the doors manually, unlike the fancy new button open ones, pick her up, set her in her seat, and buckle her in.

"I said we'll have to go soon, not today," I answer. The last place I want to be right now is around more people. Who knows what Imogene's teacher is thinking about now that she's seen me move at an inhuman pace. I can't imagine trying to make it through Target, all the way in El Dorado— a town far more populated than here— without something bad happening.

"Why?" she asks.

"Because— just not today." I shut her door before she can reply and get into my seat.

"Sissy, I'm going to be a ninja," she brags to Imogene as I buckle myself in and start the car.

"Well, I'm going to be a ballerina," Imogene brags back.

"You were that last year," Davina argues. Imogene has been a ballerina every year since she was four.

"SO!" Imogene shouts.

Their little hearts begin to pound as each of their tempers rise.

"Hey! No yelling!" I yell back, then laugh at the irony. "Let's just get home in peace, okay?"

Davina nods. "Okay, Mommy. Then can we go to the costume store?"

"Not today." I'm now dangerously on the verge of losing my patience. I really don't want to know what I might do if that happens.

"But Mom, Halloween's this weekend!" Imogene wails.

"Not. Today," I reiterate, my words sharper as I try to regain control of myself. They get the message. I slip a new movie into the van's DVD player in an attempt to distract the girls and pull out of the parking lot to head home.

I feel like beating my head on the steering wheel. These feelings are nothing new; they come with the job of being a parent. But then, add this unpredictable, seemly mood-driven thirst for blood I have burning through my body. *These* feelings are the new ones clearly amplified by stress. The bear will last me a week, my ass— it's been one day, and already I fear its power is fading. Stupid Donovan. A flash of his smiling mouth comes to mind, and I grimace. No. I need to think of something else. But what? I bite my lip, the taste of his kiss still lingering there from earlier. How he felt pressed up against me—

"Ahh!" I hit the dashboard with my palm, denting it slightly. The girls shoot their attention toward me.

"Uh, sorry. Spider," I say, wiping away the nonexistent creature's remains. Then, to lighten the mood, I force a laugh. "How about we go get costumes Friday?"

If I can eat again before then. Otherwise, watch out poor, unsuspecting Target shoppers.

Imogene and Davina turn their attention back to the movie. I take a breath, grateful that they're still young and unaware.

———

THE REST of the afternoon and evening goes well, coffee once again helps keep any cravings I fear I might have at bay. The girls are happy I don't make them take a bath, but bedtime, alone— without Phil — is a different story. Bedtime means stories and snuggles. All things I love deeply, things that strike within me a deep fear. I shake it off, my girls mean far more to me than anything. We're backlogged in bedtime books, so I settle on reading three of their favorites and draw the line there. Once they are snuggled down in their beds, I kiss their warm little foreheads and shut off the lights.

"Goodnight, girls. I love you," I say, closing the door to their room. The day is done with everyone alive and well. I reheat yet another cup of coffee and proceed to sit on the couch in front of the television aimlessly scrolling through Netflix for what feels like hours unable to decide on anything.

RING-RING. RING-RING. The time on my cracked phone screen reads a quarter to ten, which means I have actually been scrolling for hours. God, I need a hobby. "Hi, Ana."

"Hi sweetheart, just calling to check in. How was your day?" Her tone is concerned, motherly.

"Just fine. I picked up Imogene today. I didn't realize how famous I was these days, though." I laugh but, really, I want to cry from embarrassment.

"Trouble at school, dear? Or is it those damn paparazzi?"

"I don't think they count as paparazzi, but it was a little awkward with Ms. Cooper—"

"Oh, that girl! She's going to talk herself into a heap of trouble one of these days. Doesn't know when to quit!" Ana says, getting heated.

I try to calm her down before the sound of her rising blood pressure forces me to make more coffee. "It's no big deal, really."

She takes a deep breath. "Why don't I pick up Imogene the rest of the week?"

"You sure?" Hear her heartbeat slows and I'm grateful to not have to go back to the school tomorrow.

"Sure! Of course. Give it another week and you'll be old news," she says. I can feel the comfort in her voice like a warm hug.

"Thank you."

"Well, it's late, sweetie. I'm sure you're exhausted

after today. Get some rest and I'll come by in the morning for Imogene. Goodnight."

"Goodnight."

While I can't say I'm physically exhausted by any means, trying to be normal is mentally taxing. So is controlling this damn hunger. Forget rest, what I need is another bear. Donovan said he drained seven men; that would be way more than one bear. A small one, too, come to think of it. God, my life is anything but normal.

Hours pass as I try to stay distracted from my want of blood by occupying myself with Pinterest. Kitchen remodel ideas turn into searching through "thirty-minute meals" recipes, which makes me curious to see if there are any possible finds for "blood alternatives" that don't involve killing. By two-a.m. I realize there is, unfortunately, nothing to pin for that. A shrill scream pierces the air and Davina cries out, "MOMMY! MOMMY!"

I race to the girls' room faster than I've ever moved in my new life, pushed by my own fear and a desperate need to protect my daughters. I whoosh through their door, expecting to find the worst.

"MOMMY!" Davina sobs from under her blanket.

There is nothing in the room except a mess of toys, the two girls, and a faint hint of smoke that disappears within seconds of me entering. With all

Davina's yelling, I'm shocked Imogene's still sleeping peacefully. Just a nightmare then.

"Shh, I'm here, baby." I lie down beside Davina on her bed and pull back the blanket from her head.

She yells *mommy* again, crying inconsolably.

"Shhh. You're okay. It was just a dream, baby girl." I hold her in my arms, being careful not to crush her delicate frame, and sniff the air, trying to catch that tinge of smoke again.

I go over a checklist in my brain of what the burning smell could be from: the heater is turned off and their one nightlight doesn't look like it's been smoking. The only thing I can think of is someone nearby must be running their wood stove tonight. Without disturbing Davina, I try to peer past the closed curtains from where I'm sitting to see if I left the window cracked open, but I can't tell. She whimpers. Her heart is racing, and her skin is cold and clammy, but no matter what I try I can't get her to wake up fully and calm down. The last time she had night terrors she was two; nothing calmed her then, either. I just had to hold her and wait it out till she woke up on her own.

Imogene moans and hides her head under her pillow. Humming a lullaby, I stroke Davina's hair, trying my best to calm her down before she fully wakes her sister. "Mommy's here. Shhh," I remind her.

Moments later, peace returns to her sweet, tear-stained face. Her pulse settles back into a smooth, soothing rhythm as she nestles down onto my chest, the warmth from her little body soaking into my skin.

"Your heart is quiet," she mumbles sleepily, eyes still closed. She yawns, stretches out her legs, and repositions herself beside me in the crook of my arm.

"Goodnight, baby girl."

I kiss Davina on her tiny, sweaty forehead and cover us both with her blanket. Snuggling in with her for the night, I survey the room once more for evidence of smoke or fire but find nothing. I shut my eyes, enjoying the peaceful, amplified sounds of their breathing and feeling more alive— more invincible than ever. If there was something or someone in their room, I have no doubts I could have torn them apart. I'm strong enough to protect them from anything. And for the first time since I came home, I try to give myself the benefit of the doubt that no matter what, I know I will not hurt my children. Still, I hold my breath as her sweetly scented blood drifts up toward me— just in case.

14

STINKY CHEESE

The first light of morning glows softly through the sheer pink curtains. Imogene stirs in her sleep, then settles back onto her pillow while Davina rests peacefully on my arm.

It's five forty-five-a.m. Their alarm will go off in an hour for school, signaling a new day is about to begin. Tuesday— trash day; I can't forget the trash. Sliding my arm out from under Davina's sleep-heavy body, I sneak out of their room and take in a deep breath once I reach the hall. While my brain and body no longer scream for air, the practice of breathing brings me comfort, helps me feel normal. But with breath comes all the smells my home offers, and now my arm is saturated in Davina's honeysuckle scent. My thirst is growing and coffee, once again, is all I have to save me. I need to figure out how to plan a successful hunting mission on my own. Hopefully coffee can keep things at bay until tomorrow when Phil will be off his shift.

I check my phone. Five more ignored texts from Donovan, all apologizing for the info dump that he assumes has scared me off. If only that were the reason. The truth is I'm more scared of myself right now, and my inability to push his kiss from my mind. I decided instead to focus on how much I hate him for taking my humanity, being so devastatingly good looking, and making me think that damn bear would last me a whole week.

There are no texts from Phil, which is normal, I guess. He's not one to chat while working. Except he never texted me goodnight last night, and he always does that. I try not to read anything into it and grab a fistful of coffee beans, crushing them with my hands. It's way quieter than the grinder and still makes pretty delicious coffee. After slapping the last bits of grounds off my hands into the French press, I breathe in deep the smooth, earthy aroma steaming up to me as I slowly pour in the hot water. My phone rings.

"Hi pretty lady, good morning." Phil's voice is soothing to my ears. "Figured you'd be up."

"Hi there. How's saving the world going?"

"It's been crazy here, lots of weird calls. Sorry I didn't check in last night."

"It's okay. Weird calls, huh? It's not even a full moon." We laugh together, for a moment.

"Yeah, ever since that car fire, the one we saw on

239

the way to the airport, there have been a few other reports of fires and assaults flaring up around town." He hesitates. "Jon said there was another murder."

Another murder? A heaviness settles in my stomach as I remember the poor elderly woman from the parking lot. "Any news on if these are all related?"

"No, not yet— Oh, hey I have to go," he says abruptly, "but before I do, I'll be home tonight after all; they cut my shift for me. We got a new crew member, though, so a few of us that are free are going out for drinks after our shift. Bye, babe!"

"Oh, okay. See you tonight." I'm half excited he will be home early, and half disappointed he'll be going out to have fun and didn't invite me. Maybe he meant to. He usually offers, and as usual, I'd decline with some excuse involving the girls needing me home, I'm not much for social gatherings.

My throat aches, dried out from talking on the phone and I dull it with a large swig of coffee. Another murder? Red thermoses full of blood come to mind. Could this be where Donovan is getting the blood? Or what if there are others, here in town, like us? Which is entirely within the realm of possibility. Or what if the one who changed Donovan is still lurking around these parts? There is so much I want to understand, so much I should simply ask Donovan about and find answers, but as I look at my phone in a moment of weakness, my pride and fear stand firm in my need to ignore him. These unwelcome feelings I have for Donovan grow stronger every day. But my love for Phil is unwavering. It has to be. I can't bear the thought of losing him sooner than necessary. My only assurance is staying as far away from Donovan as I can.

The girls' morning alarm beeps from their room. It's six-thirty. Downing my coffee in one long gulp, I put my mom hat on. Time to get the day started.

At seven-thirty on the dot Ana walks through the door, bringing with her a box of rancid-smelling donuts, which I'm sure will be utterly scrumptious to everyone but me.

"Hi, Ana! Be right out!" I holler from the bathroom while finishing up Imogene's braid, her long soft hair threading through my fingers as I weave one strand over the other. This usually reminds me of the more pleasant parts of my childhood when my grandmother would braid my hair. Except for today, Imogene woke up in a foul mood and won't stop whining about how uneven the braid looks, and I wonder if it was more than Davina and me lying awake in that little room last night.

"Grandma!" Davina's words are garbled as if her mouth was full of marbles. Through the bathroom doorway, I catch a glimpse of her running from her bedroom to Ana, almost *whooshing* herself, with her fake vampire teeth. "Rawr!"

"Oh my goodness, you scared me!" Ana laughs.

"Okay. All done!" I say to Imogene. Her face is

scrunched up as she looks in the broken mirror, attempting to get a glimpse of her hairstyle. I really should replace it. "Go use the mirror in the living room."

She stomps out of the bathroom. I follow her to the kitchen where I find Davina with a mouthful of donut, trying her best to chew with her fake teeth in. She gives up after a few failed attempts and puts them all gooey on the table to enjoy the rest of her donut. Ana sits by her, a cup of coffee already in hand.

"Good morning, dear. Your coffee is excellent today. Have you ever considered opening a coffee shop?" Ana says between sips.

"I have, actually. Maybe someday!" I laugh. Not about to tell my mother-in-law I used my hands as a grinder. A new trend in third-wave coffee, *hand-crushed* — the hipsters would love that. In my next life, I'll open up a coffee shop and call it *Better than Blood*. I laugh out loud at the thought. At least it can give me something to look forward to.

"Mo-om. It's lumpy!" Imogene laments, walking into the kitchen.

"It's a braid. They're supposed to be lumpy." I clench my teeth. My patience is short today. Each time I'm forced to speak, the burn in my throat reminds me of Donovan and his B.S. about the bear holding me over. It's probably just a ploy for him to find time alone with me. "Eat some breakfast and you can have a donut once you're done. Hurry, school's starting soon."

"You look lovely," Ana says to Imogene, placing a kiss on her forehead. Imogene scrunches up her face and scuffles away to eat breakfast.

Ana looks at me, eyebrow raised. "She's a bit cranky this morning."

"Imogene was woken up last night. Davina had a bad dream," I explain.

"I see." Ana turns to Davina. "Honey, do you want to tell Grandma about your scary dream?"

Davina purses her lips.

"Good luck," I say. The girl is as stubborn as I am, if not more.

"Grandma, I'm going to be a ninja for Halloween," she replies instead.

"That's wonderful sweetie." Ana gives up.

"Watch me disappear like a ninja! Close your eyes!"

Ana shuts her eyes, and Davina spins around, karate chops the air, and sprints away to her room.

Ana turns to me with a huff. "Got any more coffee?"

I make another batch, this time in a more conventional manner. Ana takes her coffee to go as she and a sulking Imogene head off to school. *Good luck, Ms. Cooper*, I say to myself then chuckle quietly. Karma for her silly babbling? I can't help it, I'm hangry.

Davina races back into the kitchen yelling bye to

her sister. "What's so funny, Mommy?" She grabs hold of my hand.

"Nothing sweetie." She lets go of my hand, frowns, and darts off again.

I take the time alone to speed-clean the kitchen, actually enjoying using my new-found abilities for these things. Starting with the dishes, I'm soon on to the counters, and without much time lost I'm sweeping the floors. I slow my speed when I hear Davina run down the hall.

"Give me your hand," she demands, running into the kitchen. I comply, holding out my hand to her, and set the broom down against the counter.

"Now close your eyes," she adds.

She places something soft against my fingers and then, with her little hands, begins jamming my fingers into what feels like a baby sock. I take a peek and watch with a smile as she tries to force one of her tiny mittens onto my hand.

"I think it's too small," I whisper with a smile, kneeling down beside her.

"Your hands are cold. Mommy. You need glubs," she says, determined to still get the "glub" on me.

"Want to see a trick?" I ask. Her eyes light up. "Hold my hand in-between both of yours."

She does as I ask. "Now what, Mommy?" Four-year-olds can be so impatient.

"Wait a minute. Wait, there! See? You warmed them all up! Thank you!"

She holds my hand to her warm cheek. "It is warm! Am I magic?" she asks, her face glowing with excitement.

"You are more than magic, my darling. You are love." I give her a hug and kiss her forehead. "Now go play. Mommy has some stuff to do."

My heart might be non-functioning, but for a moment I almost felt it beating again.

Kitchen cleaned, coffee, living room cleaned, coffee, bathrooms, more coffee, bedroom— loud, squeaking breaks sound outside as I look out my bedroom window just in time to see the garbage truck pick up my neighbor's trash, then zoom right past my house and on to the next. Dammit, I forgot the trash.

"Mooo-oommmy! I'm starving!" Davina stomps into the kitchen where I am once again hand-crushing coffee. It's one-thirty, and I've yet to make her lunch between reorganizing the mess I made in my closest and scrubbing the bathrooms I simply lost track of time. Mega mom-fail, but it's hard when you don't eat on a normal schedule anymore. No more stomach grumbles to tell me it's time to eat, only the disgustingly strong desire to make myself a nice "Bloody Mary" from an actual Mary. And once again my mood sours at the thought of what my life is now.

"I'm so sorry. What do you want, PB and J?"

Please say okay, please say okay. It's quick to make and doesn't smell as bad as some other choices.

"I was thinking tuna fish," she says with attitude, taking a seat at the table. "With pickles."

Ugh, tuna is the worst smelling offender. "We're all out, sweetie. PB and J today, okay?"

She hesitates, then sets her terms. "Okay, but make it a heart sandwich."

"You got it!" I gather the fixings and pull out the heart-shaped cookie cutter.

"Thank you, Mommy," she says, with much less attitude at the sight of a heart on her plate and my mood softens a bit, it's not her fault I'm like this. I lean down and kiss the top of her head in gratitude.

I pick up my coffee mug and take a seat across from her. Davina eats quietly, her blue eyes appearing slightly grayer from the charcoal dress she's wearing today. I can't help but envision what she will look like at each stage of her life, every year growing stronger, smarter, more beautiful than the year before. I sigh, stopping a tear from building in my eye.

"Do you want some?" She holds out half of her heart to me.

I smile once again at the sentiment of her actions. "No thank you, honey. Mommy's not hungry."

"Okay, but no dessert if you don't eat your lunch," she scolds. Imogene must be rubbing off on her.

"Haha, all right." I can't help but be a little curious

as to what her dream was. I'm worried it has to do with her four-year-old mind sorting out everything going on in her life. So I ask again. "Davina sweetie, can you tell mommy about your scary dream?"

"No, I don't remember," she says through a mouthful of sandwich.

"You know you can always tell Mommy anything, right?"

A smile stretches across her face as she stands on her chair and leans over the top of the table toward me. I hold my breath as my throat burns hotter the closer she gets.

"Okay, yesterday," she pauses, her face growing serious, "I was being sneaky and ate cheese from the fridge when you weren't looking." She plops back down into her seat and picks apart the last bite of her sandwich.

"Oh, okay." Definitely not what I was expecting to hear, but that's a four-year-old for you. "Well, thank you for being honest."

"Can I be all done?" She shows me her plate of massacred bread and jelly, and I nod. She runs to dump her plate in the sink and returns to her world of play and imagination.

She is a complicated girl. Maybe I should be going to her for tips on how to be sneaky. I laugh out loud and get up to refill my mug, uncomfortable with how strong my thirst is growing. And then I remember my goal to plot out my next "hunting" trip— solo. This calls for some heavy-duty Googling.

I grab my laptop and get to work, reading everything I can on hunting without weapons. I'm surprised by the wealth of information I find. It's disgusting, what people will do even though we have grocery stores. Being my own butcher is something I would never have picked. The longer I scroll, the more blood I see, the more painful my hunger gets, almost aching into my bones. Yet, the sight of bloody animals is as tempting as it is revolting. I hold my breath and think of tuna fish sandwiches, and my hunger subsides a bit.

Ana's car pulls up in the driveway, just in time for me to make more coffee. She should appreciate that, especially if she knew it meant I won't try to eat her.

"Hi Imogene, how was school?" I ask as she bursts through the front door.

"Humph," is all she replies as she throws down her backpack and trudges through the kitchen.

"Not much has changed since this morning," Ana says, closing the front door behind her. "I tried to see what was bothering her. Says she's just tired."

"She must be exhausted."

"You must be too. How much coffee have you had today?" Ana says, peering over the open garbage can full of coffee grounds. The last thing I need is for her to be suddenly concerned about my exhaustion level.

"I'm fine," I say, pouring the hot water into the coffee press.

"Is Phil thinking of getting into hunting?" Ana asks, an air of motherly disappointment in her voice, she is strictly vegetarian after all.

"He's talked about it, but I'm not sure it's his thing. Why, did he mention it to you?" I reply, on my way to bring her a cup of coffee. Only to realize she is sitting in front of my laptop that's open to a page with a very muscular shirtless man holding three geese in one hand and a fox in the other. His face is covered in war paint and his bare chest is oiled down like he's some Rambo of the hunting world.

"You have a naked man and hunting stuff on your computer," she says, taking her coffee, her eyes glued to the screen. "Killing animals without weapons? Last I checked we live near a grocery store."

My thoughts exactly.

"Oh, that. Yeah, that was me." I close the lid on the laptop, my insides reeling with embarrassment. "I was curious if that was a thing or not, sorry." Ana does not approve of eating animals, let alone hunting them with bare hands.

She raises an eyebrow at me and smiles. "Don't worry about it, dear. No harm, no *fowl*." She laughs, a most unexpected reaction. "Oh honey, I like to look at men on the internet, too, from time to time. What can I say, I'm a human woman!" She takes a sip of coffee as I choke on mine to keep from spitting it all over her. Oh dear God, kill me now . . . again!

"Oh-OH! Human, yeah," I say, as a strange, giddy laugh escapes my lips. Inside my head I'm covering my ears, shutting my eyes, and singing as loud as I can, *LA LA LA LA LA*. But not wanting to embarrass my mother-in-law, I go along with it. "Those primal hunting men just really— really are something," I add. I want to bury myself under a rock.

"Oh, listen now, I won't say anything to Phil. Your secret's safe with me." She winks, leaning back in her chair, and confidently drinks her coffee.

"Thank you." *Can I tell you a million more?* "I'll be right back. I'm going to talk to Imogene." I take my mug with me as I escape the worst hell imaginable: talking porn with your mother-in-law.

Imogene sits alone in the living room, watching a show. I sit down beside her on the couch and wait. I've learned not to push her for answers; when something's bothering her, she usually tells me eventually if I make myself available. After a minute or two she scoots herself closer and rests her head on my shoulder, her eyes still glued to the TV screen. I place my arm around her as she looks at me; her emerald eyes tired and worried.

"How are you, sweetie?" I ask.

"I'm good," she says with a smile, her eight-year-old self finally showing through instead of the eigh-teen-year-old one.

"What was with all the grumpies today?" I smile back, tickling her side. She giggles, eyes bright, smiling.

"I don't know, I'm just tired I guess," she says, breathless from laughing. I tickle her some more.

"Are you sure?" I have an idea there is more to this than being tired, and I think it has to do with her mom going off the deep end. Guilt washes through me. Maybe I haven't been doing as good of a job as I thought of hiding all my new issues.

"I'm sure," she says, hugging me tight before sitting back to focus on her show. I'll leave it alone for now.

Out of the corner of my eye, I catch Ana slowly opening my laptop. I stand up, trying not to notice the awkward smile appearing on her face and shout, "Who wants pizza?"

She slams the lid shut. "I'll get it!" she calls from the kitchen. "Vegetarian okay? Or would you prefer meat lovers?"

15

WON'T YOU BE MY NEIGHBOR

T wo hours later, Ana returns from picking up the pizza. "Aileen, dear, why don't you come join us?" she says from the kitchen while I pretend to busy myself with laundry to avoid her.

"Oh, I'm fine. You go ahead without me," I say from the laundry room, my nose buried in a box of dryer sheets to drown out the smells. Pizza is close to tuna in levels of olfactory awfulness. Not to mention I'm still traumatized by our earlier conversation.

In my panic to announce pizza for dinner, I failed to think through the logistics of it all. As far as I know in my limited knowledge of my new self, I can't eat regular food. Or can I? Sitting on top of the washer, I pull my phone from my pocket and start a new text addressed to 007. I delete it, deciding these are the things I should figure out for myself, and join them at the table.

"Here you go." Ana hands me a large slice of vegetarian.

"Thank you," I say, trying to keep the disgust from leaking out into my words.

I slide the warm pizza into my mouth. It's not as bad as it smells— it's a thousand times worse. The once delicious cheese now tastes like dirty rubber. Ana watches me, but unable to swallow, I hold my composure and stand, holding up a finger, and nod to her, excusing myself with a smile. Slowly, I walk out of the kitchen until I'm out of sight enough to zip off to my bathroom and discreetly discard the putrid pizza. I give my mouth a rinse for good measure and think about my next move. If I don't eat, Ana will worry and think I'm getting sick again. If I do eat— the memory of the rubbery cheese skirts across my thoughts and I gag. No. Eating is not an option.

I return to the kitchen and before sitting back down I grab a tall, opaque cup from the cupboard and partially fill it with water. Desperate times call for desperate measures. I can't run to the bathroom after every "bite", but I can spit it back into this cup, pretending to take a drink.

"You all right, dear?" Ana asks.

"Sorry, I had to pee." I sit down, game plan in hand.

Holding my breath, I take a small bite and do my

best to pretend-chew it. The thought of actually chewing shoots my disgust-o-meter to the roof. Now for the cup trick. I take a sip, letting some of the water wash out with the pizza as I attempt to spit it back into the cup without Ana's noticing. Instead, water dribbles down my face. I abort the mission and pretend to swallow, a wad of soggy pizza still sitting regrettably in my mouth.

Ana looks at me and smiles. "Good pizza, huh?"

"Mmmm" is all I can say and take another bite, this time smaller, piling it on top of my previous bite.

It's do or die. I take another sip of water, and this time I don't let the water in but shove the two bites of pizza out with my tongue. Success. I look down at my nearly whole slice— twenty more bites to go or so. Couldn't she have given me a smaller piece? It's hard work keeping up this human façade. There better be a big, huge, juicy bear waiting out there for me tonight.

"Want another slice?" Ana asks me while picking off a pile of olives from another piece before dumping it on Davina's plate.

"No thank you." I stand to bring my plate and cup to the sink.

"I'll take care of that! You sit back down," Ana scolds.

"You have done so much for us. It's the least I can do." I snatch her empty plate too before she can get out of her chair, place them in the sink, and dump my pizza cup down the drain. I might have survived eating— barely— but I certainly wouldn't survive Ana finding out it all ended up in my cup.

"Well then, I'll get the girls washing! Bath time!" she sings, herding two reluctant girls toward the bathroom. They used to love bath time. Time truly changes things, I guess.

By nine-p.m., the girls are in bed and asleep. Ana left soon after bath time, and Phil is still not home. I've learned everything I possibly could about how to hunt on my own, but I'm not sure whether any of it will help me. I've cleaned the house again, and almost completely defeated the laundry monster. Minus folding, which shouldn't take too long thanks to my newly acquired speed. Once again, I find myself sitting on the couch scrolling through Netflix until I turn it off. Nothing sounds appealing. Probably because my everyday life now feels more like a movie than reality.

I text Phil for the third time since seven-thirty:

Where are you? Everything okay?

I wait ten minutes. No reply, again. Tossing my phone on the couch beside me, I'm left with nothing to distract me from my thirst and the anxiety that comes with thinking of what I'll have to do tonight to satisfy it.

My phone dings. Finally Phil's responding. Disappointment befalls me as I read my notification screen.

007: Guess what . . . I'm coming over!

I don't think that would be a good idea.

007: See you in a few! P.S. I'm bringing a snack, figured you'd be hungry.

No, please don't. Phil will be home any minute.

He doesn't reply. God help me! I've been dressed in tight leggings and a tank top all day, so I run to the unfolded clean pile on my bed in search of something less revealing. Jeans work. I slide them on and dig up one of Phil's old sweatshirts. Perfect. Hair, ponytail— okay, not much sexy about a messy ponytail. The front door opens, and I whoosh to the end of the hall, gathering my resolve to stuff down any and all feelings I may or may not have for Donovan.

"I thought I said not to come over," I whisper under my breath, knowing he can hear it loud and clear while rounding the corner into the kitchen. No need to wake the girls—

But it's Phil's voice, with a hint of a slur to it, that sounds out. "Hey babe, sorry I'm late." I can tell Phil's drank a few more than normal. It must have been a good time. "I got stuck talking with a new guy I met, when I was out with the crew." He saunters over, throwing himself at me with a hug. He reeks of beer and bourbon.

"Did you drive like this?"

"No, I walked."

Relieved, I smile. Drunk or not I'm glad he's home. Although I was hopeful Donovan would see Phil's car in the driveway and stay away. But now what? Would Donovan still try to come over? He wouldn't dare, would he?

"Everything okay?" Phil sets down his overnight bag on the edge of the table, it falls to the floor with a thump. He shrugs and leaves it on the floor.

"Yeah, all is well here." I smile, picking up his abandoned bag for him.

"So, the guy I met tonight is on his way over now."

I give him a look, then glance down at my sloppy outfit. "Why now? It's getting late."

"He just moved in a few houses down and doesn't know many people yet. Said he'd grab some drinks from his house and be right over." He pauses and looks at me for a moment, his brow furrowing. "Is that all right? I meant to call but my phone died."

"No, no, it's fine. I'm going to change." He must be drunker than he's letting on; why else would he invite a "stranger" he just met, to our house? He never invites people over.

"Okay," he says, following me to our room. "You look fine in what you have on though."

I pull off the baggy sweatshirt and tank top over my head, tossing them on the floor, and shuffle through my closet in hopes of finding a decent shirt that's not too stained. I settle on a plain grey one and as I throw it over my head Phil's jaw drops.

"Wow, what happened to your stomach?" he asks.

"Oh, right. You're probably just drunk." I laugh, hoping he won't think too much more into it.

He laughs as he moves closer. "I am not *that* drunk." Standing before me he embraces me, alcohol heavy on his breath, but it doesn't bother me. I find it quite pleasant almost intoxicating myself. I wrap my arms around his neck, he wraps his warm around my cold middle, one hand feeling over the smoothness of my tight belly.

"I tried those wraps all the moms at school are selling these days." His hand on me awakens a whole different kind of hunger, one we don't have time for now considering he has company coming, also the small fact Donovan might be showing up as well.

"Well, they seem to work miracles with how bad your skin was— uh, sorry." He drops his hands, as I place a quick kiss of forgiveness on his lips.

"No, it's fine. It was pretty severe."

Knuckles rap on the front door, in a *rat-a-tat-tat* rhythm. Phil's face lights up and he bolts for the kitchen. I'm grateful for his acceptance of the lie and glad there is one less thing I need to hide from him.

I quickly glance in the mirror one more time. I look presentable enough to meet a new neighbor, I guess. On my way down the hall, I stop midway as the strong scent of vintage leather and men's cologne hits me. Donovan is here.

I speed into the kitchen to see both mean reaching for each other. "No!" I whisper, out of breath, in fear what he might do to Phil, what Phil might try and do to him.

"Hey Phil!" Donovan embraces my husband in a friendly hug, his hands full with a thermos in each of them— one red, one blue.

"Aileen, this is Donovan Sellars." Phil smiles at me and it takes a moment for me to piece it all together. Donovan is the friend. That sneaky bastard.

Sellars. I vaguely recall him saying his last name at the farmhouse, but I swear I've heard it somewhere else. I stand there, still frozen. He's now my neighbor? He's friends with Phil?

Phil nudges my arm. "This is the guy I met earlier at the bar, the one I was just telling you about, who lives down the street?" he says in a tone usually saved for those who suffer from memory issues.

Donovan holds out his hand to me. "Well hello, Aileen. It is so nice making your acquaintance," he says with a more-British-than-usual accent.

Shocked, I stand there still staring at Donovan

while Phil fumbles around somewhere in the cupboards behind me. Donovan accentuates his smile with a nod, looking down to his hand, and clears his throat. *Play it cool, Aileen.*

"Oh, right. Yes, hello. Where are my manners?" I smile tightly. "It's nice to meet you too," I say, taking his hand, squeezing it in a death grip that would crush any human's hand.

He raises it to his mouth and kisses my knuckles. Tingles run up my arm as his soft, cold lips touch my skin.

Donovan purrs, "The pleasure is all mine."

I make it clear I'm less than impressed. "So, you moved in down the street, huh?" I ask, probing for answers as to why he is here in my house.

"From London!" Phil says, excited, while he grabs three glasses out of the cupboard.

I don't try to hide my sarcasm. "How interesting."

"He moved here to become a winemaker!" Phil adds, trying to figure out how to hold the three glasses in one hand but however many drinks he's already consumed is making it a challenge.

I've never thought to ask Donovan what he did for a living. With Phil's back turned, I give him a look, trying to piece together what he might be trying to do. He just smiles back at me. Phil turns around, holding the three glasses now in a precarious, clinking tower.

"Here, let me help you with that." Donovan reaches for two of the glasses.

"Thanks, man. Isn't he great?" Phil says to me. And for a moment, I worry if Donovan is as charming to Phil as he is to me.

"Great." My voice is icy. Phil doesn't notice, but Donovan definitely does.

My unwanted guest flicks his dark chocolate eyes up to me, amused, and fills the two glasses he's holding with a very deep burgundy, thick wine from the red thermos. He takes the last glass from Phil and fills it with an identical-looking dark wine from the blue thermos, and hands it back to him.

"You will love this!" Donovan's eyes sparkle. "It's an old family recipe. I made it myself."

He hands me my glass. The fire of my hunger burns deep within my veins from the heavenly aroma coming from the blood in my cup. My senses sharpen on the object of my desire, and for now, I'm grateful he's here.

"This is amazing," Phil says, then turns to me. "Donovan was telling me he moved here to be a winemaker."

"You said that," I say, wondering if this whole charade was all Donovan's idea just to bring me dinner. Then I remember why his last name is so familiar. "Sellars, Cellars! You're Sellars Cellars!" I shout. I've driven past the nearly completed Sellars Cellars building outside of town countless times over the last year.

"Yes, I am he." He smiles proudly with a slight bow.

Phil grins drunkenly at us, obviously pleased we seem to be getting along. "Let's enjoy this in the living room where it's more comfortable," he says, walking ahead to the couch.

Donovan and I follow, and I grab his arm. "What are you doing?" I whisper.

"Told you I'd bring a snack," he whispers back with a wink.

"No, what are you doing friending Phil?" I hiss.

Phil turns to face us and I let go of Donovan's arm before he can notice. Donovan takes a seat in the maroon wingback chair adjacent to the couch. I sit on the couch, placing myself between Donovan and Phil. I don't trust him; I know "Mr. Sellars" has feelings for me, and I fear he might be up to no good because of it and the last thing I want is Phil caught in the middle.

Donovan raises his glass. "To new friends in a new land! Cheers!"

"Cheers!" says Phil.

We all take a sip at the same time, and I try to control myself and not down the entire glass in one gulp. Donovan sneaks me another wink between sips of his "wine"; my stomach flutters.

"Donovan, my man, this is some dope shit." Phil laughs and goes back to drinking his actual— I'm hoping— wine.

"Thank you. It's all about the grapes and how long you let them age." Donovan tips his glass in my direction.

My stomach knots. I wonder how long the "grapes" in my glass have had to age— does that mean I'm drinking an elderly person? I set my half-drunk glass on the table, remembering the old woman who drove me to my change in the first place. How sweet and rich her blood was scented, how it tasted even more divine than anything I could have imagined, how she is now dead— murdered.

"You don't want it?" Phil reaches for it. His glass is empty in his other hand.

"No!" I snatch it back and chug it down, soothing the burn. "It's so good, I can't possibly share it."

"I have plenty more back at home, darlings, barrels of it," Donovan says with a laugh. The air thickens as a heavy question of not *what*, but *who* fills those barrels knocks at my conscience. Here's hoping he was just talking about the actual wine he brought for Phil.

Phil and Donovan enjoy a lively conversation on the science of making wine, while I'm stuck in the middle, keeping one eye on Donovan and the other on the clock, and my ears open in case one of the girls wakes up. The drunker Phil gets, the louder his volume grows.

Donovan refills Phil's glass, emptying the blue thermos. "Not to be a downer, but your husband told me what a horrific accident you were in. But wow, Phil, you are one lucky guy she turned out okay!"

Now my anger burns along with my hunger at Donovan. What is he doing? He of all people should know I don't need to be reminded of this, I don't think Phil needs or wants to be reminded of how he almost lost his wife.

"Yes, I am very happy to have her here with us still." Phil puts his arm around me, squeezing me into his side. His words are slurred from the wine, "She gave us quite the scare there."

"Someone was watching out for you it seems." Donovan stares into my eyes.

"You could say that," I reply, dryly.

He swirls his glass like a real wine snob. "Phil mentioned you're using running as therapy."

"Well, it's cheaper and less invasive." I turn my sarcasm on Phil. "What hasn't Phil mentioned tonight?" I nudge my husband, who's sitting pressed against my side in an attempt to not fall over. What else has he been sharing with his new "buddy"?

"Oh! I forget to mention—" a very excited, very drunk Phil says, sitting up on his own and facing me on the couch. "You shouldn't be out running on your own anymore."

I look glance at Donovan. He smiles.

"Excuse me?" I ask, now face to face with Phil.

"Yeah, it's official, *there* is a serial killer on the loose —" he burps "— in town. That woman assaulted in the parking lot your car was taken from, you know how she was murdered? But what I didn't tell you was she was left with no teeth or fingers."

I look at Donovan again and his face becomes solemn. He gives his head a slight shake as if to say he had nothing to do with it.

"I shouldn't say this," Phil's voice drops to a whisper. "But the burned woman, from the car wreck, that they can't identify, she had no teeth or fingers either. It was as if someone ripped them right off. Just like the other woman. That's why they can't identify her." Phil sits there, nodding his head. He belches again, the fruity wine stench on his breath repulsive, unlike the bourbon he was saturated in earlier. "So, I don't think running around these roads is the best idea."

"Well, then I won't run on the roads."

Phil's smile disappears. I can't help but look at Donovan to see once again if any of this has to do with him. He shakes his head again, and for a moment there seems to be a hint of fear hiding behind his dark eyes. I'm assuming that means it's not him. But *something* is involved, and an uneasiness settles into the pit of my stomach.

"I don't want you running anymore."

My frustration rises. "What am I supposed to do, then?"

"You could call the therapist, or get a treadmill?" Phil answers like a defiant teenager.

"I told you I'm not doing that," I try to keep my composure. We have a guest here, after all.

"I can't stand the idea of losing you again," my poor drunken Phil says, unraveling and on the verge of tears.

"Good lord, what did you give him?" I ask Donovan. He laughs. I turn back to Phil. "Whatever. I can't not run, and a treadmill won't cut it." What other excuses are there to go kill things?

It's useless; two glasses of Sellars Cellars wine and Phil is off dancing with the pink elephants from *Dumbo*. The one glass of blood for me certainly wasn't enough. If anything, it made my need for blood worse. I rub my throat in an attempt to put out the flames I feel inside and wonder if maybe something's wrong with me to be this thirsty, all the time.

"Phil, you look like a runner. Maybe you two could run together?" Donovan suggests in calm-mediator tone. Whatever fear he seemed to be feeling is now long gone, if it ever existed in the first place. His eyes regained their usual smug and cocky luster.

"Unfortunately, I don't think that would be the best idea, Mr. Sellars." I stand.

"Oh?" Donovan adds, playing stupid, which I know he's not, so I have to assume the worst: he knows exactly what he's doing.

"If we didn't have the kids to take care of, I'd gladly run with her," Phil says, sniffling. Then, he snaps his fingers. "But Aileen, my mom could watch the girls!"

"No, I can't ask any more of her." Plus, the last thing I want is Phil escorting me on my dinner runs.

"I'm sorry, babe." Phil grabs my arm, pulling himself to standing. "It's just not safe right now. Just give Jon some time to see what's going on with the car wrecks." He smiles, squeezing my arm tight to steady himself from falling.

I'm beginning to notice the heavy scent of alcohol in his blood, making it completely unappetizing.

Behind us, Donovan clears his throat. "If I may— and I know we just met— I'm an avid runner myself. Do it every day." I peer past Phil at Donovan, who's reclining casually in the old wingback chair, wine glass balanced on his palm. Coming in to save the day, once again. This is probably why he's here in the first place. "I live just a few houses down. If you'd like, Phil, I'd gladly accompany Aileen on her runs." He smiles at me. Yep, he knows exactly what he's doing.

As much as I want to turn down the offer, I know better. I'm too thirsty, and at least this way, Phil might ease up on me. "I will accept your offer," I say slowly, hoping Donovan won't read too far into this agreement.

"Are you sure you don't mind?" Phil asks Donovan, relieved. "That would mean a lot to me, man, thank you. She says running helps and I believe her.

She's doing so much better." Tears are oddly forming at the base of his lashes. "I just don't want her alone."

Donovan looks at me and smiles. My need to feed thanks him.

"Not a problem." Donovan pats Phil on the back, almost knocking him over. "What are new friends for?"

Almost eagerly I ask, "Feel like a run now, Mr. Sellars?"

"Aileen, it's twelve-thirty-a.m.!" Phil looks surprised, even through his drunken haze.

"Actually," Donovan interrupts, "I prefer a nice, early-morning run. Only loonies are out and about this late." Phil laughs.

"Morning it is, then." I grin. My hunger groans; I'm not sure I can wait till morning. But with Phil smelling like a bottle of old wine, I don't find his blood currently appealing. Maybe I should get him drunk more often.

Donovan fakes a yawn. "Thank you both for such a lovely evening. I'm so glad we've met." He hugs me goodbye, purposely pressing his body up against mine. The scent of his jacket, the deep warmth of his cologne paired with the coolness of his hands set way to low on my back— it's all too much. Without warning I melt inside, suddenly yearning for a repeat of Monday morning, his lips pressed on my lips— ugh, I shake the thought and push myself away praying Phil is too drunk to notice whatever that was that just happened.

Phil seems unfazed as he unsteadily escorts Donovan through the kitchen. They pause at the table as Donovan grabs the thermoses he came with. As the men briefly hug goodbye while I keep my distance, not wanting to seem any friendlier with my new "running buddy" than necessary. The positives come to mind, making this whole uncomfortable meeting of worlds all the more bearable. Phil knowing who I'm safely running with could make life easier, Donovan is now someone I don't have to lie about . . . completely.

"Bye." I wave once Donovan's out the door and on the porch.

"You better keep your eye on her, Phil, or I might take her for myself!" he says, giving Phil a wink.

"Bye, Donovan!" Phil yells out the door.

"Shh, quiet down, you'll wake the neighbors!" It's unusual to see him this drunk without being drunk myself.

Phil closes the door with a chuckle.

"Hey, pretty lady." He stumbles his way across the kitchen to me. "I'm keeping my eye on you." He laughs, pointing to his eye, almost poking it in the process.

"Hey, drunk guy."

"I'm fine, I'm fine—" Phil loses his balance, and I whoosh over and grab him, stopping his fall.

"Whoa there, tiger. Let's get you to bed."

"I'm fine," he says again, the full weight of his body slumped against mine.

I toss his arm over my shoulder and we head down the hall.

"Wow, you're strong," he slurs. Running his free hand down the front of my face, he flops my lips with his fingers, laughing as he does so.

"And you are wasted!" Now I'm feeling concerned for his well-being. He grabs my breast with a "honk" and laughs again. Annoyed, I hoist him down the hall to the bedroom.

"Stay here, I'll get you some water," I say as I lay him down on our bed.

He grabs my shirt, pulling me down on top of him. "How about I drunk-drink—" he bursts into eye-watering laughter and lets go of my shirt.

I sit up beside him. "I'll get your water now."

"No, no, don't go," he says, his arms flapping for my shirt again.

"What?" I ask, not sparing the slight annoyance in my voice. Nothing sexier than your drunk husband expressing his desire for you by dog-paddling for your chest.

He sits up onto his elbow, smiling, trying hard to catch is breath and withhold his laughter. "How about — how about I drink you?" he says in his best attempt at a seductive voice. Then he bursts out in laughter again.

Just like my desire to taste his once sweet, now

alcohol saturated blood is long gone, so is any desire to do much else with him tonight.

"Mmm. That is a tempting offer." I scrunch up my nose, get up, and stand at the door. "I'll be back with your water."

He lies back down on his pillow with a thump, giggling to himself, as I leave the room. By the time I hit the kitchen, all I hear is the loud sawing of Phil's snores. I fill a large glass with water— boy, will he need it— and grab a few aspirins as well. I return to the room, placing the water and aspirin on Phil's nightstand for when he wakes.

For once, I'm thankful not to be human anymore. His hangover won't be pleasant. But I know I don't mean that. I'd give anything to be drunk with Phil right now. To share in his headache tomorrow. To be human with the one I promised to marry, till death do us part. The phrase stings as it makes its way from my thoughts— after all, I'm not exactly alive anymore. I push it aside and instead watch the rise and fall of his chest, resting my hand on his stubbly cheek. His sleeping brow furrows at my icy touch and I catch a lone tear as it slowly trails down my face.

16

RISE AND SHINE

Darkness blankets the hills outside the window of our room as Phil stirs in his sleep, still fully clothed. I sat there watching him until about thirty minutes ago, at three-a.m., when Davina woke, screaming with another night terror. Phil didn't move an inch.

She fell back to sleep quicker this time, but not until she made sure I shut her curtains to protect her from the statue of fire she swears she saw outside her window. Although a hint of smoke hung in the air of the girls' bedroom, there was clearly no fire outside. I convinced her people were just using their wood stoves to keep warm like we do. At least she told me a little about what her dream was about. I'm hoping this phase of night terrors will pass soon, I have enough on my plate right now.

Back in our bedroom, I check on Phil for the hundredth time. The sweet smell of his blood I've grown to love has finally returned. Only a hint of wine remains.

"Good morning," I whisper in his ear, sitting beside him on the bed, already dressed and ready for my run.

"Mmmm." He hides his head under the pillow. "What time is it?" comes his muffled voice.

"It's five-forty-five," I lie. It's three-forty-five, but I changed the clocks just in case he looks. I didn't want him to worry about how early I'm leaving the house. However, I would bet he's far too hung-over to notice. I need time to feed, and I need to do it alone this time.

He moans some more.

"You don't need to get up. I'll be back before the girls' alarm. Drink this." I pull the pillow off his head.

"Thanks," he mumbles, barely audible even to my ears. "Wait. You're leaving?" He tries to sit up, then grabs his head, wincing in pain, and falls back down face first into his pillow.

I help him sit back up and shove a glass of water into one of his hands and some aspirin in the other. "I'm running with our new friend this morning, remember?"

"Huh?" He swallows the aspirin and half the glass of water with it. "Oh, right— running." He rubs his head, shoving the glass of water at me. I take it and he sinks into the pillows.

"Love you." I kiss him on the forehead.

"Mmm," is all I hear from him, followed by more snoring.

I put my phone in my sweatshirt pocket along with a taser Ana gave me last Christmas, just in case I run into any trouble. It can't hurt. I quietly close the front door behind me and hit the ground running. Like a child scared of the boogie man after hearing a scary story I— the scariest of any actual, known to me, monster— am spooked by every rustling tree branch, each dark shadow, and sound I hear. Regardless, the recent murders in our otherwise quiet town, have me on edge. The taser from Ana bounces around in my pocket as I run, which seems silly now that I think about. My hunger for blood is far more lethal than a small burst of electricity. Suddenly, what feels like a puff of air hits the back of my neck; it's probably the wind, but I don't stick around to find out and like a scared cat I whoosh away full speed ahead. In seconds I'm out of town, through the hills, and on to the highway racing toward the high country.

I'm not waiting for Donovan this time. I don't need a chaperone, and I don't need his help. Finding food is something I must learn to do on my own. The stars are hidden behind the clouds this early morning and it looks as if rain might pour down any minute. At four a.m., the highway is all mine, so instead of running through the trees, I take the road. The hard pavement under my shoes allows me to run faster than running over dirt. Soaking in the purest form of freedom I've experienced yet, I soar down the empty highway as fast as I possibly can, wind whipping through my hair, leaving my fears, my worries, my life behind.

The seven-thousand-foot elevation sign catches my eye. It's windy, but the sky is clear up here. Scattered across the black vastness billions of stars twinkle, their reflections dancing on the frost-covered treetops. I slow my pace to look at the time: four-fifteen-a.m. and no cell service, but wow, is this feeling worth it. I just ran an hour-long drive in fifteen minutes and I don't even have to catch my breath. I set an alarm on my phone for six-thirty-a.m., fifteen minutes before the girls' alarm clock would go off. Just to be safe, I change my alarm to six-twenty; I can't be late.

My sneakers hit the dirt roadside as I hike into the forest, hoping to catch the scent of something other than pine trees, something I can manage to catch and eat on my own. Though my thirst is becoming easier to control around the ones I love, I long to find a way to soothe the chronic irritation in my throat, the one soothed only by blood or coffee. I wish Donovan had brought more over last night. The barrels of blood he claims to have, tempt me, but the horrors of where they might have come from, deepen my resolve. I will not eat people.

I find the edge of the small clearing I came to on my first hunting trip and close my eyes. The tactic worked well last time, but the howling wind makes even my own footsteps hard to hear. I sit on the ground near a large fir tree, the thick silver trunk blocks the wind from rushing against my head. Moments pass as I try to focus, and finally, my ear picks up a group of firm, steady beats not too far to my right, just beyond the clearing. Instinct once again takes over as I stalk my way over to my prey.

I see my prize: ten or so deer all bedded down in the soft dirt under the trees, lying there, sheltered from the wind and the cold as if they were waiting for me. I can do this; I have to do this. Just break the neck quickly and bite. A shiver runs through me. I've never broken a chicken bone, let alone a whole live deer. If only I could eat a cheeseburger, let someone else do the dirty work for me. Or maybe Donovan will show up like he usually does. My stomach flutters at the thought of seeing him again, but I quickly shake it off. I need to do this alone.

A large buck sleeping at the head of the herd calls to me. The warmth from his body radiates toward me through the chilly air as I near him. His blood, scented with spicy notes, pairs well with the earthy aroma of the forest, not as gamey as the bear but not as sweet as a human's. I sit still beside him, inches from his strong, thick neck, just as I did before. A vein pulses under his coarse brown fur. All my hunting research has been wiped from my memory after Ana's horrific allusions to pornography, so I'm drawing a blank now as to how to kill an animal with my bare hands. I only remember "break the neck quick." I'm sure I'm strong enough physically, what I question is my resolve to go through with it. I want to stop, back away, abandon my mission, but the heat from my hunger begs me otherwise. My hands lift, outstretched towards his neck. One snap and it's over, I tell myself. Just. One. Snap. My hands defy my need for blood and throw themselves back into my pockets. The deer is still peacefully sleeping, unaware of both my presence and my moral dilemma. I can't do it, I can't take this life.

Then I remember that last moment I was alive on the plane. That moment, that heart-stopping, stomach-sinking moment, when I realized, *this is the end of my life.* The horrific pain coursing through my body— not because of the fiery death looking me in the face, but because I would no longer be there for my girls. I was leaving them motherless. That one single moment was worse than death itself. Breathless and lost, it was the most helpless feeling I'd ever experienced, until now. I was wrong; the most helpless feeling is becoming a living danger to the ones I love because I can't kill this deer. I sure as hell don't want to feel this way any longer.

The cool metal of the small taser in the bottom of my pocket brushes up against my fingertips. With a new determination, I pull it out, and without thinking, I leap onto his back and jab the taser into the side of his neck. Hoping I might simply stun him unconscious first. The buck yells out horrifying screams, sending his herd running for safety. I duck from their hooves as they jump over my head and flee toward safety, still holding the taser to the buck's neck. Burnt fur dulls my hunger as the kicking and screaming buck beneath me suffers endlessly at my hand. I can't do what I need to do, and I'm desperately wishing Donovan would have appeared so my hands could remain clean, but it's too late. With tear-filled eyes I simultaneously throw the taser away from me, wrap my arms around his neck, and twist. A loud snap echoes over the wind and his suffering ceases.

How could I be so foolish? Sobs break through my tears at the reality of what I will have to do for the rest of my immortal existence; these hands hold my children, not takes the lives of the innocent. Gently, I cradle the poor buck's head in my arms looking into his large dark, now lifeless eyes. I push aside my shame as my thirst drives me to his neck. Not bothering to tear away the fur, my teeth sink easily into the once mighty buck, and I drink until I nothing is left.

THE TOWN slowly brightens from the rising sun behind me. I did it, I fed on my own, though I'm certainly not proud of it. My phone alarm beeps, it's six-twenty. I hit snooze and set it back down on the rock beside me — the same rock on the hilltop overlooking my tiny town I sat on with Donovan only days ago. I stare down at my shadow stretching west from my feet toward the town, pointing me to my life— my old life, one now filled with lies and danger.

The alarm goes off again; a nine-minute snooze doesn't feel like a long time when you now have an eternity to live. I hit snooze again. I need to go back home; the girls will wake soon, and I'll need to be mommy again. A shudder runs through me. What kind of mother tries to kill a deer with a taser? Another shadow grows beside mine.

"You going to wake up now? Or is another nine minutes really going to help you catch up on your sleep?"

"Hello, Donovan *Sellars*," I say, unfazed by his appearance, still staring at our shadows. "I thought we wouldn't have shadows."

"There is a lot you still don't know," he says, taking a seat on the rock beside me.

"Apparently." I scoot over to create more space between us. "Like you being a winemaker? And by the way, whatever that wine was you gave Phil is nothing any human should be drinking."

"It was an experimental batch. I'll make the needed adjustments. Thank you for your feedback." He pulls a notepad and pen out of his jacket pocket.

"Seriously?" I stare at him.

"Batch too strong. Don't give to humans," he dictates out loud as he writes on his notepad, closes it up, and stuffs it and the pen back in his pocket.

"And what's this about you living on my street? Do you have any idea how creepy you are?" I'm certainly not hiding my frustration from earlier, but I know that taking it out on him won't help me feel any better.

"It's a nice neighborhood. Homes are a great investment, and it's all about location," he says, not bothered by my attitude.

"What about your farmhouse?" I jab.

I feel him look at me, can almost sense his eyebrows rising. "Feeling testy today, I see. How was 'therapy'?" he asks.

"No comment."

The calm tone in his accented voice only fuels my frustration. I want to cry again at the thought of what I did. The screams blaring from the buck who moments before peacefully slept with his herd— his family— still echo through me. The taste of every last drop of his blood flowing into my mouth, coating my throat— the warmth of his life filling my veins should leave me satisfied. But all I'm left feeling is shame: of my weakness, of what I did.

"So, you didn't like doing it on your own, did you? Clever with the taser idea, but kind of sadistic, don't you think?" He smiles his smug, stupid smile, showing all his perfectly white, perfectly dangerous teeth.

I should have known he'd be there watching me. My anger rises. "You are unbelievable!"

"I promised to be your running buddy, remember? You seem to have forgotten."

"I don't need a guardian." I stand up, grabbing my phone off the rock.

"Of course you don't." He stands too, looking me in the eye. His dark brown eyes filled with intensity. "But you do. Need. Me." His face moving closer to mine with each word. His lips only inches from mine, their memory still fresh from Monday's kiss. My lips quiver, begging for more. My alarm goes off again, cooling whatever is trying to build between us.

I back away. "I need to go home and be Mom now." And run down the hill to the road that leads back to town.

Donovan is right beside me. "Slow down."

"What do you think you're doing?" I retort, running faster. He catches up.

"Hello? Running buddy? What would Phil think if you were out all alone?" he says, grabbing me by the shoulder. "Now, slow down before you attract unwanted attention."

I shrug his hand off my shoulder. "Right, because you and Phil are best buds now. Is it because I never texted you back? I ignore you and you push your way into my life regardless?" Still, he's right. I slow to a normal running speed as the town appears in the distance. After running full speed down the highway earlier, I now feel like I'm crawling.

"The lack of speed is getting to you, isn't it?" He smiles, slowing to my pace. "Dare I say, vampire looks good on you?"

I take a few steps quicker to stay ahead of him ignoring his comment, growing angrier because he's not wrong. "You didn't answer my question."

"Phil seems like a lovely fellow. A very nice guy to talk with, who smells wonderful, by the way. How have you not tasted that yet?" he says, catching up with me again, wearing a devious half-smile.

"Are you serious?" I stop running, now only yards from the edge of town. A fierce protectiveness is rising within me. "What do you want from him?"

"Cool it, love. Nothing to get huffy about." He faces me and grabs my left hand gently running his thumb over the place my wedding ring used to be. "Just seeing what I'm up against is all."

I snatch my hand back. "What is that supposed to mean?"

"We have forever to worry about that, remember?" Still smiling, he walks on ahead.

"We need to talk about what happened on Monday," I say, still standing firm and feeling the need to redefine lines.

He pauses and turns around. Good. That wiped the smile off his face. "I already apologized for kissing you."

"I know, but what I am concerned about is you not hearing me when I say how much I need you right now as a friend. You friending my husband to get a feel for what you're 'up against' doesn't seem very friendly."

"Well, it's true. Do you plan on changing him?" he asks. "Because I get the feeling you love him and wouldn't wish this life on him, am I right?"

"If he wanted this— maybe, I don't know." The truth is, he's right, again. Phil has already mentioned not wanting to live forever if given the choice. A minivan drives down the otherwise deserted road. I turn my head away and wait as it passes. "Regardless, right now he is here with me, and I love my husband and my girls. They are my whole life, my reason for living. They are the reason I killed that poor deer. You can't just run in, save my life, and expect me to leave them behind."

He takes a breath, for effect, I'm sure, and looks me in the eyes. "You're right, I'm sorry. Friends?" he asks with a large grin, leaning in for a hug.

"Just friends," I say. He embraces me, but his hug makes him a liar as he presses his hips against mine just like he did last night. Once again I find myself melting at his touch. And worst of all, I enjoy it. My mind drifts as I imagine what it would be like to give in, to sink my mouth into his, let him tangle his hands through my hair. Then reality pulls me back.

Pushing myself away from him I repeat, "Just. Friends."

"All right." He nods, seriously.

I stare at him a moment longer, unconvinced until he motions us forward. We start walking, reaching the neighborhood section of town.

It's too quiet, somehow. I blurt out, "Did you ever find who changed you?"

"I'd rather discuss your tasering technique." His eyes turn sad, and his brow furrows as if the memory still hurts all these years later.

"Please?" I ask as we near the start of my— our— street. The desire to know who else is out there is growing. We can't be the only two creatures like us in the world. "I was wondering about the violence happening around this usually quiet town. People being murdered, gruesomely at that. Are there more like us, here?"

He sighs, relaxing his forehead and giving in. "After being rejected by my wife I ran off to the mines and spent years alone, hating what I had become. Not knowing what else to do, I put that energy into mining in hopes of building wealth for my eternal future. Yet I found myself constantly fighting this strange, compelling urge to find the one who made me. No matter how hard I tried to ignore it, something inside me was drawing me to the creature. Only I didn't know where it was drawing me to." He stops, and I think I understand what he means. This draw I have to him is one I can't ignore, no matter how hard I try.

We're at my front door. It's six-forty-three and he still didn't answer my question. "So you never found who did this to you?"

"Don't you need to go be a mum now?" Agitated he motions his hands up the path toward my front door.

I stare back, hopeful he will share more of his story.

Donovan sighs then answers, "No, I never found who did this to me. Happy?" He pauses, his eyes drifting back to the hills we came from. Something tells me he isn't telling me everything.

"But what about others?" I beg, wondering if other creatures might be around here and what threat they could pose to my family.

"Speaking of butts, you have a nice one." He forces a laugh, switching the subject. He doesn't want to talk about it now, fine. I'll get it out of him sooner or later.

"You are impossible. Same time tomorrow?"

"I'll be counting the seconds till I see you again, *friend*." In a flash, he's gone.

As I sneak into the kitchen, still dim from the early morning light, I'm welcomed by a familiar heartbeat. Only it's racing. Phil sits at the table, arms are crossed in front of his chest as he leans back into his chair, his blood now smelling clear of alcohol.

"And how's Mr. Tipsy feeling?" I ask timidly, he doesn't look well.

"Not great. I woke up to find you gone . . . again, and now you're back and a mess." Phil gestures with his hand in exasperation. "I thought I said it wasn't safe to be out? Do you have any idea what this does to me?"

"I went running with Donovan, remember?" Playing up the innocent card, hoping to calm the angry tension sizzling out of him. I look down at my shirt at the dark-brown streaks of blood mixed with dirt all over the front of me. I don't want to know what my face looks like.

"The new guy down the street?" A look of confusion crosses Phil's face, followed by agitation. "You just met him last night— I just met him last night!"

"Do you not remember our discussion?" The mess all over me will have to wait.

Phil tents his fingers over his eyes. The aspirin must not be working. "I remember being at the bar with the guys for the new girl we hired. Then meeting Donovan, that really great wine he brought over, and me telling you it's not safe to run." He drops his hands back on the table. "Yet off you go running— is that blood on your neck?" He takes a deep breath, his heart rate speeds up.

"Oh, I tripped but I'm fine." I rub at my neck with my hands. "Don't you remember? You didn't want me to run *alone*, and Donovan offered to run with me. I thought this was okay with you. At least you were happy about it last night; his offer had you in tears— did you say new *girl?*" My stomach flips as I watch him sit back in his chair, most likely running through his memory of last night.

"Right, okay. My head hurts, I need a shower and by the looks of it so do you," he says. Ignoring my question, he gets up from the table and heads toward the hall.

"Wait a minute. I want to hear about this new *girl*. You never mentioned the new guy was a woman," I hiss, keeping my voice quiet as we pass the girls' room, then continue down the hall to our room, where I close the door behind us.

"Why does it matter? You jealous or something?" he asks with a strange, flirty smile. He takes off his shirt and pants, tossing them along with his frustration on the bed.

Me, jealous? What do I have to be jealous of? I'm only feeling slightly betrayed he didn't tell me it was a woman in the first place. "No, I'm just surprised you were out with another woman and didn't think to tell me."

"I wasn't *out* with another woman. It was with a bunch of us from the firehouse, welcoming the new hire. Like we always do," he says, brow furrowed, arms crossed, as he stands opposite me in his boxer briefs.

Is this what this new girl will get to see every time

they work together? I look over his toned, tall body. I am not okay with him sharing a firehouse with another woman. So yes, I am jealous and a complete hypocrite. "Well, you failed to mention the part about her being a woman," I huff, sitting down on the edge of the bed.

"Oh, like you're one to talk. What about your running buddy? You don't see me having a problem with that now, do you?" He hastily grabs clean clothes from the dresser.

"Is that what this is about? What am I supposed to do? You won't let me run by myself!" I say, feeling more misled by the minute.

He's pacing now. "Uh, well, I don't know, maybe instead of running from your problems you could call the therapist from the hospital back."

"Well, you survive a plane crash and tell me how you feel!" I sit back against the headboard and hug a pillow, realizing too late that I'm covered in deer blood and it's now on my pillow— dammit, more laundry. I throw the pillow off the bed.

"Give me one reason why talking to a doctor, who's trained to help trauma victims, won't help you?" Phil softens his tone and comes to sit near me on the bed, lifting my hands off the comforter and holding them in his, talking at me like I'm some child. I know how hard this must be for him. But currently my frustration is getting the best of me and I literally do bite.

I fake the calmest voice I can find. "You know what's not helping? The idea of you sharing a fire-house with another woman!" I stand up, wishing to not be in the same room as him right now. Who knows what I might do while angry.

"Why does she have anything to do with this?"

"I don't like you not mentioning she was a woman." I take an unneeded breath and count to five in hopes of calming my jealous rage. "I don't like you not inviting me to have drinks like you usually do. Why can't you support me in what I feel helps me best?"

"First of all, I always invite you and you never want to come, last night my phone died. Second, how has everything I've done for you not been supportive? Your erratic behavior, sneaking out at all hours of the night. I've been supportive by giving you privacy, letting you work through this on your own timing, because clearly, you haven't needed me."

Shame wells up within me. "Of course I need you. I couldn't have survived this without you." Thanks to my complicated relationship with Dono-van, I'm starting to assume the worst when it comes to male-female friendships.

"I can't help but feel there's something you aren't telling me. Like it's trapped inside somewhere. Like what happened to you the night we found you lying in the road?" Tears well up in his blue eyes, and his face is full of hurt.

"I— I just can't. I'm sorry." I walk over to his half-naked body and give him a hug. The sensation of his body warming mine, as well as the smell of his fading deodorant mixed with leftover wine, comforts me. I breathe him in, but not without my constant dull burn to remind me of what I really am. God, I hate this. I hate my secrets. It's been less than a week and already they're tearing us apart. Us— the whole reason for everything I've done. I even killed a deer— with a taser— for us, and it's all falling to pieces in front of me. I just wish the truth would help.

He takes a deep breath. "I'm sorry, too. You have been through more than I can imagine. And if running helps, then run." He kisses the top of my head and then, after a moment, adds, "I trust you."

His kiss brings me comfort, but I can't help but feel the hesitation hidden in his words.

He shimmies off his boxer briefs and tosses them in the laundry basket. "I'll be in the shower." Standing naked, he gives me a sad smile and disappears into the bathroom, flicking on the light as he closes the door.

The words, *I trust you*, stab deep. I can't think of that last honest excuse I gave of where I was going since the crash. Since then, it's been nothing but lies. I'm beginning to question whether I'm doing this for love or for my own selfish desire to hold off the inevitable of losing him and the girls. Am I simply living a bittersweet fantasy life? A life I thought I could hold on to? This illusion is only made possible with lies and secrets, with each lie thickening a wall I'm forced to build in order to keep the life I once had, all while severing the closeness I long to keep. Donovan's words, like poison, flow through my mind: *I can be your forever.* Donovan, the only one who can truly pass through my walls.

THE KISS OF DEATH

Imogene is at school. Wednesdays are usually her favorite day because she gets to do office runs for Ms. Cooper. Davina persuaded Phil to a park date, which I gladly encouraged, even though the sky is threatening rain again. I need some time alone to think, to sort out these strange, ever-growing feelings for someone who's not my husband. I'm also in desperate need of a shower.

I lock all the doors, clean up the mess of our rushed morning, and start a load of laundry, throwing in the bedsheets I so carelessly sat on while arguing with Phil. I throw out the deer-blood-stained pillowcase, knowing that stain will never wash out. I don't want to remember what I did to that poor deer every time I see its blood stained on my bed.

The house is quiet as I stand in the shower alone,

my hair full of shampoo, attempting to scrub away the filth growing inside me. Thoughts of Phil and I in this same shower following our passion-filled morning the day of the plane crash rush into my mind. Standing together under this waterfall of mixed emotions, I imagine his arms embracing me from behind. If he were here now, the front of his body would be against my back, while his firm yet soft hands could explore the new-to-him smoothness of my miraculously healed belly. Right now, I want nothing more than to feel his hot breath on the back of my neck as he exhales with each kiss he gives, sending chills down my spine that excite every inch of my cold skin. Imagining the sound of his heart beating with passion for the wife he loves and trusts— a trust I worry I don't deserve to have. The new girl at the fire station rudely pushes her way into my fantasy, shattering my otherwise pleasant thoughts. I have no clue what she looks like, but I can only imagine a fit, hot firefighter, centerfold-of-the-station type. A small, jealous flame, like a match, lights deep within my frozen heart.

Hot water pours down my back as my tumultuous mind runs wild with fabricated stories, only amplifying these unnecessary thoughts about a woman I've never met. Could it be Phil was hiding the fact the new hire was a woman to protect me? Or was he hoping I might never find out? Which is silly to think

— I know a lot about what goes on around the station; you can't hide things in a small town for long.

I try to stop my insecurities from growing like cancer, invading my every thought. I rinse the shampoo from my hair, visualizing the jealousy washing from me as well. Phil hasn't done anything wrong, and in reality, he probably didn't think it a big deal that the new hire was a woman. I wouldn't have given it a second thought if she was a man, but my insecurities are getting the best of me today. The truth about what I am is bound to leak out eventually, and what if Phil does leave me? Any sane person would, right? He deserves someone he can grow old with, and I will never grow old. Angry, bitter tears pour from my eyes and trickle down my body, mixing with the swirling water headed down the drain, much like my future. I slide down the wall to the shower floor, wishing I could melt into the drain myself.

The creak of the front door pulls me off the shower floor and back to the task. The bathroom door opens. I squeeze out a healthy portion of conditioner to make up for how long I left the shampoo in.

"Back so soon? Did it start raining or something?" I ask, sniffling away my tears while squishing the conditioner through the ends of my hair. No one answers. It must have been Davina on one of her ninja missions or something.

The light, airy scent of my conditioner soothes my unrest, reminding me of a day at the spa. Only I don't remember it smelling quite so musky until I realize what I'm smelling is more than my conditioner, it's Donovan.

"Donovan!" I hiss, mostly to myself, but knowing he'll hear it if he is here.

No answer again, but I'm certain that's his cologne floating in the air. Quickly, I rinse the conditioner from my hair, turn off the water, and open the shower door just enough to poke my head out. The bathroom is empty, but the bathroom door has definitely been opened by someone. I listen for the sounds of Davina or Phil, hearing nothing except the quiet emptiness of the house. I reach out for my towel, but my hand hits the cold, hard wall under the towel bar instead. I look down. No towel on the floor; it's nowhere to be found.

"Missing something?" Through the partially opened shower door, I see a hand pop into the doorway of the bathroom, holding my grey towel.

"Seriously? I am in no mood for this right now." I growl, still hiding behind the frosted glass.

The hand dangles my towel. "I won't look, I swear." And although I can't see it, I can feel Donovan's smile plastered to his smug face.

"Why are you here?" I inch out of the shower and pressing myself against the wall to stay out of view from the bathroom door. I don't want him seeing anything he might hope to be seeing.

"There's something I need to tell you."

Snatching the towel from his hand, I wrap it tightly around me. "And you had to tell me now? I just saw you an hour ago. Can't it wait till I get dressed?"

Donovan comes around the corner and leans against the doorframe. He smiles like this is some fun game. "Aileen, I've been around over a hundred years; it's nothing I haven't seen."

I narrow my eyes at him. "What is it that's so important?"

He advances toward me. The bathroom isn't that big; he's inches from me in two seconds.

I take a step back, he stops. Sadness sets into his dark eyes as he stares into mine, both our feet frozen where we stand and again my feelings for him engage like a magnet and I want him closer.

"I'm sorry," he says. "The smell of your shampoo reminds me of . . . " He stops and stares as if lost in a memory.

"Your wife?" I tighten the towel around me even more, straining to keep an ear out for Phil's imminent arrival.

"I haven't spoken of her in over a century, and now thanks to you . . ." He looks down at the floor.

Something about his sadness, in this moment, captivates me. Maybe it's my own sadness connecting to his, or perhaps when he's sad it's the only time he seems human. I walk toward him, drawn to him by this hold he has on my dead heart. His eyes showing gentler emotions, ones I've yet to see from him. I place my hand on the side of his strong cheek. He leans his head into my hand as I take his sadness on as my own. Like we become the same person each time we touch.

"What did you need to tell me, Donovan?" I ask again, softer, questioning why I'm still standing here. But I can't make myself leave his presence.

"You have captured my heart, consumed my every thought. I can't even hunt without your voice saying not to harm people echoing in my mind— Aileen, you are making me human again." He places his hand on my cheek. "And I don't know what to do about that."

His hand is gentle, reminding me of the comfort it brought me on the plane. My mind goes numb, and all the feelings I've been fighting for him rage through me unbridled. Feelings I haven't felt since the first time I met Phil. But I don't love Donovan, do I? I can't. The bathroom swirls around us and nothing else matters, and for a moment it's as if we are the only people left in the world.

I drop my hand from his face, and he drops his from mine, breaking me from this trance as a new kind of fear streaks through me. A fear of what this deep, primal part of me wants. I find my resolve and take control of my thoughts, pushing aside the monster taking over within me.

"So you break into my house and steal my towel while I'm in the shower because you don't like feeling human?" Now perplexed as to why he's really here.

He shrugs while managing to look contrite. "I guess so. I'm sorry, I shouldn't have come."

The sadness in his eyes deepens, hurt spreading across his brow as he turns to leave. It tugs at my heartstrings.

"It's okay to be human." It's good to encourage his humanity, right? If he can be human, then there is hope for me too.

He stops and adjusts the lapel on his jacket as he turns to face me, grabbing my hand. "Well darling, I don't know if I like it, that's all."

I look up into his deep brown eyes, so soft, so vulnerable. An overwhelming need to hold him in my arms, to repay the comfort he brought me on the plane, for this odd new life he's gifted me, wants to burst out of my skin.

"I do," I reply. "Human looks good on you." I catch myself biting my bottom lip and stop, but it's too late; the monster within me who wants Donovan tears herself loose from my hold. He sees it as an invitation and in a flash, backs me up against the cold glass shower door. This new fear of my primal self and what it's capable of grows but is quickly overpowered by an even more sinister, animal desire, shutting off any of my better senses.

Breathless he asks, "Will you teach me? I fear I

might have forgotten how."

I grip my towel, my hand wedged between my chest, his body firmly pressed against me. As he leans his head in, resting his forehead on mine, he whispers with a voice like velvet, "Will you?" His lips hover so near the exhale of his request tickles my lips.

My mind goes numb as all propriety ceases to exist. I'm no longer here, in my bathroom with a devastatingly beautiful Donovan. The Aileen I'm fighting so hard to hold on to suddenly disappears without a trace. And before I can stop myself, my chin tips up to his face.

Electricity ignites as our lips collide and we both lose ourselves in each other. I wrap my arms up around his neck, threading my fingers through his thick, soft hair. His hands eagerly slide up and down my back, pulling me tight up against him. My towel falls to my feet. I let it. The soft leather of his jacket brushes up against my naked chest and a burning passion for more than just this kiss of death rages within me.

My better senses return. I need to stop, but I want to keep going. I tear my lips away from his, as an instant sting of regret reverberates in my still fuzzy brain.

"You are so beautiful." He leans back in for more.

"I can't do this," I whisper, kneeling down to I grab my towel off the floor. I wrap it around my shame, unable to look him in his cold, sad eyes, afraid that if I do I'll only lose myself further.

He doesn't say a word and I watch his black combat-style boots as they back away toward the door. Tears fall from my cheeks as the breeze of him leaving blows gently against my wet hair. What is wrong with me? With him, there's no telling what I might do. And this terrifies me more than anything.

Eventually, I get up, splash some water on my face in hopes of washing off the kiss, but it's no use. My lips still burn from the slight scruff of his upper lip. What's done is done. I dress in another pair of yoga pants and a wrinkled shirt I dug out of the clean, to-be-folded pile by my bed. Mixed with Donovan's signature scent left floating in the air is an even more desirable one coming from a familiar red thermos sitting on Phil's nightstand by the bathroom door. A sticky note on it reads, *"Thought you could use this later. Love, D."*

I want to be repulsed by the note and all things related to him, but I can't. Instead I grab the thermos. The now-familiar metal smooth under my hand. Temptation emanating from the lid. I take a sip; it's still warm, but I don't care about who or where this came from. At this moment I don't care about anything. My animal senses take over again as they did with the bear and the deer— and Donovan— and I douse the flames of my hunger, lust, and guilt, drinking every last drop.

Now I am far from satisfied and my insides hurt as if they were being split in two. My old self struggles to find balance with this monster I am. This monster that daily grows stronger, more primal, closer to taking over without fear of consequence.

I'm not just losing control, I'm losing myself.

18

POINTING FINGERS

The lock turns in the front door as I rinse out the last bit of blood from the empty thermos and stash it under the bathroom sink alongside my dignity. The front door creaks open, then slams shut as small feet patter across the kitchen floor. The TV turns on, soon joined by giggles from a little girl watching her favorite show. I wonder where Phil is; his footsteps were unaccounted for with Davina's. I look out my bedroom window, which faces the front yard. Phil and Sheriff Jon are talking at the end of the driveway, Jon's cruiser parked more crooked than usual. Phil's back is to me, muffling the words exchanged. I crack the window to listen.

"It was written with the teeth?" Phil asks, "and you're sure they are human?"

"Looked pretty darn human to me, I'd have to see the official report to confirm. The fingers were certainly human." Jon says, his eyes weary as if he's on the brink of exhaustion.

My stomach churns; it's either the talk of teeth and human fingers, or my guilt from kissing a man that isn't my husband. Maybe a little of both I'd assume. My phone dings. I grab it off the top of my dresser, sit's Donovan.

007: We need to talk, now.

No annoying note, no weird, kissy-cat emoji.

Why?

007: Are you okay? Is everyone okay?

We're fine, why?

007: Say you need to go for a run.

I don't think that's a good idea.

The last thing I want is to be alone with him again. No telling what this monster inside me will do. I peek back out the window at Phil and Jon.

"Does this have any connection to your Jane Doe?" Phil runs his hand nervously through his hair. "And no clue at all as to who might be behind this?"

Jane Doe? Teeth, fingers, they did mention her teeth were missing as well as fingers. My stomach churns again, could a monster even worse than me, worse than Donovan, be on the loose? Who else would do such a thing aside from a serial killer?

007: Forget about earlier. This is important. Please?

How important?

The sheriff's voice booms in through the window. "Nothing yet on who's behind this, but school is canceled till further notice."

007: Very.

Life and death very?

Seconds pass with no reply, only the dot, dot, dot waving back and forth, stopping then reappearing then stopping again in the message window until he finally sends back a simple *Yes*.

I stash my phone in the waistband of my yoga pants and dash out of my room, through the living room past Davina, hoping she won't see me, and stop at the front door. Before I open it and step outside, I take a deep breath. What happened with Donovan earlier can be dealt with another time; right now I need to know what's going on and decide whether it's worth risking my fidelity to meet with him. Phil turns around to look at me as I open the creaky front door, but I can't bring myself to look at him. Jon offers a very forced half-smile. Something big is happening.

"Why is school canceled?" I ask, trying to ignoring the shake in my voice as I walk up to them.

"Are you okay?" Phil's face is creased with concern. "You look like a ghost."

"I've been better. I heard you talking through the window, something about human teeth and fingers, and school being canceled. Please tell me what's going on. I'm freaking out."

Jon clears his throat. "Someone left a note, of sorts written in teeth and fingers on the elementary school blacktop."

"What?" My stomach twists.

He nods. "Yup. Sometime between school starting and the first recess. Thankfully a yard duty found it first. They're sending the kids home as a precaution." He must see the panic forming on my face because he quickly adds, "Don't worry, Ana is on her way with Imogene."

Relief washes over me knowing Imogene and the other children are safe. But whoever did this is sick, evil maybe and I can't help but think it's related to Donovan's wanting to talk. He wouldn't do this, would he? He may be trouble, but he's not evil.

"The scary part is how much this might be related

to our Jane, and the elderly woman, only there were far more fingers and teeth than just two bodies. But why do this at the school?" the sheriff asks, rubbing his fingers on his mustache as he thinks out loud.

Something lukewarm rises up into my throat, and I choke it back down. There are more bodies?

"Are you sure you're all right?" Phil asks.

"I'm fine." I nod my head, thankful the thermos full of blood seems to be settling in my stomach— for now. Turning to Jon, I ask, "What did the note say?"

He fiddles with his badge for a moment before answering. "Eh, it's pretty cryptic, some weird something-or-other."

I frown, hoping he will explain further, but he doesn't.

Jon clears his throat to break the awkward silence. He's already shared more than he should. "Well, I best be going. Take care, guys, and hey, Aileen?"

"Hmm?"

"Listen to Phil about not running alone. We'll figure this out soon."

"Thanks, Jon, you're a good friend," Phil says, waving as the sheriff walks back to his squad SUV.

"Oh, by the way, good for you guys hiring a woman! I hear she's very exotic-looking. Wonder if she's single." Jon grins as he shuts his car door.

Phil cringes when I give him a look.

Jon drives off just as Ana pulls up with Imogene. I ignore what Jon said about miss exotic firefighter and rush over to Ana's car, relieved to know for certain Imogene is safe.

"You okay, honey?" I ask, looking her over for blood, marks, any kind of familiar or unfamiliar scents.

"I'm fine! Why are you smelling me?" she says with a smile, seemingly unaware. "They canceled school today!" she adds. "For the rest of the week even!"

"Go inside with your sister," Ana tells Imogene. Her hands are shaking as she gives Imogene her backpack.

It must be bad if Ana's rattled. The three of us adults stand in the driveway, silent until Imogene is safe inside, the door shut behind her.

"Well, what did Jonny have to say?" Ana asks, trying to mask the quiver in her voice, looking as if she's on the verge of tears. "It's a mess over there with parents and police. People talking about hearing there's dead—" Ana pauses, her voice growing higher as a tear escapes, "kids on the blacktop, and, and something about a bloody note reading, *You're mine, forever*—"

"No, mom. Fingers. There was a note written in fingers and teeth, adult ones. The kids are all fine," Phil interrupts.

I swallow back the disgust, even so. Fingers and teeth are pretty horrible, either way. They belonged to someone at some point.

"Oh thank God!" Ana cries. "Parents are going crazy over there. I was scared out of my mind! I had no idea what to tell Imogene. She kept asking why all the sheriffs were at school. The poor girl's been through enough these last few weeks." Ana glances at me. "Are you okay, dear? You look pale."

"I'm fine, Ana." But my thoughts center back on the note. I'm not sure why it would be, but I can't help but wonder if somehow, it was meant for me.

She hesitates, then focuses her attention back to Phil. I head back inside the house and watch them from the kitchen window as I compulsively crush a fistful of beans to make a fresh pot of coffee, figuring out my options for getting out to get some answers from Donovan. My only option would be to just leave, but I can't do that to my family, not now. And I'd say right now is not an appropriate time to tell Phil I'm going for a run.

From here I can see Phil and Ana still talking outside in the driveway, with the addition of Mr. Gerigson, who must be wanting in on the town gossip. I slap the last of grounds from my hands into the French press and heat some water on the stove. The landline rings, and I turn towards it curiously. It never rings; the only reason we have one is for power outages. I let it go to voicemail. After the beep, a familiar and pleasant female voice floats through the speaker.

"*Hello, this message is for Aileen Ross. This is Angela*

Summers calling from the National Transportation Safety Board
—" A wave of nausea passes through me, sending me
diving toward the sink as my stomach empties everything from the thermos and the deer down the drain.
Could today get any worse?

The door opens, and Phil and Ana walk in just as
the message is ending.

"Who was that?" Phil asks.

"The NTSB again," I reply, hoping no bloody
remnants are dribbling down my chin. I drag the back
of my hand across my mouth just in case.

"You really should talk to them and get it over
with. It will help in their investigation of the crash,"
Phil says, grabbing four plates out of the cupboard
and placing them on the counter.

"What's there to say— really bad storm, plus
plane, plus bad luck, equals plane crash?" What more
is there to think of it? I pour hot water into the coffee
press and focus on the swelling grounds rising up on
the water.

"Maybe they think the cause of the crash was
more than the storm," Phil says ominously. "You are
their only witness after all."

His words make me stop still. My stomach drops
at the thought. Of course it was the storm. It is ridiculous to think otherwise. But... what if he's right? I
push the idea aside, convincing myself it's the stress of
the murders getting to me.

"Want some coffee?" I ask Ana, abruptly.

Before she darts her way off to the bathroom she nods. "Yes please."

"How about you?" I ask Phil.

"No. Want me to make you some lunch?" He walks past me to the refrigerator and opens the door. I hold my breath to let the pent-up smelly food air disperse for a moment.

"I'll stick with coffee for now."

"You sure?" he asks, peeking at me over the open refrigerator door. "And are you sure you're feeling okay? You do look pale."

"Yeah, I'm fine," I answer, wondering if all he recognizes about my new self is my less-than-alive skin tone.

He eyes me for another minute, then pulls out peanut butter and strawberry jam. I'm relieved once the refrigerator door shuts and thankful he picked the less stinky lunch option. I grab the bread next to the coffee press on the counter and slide it over to Phil. He fumbles with the jar in his hand, shouting as it falls. Without thinking, in a flash, I grab the falling jar and set it back on the counter. Just barely avoiding a sticky, glass-laden mess all over the kitchen floor. Phil stares at me the same way Ms. Cooper did the other day at school when I moved too fast to stop the pile on her desk from toppling, his wrinkled brow splattered with questions.

"What? You okay? You're looking at me weird." I

play innocent, hoping he will ignore what just took place.

"How'd you do that?" he asks, his face frozen in confusion, my question unheard.

"Do what?" I play dumb, pouring the hot water into the coffee press.

"The jar, it was falling one second, and now it's on the counter by your hand."

"I don't know what you're talking about," I reply, taking a mug from the cupboard.

"The jar, the jar! How's it back on the counter? You saw it fall, right?" His face is flushed, eyes wide in disbelief.

I'd laugh if I weren't so scared of revealing myself to him.

I pull another cup from the cupboard and motion toward him. "Are you sure you're not still drunk from last night? Coffee?"

"No." He doesn't look amused. "I swear the jar just fell!" He grabs a fistful of his sandy blond hair, and for a second, I fear he might rip it right out.

"The jar looks fine to me, right on the counter where you left it."

Ana enters the room, gives her son a double-take, and her face takes on his same quizzical expression. She looks from him to me, "Everything okay?"

I shrug my shoulders and give her an I-don't-know smile as I press down on the coffee plunger for the

French press. She pats Phil on the shoulder and takes over the sandwich-making.

"You want one too, Phil? Or just the girls?"

"Huh?" He snaps out of his trance. "Oh right. Yes, please. Thanks, Mom," he adds as he walks over to the kitchen table, shaking his head and muttering to himself.

"You aren't yourself, Philbert. If I didn't know any better . . . " Ana swoops over and squishes his cheeks between her hands and stares him in the eyes. "Let me smell your breath!" she demands.

"Mom! What are you doing?" Phil says, trying to wiggle his way out of her iron grip. "I'm fine. God, you haven't done that to me since High School."

She narrows her eyes. "Is something going on? Are you high?"

I stand back against the counter and watch Ana, imagining what she would have been like as a mom in high school— her stern, reddening face and slit eyes that burned into Phil for information seconds ago. I want to laugh, especially since he's only in shock from an unexplained teleporting jelly jar, but now would not be the appropriate time.

"Mom, I'm not high. What in the world would make you think that?" He slowly sits back in his chair, away from his mother.

"I just don't know! I walk in here, you had this crazed and dazed look on your face. This day has got me all up in a tizzy. Here's your sandwich," she says curtly, as she grabs a plate off the counter and plops a half-made peanut butter jelly in front of Phil, then storms out of the room. I hear her quickening stomps as she makes her way back to the bathroom and quietly shuts the door. Not typical for Ana to present less-than-best food.

I stifle a laugh. "Wow, I'd hate to have been you in high school."

He glares at me. "What is going on here? Jars are falling then not falling. My mother is so upset she's losing her mind."

I don't know what to say. The truth would be helpful right now, right? Or would it? Donovan's wife leaving him after he told her the truth makes me think otherwise.

Phil waits on the other side of the table, then continues. "Ever since you've come home things have been off. And not just-tragedy-happened-to-you off— it's almost as if—" he stops.

"As if what?" I hold my breath.

"Almost as if you're changing into a completely different person."

His eyes meet mine and I swallow down a sob. He's one hundred percent right. But this hasn't just changed just me; I can see now, it's changing him too, it's changing us. The way he looks at me and acts around me is different since the plane crash. The room begins to close in on me as the sound of cartoons, giggles, and Phil's breathing swarm around me. I could tell him everything— I should do it. Just open my mouth and say it out loud.

I stand up and gather my nerve. "I am—"

A siren blares from Phil's pocket, his ringtone for work. He answers and I hear a woman's voice on the other end; it must be the new-hire. Her voice sounds sweet, almost familiar, and worst of all it carries a hint of sexy. So she's exotic and sexy, great. "Where's the chief? Okay Indy, I'll be right there." He slips his phone back into his pocket.

"So, they need to you fill in?"

"Indy just asked if I could fill in until tomorrow afternoon. Jake is taking the day off, some family emergency," he says, removing his running shoes.

"Uh-huh," escapes my lips.

"What's wrong?"

My face must be showing my feelings more than I'd like it to. "Nothing's wrong." I look down at my fingers to find any imperfections to pick at. Of course they're nothing short of perfect.

"Are you still being weird about the new-hire being a woman? You can come down and meet her if you'd like. If that will make you feel better."

The thought of facing Miss Exotic Sexy Fire-fighter Pants makes my stomach turn. I pick at my perfect nails anyway. In all reality, there is nothing he can say to help me shake this jealousy. "No. I'm fine, really."

Phil looks at me, unconvinced. "You're not okay.

If it helps, she sleeps in her own area of the fire-house." He walks off to grab his work shoes from the laundry room.

"Be safe, that's all I care about. This chick is the least of my worries with a job like you have."

He sits back down in a dining chair for a moment, to slip on his shoes. "You two would probably get along well, you know." He then stands up and walks toward the hall to get his bag, already packed for his shift. "You're both stubborn."

"So, you know her well enough to know she's stubborn?" I can't help it— it slips out of my mouth and by the hurt in his eyes, I wish I'd kept it in my head.

"You really want to go there?" He pokes his head out from the hallway. I may as well have slapped him seeing the injury written across his face. Fighting won't help me feel any better. No need to give him a reason to cozy up to anyone else.

"Sorry, it's fine, really. I trust you." I muster up the most honest smile I can without baring teeth. "Be careful, okay?"

He disappears down the hall to say goodbye to the girls. I'm seriously contemplating changing my stance on using humans as a food source. Indy might make a sweet treat. But the truth is, I'm the one not to be trusted. Shame tingles from my lips recalling Dono-van's mouth on mine. At this point, if anyone needs to worry about our marriage, it's Phil.

Ana creeps into the kitchen. "Everything okay, sweetie?"

"Everything's fine," I say, trying to make my voice sound normal, standing up to grab Phil's plate of the half-eaten sandwich.

"He's a good man, honey. You have nothing to worry about. Plus, you know I'd paint his backside red if he ever hurt you in any way. I threatened him with that on your wedding day." She smiles, giving me a wink and a pat on the back. "I love my boys, but you were the daughter I always longed for."

"I know Ana, thank you." Now I'm terrified of what she'd do if she knew what I was doing earlier this morning. Actually, she might be more upset about me killing a deer than kissing another man.

"Can I get you anything?"

"No, thank you."

When she heads back to the living room, I let loose a frustrated breath, and settle down into one of the chairs at the kitchen table, dropping my head on top of it harder than I realize. A loud crack and pop erupts and wood splinters under my forehead. Clearly, I don't know my own strength. I stair at the crack stretching from where my head landed into the middle of the table. "Shoot."

Footsteps speed down the hall. I quickly try to cover the crack with Phil's plate and stand up, away from it.

Ana rushes back into the kitchen, eyes wide. "You okay? I thought I heard something break!"

"Must have been something outside." I hastily shove a bite of Phil's nasty half-eaten sandwich into my mouth. What's more normal than eating lunch, right? Only it's tastes like sandpaper that's been dragged through dirty dishwater.

"All right, just checking." On her way out, she almost bumps into Phil. I take the second to spit out the chunk of sandwich into the napkin on the table by Phil's plate.

"What was that sound?" Phil asks as he slings the overnight bag over his shoulder.

"Must have been something outside," Ana says, giving her son a hug. "You be careful at work, dear."

He kisses her on the cheek. "I always am, Ma."

I make my way over to them hoping not to draw attention to the crack in the table and stand beside Phil.

"I'll just leave you two alone." Ana winks and hurries back into the living room.

"I'm sorry." I give Phil a hug. His warm arms tighten around me while I try my best not to burst out crying or squeeze him too hard again. "I don't mean to act so jealously."

"It's okay," he says, kissing me on the forehead. "I love you."

Sniffling, I step back, wiping my nose with the back of my hand. "I love you too."

"Try and have some fun while I'm gone. Okay? It might help you feel better."

"Maybe I'll take the girls shopping in El Dorado. I promised them costumes." Getting out of town sounds like a good idea. Give me some space away from anywhere Donovan might be.

"They'll like that." He smiles. Then he heads out the door.

19

PANIC IN AISLE FIVE

E ven for a Thursday afternoon, Target's parking lot in El Dorado is no joke. People scattering to and fro, grabbing their last-minute costumes and treats for the weekend's festivities. At least I'm not the only one who waited.

We find a spot further out than necessary because I don't like to cram my van into tight spots just to be closer. With my venti cup of coffee I grabbed at a drive-thru Starbucks on my way into town in one hand, my girls both trying to hold my other, I'm pulled toward the bright red-and-white bulls-eye if Target. I pause to take a sip; here goes nothing.

"Come on, Mom!" Imogene scolds as we walk through the automatic glass doors.

As we step into Target, I'm blasted with every delicious scent imaginable. Donovan was right about the variation in human blood. From sweet to spicy, the range is like stepping into a world market of culinary delicacies. I take another drink of coffee and hold my breath as we search for where they're hiding the Halloween items.

The barren costume aisle doesn't look promising. It's already been moved to the back corner of the store to make room for Christmas decorations. Forget Thanksgiving— all those items are just as picked over, joining Halloween in the corner. Note to self: buy Halloween costumes and Thanksgiving decorations in summer next year. At least now they're all fifty percent off.

"Mom! Mom! Look!" Davina squeals, holding a black-and-purple Dracula-style cape accompanied by fake blood capsules and a wooden stake attached to the hanger.

Laughter bursts out deep from my gut at the ridiculous caricature of a cheaply made Dracula costume. "What happened to being a ninja?"

"I want this! I want to be a blood-sucking vampire!" She lets out a wicked laugh.

"Where in the world did you learn about blood-sucking vampires?" I ask, shocked. Last I checked, she's never even watched a scary movie.

"Sissy told me." She sticks her tongue out at Imogene.

"Where did *you* learn about it?" I redirect my focus to Imogene.

"Eric told me his daddy lets him watch scary

vampire movies." Oh, the joys of school-aged children.

Davina tugs on the edge of my shirt. "Please, Mommy! I want to be a vampire! I can be a good one! I promise I won't bite anyone!"

Part of me wants to slap it out of her hand and tell her no. Why would you choose this? But the sad, hope-filled look on her face makes it impossible for me to say no. Besides, she already has the plastic fangs.

"Okay, fine. *Good* vampire it is!" I wonder whether *good* and *vampire* are two words that can coexist at all.

"I already have my costume, Mom. I'll use the same one from last year," Imogene says, sounding once again way older than eight. I wish she'd just be an eight-year-old. Now, more than ever, I'm in no hurry for either of them to grow up too fast.

"Okay! We're all set then." Davina hands me her costume and as we turn to head toward check out an unwelcome fragrance wafts past my nose. My senses stand on edge and every muscle in my body is at full attention, ready for anything. Donovan is here. I don't want to see him— not now, not around the girls. Not with how I seem to lose control every time I'm with him. "Come on, quick. We need to go."

They seem to hear the urgency in my voice and their confused eyes stare into mine. I stuff the costume under my arm and grab their hands. As we rush past the toy aisles, Davina tries to stop by the Legos. I pull her away.

"What's wrong, Mommy?" Imogene asks, her voice nervous, probably from the quick pace I'm dragging them at.

"Everything's fine." I hesitate, slowing down a little. I don't want to scare them, but I don't know how strong this monster within me has grown. I can't control myself when I'm around him. What if I can't stop myself from kissing him, even in front of the girls? *Get ahold of yourself, Aileen.* I am stronger than this.

I change course, cutting through linens, the items on the shelves a blur as we whizz past as I try to outrun my demons. Doing all I can to find my resolve to face him, only if necessary. The girls shuffle their little feet, their legs barely keeping up with mine even with me slowing pace. Now, only yards away from the checkout stands, his scent grows stronger. I debate dashing away with the girls, I could tuck them each under an arm, no problem, and rush toward the safety of our car— but what if I'm wrong? Anyone could smell like that, right? I'm not sure my paranoia is real enough to expose my secrets to the world, especially to my children. But if it is him, he's here somewhere and close. I stop in the middle of the busy main store aisle and close my eyes.

Davina taps my arm, dancing in place. "I have to go potty."

"Shhh." I hold my hand up, smelling, listening, trying to calm myself down before I let him get the best of me.

"Where are you?" I whisper at the fluorescent lights above me. Surely I can control myself. Anger flashes through me, how dare he put me in this position. It was bad enough him coming to my house—befriending my husband— but to follow me when I'm out with my daughters?

"We're right here," Imogene says, looking at me like the crazy woman I am.

"Can I help you find anything, ma'am?" a young man's squeaky voice says to my right.

Relief washes over me at the sight of a tall, teenage store employee dressed in khakis and a red shirt. He peeks out timidly from behind the end cap next to the laundry aisle. I gather my frazzled thoughts with an almost deranged giggle as I realize he smells just like Donovan.

"Oh, no. I'm fine."

He gives me a nod and turns back to where he came from.

A thought comes to mind. "Wait!" I yell at the Target employee.

His eyebrows are raised, ready for my request. "Yes?"

"What cologne are you wearing?"

His heart rate speeds up as his face flushes. I've embarrassed him. "I— I have no idea," he says, the redness in his face growing deeper. "My mom bought it for me. I think it's from Macy's or somewhere fancy she shops."

"You smell very nice." And not just his cologne. Embarrassment, I notice, lets out an extra sweet almost sugary scent like melting caramel. His blush deepens, and I realize in horror he must think I'm flirting with him. Pulling the girls with me toward the front of the store, I head for the exit, almost running.

"Ma'am!" the young employee yells after me as we walk through the door, "EXCUSE ME, MA'AM!" Alarms blare as a couple other employees meet me at the front and I realize I've almost become a shoplifter in my distraction.

Mortified, I rush the girls and me to the checkout. The woman ringing me up gives me the stink-eye while I apologetically pay $39.99 for our nearly stolen, possibly inaccurate, last-minute Dracula costume. Of course, the costume she wanted was not one of the ones on sale.

BY THE TIME I got through purchasing my almost stolen goods, taking both girls to the restroom, buying them dinner from the Target food court, it's nearly six-thirty-p.m. by the time we leave El Dorado. The girls zone out on a movie as we drive home, front windows-down. The cool fall air clears my senses of all the overwhelming scents of Target. To the right of us a magnificent autumn sunset blankets the sky with cotton candy pink clouds that drift into the vibrant orange western horizon.

The blood-red sun reminds me of the poor Target employee and the sweet scent of his embarrassment. I can't go anywhere without the temptation of blood; I am a predator, sensing the fear and weakness in those around me. Is it only a matter of time before I completely become this monster inside me? How long can I keep myself together when I feel like I'm splitting in two? It hasn't even been a full week and already I fear I'm losing control. No answers come to mind, so instead, I clench the wheel and focus ahead on the coming twilight. Just as we reach the Amador County- El Dorado line, the first stars make their appearance as the sun finally sinks down behind the hills.

I pull into our driveway a little after seven-thirty, trying my best to prepare myself for another night alone with the girls. I can do this— I have to. They run inside and straight to their bedroom. Memories of those first few nights I spent home alone with newborn Imogene when Phil was in fire training flood my mind. How I'd stay up all hours of the night, knowing the minute I fall asleep she'd wake up and need me. How lonely those nights were, the TV my only companion. It was good at drowning out any worrisome noises I'd hear in the night. At least now I know I could hold my own against any scary noises. I find comfort in that.

I give out the bedtime orders as I shut and lock the front door. "Please brush your teeth and get in jammies; it's bedtime."

All I hear is giggling from Imogene while Davina makes muffled scary noises with— I can only assume — her vampire teeth.

"Please girls, you can play with your costumes tomorrow." Today has been overwhelming, and now all I want is for them to go to bed so I can have some quiet time to myself. Maybe I'll actually find a show I want to watch.

Begrudgingly, they get themselves ready for bed and the three of us sit together, one girl on either side of me, on Imogene's bed for our nighttime routine.

"Anyone want to tell me their favorite part of your day?"

"No school!" Imogene exclaims. Glad to know that was a positive part of her day. Had she known the real reason for school not being in session, that might be a different story.

"My favorite part was going to Target!" Davina says, bouncing on the comforter. A girl after her mom's own heart.

"I liked that part too," Imogene adds.

"Me too. Time to sleep now." I kiss Imogene on the forehead.

Davina looks at me with worry in her eyes.

I kiss her forehead too. "What's wrong, baby?"

"How long can people live?" She curls up tighter against me, her big blue eyes search mine. I'm not sure how ready I am to talk about such things. This would be a hard enough topic to talk about before my change, but now? What do I say when someone like me will live forever?

Imogene sits up, interjecting, "Most people don't make it past 75."

"That's not necessarily true." My voice is a whisper. "But why do you want to know?"

Davina is clearly disappointed by her sister's response. "I'm just trying to figure out how long people can live. You know, like a thousand years old?"

"Well, if you take good care of yourself, and you make good choices and eat healthy foods and be kind, then I think you could live to be over one hundred."

Her eyes widen in amazement as she mulls over what I just said to her. But who am I kidding? All of that is sadly untrue most of the time. I took care of myself, made good choices, except the choice to get on that plane. Technically speaking, someone like me can live more than a thousand years— or however long immortality is, I guess. But what good is immortality when one day everyone I ever loved will be gone and I'll still be here? Worst of all, in a thousand years, this current life of mine will have been but a moment, a quick flash in the light of eternity. Is it possible I could forget my beautiful, sweet girls in that expanse of time? Tears well up as I hug them both close, all of us sitting there in the middle of Imogene's bed, with me wanting more than anything to hold them like this forever. A dark thought forms. I could freeze this moment. I quickly blink the awful idea away. I would never wish *this* on them, ever. Especially so young.

My voice comes out thick. "Time to get to bed."

Davina runs to her bed without a fuss. Imogene pulls her covers over herself.

"Goodnight girls," I whisper, slowly backing out of their room, the burn now deep into my bones from the concentrated smell of their young blood. Wishing for once I could sleep to speed up time till the morning, I shut their door.

In the hall, my hair stands on end. I'm not alone.

I turn the corner from the hall into the kitchen. Donovan sits at the table fingering the large crack across its top with a gas-station-soda-size thermos in front of him. "Thought you could use this. I didn't realize you were drinking so much coffee. No wonder you're always hungry. Consider it an apology for my intrusion earlier."

"You need to leave. Phil will be home any minute," I lie, keeping as much space between myself and him as possible. "And what is wrong with coffee?"

"What's wrong with coffee is that it will dehydrate you quicker than anything. And for someone who doesn't like to kill things, I'd think that's the last thing you'd want." He flashes his flawlessly white teeth as he smiles.

What he says makes sense, but the last thing I want to give up right now is coffee. "It helps with the cravings. I don't really know why."

"Well, smoking helps curb an appetite, doesn't mean it's good for you."

"I'll stick to what keeps me safe around my kids. Regardless, you need to leave, I don't trust . . . " I trail off.

Donovan cocks an eyebrow. "Me?"

"I don't trust myself with you." A flutter rushes through me. Perhaps admitting the truth might free me from these feelings I have for him. Get them out in the open, deal with them, and move on.

I hate that he looks so pleased by the idea, but thankfully he doesn't latch onto the statement and needle me for more information. Instead, he dangles the thermos out towards me, his firm, perfectly stubbled jaw supports his dazzling smile. "You sure you aren't even the slightest bit thirsty? Come on. I know being out around people must have been terribly hard for you."

"No, thank you." I cross my arms in front of me and stare down at the floor. My mouth waters, for the blood and for Donovan. The memory of his lips on mine, his hands embracing me, the warm scent of his cologne, and how he makes me melt with every touch. He needs to leave.

"You know you can't keep this part of yourself locked up forever. It's not in your nature."

I stare at his peace offering until my thirst reaches a point of desperation. I give in to the blood, taking a seat at the table across from him. Distance is critical right now.

"It's not human, I swear," Donovan says almost jokingly, pushing the container closer.

With those words I grab it and take a sip of the rich liquid inside, then another, and another.

"It's still warm," I moan, losing myself in the ecstasy of my addiction. For a moment, nothing else matters.

Donovan's tight voice breaks through my blood-haze. "We need to talk."

I set down the thermos and wipe my mouth with my sleeve. "Okay."

All of his playfulness from before is gone. "I wasn't completely honest with you earlier."

Unease floods through me. "Which part? You mean earlier when you gave me your sob story about feeling human and playing to my uncontrollable urges to help you? That was a lie?" Is this what he does? Feeds me blood and then lies to get what he wants from me?

"Listen, that wasn't a sob story. I meant every word—" He holds up a hand in defense.

"No, you listen!" The realization of what he's been doing to me begins to boil up inside me.

"Because of you, my life has turned upside down. I've put my children, my marriage at risk. I can't trust myself anymore, especially around you. Why can't I get away from you? Why can't I get you out of my mind?"

"Aileen," he starts, but again I roll right over his words.

"Why am I so dependent on you? I want my life back, Donovan." I slump back into my chair, too upset at myself for tears.

His face is sober. "Your life that you have now is because of me, love."

"You are really something, aren't you? And to think I found you charming—"

"You find me charming?" he acts surprised, playing modest for once.

"*Found*."

"You wouldn't be here if it weren't for me, remember that," he says, reiterating the point with more force. I hate him for it, but at the same time he's right, and again I fall for the sadness spreading across his face.

"Now, back to why I'm here tonight. You asked if I found the one who changed me, and the truth is I didn't."

"You said that already."

"I didn't find Catherine; she found me—" he stops and stands at attention as screams ring out from my daughters' room— both of them this time. "Stay inside," he commands as he disappears out the back door.

I rush into the girls' room.

"Mommy!" Imogene screams, pointing toward the window.

I run toward it, and horror slams into me at the sight of what's just outside.

A woman, clothed in fire stands on the other side of the window. My mind shoots back to the woman in the mirror from my nightmare after the crash. Only this time, it's no dream. She reaches out to me, peering into my soul with her violet-blue eyes, flames reflecting through the black of her pupils, as a wicked smile reaches far across her flaming face when she realizes my recognition of her— the lavender-eyed woman from the plane.

I whisper to the girls, in shock, "Hide."

They both dive under their blankets. I try to catch up with the thoughts racing through my head so I can contemplate my next move. I want to tear through the glass, grab her— flames and all— with my bare hands for doing this to my children, for tormenting them with false nightmares. Because this is the scent, that burning smell, this is what's been plaguing my poor babies. Not just me. My hands curl into fists at my side as we lock eyes.

She touches the glass with a finger and yanks her hand back as something distracts her from behind. The flames extinguish in an instant as she whirls around faster than the human eye could see, and takes off into the darkness, followed by Donovan. In seconds they're gone, disappearing into the night. The only remnant of what happened is smoky air and a fingerprint-sized spot of melted glass on the window-pane. I suck in a breath, still nearly frozen in stunned anger and fear. The girl's uncontrollable sobs snap me out of it.

"Shh. It's okay, I'm here." I scoop up Davina from beneath the covers and bring her to sit with me on Imogene's bed. Their shaking bodies hot and sweaty, hearts racing. The terror of the night causes their blood to sour but smell stronger than ever, and I'm thankful for the blood Donovan brought. He saves the day once again. That bastard.

"Is the fire going to get me?" Davina cries.

"No fire is going to get you sweetheart. Is this what's been waking you up?"

"Yes!" she wails.

"Shh baby girl, there's nothing there now. I'm here. It's all just a bad dream." I only wish that were true.

"It's not a dream— I saw it too! Close the curtains! Close them!" Imogene sobs.

They huddle close together, hiding under Imogene's teal, chunky-knit blanket as I get up to close the curtains. Summoning as much of that mama-bear instinct from before as I can, I open one of the curtains further with a firm hand and peer into the night. Even with my super-vision there is nothing to be seen in the dark outside. Whatever she wanted, she's gone— chased off by my knight in shining leather. After checking the locks on the window, I shut the curtains tight.

"Everything is going to be okay," I tell the girls. At least that's what I'd like them to believe. Reassuring myself that I am powerful enough to protect these two against anything, yet Donovan proves how much I need him. How much *we* need him. Although, if it wasn't for leaving the girls alone and susceptible to danger, I think I could have taken care of it just fine myself. I take a breath to cool the rage building inside me.

"I'm scared," Imogene says, still hiding, fingers glued to the edges of her blanket to protect herself from the outside world. I know how she feels.

"You can both sleep in my room tonight, okay?"

"With you?" Imogene asks, her sobs muffled.

"Yes, with me." They stay silent for a moment. Then, I see Imogene's white knuckles slowly release their hold on the edge of the blanket. I help uncover Imogene lying on her bed, and then Davina, who's holding on tightly to her sister. Effortlessly I hoist them both up into my arms, one on each hip and carry them to my room.

Davina points to the open curtains in my room, still shaking with fear. "What if she comes back to your window next time?"

"If she comes back, Mommy will get her. Okay?"

"No!" Imogene yells. "What if you get hurt?"

"Okay sweetie. I'll call Sheriff Harker, is that better?" I set them on my bed and close up the curtains, checking the locks just to be sure.

"No, call Daddy! He will put out her fire! I don't want anything to happen to you again, Mommy," Imogene says.

Her tear-stained face, so broken and filled with sorrow. Breaks my heart knowing how much these girls have been through these last few weeks. And now this?

"Okay, we'll call Daddy." I debate giving Phil a call, but this is something I don't want him getting mixed up in anymore than he needs to. I'm not sure he would believe my description of a burning woman at the window, or that she was on my flight. I don't need to give him another reason to think I'm crazy.

Snuggling down between the girls on my bed, I reach the covers up all around us. They nestle down on each side of me, shivering slightly from my cold, undead body until I tuck the blankets between them and me. We'll all be warm soon enough.

"Sleep now, okay? All will be better in the morning." I kiss their cheeks and stroke both of their foreheads gently.

Eventually they each yawn, and the fear erases from their crinkled brows as they fall asleep. Eyelids begin to flutter, and I pray they may enter into a peaceful dreamland instead of one filled with heartache and horror. As they sleep, I watch. Listening to every rise and fall of their little bodies, their tiny snores, and the steady beat of their hearts. When they were newborns, I would find myself staring at them, lost in a place between pure peaceful-ness and heartbreak. Fearful that at any moment their breath might cease, and I would helplessly lose them forever. Tonight feels a lot like that. As strong as I am I can't help but feel helpless, worried I won't be able to protect them forever. A tear drops onto my shoulder off the left side of my face, another off the right. Back and forth they silently fall from a place within me once again lost between peace and sadness, knowing one day I *will* lose them. But I swear to God, it won't be at the hand of some crazy bitch on fire, or whoever-whatever that was Donovan chased off.

She found me, echoes in my mind. *Catherine* is the one who changed Donovan. That must be the woman in the window, the woman from the plane. Somehow, deep down I know it to be true. Now, she's threat-ening my children. And once again, I can't help but wonder what else is Donovan not telling me.

20

TRUTH BE TOLD

The early morning light glows from behind my bedroom curtains as the girls' clock beeps from their empty room. Six-forty-five. Only there's no school again today; I forgot to unset their alarm.

The girls have finally migrated away from me enough that I can sneak out of bed without disturbing them. I double-check the locks on the windows in my room and theirs, turn off their alarm, and head to the kitchen in search of my phone. There it is, right where I left it, next to the empty super-sized thermos and the foot-long crack on my kitchen table. I expected to see a text from Donovan or maybe even the man himself sitting there, but the only notification on my phone is another missed call from Angela Summers at the NTSB. I send Donovan a text.

What was that last night?

Ten minutes pass by with no reply. I get up and fill the kettle with water, placing it on the stove. Coffee sounds reassuring right now, but what would be nicer is to hear from Donovan. The water boils as I hand-crush the beans and toss them into the French press. The warm aroma of the coffee as I pour hot water over the beans soothes my nerves. I place the plunger lid on top of the French press, pull up my chair to the counter, and sit, watching the coffee like it's about to do some amazing trick. Until disappointed, I remember I shouldn't drink coffee, and there's still no reply from Donovan.

Catherine.

The name burns into my mind. It has to be her, behind the murders, and fingers and teeth, and fires. Could she have been the cause of the crash as well? Donovan did describe his creator as a monster, a creature that attacked him and left him alone to change. Now I'm even more convinced Catherine is the one appearing on fire, to my children. Worry sets in and I send another text to Donovan.

Where are you?

I wait but still no response and I wonder if someone like us can get hurt— or worse, be killed? My mind races through all the things I have yet to ask

Donovan about this new life of mine. Again, assuming the fiery woman is Catherine, how did she set herself on fire but not burn? The plane crash comes to mind, I was on fire, and yet, here I am, unburned. As I set my phone back down on the counter, it rings.

"Hey!" I snap before looking at the caller ID, impatient for news about what is going on.

"Good morning to you too," Phil says.

"Oh, hi. Sorry, it was a long night." I try to switch gears after assuming the caller to be Donovan, not my husband.

"Everything okay?"

"The girls both woke up with nightmares, so it was eventful, to say the least. Everything okay with you?" I relax a little from the much-needed comfort I find in his voice.

"There was a big fire last night. . . " He pauses. There's a shake in his words; my nerves begin to shake as well.

"What burned?" He's fought many fires, but he's never sounded like this telling me about it. Anxious, I hold my breath.

"The Sellars Cellars place. Got called around ten-o-clock last night. It took us all night to put it out," he says, his voice quivering more.

"You sound upset." My head is swirling, piecing together the events of last night. Donovan came over to talk about *her, Catherine,* that monster from my nightmare, terrorist to my children, and again he protected us. Now his building burned down, and he's MIA.

"I'm fine— well no, I'm not fine." He pauses again. Is he simply rattled, or is that fear I'm actually hearing in his voice? He takes a breath and continues. "I don't understand, how these things are here—" rambling his words become one unintelligible mass, he stops and clears his throat. Sheriff Jon is in the background asking for the phone. I hear more murmurs from Phil, clearly in shock of his findings, then Jon begins to talk.

"Aileen, we found some disturbing evidence here concerning you, and Phil and I think it would be best if you took the girls to Ana's house till we have more answers. You shouldn't be alone right now." Jon's tired voice shakes as well. "I'll send someone over if you'd like."

"No, I can take them myself. What did you find?" Whatever it is, it has to be bad for both of them to be so nervous.

Nothing but silence falls on the line, and then Phil whispers Jon an okay to continue. Jon takes a deep, drawn out breath.

"I really shouldn't say, but since it concerns you— while searching for the cause of the fire— we found in Mr. Sellars' office area— well, what's left of it— a charred green purse with your cell phone, wallet, and what's left of your boarding pass from your flight inside it."

"What?" Shock shivers through me.

"I know it sounds impossible, I can't explain this — also, we found a bloody knife, a few teeth, and a pinky finger. We're sending them over to the station now to see if it's a match to any of the ones at the school."

My phone drops from my shaking hand to the floor.

"Aileen? You still there? You okay?" Jon's tinny-sounding voice speaks from the floor. I scramble to pick up the phone.

"Yeah, I'm here," I say, putting it to my ear. "Have you found Don— I mean Mr. Sellars?"

He takes another tired breath. "No one seems to have been in the building. We sent an officer to his home and no one was there. I'll head over there later myself to check again. Are you sure you don't want me to send an officer over to help you?"

I hear more muffled sounds of the phone being passed as Phil demands it back. "You'll take the girls there now? Please?" Phil begs, clearly upset, he starts rambling again. "The incident at the school! This connects him, Aileen! I let him into our house, you went running with him . . . I didn't know. I'm sorry, I didn't know he was dangerous or stalking you."

Stalking. That's one way to put it.

I try to console him. "It's okay, I'm okay. You didn't know."

"No, it's not okay! How the hell did he have your things? You didn't come into the hospital with them. The nurse said you had nothing on you." His voice is shaking more than ever. "He would have had to have been at the crash site. Have you talked to the NTSB yet? They need to know this. This has to point to something, involving something— and the unidentified woman, the woman from the parking lot, they were missing fingers and teeth!"

It pains me that he has to re-live that day and now this connects directly to me, his wife. I'm sure this only adds to his anguish.

"We'll find him, Phil, and get some answers," Jon says in the background, "You just tell her to get out of that house; he lives on your street."

"You need to take the girls to Mom's, please. I'll meet you there as soon as I can leave. I— uh, we have more to investigate with this fire."

"Okay. Does your mom know anything yet?"

"No, I haven't told her. She's going to freak out."

"I'll tell her, okay? You just get through your shift. We will be all right. I love you; stay safe."

I hear him take a long breath of relief.

Indy's voice rings out in the background, "I think I found the cause of the fire!" There's still something familiar about it I can't place, but feel like I've heard before. My hunger burns at the thought of her there with Phil, but I push it aside. There are more important things at stake right now.

"I've got to go," he says just before he hangs up.

I sit down with my coffee, that I'm not supposed to drink, to gather my thoughts, which are whirling with questions about why the teeth, fingers, the burned woman from the crash, why Donovan would have my things unless he, is the cause of all this. It doesn't make sense, and my thoughts turn to Catherine. Could she be behind all this? If only I could talk to him, find out what is going on. I text him again.

Donovan?

Still nothing. Something has happened to him; it's almost as if I can feel it in my bones. I need to find him, and his house sounds like a good place to start looking. I dump my forbidden coffee down the drain, clean up the kitchen, and whoosh into the girls' room to pack up their clothes for Ana's. I spot the Target bag with Davina's Halloween costume in it and grab it, along with Imogene's ballerina costume from last year that she already laid out neatly on her dresser. They deserve some fun after last night, and tonight is the night our town puts on its big Halloween celebration on Main Street. It's always on the closest Friday night to the actual Halloween.

I sneak into my room, peeking at Davina and Imogene and listening for the soft rise and fall of their breath, and change into my most normal-looking clothes: blue skinny jeans and a grey t-shirt. I decide to grab my favorite navy, bulky-knit sweater because it is October. Before waking the girls, I slip out of the room and give Ana a quick call.

"Hello sweetie, Happy Halloween!" Ana loves the holidays.

"Hi Ana, would you mind if I brought the girls over for the day?" I reply in the most normal, cheery voice I can come up with.

"Of course, see you soon!"

Well, that was easy, I think as I hang up. No need to mention the fire, or the found fingers and teeth, or the burning woman at the window. It will only make the pit bull in her come out. I need to find Donovan, and I don't want Ana getting in the way of my search. A smile crosses my face for the first time this morning, thinking of what her reaction would be to all this. She'd probably fly us all to some obscure island where we would peacefully live out our days in hiding. Not a bad idea really. My smile fades thinking of what her reaction will be when Phil comes home later and she learns I lied to her.

I wake up the girls, Halloween costumes in hand, hoping to distract them from last night's terror. I gently stroke their cheeks with my cold hand. They yawn simultaneously, arching into a satisfying stretch. Davina's eyes open, and she squeals with delight.

Sitting up, she grabs her Dracula costume out of my hand.

"Good morning sweetie. Happy Halloween!" I smile.

Imogene is slower to rise. She moans, facedown into the bed. "I'm so tired."

"Sissy! It's Halloween celebration day— wake up!" Davina yells as she begins to jump on the bed, much to her sister's displeasure.

"Come on Imogene, wake up. We're going to go to Grandma's now."

Finally, Imogene wakes up enough to see her costume, which brings a sparkle to her eyes as a smile forms on her face.

"Can I wear this to Grandma's?" Davina asks, still jumping on the bed.

"Sure!" I answer, feeling grateful that they both seem fairly unaffected by last night. Perhaps they might recall it only as a nightmare. "You two get dressed and we'll head to Grandma's."

Imogene frowns. "But what about breakfast? I'm hungry!"

"You can eat at Grandma's."

Ana lives a few streets over and across from the old downtown main street that is already decorated to the nines for tonight's celebration. We pull up to her house, historic like the rest of the town. I think hers was built in 1896, one of the older ones. I love her house— the white picket fence, and lush garden surrounding it, which Ana meticulously tends to like it's her child.

The front door swings open and, as usual, Ana comes rushing out to greet us, this time wearing a ridiculous headband with flopping bats wired up from the brim.

"Grandma!" the girls yell, running from the car to give Ana a big hug and almost knocking her over in the process.

"Well, what have we here?" She claps her hands together. "I see a vampire and a ballerina! What did you do with my grandkids?"

The girls giggle and run inside. I grab their bags and walk toward Ana. She rushes at me, the smile she had for the girls gone now, replaced by a grim expression. She grabs me by the arms and stares me in the eyes. What does she know?

"Did you hear about that winery burning down last night? Isn't that terrible?" She loosens her grip on my arms. "Not that we needed another winery."

I take a moment to feel grateful she isn't fully up to date on things.

"Phil told me this morning. That is terrible." Guilt creeps in, or is it fear? Once Ana knows I didn't tell her Phil's whole message, I won't ever hear the end of it.

"What is going on in this town? Unsolved murders, fires breaking out," she sighs, picking up the girls' bags from me. "It used to be such a safe place."

"I can get those."

"No, I need something to do." She turns to head into the house. "Aren't you coming?"

"Phil had a rough night. I thought I'd surprise him with some coffee at the station."

"I'm sure he'd love that," she says, smiling.

"Thanks Ana." I pause, wondering how many lies I can pile on here as I have no intention of finding Phil, but Donovan. "And if you don't mind, maybe I'll get some grocery shopping done too. I'll be back before dinner, and then we'll take the girls down to Main Street for the party, okay?"

"I was thinking pizza," she says pointedly as a mischievous grin appears on her face. "You want a combo this time?" She laughs with a wink and nod, and I wonder if she will ever let the hunting man on my computer she thought was porn, go.

"Oh, you!" I return the laugh as my embarrassment begins to take over.

"I'm sorry, I couldn't help it. You take all the time you need, darling. We'll have fun here," she waves, chuckling. I go back to my car, letting the smile drop from my face. It's time to get answers.

STORM CLOUDS ACCUMULATE overhead as thunder rumbles off in the distance. Due to the strange happenings around town and the impending storm, the overly-decorated Main Street is currently a ghost town, the darkening sky only adds to the eeriness of the holiday. I park my car in the community lot behind the pizza place and wonder if anyone will actually be attending the festivities tonight.

Still no word from Donovan. Something big is brewing, and the urgency to find him grows stronger by the minute. I pocket my phone and car's key fob, stash my purse with the rest of my keys under the seat, and head out on foot. The once pleasant smell of pepperoni and cheese forces me to hold my breath as I walk by.

Each well-preserved historical home I pass is cheerfully decorated for tonight, which feels odd, given the circumstances right now. But this is what brought us to this old gold-mining town in the first place: the feeling of living in another place and time, the quaint community with small-town charm. I walk toward my street— Donovan's street. The wind picks up as I approach his house. Not much different than my own. Old like mine, but more of a shotgun style, smaller, but with a "Sellers Cellars" sign sitting in his front window. I look down the street toward my house, feeling like an unwelcome stranger in a familiar place. With no one in sight, I knock on the front door, hoping he'll open it and tell me all is well. No one answers.

I knock again and wait. Still nothing. I sneak around to the back of his house, which opens up into the same oak-filled fields that mine does, but with more open farmland. Black-and-white cows spot the hillsides, and my throat constricts, curious at the thought of what a cow's blood might taste like, wondering if that is what Donovan brought me last night. I test the back door, and to my surprise, the knob turns with ease under my hand.

I slowly open the door and step into the kitchen. "Donovan? Are you here?" No answer; I close the door behind me. "Hello? Where are you?" Still, no answer.

All is quiet except for the fast-paced ticking of an antique clock on the fireplace mantle in the living room, next to a photograph of a tall white farmhouse — the same one Donovan took me to. The air is thick with Donovan's scent, but it's stale, he isn't here. My worry increases as I continue into the depths of Donovan's house in hopes of finding something, even if I can't find him.

An old, thick, leather-bound journal sits open on a Dresden table folded up against the wall across from me. Curiosity compels me toward the book— it is open, after all. Justifiably, if it was meant to be private, it wouldn't be left out like this on the table. Knowing Donovan, he probably left it here in hopes that I would find it.

Inside the journal, pages are decorated with the most beautiful penmanship I've ever seen. If I didn't know any better, I'd say ink and quill were used. In fact, the date at the top of the page sitting open reads *April 11, 1872*, and under it is an eloquently hand-scribed recipe of sorts. I start to read it and find note after note explaining the proper way to ferment the perfect merlot. I flip to the next page, *June 28, 1879*. This one is all about chardonnay, with a beautiful grapevine drawn in detail across the bottom of the page. I skim page after page, year after year, with headings listing countries from all over the world. Anything and everything he wrote down was about grapes, vineyards, weather, location— copious notes on creating the perfect wine. Donovan would have had to travel all over the world to obtain such detailed information. I wouldn't be surprised; he has been alive for 150 years or so.

I turn to the pages near the end of the journal; the one I open to has a name written at the top.

Catherine's Cabernet

This too has a recipe, but it's written in French. There is a tenderness and intimacy almost to the lettering and the beautiful line drawings in the margins. If this is the same monster that left him alone all those years ago it doesn't add up to the personalization of this recipe he so clearly made for her. Were they lovers? The thought stings as I think about our kiss, the way he's thrown himself at me, all while withholding the fact his jealous ex-girlfriend was around. The pages scripted in French, go on until the last page dated July 5, 1905. I set down the journal as anger and betrayal builds within me and look through the other papers scattered around the table, all of which feature the same flawless penmanship but now written with a modern pen.

One paper in particular stands out.

Aileen's Merlot

Drawn across the top in beautiful filigreed letter-ing, and "too strong" scribbled boldly in the margins. I pick it up, scanning the description. This must be the wine he brought to our home. I let out a bitter laugh, thinking about how wasted Phil got off this stuff, then scoff at the fact this liar, Donovan, created a wine for me just like he did for Catherine before I notice the date at the top of the page. *August 3, 2015.* I blink and read the date again. Confusion and fear override my growing jealousy for whoever Catherine was to him. This blend was created almost two months ago, far before I ever met him on the plane. I flip the page over to find my address, my phone number, stores I shop at, places I dine— my trip to Miami. Flight 29, seat 21-B. Dates and times of my whole life for the past two months.

The bulkiness of my sweater weighs heavy on my body as if it suddenly shrunk and is too tight. I shed it, unthinking, and throw it on the floor as I gasp for unneeded breaths. The room spins as fast as my whirling thoughts. My found purse and phone from the plane in his office near teeth and a finger possibly connected to the ones at the school, the message *You're mine, forever*, the unidentifiable woman in the car fire, the elderly woman murdered in the parking lot. My lips burn from the kisses we shared as betrayal stabs deep into my cold, dead heart, shattering my empty soul. He wanted me. Nothing makes sense, yet at the same time, everything makes sense. Phil's words bounce around inside my head once again, *Maybe they think the cause of the crash was more than the storm.*

"Donovan!" a male voice yells, followed by three bangs on the door, fists pounding away at it. "This is Sheriff Harker, open up!"

I whoosh out the back door as fast as I possibly can and just keep going. The grass is a blur under my feet, trees blend into a Monet of green beside me to my left, and then, about a mile or two out, I stop. Just off to my right, not too far in the distance, sits the old, tall farmhouse from the photograph. If Donovan is anywhere right now, it's here, and I'm hungry for some answers. Lightning flashes and thunder rolls not too far behind. If that's not ominous, I don't know what is.

The farmhouse looks altered today under the dark, storm-clouded sky. Perhaps I simply see things differently now than the night I left this house after learning my life had changed forever. This house brought me my first taste of blood and felt through its floorboards the final beats of my heart. It was here I first saw the world through new eyes— immortal eyes.

I can almost imagine a time long ago, walking up to this house from the green pastures, with laundry drying out on the line, maybe chickens and goats wandering about. Inside, a human Donovan with his human wife living happily together, hopeful for their future, only to have it end in darkness and devastation. I stare at the house's peeling paint and see only the death it represents now that the life of it has long been stripped from its bones.

My pocket vibrates, and I fumble my phone out. It's Phil. I watch the screen pulse his number over and over until it stops, and painfully place it back in my pocket. I can't talk to Phil right now. I need to find Donovan. I know he's in here. I can feel it. Alone, I stand staring at the old farmhouse, willing myself to face the one I thought I could trust.

Again, my pocket vibrates, and again, I ignore it.

I reach the splintered wooden steps that lead up to the back door, carefully stepping on each rotting plank as it creaks and groans under my feet. Rain begins to pitter-patter off the rusty tin roof. I reach for the doorknob and pause to take a breath. The knob is stiff, clicking as it turns under my hand, and with a light shove, the old door opens into a dilapidated kitchen that smells a lot like burning leather.

A large crash echoes throughout the house as a woman's voice softly speaks something in French.

"Aileen!" Donovan shouts to me from the living room.

I run into the living room just as Donovan falls from a cracked wall to the floor. Simultaneously a woman cloaked in a black robe, with stringy hair attached to a mostly burnt scalp rushes at me. The woman who was on fire outside my children's window slams me into the wall behind me pinning me back with her burnt arms. My stomach turns at the stench and sight of her. Her violet eyes stare at me from a gruesome face. Before I can even blink Donovan pulls her off me and she disappears out the front door. And now I'm certain— the woman in my seat on the plane, the woman burning in the window— is Catherine.

Donovan brushes the plaster from the crumbling wall off his back. "Thank God you're all right." His leather jacket is torn and charred, explaining the smell of burnt leather stinking up the room. He places a hand on either side of my face, as feelings for him flood through me regardless of the thousands of questions swirling around in my head. I'm frozen, unable to move, shocked and confused as to what Catherine would want. Why she would do this. I look into his eyes, the soft pressure of his hands on my face is soothing. With a single touch, nothing else seems to matter. He stares at me with breathless silence as one of his arms finds its way down to the small of my back, pressing me into his body. My lips tingle waiting to meet his once again, and my fuzzy mind is torn between seeing him as someone I can trust and someone I should stay far away from. A part of me could stay in his embrace forever— *You're mine, forever.* I push myself back as a sad longing replaces his passion-filled eyes.

"Stay away from me," I manage to say, realizing how strong his hold on me has become, hating the both of us for it.

He steps aside, giving me space. "What's wrong?"

"She was on the plane!" I back away from him and stand by the fireplace. "She threatened my family—"

He cuts me off. "I'm sorry, I came to tell you everything last night. Unfortunately, she arrived before I could. She'll be back as soon as she finds some blood to heal her burns." He rolls his eyes. "Catherine always had a dramatic flair about her, with the whole fire thing. It's tiresome, really."

"I don't understand."

"Doesn't matter, we have to leave, and we have to leave *now* before her strength comes back." His voice is urgent.

"I'm not going anywhere with you."

"Do you want death and destruction to come upon everyone and everything you love?" he asks, his usual charm hidden under a mask of fear. "This isn't the first time Catherine found me."

Remembering the name from his recipe book I whisper, "Catherine's Cabernet."

"What did you say?" His eyes widen as he straightens up.

"Aileen's Merlot," I add, strength growing from my voice. He stands and his brow furrows as he walks toward me. I move away from the fireplace to the doorway between the living room and the kitchen from which I entered.

He stops to lean on the fireplace mantle and adjusts his disheveled hair in the mirror above it. "You know, breaking and entering is a prosecutable offense, darling."

"So is stalking." This grabs his attention. "Did you love her? Do you still love her? The recipe title in her name, all written in French. Were you really abandoned by her as you said?"

"Oh, she abandoned me all right." He clears his throat. "Let me explain a little something to you, a lesson in vampire 101, so to speak. You see, love, when a vampire creates someone new they leave a part of their—" he pauses, searching for the right word with his hand "— essence, let's say, within their creation. This essence creates a bond, a very strong bond that draws the creation to their creator, making them dependent on them. Forcing them to need their creator for their very survival. Like a newborn and its mother." He runs at me, pushing me back, up against a wall, his face close to mine and suddenly all my anger, doubt, everything fades and I want nothing more than his lips on mine again. He backs off and smiles.

"I know you felt that. I feel it too. This is why even though Catherine, lovely girl that she is, left me to change on my own, the moment she came back to me I couldn't help but be enamored of her. Even though when it came to her feelings for me, she was more interested in the wealth I had accrued. Working in the mines day and night all alone those first few years after Rebekah rejected me built me quite the nest egg."

"But the note at the school, *You're mine, forever*, written in teeth and fingers? I need to know . . . was that you?"

He looks offended by the idea, shaking his head. "That would be Catherine, love. I know her well. After all, we spent years together. She showed me the world, and during that time taught me winemaking, how to be free, and everything she knew about being a vampire. Only everything she knew ended up being dark and twisted, she was hellbent on consuming anything and everything she wanted. As the years went on, she grew increasingly jealous of any woman who would even dare to look my way. Bodies started to pile up, along with reports of missing women, everywhere we went. I knew it was her, thanks to her strange obsession with burning and dismembering parts of her victims. I grew tired of her paranoia and destruction and left to start a life of my own, far away from her. The only way to break our connection is distance. So, I came back to America, to Amador County, the last place I thought she'd find me."

Anger and betrayal bubble up inside me. "Is this why you changed me? Because you were lonely and wanted someone new? Someone you could create yourself, who would be drawn to you with their affections and love, like you were to Catherine?"

"Of course not!"

Bitterness laces my voice. "You know, for a split second I actually thought it was sweet, you naming a wine after me . . . until I saw the date you wrote it. Two months before we met on that plane. Did you crash the plane too, or was that a nice coincidence?"

"Aileen, I wanted you from the first time I saw you walking around town after I moved back here." His words are soft. "So I watched you, and I fell in love with what you were— human. When I heard you were going on a trip alone, I saw it as a chance to get to know you personally. You made me long to be human again, it was selfish of me. I was so lonely. I didn't realize Catherine was on the flight too until I sat in your seat and smelled her. I didn't know she found me, that she knew about you."

I stare up at him. "So she went on that flight to do what? Check me out? Hurt me?"

"I can't say. But when the plane began to go down, I was presented the opportunity to save your life, and so I did. I'm sorry, but I don't regret changing you because you changed me, Aileen. Your drive to hold on to your humanity, the love for your family . . . it made me feel something I haven't felt in a long time. Something Catherine took from me." Donovan pauses, his eyes are hopeful as he holds out his hand out toward me. "Come with me, please?"

I fold my arms in front of my chest and shake my head. "I won't leave my family. I need to protect them."

He takes a breath. "Let's just say Catherine is the unforgiving, jealous type and she doesn't like that I love you and will stop at nothing to destroy both our chances at happiness. You're lucky all she's done to your children is scare them. If we go, she'll probably leave them alone. She'll be too busy searching for me." His hand is still outstretched toward me. "I'll take you up north to some old friends of mine, they are more like us. We'll be safe with their numbers; we can have a life together there."

I fight the feelings building up inside me. Every time his sadness shows so does his humanity. It's irresistible to me, but now that the truth about Catherine is out, I have to fight it. The thought of other beings like us is intriguing, but my family needs me now more than ever. Slowly, I shake my head. "I won't leave. Catherine is your mess, not mine. Leave me out of this, Donovan."

I turn around and walk out the back door.

"Aileen, wait!" he yells after me. "She will find you!"

But I don't wait. I don't want to care about him, or our connection, or Catherine. All I want to care about is the safety of my family. Without me, they are vulnerable to anything. Every lie, every secret, is worth it for their safety. I run as fast as I can, racing against the storm brewing worse in the sky, praying no one sees me and that Catherine has as much trouble hunting for blood as I do. Only I doubt that's the case.

I BURST in the door at Ana's. The house is quiet.

"Hello?" The worst leaps to my mind as I gaze around the dimly light entryway. I hear a thump to my left. Why did I leave them? I should have stayed. Screw Donovan and looking for answers.

"RAAAAAWRRRR!" Davina jumps out of the hallway and my breath catches. She's dressed as the cutest Dracula I've ever seen. I'm relieved to see she's safe.

"Oh sweetie, you scared me! Where's your daddy?" I ask, trying to hide the frantic note in my voice.

"I don't know," she says, shrugging her shoulders.

"Can we go trick-or-treating downtown yet? Is it time?" Imogene says from the kitchen, flipping on the foyer light.

Ana walks up to me, her face stern. "Where were you, young lady? And what are you doing walking around in weather like this, wearing that?" She points to my grey T-shirt and I realize my sweater is still in Donovan's house.

"Something came up. Is Phil here?" I ask, ignoring her question about the sweater.

"No, he was here a little bit ago. He said he was trying to get ahold of you but then got a call himself and left; I thought maybe it was you calling him back."

My phone begins to vibrate in my pocket. It's Phil, thank God. I answer, not hiding the urgency in my voice. "Where are you? I'm at Ana's."

"I don't care where you are now; where were you?" he snaps.

"I had some stuff to do today, and then I was going to grab some pizza on my way back." It's the best excuse I can muster right now— only I never did get the pizza.

His voice quivers with anger. "Bullshit, Aileen. Why are you lying to me?"

Ana looks at me, then hustles the girls back into the kitchen, where I see two boxes of pizza sitting on the table.

"I'm not lying." Technically I did have stuff to do.

"Bull. Shit," he says again. "I know you're lying. I stopped in the pizza place after Mom said you never came home with the pizza. They said they hadn't seen you at all but then, funny thing, I look and see your van in the parking lot."

"It's all really hard to explain right now. Where are you?" I'd much rather talk about this here, where I know we are all together and safe.

"I'm at the house. There's much more we need to talk about, and I don't want to do it around the girls." He hangs up. I release a tight breath.

Ana pops back into the foyer with me. Her voice is softer this time. "Everything all right?"

I shake my head no as the reality of what's happening begins to overwhelm me.

"So, you're having a fight," she says matter-of-factly, rubbing my back. "You two love each other, and these last two weeks, you've both been through a lot. But remember, nothing is too big for a love like yours."

Tears flow freely as I embrace my mother-in-law, crying into her soft shoulder, not caring how tempting her blood smells this close to her veins. In the light of everything going on right now, I've momentarily lost my appetite. The hug of a mother brings comfort in the darkest of moments. Except for this one, I fear nothing can fix the mess I've made. She lets go and grabs a sweater from the hall closet, placing it over my shoulders.

"I hope you're right, Ana," I say, threading my arms into the sleeves. "I need to go. Please keep the girls inside— the weather is getting bad out there. Forget trick-or-treating. And keep the door locked. *Please*." The sky has grown darker as the storm settles in overhead. Wind whistles across the rattling antique windows in Ana's house.

"Don't you worry about them. We'll have some fun here." She smiles. "Go to him, sweetie. You two will work this out."

21

THE END IS NEAR

Frozen, I stand at the end of the driveway, my feet not yet willing to advance. Storm clouds swirl above the rooftop as lightning tears across the sky, and the thunder claps its mighty hands in approval of its terrifying production. Our home, once so full of warmth and love, is now cold and broken. I want to go back, back to the day I left for my trip, and never leave. I long for my life to be as it was before when I was alive. Memories of walking through these doors to the happy faces of Phil and the girls slip away as I open the creaky front door and see Phil standing like a stranger, alone in a darkened kitchen, still in his fire gear. Here's hoping Ana is right and our love can make it through anything.

"Hi," nervously escapes my lips, along with a half-smile, as I close the door behind me. Phil's anger pulsing from his fast-beating heart and flowing through his veins awakens my hunger, and what usually is a subtle burn instead ignites a roaring blaze within me.

"Would you like to tell me where you were?" he asks, his face like stone, as he sets my sweater on the table next to him. The one I left at Donovan's.

I bite down on my lower lip to hold off the sobs that want to break free and simply answer, "No." But even the tiny breath it took to answer stoked the beast growing inside me.

"Jon found it at Sellars' house down the street." Phil pulls out a black phone that's not his own and begins to read, "Until then I'll drink to the taste of your lips."

My ears ring as I realize what he's reading.

Phil scrolls a bit, then continues, his voice shaking. "Talk felt good, sorry about the kiss." He opens his mouth to read another but instead slams the phone down on the table.

"Phil . . . I can explain." Tears fall uninvited as I do everything I can to regain control over myself.

"How long has this been going on with you two?"

"This isn't what you think," I start, but isn't that what every cheating person says? Every breath I take to speak draws his scent into me and I can barely contain myself as the intense hunger snags at me. I grab tight to the kitchen counter to my right.

"What am I supposed to think?" His heart beats faster than ever. He falls into his chair, fists clenched.

My hunger swirls into my brain, distracting me from the question at hand. I hold my breath, but it's too late.

"Tell me! What am I supposed to think?" he shouts through tears, kicking his chair back as he stands again.

"It's complicated!" I force my words painfully, saving what little air is left in my lungs. Hoping I won't have to breathe in again. My head spins, mouth waters, with each juicy pump of the vein on his neck that grows bigger from every beat of his wounded heart.

"I tell you this man is stalking you." He starts ticking off on his fingers. "I find your things from your flight in his burnt-up office, your sweater in his house, and text messages from you on his phone! I ask you to simply go to my mom's so I know you're safe, and what do you do?" He pauses. "You lie to my mom, you lie to me. The lies . . . Aileen, where were you?"

He waits. I back up against the front door, shaking my head no, my body vibrating as I try my best to stop the monster who's now fully awakened, from tearing apart my husband. My thirst now worse than ever, clawing at my throat, burning me up from within. Lightning flashes, exposing the sad, broken expression on his face. I look to the floor as it waves under my feet and grab the counter tighter to steady my stance. My veins burn like the flames threatening to devour what's left of my humanity.

"Ever since the crash you've been different. Something is going on with you. What are you not telling me?" He takes a step toward me.

"Stop!" I scream. He freezes, looking at me like I'm some crazy person. "Stay back!" I plead, terrified of what I so desperately wish to do to him.

He ignores me, moving closer. "I need some answers, Aileen."

My primal instincts push and shove their way to the front of my brain, I can't hold it back much longer. My thoughts are foggy and jumbled as I fight to hold on to my humanity. If I inch back any further against the door, I'll go through it. With one hand I grasp the knob behind me just in case I need to flee, but even if I do, who will protect him if Catherine is truly out to destroy me?

"Please?" he asks, walking closer and closer.

"Stop, please!" I growl through tightly clenched teeth.

"Why do you push me away?" He continues toward me. "You won't open up to me about the crash, you keep running off and disappearing . . . what happened to you?"

"He was on the plane!" I shout, holding my mouth tight with my free hand, ceasing my breath as tears flow down my cheeks like the truth so desperately wanting to escape my lips.

Phil stops in his tracks. "Who was on the plane?"

I tighten my grip on the doorknob.

"Donovan," I say breathlessly.

Confusion floods his face, followed by all his jumbled thoughts attempting to form themselves into coherent words. "But how is that possible? There were no other survivors."

My eyes meet his, but I can't answer for fear I'll give in. Desperate to feed on his blood.

"Were you two going on that trip together?" he finally asks, sadness distorting his lips into an unfixable frown.

I shake my head, mouthing the word "No," begging for these terrifying urges to rip apart my husband to pass.

Looking lost, he backs up to the table and sits down. His distance gives little comfort but enough for me to take a quick breath.

The doorknob crumples beneath my hand as I grip tighter. I tell him, "Donovan is the reason I survived."

"What do you mean?"

Before I can answer, burnt leather fills the room.

"It means *I* am the one who saved her life, and now apparently I need to save yours from your hungry wife," Donovan says, walking out of the shadows from my living room. He looks at me. "Sorry, I didn't bring you a snack this time."

"Get the hell out of my house!" Phil yells as he stands once again.

Donovan keeps his gaze fixed on me as if he wishes to control me with a glance, ignoring Phil.

"I don't need your help, Donovan," I growl, digging my other hand's fingers into the countertop as if it might anchor me down. I'm torn between rushing to Phil's side to protect him from Donovan and the hunger that's forcing me back.

"No, love, I believe you do need my help." Donovan turns to my husband. "That is the look of a very hungry girl, Phil, and if you were smart, you'd leave."

"I'm not going anywhere." Phil rushes towards Donovan, fist aimed at his face. Donovan grabs Phil's hand in his, mid punch. His bones crack under Donovan's grip.

Phil yells out in pain as he falls to his knees, his wounded hand still caught in Donovan's.

I stand against the front door, pinned back by my blinding hunger, fighting off every urge to run to Phil and sink my teeth into him, so I can focus on how to save him from Donovan's grasp.

"You really shouldn't do that," Donovan says. "See, now you're going to start turning all black and blue, which is really going to make her even more hungry." He adds, looking over at me, "Isn't it weird how you can smell bruising?"

"What are you doing?" I gasp, every word I speak brings pain throughout my body.

"Rescuing your husband from what you really are. By the way, have you told him yet?" He smiles, finally letting go of Phil's hand and he walks toward me.

"You need to leave," I utter through the pain. Every inhale of Phil's scent leaves me swirling deeper into the madness. Behind Donovan, Phil rises and runs at him.

Eyes still on me, Donovan reaches back and grabs Phil by the neck. Spinning around he slams my husband up against the far kitchen wall, drywall cracking beneath him as a flash of lightning fills the room.

"No!" Frozen in fear, unsure of what to do. Do I rush over there and fight off Donovan, who is much stronger and faster than I, all the while revealing what I am to Phil? Or do I let the two of them fight it out — a fight which Phil will surely lose, either at Donovan's hand or mine?

Phil tries to swing his arms at Donovan to no avail.

"Don't move or I'll snap your puny little neck," Donovan whispers, tightening his grip on Phil's neck. "I'm doing you a favor, really."

"Just stop!" I watch as the wall crumbles out from behind Phil and falls slowly to the floor. I focus all my efforts on regaining control of myself, to no avail.

"I get it," Donovan says. "You don't want to move too quick, give up what you are because then Phil might not want to keep you around. I know, I've been there, done that. But you see, the best thing you can do right now for Phil is leave, get yourself a nice warm meal, and then we can all talk about this like normal, civilized people."

Phil gasps for air. I have to fight— who cares if Phil sees my secret? His life is more important. Like lightning, let go of the doorknob and rush to grab Donovan by the shoulders, throwing him to the opposite side of the kitchen. Finally feeling the full extent of my power. My strength is not too far off of Donovan's. Phil collapses on the ground, rubbing his neck and coughing, while on the other side of the kitchen my dishes in the cupboard shatter under the force of Donovan's body having been thrown into them.

"Are you okay?"

Phil nods his head in shock.

"You need to get out of here."

His voice is hoarse from being choked. "I'm not leaving you with that psycho."

Phil's blood rushing to his bruising neck calls to me and the monster within me breaks free again. Phil's eyes are wide with terror, but in the moment, all I see is a meal. Donovan charges at me, tackling me off my path, sending us both flying into the kitchen table. The wood explodes from under us, cracking and splintering as we both fall down onto it. A sharp pain pierces into me as a wooden slab of the broken table stabs straight through my right side spilling out copious amounts of oily, black blood.

I cry out, breathing through my pain, trying quickly to extricate myself from the wood. My loss of blood subdues the bloodthirsty monster I felt like only seconds ago.

"Aileen! Oh, God!" Phil yells as lightning flashes outside, illuminating the black ooze flowing from me, spreading across my torn shirt like ink. I push myself forward, dragging myself off the plank that stabbed through my side. Phil watches me in horror. I scream as the rough wood scrapes again my insides as I pull out the board, freeing myself.

Phil runs blindly to me. Donovan yells for him to stay away and in the process shoves him back, accidentally throwing him hard into the wall. Too hard.

"No!" I scream from the depths of my being, reaching out to Phil. I'm still incapacitated from the gaping hole through my side and weak from the loss of blood.

Everything falls silent as Phil's limp body collapses to the floor.

Ugly, angry tears build from a deep lump quickly expanding in my throat as I stare at his lifeless body. But I can still hear it, his heart! It's still beating—slower and slower. He's alive.

I crawl to him as fast as I can through the pain, through my weakness. Donovan grabs me by the shoulders.

"Don't, Aileen! You'll never be able to forgive yourself," he says in a solemn tone.

"You did this!" I cry, trying to shove him off me as tears stream down my face.

Donovan looks me in the eyes and releases my shoulders. The pain in my side is too great for me to move fast.

"I didn't mean to," Donovan's voice is ragged. "I swear. I was trying to stop you from doing something you'd regret."

"I was fine before you showed up. I would never have hurt him." I will myself to believe this and raise my chin. Even though I know it's a lie. "I was fine before you showed up in my life at all. Look what you did!"

I finally make it to Phil and stroke the side of his face with my hand, at a loss for what to do. "I'm so sorry." Loud sobs tear through my body, not just because he's hurt, but because I lost control, I *wanted* to hurt him. He was nothing more than a meal, and if it wasn't for Donovan, he would have been.

Phil's heart begins to beat sporadically.

"Stay with me, Phil!" I pound my fist onto his chest, cracking his sternum. The rhythm steadies. "Stay with me!" I cry, fumbling for my phone in my pocket to call 9-1-1. "Oh God, oh God," I moan.

"That's not going to help him," Donovan walks over to the kitchen window, staring out of it. "His neck is broken. I heard it snap."

"No!" I pound on Phil's chest again to try and steady his failing heart, then let my head fall next to his, weeping uncontrollably. My mind spirals out and away from me too quickly for me to catch up to reality, brought back only by Phil's weakly pumping blood. Donovan swoops down by my side on the floor. I survived a plane crash, but now I feel I could die of a broken heart.

"Maybe this all happened for a reason," Donovan says, brushing a tendril of hair away from my face. I slap his hand away.

"Don't touch me. This happened because you can't leave me alone. Now get out of my house." Tears fall, pain radiates from my side, from my dead heart. I'm losing everything. Lightning strikes as thunder shakes the walls.

"This was bound to happen eventually. He's human, he's weak. Nothing like us." Donovan gets up, looking down at me. Phil's heartbeat wanes even more.

When I think this night can't get any worse, it does. I snap up my head as smoke fills the room. Catherine steps into the kitchen, laughing. Clad in tight black pants, a pristine white silk blouse and tall red stiletto heels. This time in her full unburned glory. The happy, smiling woman from the plane no longer existing in this version of her. I stare in a grief-struck haze, as she moves closer. A fire burns behind her, trailing from the back sliding door, through the living room, she clicks on a lighter and sets a dishtowel on a cabinet knob aflame, dousing it with a small bottle of liquor she holds in her other hand.

"Oops." She throws the rest of the bottle behind her, glass shattering within the growing flames, and wipes her hand on her tight leather pants. "Well Donovan dear, look what trouble you've found yourself in now," she says, through a thick French accent. Her violet eyes glare down at Phil and me before she turns to Donovan. "Come along, leave this sorry excuse for a vampire to her dying human. You've had your fun away from me, and you have no idea how much trouble I've had to go through to get you back. Let's go." She claps her hands as if Donovan is her puppy.

"Go away, you flaming bitch!" I cry out, too weak to do anything more.

She zips over to me, peers down with disdain and jabs her red stilettoed heel into the wound in my back. I hold in my cry.

"You were supposed to die you know. On the plane. I thought that would rid Donovan of his affection for you, punish him for his transgressions against me."

"Catherine . . . " his voice is pained as she stands

face to face with him. Her finger caresses the side of his cheek, pausing on his supple lips.

"I didn't think you had it in you Donovan, you always hated the hold I had on you. Never thought you'd place it on another."

"Leave. Just leave." He growls.

Catherine laughs, her eyes wide, almost surprised. "You're too cute, she's not going to want you now regardless of your bond. Can't you smell it, mon amour? She's almost out of blood and I doubt she'd take her pathetic human's." Her smile fades as she grabs a slab of wood from the shattered table and throws it like a spear into Donovan's shoulder. He doesn't even flinch. "Once you pull that out, and your better judgement returns, come find me. It's getting quite warm in here and I have another job to attend to." And in a flash, she disappears.

Donovan looks at me, oily black blood dripping from his shoulder. "Aileen . . . "

"Your master is calling, go!" I yell at him between tears, heaped over Phil, pressing myself into him. She's right, I can almost feel my body growing stiff as it begins to run dry. The pool of black flooding the floor beneath me.

"She's nothing, Aileen, come with me. You just need a little blood and you'll heal. You can take some of mine to hold you over. Please, I can't go back to her. I won't. It's just a scratch, I can still carry you out. I can't let you can't die, Aileen," Donovan says gently, wincing as he pulls the wood from his shoulder.

"I can take care of myself." I shake my head, choking out the words. "I won't leave him."

Phil's heart stutters as I look at his face. Deep lines crease the corners of his closed eyes, his brow permanently furrowed as he lies there, still and helpless. My human husband, weak and frail.

"Fine then, you're on your own."

Ignoring Donovan, I caress Phil's stubbled cheek. The warmth is quickly fading from his skin. Donovan touches my shoulder and feelings surge within me as I face my dying future with Phil and fading immortality with Donovan. His fingers linger for a moment before he removes his hand and his hold on my heart.

"This is your fault, Donovan. You know, I never asked for this." Bitter tears stream down my cheek as I stare into his dark eyes.

He takes a slow breath as if defeated. "You're right. I'll find her and run her out of town, I'll keep her away from you best I can." He juts his chin toward Phil. "You've lost too much blood to survive the fire. He's not going to survive the smoke, even if he wasn't this injured. Since you won't take help from me, do what you need to do to get yourself out and as far away from here as possible. Please, I can't stand the thought of this world without you." He pauses, then opens his mouth as if to say something more but instead, quick as a whisper, whooshes away. Something empties inside me, and I bury my face into Phil's chest.

Lightning and thunder crash again, hitting the house. Loud pops and snaps blare from the other side of the wall as the huge old oak on the side of our house comes crashing down into the kitchen beside us, missing Phil's head by mere inches. Rain pours in through the hole from the tree, and the smoke grows thicker, the flames hotter consuming my home behind me. But nothing else matters.

"Phil, stay with me." I try to stand, but my strength is gone. I need blood.

An orange glow appears on the crumbling wall in front of me as I watch my shadow dance and flicker from the flames I know are right behind me. The fire cracks and pops as it delights in its destruction. Phil's heart continues to slow.

"Phil? Please wake up. Please be okay. We need to get out of here." I wrap my arms around him, but the pain is so great from my side that I let out a scream as I try my best to find the strength to lift him. I have none. Catherine's right, I'm dying. The flames burn hot behind my back, and suddenly it's as if I'm back on the plane, watching helplessly as the fire grows closer and closer. Only this time it will take us both. The girls will be orphans. I shut my eyes tight.

"Damn you, Donovan!" I shout in vain, wondering if he's still nearby and at any moment will rush in to save the day like he always does. Like he was trying to do earlier, saving me from hurting Phil, and now we're here in this mess because of my inability to just admit what I've become. To accept I'm no longer human. To accept this is a life I can no longer be a part of.

As I run my fingers through Phil's wet hair, his heart skips a beat. Then another and another. I pound on his chest and his breathing stops. The flames grow closer.

"No!" I cry, "No, no, no, no!" I beat his chest, again and again, breathing into his mouth, praying for his heart to beat stronger, for his breath to return.

Nothing.

The lump in my throat grows bigger. Unable to bear the thought of the girls losing both their parents tonight a new determination rises within me. My shaky hand pulls his wrist toward my lips. Donovan's words echo through my mind: *You just need a little blood and you'll heal. Just a little.* The orange glow from the fire illuminates Phil's face, his lips turning blue from lack of oxygen. Donovan's right, *just a little.*

"Forgive me," I whisper, crying as my teeth sink into the soft flesh of his wrist.

Waves of euphoria consume me as Phil's blood flows like honey down into my veins, whisking me away to a different world, one full of love and happiness and warmth. Far away from the flames threatening to consume us. Far from Catherine, from Donovan. Far from the monster I was moments ago.

The pain in my side disappears. My wound knitting itself back together as I suck down the sweetest taste my tongue has ever known.

My mind screams at me to stop as sirens blare from down the road, snapping me back to reality. The flames, now only inches from us, are fended off only by the downpour of rain flowing into the house from the fallen tree. Red and blue lights blink through the windows. I throw Phil's arm from my mouth and on accident tear a large gash in the process. I frantically feel for a pulse. Still there, but barely. Blood pours from his wrist, I tear his shirt and tie it tight around his wound.

"Stay with me!" I whisper in his ear, hoping and praying I did it right, that this will save him as it did me. Hoping he will find a way to forgive me if this works.

With my strength returning little by little as his blood flows through my body, I hook my arms under Phil's shoulders and drag his limp frame out the front door toward the first responders on the front lawn.

"Help him!" I yell to them, licking away the last bit of blood remaining on my lips.

"I'm sorry," I whisper. Kissing him on the forehead, and step back to make room for the paramedics.

They go to work on him, strapping him to the gurney and loading him into the ambulance and out of the rain. Poking and prodding, they ask him questions he isn't awake to answer. They place an airbag over his mouth and it breathes for him as they try and stabilize him. The lump in my throat returns.

"Help him, please," I cry as a young firefighter wraps a blanket around my shoulders and I watch behind me as my home is consumed in flames.

"Is there anyone else in the house?" he asks.

"No, just us. The tree hit him— help him!" I plead.

"Are you okay ma'am? Are you injured."

"I'm fine. Just help him." No longer can I see clearly through my tears as I watch the emergency crews performing CPR on my failing Phil.

"He's coding!" shouts one of the EMTs, continuing to pump air into his still-dying body.

I try to listen in for a heartbeat, but it's hard to hear over all the commotion. All I catch is the fast-paced, frantic beating of the emergency crew's hearts. Oh God, I did it wrong! I took too much blood! My heart sinks and I'm overcome with regret— regret over keeping this a secret, for staying around and putting him in danger.

I can hear the electrical current charge.

"CLEAR!"

I watch in horror as Phil's body convulses under the current as electricity breaks and cracks through him.

"Again!" they yell. "Clear!"

Again, his lifeless body convulses. Again, I hear the current tear through him.

"Oh, God!" I cry, covering my face with the blanket.

Then one paramedic says, "We have a pulse!" and they shut the ambulance door and drive away without me.

I want to flee, to run away, in hopes that the rest of my family will be able to live a life safely, without me. But how can I leave them— especially if I end up having failed at saving Phil?

"He will be okay," the young firefighter says and walks away to join his crew as they attempt to save my home.

"What did I do?" I whisper to myself, watching the ambulance fade off down the road, past an ever-growing mob of spectators— neighbors and random cars driving by, mostly. Phil wouldn't have wanted this, but I can't imagine doing this life without him, putting the girls through another tragedy. Maybe my bite didn't work and he really will be okay on his own . . . except for his broken neck, which will probably leave him paralyzed.

Lights flashing, sirens blazing, a sheriff's SUV zooms past the ambulance in the opposite direction and into my driveway. Jon bursts out of his cruiser, sheltering his face from the rain.

"Back it up, people! Go home! There's nothing to see!" He waves his arms at the spectators. They slowly disperse, a cloud of whispers and gossip following them as they walk away. Once again, I'll be the talk of the town, but I'm too distraught to listen or care about what they have to say.

"Aileen! You all right? I heard about Phil on the radio and came right away." Teary-eyed, Jon rushes up to me, embracing me in a tight hug.

"No," I say, watching as the fire crews attempt to save whatever might be left of my house.

"You're soaking wet. Get in my car," he demands. "I'll take you to the hospital."

Numb, I do as he asks, sliding into the passenger seat of his cruiser. The moment is reminiscent of the night he and Phil found me lying in the middle of the highway. If only I had just come clean then, maybe this wouldn't have happened. Jon takes his seat next to me.

"Did you call Ana?" I ask, hoping I don't have to do that myself.

"I just came from there, actually." He takes a deep breath. "Ana called me over after your girls told her about a woman on fire looking through their window. Why didn't you call the police last night?"

"Can we talk about this later?" I have no idea how to explain this to Phil— if he wakes up— let alone Jon.

"Okay," he says, buckling up and putting the car in gear.

As we drive away another fire engine slows as it

drives past Jon's SUV. Lighting flashes, illuminating the face of the engine's driver, I see it clearly— her glowing white teeth, lavender-blue eyes— I catch my breath as she looks over at me and winks with a wicked smile before driving past.

"Indy?" I whisper to myself in disbelief clearly seeing Catherine in the driver's seat.

Jon speeds down the road while I stare back through the side mirror, watching as the fire engine pulls up to my burning house.

22

REMEMBER, REMEMBER

Beep, beep, beep, beep.

My only companion for the last five days, minus the doctors and nurses coming in and going out to check on an unconscious Phil every few hours. He's been out far longer than I was after Donovan bit me. *I must have done it wrong*, I think for the hundredth time. I curse Donovan for not telling me more, for getting me into this mess in the first place, for at least the millionth time.

Ana, once again, is graciously entertaining the girls, distracting them from the tragic unknown fate of their father as well as the loss of our home. I want them as far away from Amador County as they can be, but Ana wants to be close in case Phil takes a turn for the worst. I hope Catherine is satisfied with the damage that's been done. Donovan is hers for all I care.

Phil's chest rises and falls, rises and falls with the help of a machine. I watch from the peach-colored plastic chair at his bedside, much like the one he sat in when I was here. Each of his precious breaths is provided by the tube running down his throat into his lungs. The doctor said his spinal cord is severed and he will never walk or have use of his arms again. He's lucky to be alive at all. I choke down the guilt, this horrible guilt, knowing this isn't what he would want, no matter what the outcome. I keep replaying our final conversation but dread rips at my already torn heart. I love my husband, but this new creature that I have become, the powerful draw I have to my creator — to Donovan— is something I can't ignore no matter how hard I try. Could it be that I love Donovan too? No, I can't. He is the reason I'm here, *we* are here. I hate him.

I hold Phil's limp hand in mine, hoping it somehow lets him know I am here. Lets him know how much I want to be here, to be with *him*. Time passes slowly as I sit, listening to the monitor, finding comfort in the rhythm it plays. Assuring myself with each beat, he still has a chance, offering me hope we can fix all I've broken between us. A chance for him to know the truth of what I am.

Hope.

Ashamed, I look at the white-bandaged wrist around the hand I'm holding. The only positive thing resulting from my seemingly failed bite was fulfilling my hunger enough to get him out of the house alive. Human blood lasts longer than animal blood, but I took too much. Far too much. The doctor told me he was so low on blood from the gash on his wrist that he almost needed a transfusion. When asked how he got injured, I again blamed the tree. They didn't press me further. Why would they?

Knuckles rap on the door as a worn-down Jon in civilian attire peeks his head in. His mustache is flecked with even more white now and he hasn't shaved the rest of his beard since Phil's injury. Trying the best he can to stick a friendly smile on his face, he walks in with two to-go cups of coffee.

"They were out of creamer." He hands me a paper cup. Each morning before his shift he's made the hour-long drive to El Dorado City hospital to see Phil. He always brings coffee, then sits with me in silence. Then he leaves.

"Thank you, Jon, I appreciate it." I pretend to drink it. I don't want to hurt his feelings, but I've since given up my vice in hopes I can feed less. A hospital full of blood isn't the best place for someone like me. I'm trying to avoid causing injury to others.

Jon greets Phil with a pat on the foot, and instead of his usual silent visit, where he sits and says nothing, he pulls up a chair and tells me, "I have some news."

"Oh?"

He nods. "We've had a break in the Jane Doe

case. Normally I'd share this with Phil, but——" he looks at Phil's still body, run by machines and sighs.

I set down my coffee on the table beside the hospital bed and give my attention to Jon.

"What did you find?" I ask though I'm fairly certain Donovan or Catherine are the ones behind it all.

"The teeth and fingers found at the school and the Sellers place were a match to our Jane and the elderly woman, Susan. We were able to then identify our Jane as Indy Goddard from Seabright County." His face turns pale, as he continues. "According to her parents, she was on her way up for a job with Amador County Fire. Which makes no sense because I just saw Indy Goddard at the fire station yesterday, and she's very much alive with a full set of white teeth and all ten fingers."

"That is. . . strange," I stammer out. I knew I wasn't seeing things the night of Phil's accident. That was Catherine behind the wheel of the fire engine. I don't share this with Jon, he doesn't need to get mixed up in this mess I've fallen into. But why kill the real Indy and take her identity?

"Well, I better go. With this turn in the case I have lots of work to do. Someone messed something up real bad." He stands and pats me on the shoulder. "I'll come back later and sit with him, you look like you could use some rest."

"Thanks, Jon, but I'm fine." I'm not leaving Phil.

After Jon walks out of the room, I scan my husband's pale, lifeless face and pray he's still human — that I failed in taking away his mortality. The more removed I am from the terror and confusion of that night in our house, the more I become convinced I made a mistake. He wouldn't want this "gift" I'm cursed with. He'd rather be dead, *real* dead.

Something cold and wet drips onto my hand that's holding his. Horrified, I look down to see black ooze leaking from his bandage.

"No!" I peel it away for a better look as his hand jerks away from me. Phil sits up gasping for air, stopped by the tube shoved down his throat.

"Stop, you're okay!" I whisper, hoping to calm him down.

He grasps at his face with his hands and rips the tube out, gagging as he throws it to the ground, taking a deep breath on his own. I stare back, wide-eyed. Swallowing down the shock.

It worked.

"Aileen?" He stares at me. At first his eyes are bright with happiness, and it's a welcome sight. But his brow quickly wrinkles. His heart rate spikes on the monitor to his left. "What did you do to me?" He touches his wrist with his other hand and stares at the black ooze dripping off his fingers, his eyes wide and full of fear.

"You're going to be okay," I say, reaching out to

touch his arm, hoping perhaps our bond might calm him.

"Don't . . . " he snarls. "Get away from me."

I step back as he tries to get up from the hospital bed and look at the closed room door, hoping the nurses don't hear him yelling.

"Just calm down. Everything is going to be fine."

"What are you?" he says, backing away from me toward the hospital room door, panicked. "Tell me now!" Stopped by the tubes and wires attached to him, he rips them off. The heart rate monitor blares its siren, and I rush to unplug it before anyone hears, knowing it still only buys me a few extra seconds. Now is not the time for him to be around other people— day five is when my blood lust took over, and a hospital has a lot more bleeding people than a parking lot.

"We need to get you out of here."

"I remember what happened in our kitchen. I could hear everything. The way you looked at me— like you wanted to *kill* me— you were like an animal. No more lies, tell me, what are you, Aileen?"

Facing the truth is more painful than I could have imagined. I *did* want to kill him. Frozen I stand, facing the man I love more than anything in the world. The man I just cursed by saving his life. Cursed him because of my inability to imagine eternity without him. Cursed him because I was too selfish to accept my fate on my own. I'm no better than Donovan, am I?

"Answer me!" He stares at his wrist, feeling his neck where the bruises have already healed. Then flicks back his blue eyes to me, face full of disgust. Just like Donovan said he would.

"It's . . . complicated," I say, stalling the inevitable.

He grits his teeth, rage-fueled tears pooling in his eyes. His heart is weakening with each shallow breath he takes. Gasping for air, he grabs frantically at his chest. I remember feeling the way he feels right now, lying on the old worn floorboard of Donovan's farm-house. The fear, the pain— he's running out of time, he needs to replace his blood and complete his change. Or else. Footsteps squeak down the hall from outside the door. We're running out of time in more than one way.

"I'm— I'm the same thing you are," I whisper, trying to be strong. Trying to not fall in a puddle of shame on the floor for the mess I've made with all my lies.

"What?" he demands as he falls to his knees, pain carved into his brow, his hand clenched to his chest over his barely-beating heart. He needs blood *now*.

I look into Phil's terrified eyes. His pupils so dilated the blue is barely visible amongst the black. And for the first time, I'm ready to accept what I've become, for Phil. I don't know what our forever will hold, but enough damage has been caused in the wake of my denial. I take in a breath to hold back my tears, and as I exhale, I whisper the one truth I should have admitted to him— to myself— a long time ago.

Two words: "A vampire."

"Stop, lying to me!" he screams, as a tall male nurse storms the room.

"Sir, you're going to need to calm down." The nurse grabs Phil off the floor and with ease holds Phil's kicking and screaming body and asks, "What happened?" The name tag on his chest reads Elmer. I vaguely register it in the chaos. But something about him tugs at me, the way he effortlessly hoisted Phil up off the floor.

"He woke up, he's confused, help him please," I beg, knowing there isn't much he can do for him.

"We need sedation!" Elmer yells over his shoulder for back up, and another two nurses, one male one female join him. A doctor follows, syringe in hand as the two male nurses hold him down. The doctor stabs him in the arm as Phil stares into my eyes, his filled with terror and betrayal before they flutter shut. The nurses lift Phil back onto the bed and reattach his monitors.

He needs blood, I think silently.

The doctor speaks to me, but nothing he says registers either. Something about a miraculous recovery because Phil was up, clearly not paralyzed at all, but all I can focus on is how I'm going to get him blood.

"Why don't you head home while he rests. Get some rest yourself. We'll take good care of him. It can be very unnerving to wake up from a coma." The doctor rests his hand on my shoulder. I must look like I'm in shock as well.

If I leave, I can go find him blood, stick it in a thermos just like Donovan did for me.

Phil lies motionless on the hospital bed, as they strap his body down as a precaution. Elmer nods to me, his amber eyes flashing against the rich bronze of his skin, his smile both calming and unnerving. There is something about him, something . . . different. "Okay, I'll be back in less than an hour."

"Take your time," the doctor says as he heads back over to Phil to check on his monitors.

Only Phil doesn't have time, I don't think. I leave the room and try to figure out where in the world I'm going to find a blood source around El Dorado. Cows, there are a lot of cows here. I jump in my car to try and find the nearest place to buy a thermos. I rush into a sporting goods store and purchase the largest canteen they have— sixty-four ounces should do the trick. I buy two just in case.

Grazing pasture surrounds the outer edge of town. I drive a few miles out before I turn down a dirt road in hopes I might find a cow hidden amongst the hills and oak trees. Somewhere I could kill it without calling attention. Away from the farmhouses, and highway, and the town. An old rock wall stands not too far out near a gathering of cattle chewing their morning cud. A large female sits alone, off to the side near the rock wall, under the shade of a large oak. In seconds and without her notice, I'm at the cow. I throw my arms around her warm fuzzy neck, the snap her vertebrae makes as I twist sends a chill down my spine. She didn't even make a sound as her cud fell from her mouth and onto the grass at my feet. The other cows are still chewing, peacefully unaware of my presence or the demise of their sister.

With the canteens ready, I open her neck as sweet, thick blood pours into it quickly filling the first sixty-four ounces, then the second. I consume the rest of her, and for a moment all my stress fades away, as her life force becomes mine. Empowered at my strength, how I killed with ease, no suffering like the buck did, no need for a taser. I am the weapon now. I am a vampire. The word stings as I think it, but my denial of what I am has only destroyed what I longed to keep.

No more lies.

Unwilling to let those words be the last I hear from my husband, I rush back to my car and drive as fast as I can to the hospital. Parking, I stuff the canteen's in the bag they came in and grab my phone from my van's center consul as it rings.

"Hello?"

"Aileen? Hi, this is Elmer, from the hospital. We need you to come back."

"I'm here, I'll be up in a minute."

Something in his tone, tells me I'm too late. Tears well up behind my lashes as I walk as fast as I can get away with to the stairwell and race to the third floor. Elmer waits for me outside Phil's room. I wasn't even gone an hour.

"Aileen, I am so sorry but . . . " I brace myself for the worst, knowing it would be for the best. Knowing he would get his eternity, a death he would have wanted over *this* life I forced him into. "There's been a problem."

"What kind of problem?" I clench the bag tight within my hand, maybe there's still time.

Elmer sets his hand on the handle of Phil's hospital room door. Before it's cracked even an inch, I can smell it.

"Oh no," escapes my lips and Elmer opens the door wider. The heavy scent of human blood wafts from within the room.

He points to the bag in my hand, "You're not going to need that, unless you get hungry on the road."

"Excuse me?" I narrow my eyes at him. How would he know what's in my bag, unless— but the thought stops dead in its tracks as we step over the threshold.

The overhead lights seem far too bright and cheery for such tragedy beneath them. The once white sheet is now a dripping a deep crimson. The doctor and two other nurses lay dead— no, massacred is more like it— throughout the room.

Phil is gone.

Elmer shuts the door behind him and gazes at the bloody sight. He doesn't look phased. I take notice of the ashy undertone of his bronze skin. His other-worldly white teeth. His lack of a heartbeat. Suddenly, I understand.

"You're a—"

"I'm a friend, and right now you have a mess to clean up. I'll take care of this here. He said to meet him in the forest by nightfall, that you would know where." Elmer opens the door slightly and peeks out. "Oh, and this was left for you." He pulls a purple, lavender-scented envelope, complete with blood splatter, from the pocket of his scrubs.

My head is spinning as I take the card from him. Elmer doesn't need to say who "he" is. He pulls out one of the canteens from my bag, "Do you mind?" But before I can answer he disappears out the door into the hall. In shock I hold the envelope addressed to me, trying to process the scene before me. Phil's gone.

I tear it open. It's a sympathy card with a field of flowers painted in watercolor reading a generic, "Sorry for your loss," on the cover. The inside is blank, aside from a hand-written note in black ink:

He is mine now.

Love, "C"

EPILOGUE

Snow blankets the forest floor, tinted blue from the bright November moon above. I wait by a tall cedar a few yards away from the quiet mountain highway. Guilt pushing on the seams of my dead heart. As far as Ana and the girls are concerned Phil has been transferred to a hospital in Atlanta for emergency experimental surgery to place an implant that might help him regain movement. He had to leave fast, no time for them to say goodbye. Ana had her words with me on the phone, especially when she found out I was already on the medical plane waiting for take-off with him. I asked her to please tell the girls I love them. I promised to call back as soon as he's out of surgery.

The ground vibrates from a vehicle fast approaching. I push aside all thoughts of my former life and focus on the task ahead, to getting Phil back. To ignore the terrible pain radiating from the empty hole carved within my chest at the thought of leaving my children, our children. They'll be safer this way. It's the *only* way to make right what I made so wrong.

Headlights beam into the tree line as an old Jeep appears, roaring to a stop at the side of the road. *He said to meet him in the forest by nightfall*— *he* is the last person I want to be seeing right now. *He* is the reason my life has fallen apart. *He* is the only one I have, and once again, I need him.

Donovan's boots crunch in the snow as he passes in front of the headlights to the other side and opens the passenger door. I take a breath, finding the resolve I need to do this and walk to the car.

"If this is going to work, we need to just be friends. Promise?"

He nods his head, but we both know the truth, a friendship isn't possible with us.

"Get in, love." He holds the door and waits as I slide into the worn leather seat before shutting it. In a flash Donovan is in the driver's seat, hands set on the steering wheel, determination in his eyes. "Now, let's go find your husband."

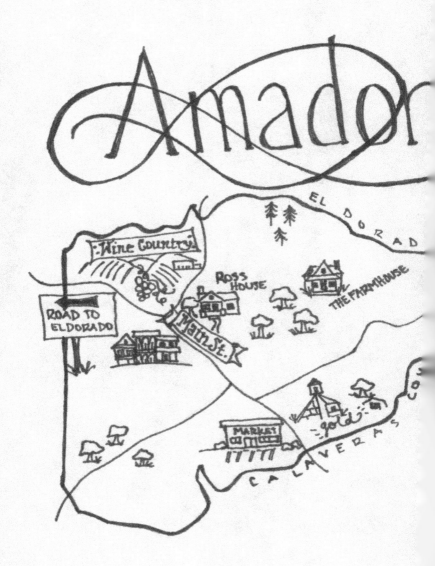

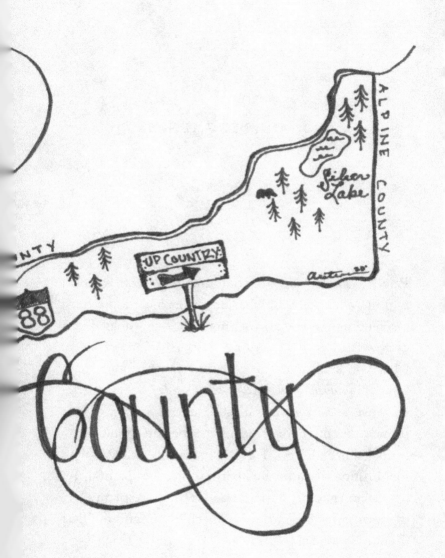

ALPINE COUNTY

Silver Lake

UP COUNTRY

Austin '20

...UNTY

88

County

ACKNOWLEDGMENTS

Peter— Thank you for your unending love, support and understanding in what has been one of the most challenging endeavors of my life. You helped me discover my love of writing. And I will never forget what you said to me after I told you my idea for a screenplay *about a mom whose plane crashes but she survives mysteriously unharmed*, you said, and I quote, "That sounds expensive for a movie, maybe you should write a book instead." So, I did. Thank you walking with me through this amazing, hard, sometimes painful, yet joyous journey of writing. You are the love of my life, the most amazing father to our children, and my best friend. I love you.

My Children— Okay kids, I know mommy had many moments during this process where I probably came across as downright crazy, but thank you for always believing in me. I love you all more than you could ever know.

M, I still have your cover idea drawing, and while it won't be the one we use, I will forever cherish your thoughtfulness and creativity. I can't wait to see where your imagination takes you my dear.

S, you have been my number one fan throughout this process. Every time you asked if my book was published yet, or when you could put it on our bookshelf, it made me both cry and smile to see your excitement for me. Your love for reading makes my heart soar and I promise, someday when you are old enough, you can read my book.

J, you once made me a pin, all by yourself when you were about 4, that said "100%" and told me it was because I was writing a good book, thank you for believing in me you have no idea how much that meant to me.

Amberly— Thank you for your amazing editing skills. For your honesty. The many rounds of edits and back and forth emails and track changes. You helped me, a brand new writer who had no idea what she was doing, get a start in this world of writing, for that I will be forever grateful.

Jana— Thank you for all our walks around the neighborhood with my triple wide stroller as you let me bounce idea after idea about Aileen off you. You have been there since her inception, you introduced me to Amberly who helped me get this story ready for querying. Also, thank you for talking me out of using the title "Vampire Mom".

Tarrah— Thank you for coming into my life, for asking me to do your hair what feels like a lifetime ago. Thank you for your advice on fire "engine" not truck. Thank you for introducing me to "fancy drinks", fried eggs, Renaissance Fairs, pretty rocks, butterflies, and for becoming the best friend a girl could ask for.

My parents— Thank you for instilling in me a love for reading and for all those years you drove me to elementary school so I could learn how to read and write all those words.

To my beautiful grandmother Rosalie— I know deep down in my heart you would have been my biggest fan. You always encouraged me to dream and I thank you for that. I miss you deeply.

Everly— Writer Mom's Inc. wouldn't be what it is today without you by my side. Thank you for listening to all my millions of ideas no matter how far-fetched they may be.

My critique partners (and friends) Amanda and Kelly — Thank you for being so generous with your time with helping me shape Remaining Aileen into the story she was meant to be.

M.M. Finck— For your amazing Query Quill services that helped me see what I could not see.

My Amador County Writer Mom Muffin Meetings— I don't know why I named us that. It sort of just happened as I wrote this... but it's in a book now, so... yeah. Thank you for your friendship and all your writerly support. I truly enjoy the times we spend together.

I want to make a special mention to all the Writer Moms in Writer Moms Inc.— Keep writing and never give up on your dreams. This writing life is tough. There is rarely a balance to be found, but I think as long as we all have each other we will figure it out something eventually! Thank you for being there for me.

COMING SOON
Book Two
ALL THAT REMAINS

ALL THAT REMAINS

CHAPTER ONE

Oh, you'll do just fine. I run my tongue slowly over my lips. Flames lick up my throat, ignited by the man in faded denim. The fabric of his thin, black shirt strains around broad, muscular shoulders. Beads of sticky, salty sweat drip down the side of his dark-russet skin, right over the hard throbbing of his carotid artery—

"Hungry, love?" Donovan opens the driver's side door to the old Jeep and slides in beside me. It breaks my trance on the unsuspecting man pumping his gas on the other side of the station. "I thought you only went for the four-legged variety." Donovan turns the key in the ignition with an annoyingly satisfied smile on his irritatingly-handsome face. The engine roars to life, filling the cabin with noxious fumes. It takes the edge off my ever-growing appetite for blood.

I look away from Donovan, back out the window as my fantasy meal steps into his car and drives off.

"Shut it, I'm fine." But both of us know that's a lie. I'm not fine. I may never be fine again. "What I really need right now, is coffee." Real coffee, not the gas station sludge of the randomly placed, outdated stations that lie along Nevada's Interstate 80.

Donovan scoffs, but even so his smooth, British accent is melodic, "Coffee? Stop kidding yourself, what you *need* is blood."

Unfortunately, my scratchy throat agrees with Donovan, no matter how much I try to deny it— I do need blood.

But non-human blood is hard to find in a desert.

My hunger spikes and I squeeze my eyes, trying to shut out the hunger. But it's only replaced by the equally painful memories of my last moments with Phil. That look on his face of complete and utter betrayal. His stormy-ocean-blue eyes that stared at me, full of disgust, when I told him I was a vampire— *he* was a vampire.

The cool sensation of a tear tingles in the corner of my eye, I quickly wipe it away just in time to see the sign for Elko, population twenty-thousand. Not much more than a few old casinos, a dinner, fast food, and a few Ma and Pa shops. However, it's by far the largest town we've driven through since Reno. I don't care about the size though, what draws my attention is the bright green and white sign of salvation: *Starbucks Drive-Thru.*

"Pull off here," I command, then when Donovan gives me a look, add a begrudging, "Please."

Instead of stopping, or even fully acknowledging my request, he steps on the accelerator. I watch as Starbucks fades away in the side-view mirror.

"What the hell was that for?" I murmur, looking forward in hopes of seeing a second sign. What are the odds they might have two? One on the way in, one on the way out? But Elko isn't *that* big.

"I'm cutting you off, love. It's for your own good."

Pent up anger rises as I stare at him, my *maker*, who's currently acting like my father, and a low growl escapes between my clenched teeth.

"Someone's grumpy." Donovan stares ahead as he changes lanes, cutting off a poor, slow-moving Winnebago, clearly unimpressed.

"My husband is gone, stolen by *your* psychotic, fire-loving ex and you are now depriving me of the one thing that will bring me some glimpse of normality. I don't care if it dehydrates me, I'll just match every other damn human in this hell-hole of a dessert."

Donovan finally looks at me, his dark eyes sharp with a warning. "You aren't human anymore, Aileen. It's time you accept that." He pauses and a half-smile grows on the left side of his strong-angular face. "Blood only for this trip. Unless you're willing to do more than grab coffee from the drive-thru barista." His smile turns full as he laughs at himself, that or from the look of pure disgust I'm sure I'm wearing at the thought of eating the poor Starbucks barista.

The memory of my last taste of human blood still lingers on my guilty tongue; warm, silky, and sweet. The salty tang of Phil's cold skin under my lips. How my dead heart shattered knowing I took far more than just his blood. I selfishly stole his life. He didn't want to live forever. He said so himself.

I readjust in my seat. It doesn't matter how much I try to convince myself it was my only choice. It was a lie to think we were both going to die. The truth is, I could have made it out without him.

The silence is thick, even in this old, noisy Jeep. There is so much I want to say to Donovan and I'm sure he has his fair share of words as well. Both of us are wounded by the other. But since starting this trip neither of us has spoken out-loud what happened the night I turned Phil into a vampire. I chose my dying husband over Donovan regardless of our forever bond as creator and creation.

Donovan turns on the radio and hums along to a fuzzy country tune that blips in and out of reception. I try not to smile, but every time he does something human I can't help but feel something for him. Then I remind myself I have no real choice but to feel something for him. Thanks to our bond. Being this close in proximity I could hardly help it if I tried. Only distance can lessen our connection.

I remind myself Donovan did this to me. He

turned me into a monster. He is the one that hurt Phil. The one who threw him into the wall and broke his neck— because of me.

I should be angrier at Donovan, but it's myself I can never forgive. I repeat to myself the mantra I've been saying in my head since I stepped into this vehicle; Donovan is my only chance to save Phil, to get him back, to bring him home to our two beautiful daughters— our family. Our home. But our home is gone, destroyed by the one who made Donovan.

Staring out at the desolate view, overwhelming thoughts flood into my mind. It hurts, how desperately I long for life to be as it was, before I was a vampire. Before I stepped on that plane.

"Feeling broody, are we?"

I snap back, not withholding my frustration, "I'm a vampire, isn't broody our thing?"

He looks at me, pretending to be offended, when his phone rings. I hold my breath, praying fervently it's news on Phil's location. The call we've been aimlessly driving around the Nevada desert waiting for. Donovan doesn't say hello when he answers, but with my keen hearing I can make out Elmer's voice on the other side. After finding Phil missing at the hospital Elmer— a nurse and vampire— took off ahead of us at Donovan's request. Apparently, Elmer is really good at finding what needs to be found and hiding what shouldn't be seen. Example, messy vampiric activity. I hear Elmer report a recent string of arsons and homicides of mostly vagrants and dancing girls in—

"Let me guess," Donovan interrupts, "Vegas?"

I faintly hear Elmer respond, "Yup, I'll meet you there."

With a pained sigh, Donovan hangs up. He takes the next exit for Las Vegas. Only 382 miles away.

We sit again in silence for a while, until I can't help but ask, "Vegas huh?"

I stare down at my hastily purchased, ill-fitting mom jeans, gray t-shirt, and off-brand sneakers, feeling grossly underdressed for our destination. Since everything I own burned to the ground the night I changed Phil. I only have a few items I picked up at Target in between visits to Phil and checking in with my daughters who are currently staying with Ana. I hold back worry over my children. I know my mother-in-law is more than capable of caring for them. But it hurts. I pick at the hem of my stupid tee, hating everything.

Donovan, glances over at me, a smile curling his lip as if he's pleased I was the one to break and speak first. "Gee, don't look so excited, we'll stop and get you something more suitable to wear."

Even after being on the road for the last five hours he still looks sickeningly amazing in his dark jeans and a white tee, topped with his signature vintage leather jacket.

"Fine," I say tightly.

"This could be fun, you know. Vegas is truly a vampire's paradise. You know there are clubs where humans offer themselves willingly, simply for a chance to *know* we exist. And sometimes, for more…"

A shiver runs up my spine at the thought of a bunch of people piled up like items at a buffet. *Yes, I'll take the middle-aged brunette with a side of tan blond, please.*

"I'll take your word for it…" I suddenly have no regrets that I've never been to Las Vegas. It didn't appeal to me after having kids. I figured my time for partying in tiny dresses, wearing stripper-worthy heels at smoky Vegas nightclubs had long since expired on my "to-do" list. I knew it was known for being the capital of debauchery and sinful pleasure, I never would have imagined the Sin City itself could be *that* bad. A place where people not only gambled away their money but their lives simply to know an apparently well-kept secret of the universe— that vampires are real.

"Suite yourself. You'll see what I mean soon enough," he offers casually. As if we are simply headed to a weekend getaway, not a potentially dangerous rescue mission, trying to save the love of my life from a deranged vampire ex-girlfriend.

"Do you really think she's there?" From the sound of it people willingly die in Vegas all the time. A string of killings doesn't necessarily mean vampires— or a specific vampire to be exact— did it. "What makes Elmer so sure we should be headed there?"

"Believe me, he knows Catherine." His hands tighten around the steering wheel.

I hesitate, but ask anyway, "Did she change him too?"

"Yes, and he will never forgive her for it. But that's his story." Donovan looks ahead at the road. I get the feeling he doesn't want to say anything more about Elmer and Catherine's past and I don't push the subject.

Elmer isn't the only one who hates Catherine. That violet-eyed monster is the salt in the festering wound of my new undead existence. She didn't have to take Phil to spite me, Donovan was hers for all I cared. Yes, Donovan made me, we now share an eternal bond which makes things *complicated* between us. But Phil is my husband, my true love, the father of my children, the man I long to spend my forever with — that is if he will still have me after all this.

Suddenly, my emotions flare as strong as the hunger within me. Tears I've been holding back since finding Phil gone, since leaving my life, and my daughters behind burst free. I wipe at my face with my grimy sleeve, but I can't keep the tears at bay no matter how hard I try. It wasn't easy leaving my daughters. And my heart broke hearing Ana's eagerness over the phone to join me when I told her the lie about Phil being flown to Atlanta for experimental surgery. A surgery that could possibly restore his spine. Through tears I assured her Davina and Imogene needed her, now more than ever. Plus, I claimed I was already on the plane and there was no time to wait. But there is no hospital in Atlanta, and Phil is gone, taken by a vengeful vampire.

Donovan's face softens as he looks over at me and rests his hand on my knee. With his touch the bond between us burns anew, something I've been trying to avoid, but right now I'll take the calming effect his touch brings me.

"Why is she doing this?" I choke out as I reign in my emotions and glance down at his fingers splayed out on my knee.

Donovan abruptly removes his hand and meets my eyes with his dark, sultry brown eyes.

"Sorry," he says.

A moment of longing tugs on my dead heart, and I wish he'd place it back. But it's for the best that we maintain distance. Just friends. That's what I'd told him before he'd promised to help me track Phil down. *Just friends.*

"It's fine." I take a steadying breath and pick at my too-perfect cuticles to distract myself from wanting to instinctively grab Donovan's hand. Because as hard as this all is, at least I have him by my side to help me fix all that is broken in my life. At least I'm not alone.

Donovan clears his throat. "Catherine believes in justice. In retribution. Eye for an eye sort of thing. In her sick, twisted mind you took me away from her."

Except I didn't. It's not my fault Donovan chose to stalk me, then save my life.

"So now, to keep the balance, she must take something away from you. It's a game she plays," he pauses. "Aileen, I truly am sorry."

"You said that."

"No, *for everything.*" His voice is soft.

I stare over at him, he won't look at me but I can see the lines of sadness drawn on his ivory face. Something in me hurts to see him sad, even with everything that's happened. I sigh, "What's done is done. Right now, the only thing that matters is finding Phil."

And hopefully *when* we find Phi, I can beg his forgiveness. Convince him that our love, this life we built together, is worth fighting for. But are we too far gone? Is it too late? I watch out my window as the desert zooms quickly by and think about how everything in my life went so wrong so fast.

Three weeks ago, I was a mom, a wife, a human.

Three weeks ago, I was alive, and now I'm not.

An encore of tears threatens to spill over my eyes.

"Aileen? You okay?"

I feel Donovan's gaze on the side of my face but I don't look at him. I can't. I manage to nod. "Mmm-hmm."

But I'm not okay.

I am a vampire.

418

ABOUT THE AUTHOR

Autumn lives with her husband and three kids in a deep, dark, magical forest in Northern California. Fluent in typo and fueled by caffeine, she writes Women's Fiction with characters that bite.

She is also the co-founder of Writer Moms Inc, a community for moms who write.

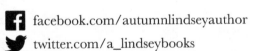

facebook.com/autumnlindseyauthor

twitter.com/a_lindseybooks

instagram.com/autumnlindseyauthor

CPSIA information can be obtained
at www.ICGtesting.com
Printed in the USA
FSHW010226090721
82992FS

9 781735 053615